THE
MIRACULOUS
LIFE
OF
RUPERT
ROCKET

THE
MIRACULOUS
LIFE
OF
RUPERT
ROCKET

A Novel of the Fae by
Mark Salzwedel

QUEER SPACE
New Orleans & New York

Published in the United States of America by
Queer Space
A Rebel Satori Imprint
www.rebelsatoripress.com

Paperback ISBN: 978-1-60864-303-5

"The princess, in her fifteenth year, will prick herself on a spindle and fall dead."

Without a word, she turned and left the hall. The guests were startled when the twelfth fairy, who still had a wish to bestow, came forth. Because she could not lift the evil spell—only soften it—said, "The princess shall not die. She will fall into a hundred-year sleep."

from "Dornröschen"
by the Brothers Grimm

CHAPTER 1: ZELDA

By the spring of 1942, the Nazis had already annexed Austria and invaded Poland, France, Czechoslovakia, Libya, Yugoslavia, Greece, Western Russia, and Estonia. They broke a treaty and amassed a navy capable of invading England. And they had been shipping Jews and other "undesirable races" to forced labor camps for seven years and had started sending them to death camps. German-Americans like Griselda Becker were often reviled, representing to their neighbors all of the horrific acts committed by the nation they had fled.

Everyone called her Zelda. She, her parents, and her seven siblings had emigrated from Germany nineteen years before. She had graduated from the second of two high schools in Sheboygan, Wisconsin, and was already twenty-four. She wrote frequent letters to her high school boyfriend, Thomas Kellerman, who had just been drafted to serve as a German translator in London for the U.S. Navy. She panicked with every report that London had been bombed by the Nazis and checked her mailbox every day awaiting news Thomas was all right.

Zelda expected to welcome him home in early 1943, after his year of compulsory service was to end. But about that time, she ripped open and read the letter in which she fully expected him to say he was on his way home to her. Instead, she gasped and started to cry. It announced that his commission was being extended. His commanding officer wanted him to assist with a new air campaign. "I don't know when I shall be returning," he wrote.

This began the series of events Zelda would later refer to as the "troubles."

The next day, Zelda caught sight of Patricia in line to punch in at the plumbing factory where she worked. She quickly ducked behind a pillar in embarrassment; she looked like a hobo by comparison in her dirty coveralls and kerchief. Patricia

1

had a cold wave, a fancy blouse and skirt, and the rarest of luxuries: nylon stockings.

After dating Zelda through her junior year, Thomas had started dating Patricia instead, an Irish girl with reddish-brown hair; pale, freckled skin; mousy cuteness; and an ethnic group more established than his. Zelda took part of her lunch break from working on the assembly line to drop by the personnel department. The secretary there confirmed that a Patricia Connor had been hired in the steno pool for the executives. When she punched out at the end of her shift, Patricia was waiting for her. She pulled a pair of air mail envelopes out of her black, patent-leather purse.

"He's been writing to me too, Zelda," she taunted.

"President Roosevelt? I didn't know you knew him as well."

She was determined not to let Patricia get her goat, so she lifted her chin and started to walk past her. But she stopped when Patricia confirmed they were from England, from Thomas. Zelda tried to look at the envelopes, but Patricia quickly slipped them back into her purse and closed it. "I think Thomas wants me back."

"I doubt it." Zelda turned away from her but didn't leave yet.

"Why else would he write to me?"

Zelda couldn't think of an explanation, so she finally stormed off and walked at a brisk clip all the way back home. When Thomas had broken things off with Patricia a year before being drafted, he told Zelda he wanted her back and had only been using Patricia to deflect the epithets and bullying so many German immigrants were suffering at the time.

When she arrived at the home provided by her employer and shared with her older brother Horst, he was working a later shift, and only Madeleine, his fiancée was there. She offered Zelda some soup, but Zelda waved her off and closed her bedroom door. She pulled out her writing tablet and the fancy new fountain pen her sister Ingrid had given her for Christmas and started composing a letter in German to send to Thomas. She threw the question into one of her last paragraphs: *Have you written to Patricia by chance?*

One letter from Thomas must have overlapped, but in the following one

2

a month later, the answer came, near the beginning: *No, I haven't written to Patricia.*

The following day, both she and Horst had a day off. Zelda had made a habit of carrying Thomas's most recent letter with her everywhere, so when she appeared at breakfast, Horst pointed at it. "Your Shakespeare has written you another sonnet?"

"I am in a bit of a quandary," she replied. "Thomas's ex-girlfriend claims he has written to her. Thomas claims he has not."

"One of them is lying." Horst smirked.

"Undoubtedly," she acknowledged, "but I can't easily get at the truth. If I press it with Thomas, he will think I don't trust him. And I cannot demand to examine Patricia's mail."

"So, you are left with uncertainty," Horst said, switching to English. "Watch what they do. Actions speak louder than words."

But Thomas's letters continued to arrive at a rate of one or two a month, and they were filled with as much ardor as ever. And Patricia pulled out ever-thicker bundles of air mail envelopes and waved them at Zelda whenever they encountered each other.

In the summer of 1943, the garbage men spilled waste on their lawn. That brought the rats. They usually didn't show up during the day, but when they did, Zelda shrieked with horror. Not long after that, the nests of vermin under their front steps and in their backyard drew every stray cat for miles. And then the cats wouldn't leave for months.

A few months later, after the cold Wisconsin winter had dumped a foot of snow on the ground, Zelda's older sister Ingrid was sick for weeks with pneumonia. The roof of the house Zelda shared with her brother started leaking every time it was warm enough for the snow to melt. Zelda's hours at the factory were cut in half. And Thomas wrote to say that he had dreams of living in another big city like London when he was discharged, bigger than Sheboygan.

In the summer of 1944, right in the middle of the troubles, Zelda was walking home from work at one-thirty in the afternoon. She decided to take a detour. She walked down by the river, reliving in her mind all the times she and Thomas had strolled there hand in hand before he was drafted.

On one of the wooden benches along the river path, she saw a woman who seemed older than her mother wrapped in a patchwork coat. She hummed a melody Zelda didn't think she knew, and yet it sounded familiar. She stopped to ask the woman what the tune was, and she noticed how pointed the woman's ears were and how unusually long her earlobes.

"It's a ditty me mother taught me," the woman said in a cheerful Irish accent. She patted the bench beside her in invitation. "I really don't know the name of it. Come have a sit with an old woman."

"That's quite remarkable," Zelda said as she sat next to her. "You answered the question I was just about to ask you."

"I could see it in your eyes, cailín." The woman chuckled. "And two out of every three who pass by here ask me the very same question."

"I've walked this path many times." Zelda noticed the woman's graying red hair and green eyes. "I don't believe I've ever seen you here before."

"I come here from time to time," the woman said.

She hummed a bit of the song again, and Zelda just sat and listened. It seemed to have happy and sad moments. It could have been a love song as easily as a drinking song. "Do you know the lyrics?"

"Something about paying a fairy in cream, I seem to remember." The woman winked at Zelda. "So, what brings a young girl like you out here so early in the afternoon?"

"I work at the Kohler plant." Zelda turned and gestured toward the buildings in the distance. "Demand has dropped off, so I'm only working half-shifts now."

"How unfortunate for you."

"It's not enough money any more to help out my brother with the home repairs and groceries. It looks like we will have to pay to have the roof reshingled at some point."

"How unfortunate for you."

"And I'm missing my sweetheart so terribly. He's serving in England, I'm

4

worried for his safety, and he doesn't know when he can come home yet."

"How unfortunate for you, my dear." The woman scooted a bit closer and put a hand on Zelda's shoulder. She whispered, "I had heard that my sister had made a deal near here, and I think you must have been the target."

Zelda leaned away from the woman. "I'm certain I have no idea why your sister's bargains would have anything to do with me."

"Do you have any enemies?" The woman withdrew her hand again and gathered her coat around herself more tightly.

"None that I know of." Zelda felt she got on well with everyone.

The woman turned her head as if she were listening to something in the breeze. "Connor. Someone named Connor?"

"You know Patricia Connor? She's a local girl who also works at the factory with me."

"I heard she is also in love with your boyfriend in England."

Zelda grimaced. "I doubt it." She reviewed everything Thomas had said about her, and it never seemed she was ever more than a temporary escort for him. "She claims he has been writing her letters."

"I definitely see my sister's hand in this." The woman folded her arms and turned away from Zelda.

Zelda wondered whether the woman was crazy or really did know of some conspiracy between Patricia and her sister. After a few moments, she called back over her shoulder, "No one deserves so much tragedy." She looked around as if she were concerned they would be overheard and then continued, "What would you say if someone could turn all your bad luck into good, so you would live a charmed life?"

Zelda chuckled. "I can't think of anyone who would turn that down—least of all me!"

"Fair enough." The woman grinned and reached up to scratch one of her pointed ears. "What if someone could bring you good luck for only a certain amount of time, and then your life would get bad again? Would you still want happiness, if you knew it was going to end?"

"How long a time?" Zelda appreciated the entertainment value of the woman's hypothetical scenario.

The woman turned to gaze out at the river. "Let's say twenty-five years."

"And I couldn't renew the good luck for an additional twenty-five years after that?"

"For the sake of argument, let's say no." She looked at Zelda again. "You would have phenomenally good luck for twenty-five years, and then you would start to lose everything you had gained. You see, cailín, some folk don't want to deal with the disappointment that they'll lose everything eventually."

"I'm not sure any of us can expect more than that from life," Zelda said. "Life is often full of sorrow and disappointment, even before friends and family move away or die. If I knew I could have twenty-five whole years of bliss and good fortune, I would happily pay the price and live off my memories."

The woman stood and faced Zelda. "If it be in my power to grant you relief from this curse for twenty-five years, so be it." The woman smiled. "Thank you for the chat, my dear. I suppose I should be heading home now."

Zelda stood also and smiled. "I enjoyed the chat as well. And thank you for suggesting the possible change in my fortune."

The woman took a few steps away and then turned back and winked at Zelda. "It is the least I could do for you, child."

CHAPTER 2: CAROLINE

In July of 1969, when other young women were still flocking to San Francisco to catch the last gasps of hippie culture and the Summer of Love, Caroline Kellerman was moving away. She said goodbye to her roommates and wrote out directions for Fred to get to her mom and dad's place in Sheboygan, Wisconsin. She promised to call for him when their baby was born. He said he would then quit his job and join her and stay until the baby was old enough to travel back to San Francisco and their new life together.

Caroline's mother had sent her a ticket. She insisted Caroline take a bus rather than hitchhike, since Caroline was already four or five months pregnant. She and her roommates often hung out at the Transbay Terminal south of Market passing out flowers to the commuters, so she knew where to go to catch the Greyhound bus back to Wisconsin. All of her belongings and any clothing she wanted to keep had been stuffed into an army-surplus backpack and a large flower-print purse with a wooden handle. The bus driver stowed her pack and took her ticket. She took an open seat in the back of the bus by the window and set her purse down on the seat beside herself to discourage anyone else from sitting there. Her increased girth and distaste for tight quarters seemed to justify it.

The ride across the Rocky Mountains and through the farmlands of the plains was so peaceful and beautiful, they took Caroline's mind off her occasional nausea and the baby's frequent kicking. Fred had been so good about massaging her as her stomach had begun to swell. She wondered how her very conservative mother would welcome her pregnant and unwed daughter back after six years away. In the first two phone calls with her mother, Caroline had to endure considerable criticism. But her mother had at least promised to arrange medical appointments for Caroline once she arrived, so she took that as some progress. Her mother had more than once told her of the years she had pursued her father before, during, and after his time serving in World War II, so Caroline knew she had a romantic side beneath her righteous exterior.

Caroline's father politely gave the horn of their Chevrolet Impala a single, short beep when she exited the bus terminal downtown. Her mother got out of the car and met Caroline on the sidewalk for a big hug. "You look beautiful, Caroline." She held her at arm's length and smiled. "You are absolutely glowing. I hope the bus ride wasn't too hard on you, darling."

"It was fine, Mom. I did some writing in my journal."

Her father finally got out of the car as well. He had picked up her backpack and gave her a very light hug. "Good to see you again, Schatz. Let me put this in the trunk." His voice was as deep and heavily accented as she remembered from her first eighteen years living with him.

"I hope I didn't take you away from work, Dad," she called after him.

"No, no," he called back from behind the open trunk. "I have managers at both restaurants."

Her mother opened the back door for her and beckoned her to sit down. "You're going to love our new house. There's a bedroom for you, and we can turn the other into a nursery. We have it all set up."

Once they were all three in the car and underway, her mother turned around. "I'm sorry Fred couldn't join you. We have plenty of room."

"It's not that, Mom." She had already explained this to her mother over the phone. "Fred has a job, and he wants to save up some money during the last few months so you won't have to support us."

Her father continued to look at the road ahead. "We have the space, and we often have more food than your mother and I can eat with all the extra from the restaurants. So it wouldn't be a burden on us at all."

"He'll be here once the baby is born." Caroline hoped that would end her parents' second guessing.

They rode in silence for a couple of minutes. Caroline decided to change the subject. "It will feel odd not going back to the apartment where I grew up."

"That cramped place above the restaurant on Geele?" Her mother was incredulous. "We have a real house now. You're going to love it."

The house was in an older neighborhood in Erie Hill, closer to downtown and finally only a few blocks from the river walk and park her parents loved. There were trees in the front yard and a big picture window looking out of the first floor, and a big balcony above the front door. When she went inside, she kept looking around for familiar things, but they were few.

Her mother read her disappointment. "We had so much more space here, we decided to get new furniture," she said somewhat apologetically. She tapped her husband absent-mindedly on the arm without looking at him. "Let's show her her room first."

The bedroom she was led into was right next to the master bedroom upstairs and had a second doorway into another bathroom. Caroline's father hefted the backpack onto the queen-size bed. "We were thinking of taking you to the restaurant for dinner tonight," he announced. She saw him smile with pride for a moment. "Sylvia and Angelo and Roger made me promise to bring you by as soon as you got in."

"I don't think she ever met Roger," her mother argued.

"Well, I told him all about her, and he's excited to meet her." Her father gave Caroline a peck on the cheek. "I'm going back downstairs to make some calls. We can head over in an hour or two once you're settled." He exited without waiting for a response.

Caroline's mother sat down on the bed and repositioned the duffel bag. "He's actually been very excited to have you back. He keeps mentioning it every day."

Caroline sat down in a wicker chair facing her mother. "I'm glad I was able to make it back in time to celebrate Dad's birthday and your wedding anniversary next month."

"If you need to go shopping for gifts, let me know. There's a new mall that just opened up on the west side . . ."

"Do you have something in mind to give Dad for your anniversary already?"

Caroline's mother smiled broadly. "I picked out a nice wristwatch with a diamond on the face."

"I think you're a little ahead, Mom." One of her childhood projects had been to memorize the traditional anniversary gifts. "Diamonds are for the sixtieth anniversary."

"Oh." Her mother looked slightly distressed. "I already put a down payment on it. What would be more appropriate?"

"You were married the year before I was born, so this would be your twenty-fifth anniversary, wouldn't it?"

Her mother's face slowly evolved into worry and fear. "It can't be time already," she whispered seemingly to herself. "I had put it out of my mind the past few years." Suddenly, she put her face in her hands and lay down on the bed weeping.

"Mom! Mom! What's wrong?" Caroline tried to stroke her mother's shoulder and back to calm her.

Caroline's father appeared in the doorway. "What happened?" he asked.

Her mother was still weeping uncontrollably. "She seemed to get upset when I reminded her your anniversary was coming up next month." She got up from the bed to allow her father to get closer to her mother.

"Zelda, sweetie," he whispered to her as he sat down and stroked her auburn hair, "it's going to be all right. Everything's going to be all right."

Caroline went downstairs to leave them alone to sort things out. After an hour or so, her father came down and announced that her mother would stay behind to rest while he took Caroline to the restaurant.

When Caroline returned to the house after dinner that night, she found her mother in the dining room rifling through a shoebox full of blue airmail envelopes. "What are you looking for, Mom?" she asked softly.

When Zelda looked up, her eyes were red and puffy from extended crying. Caroline wondered if she had been crying the entire time she and her father had been out. Zelda's voice cracked while she spoke. "I think it was in the summer, just before . . . just before your father returned home from England."

Caroline leaned forward to get a better look at the envelopes her mother had removed from the box. "These are your letters to Dad?"

"And his to me." She pulled a single new envelope from the box. She pulled the letter out of the envelope, let out a sigh, and pointed at it several times. "This is the one. It was in July 1944. I met a woman down by the river, and I told your father about how odd it was."

Caroline didn't grasp any significance to what she was saying, so she fished for some other connection. "I think you told me Dad came home a couple of weeks later, and you got married in August, right?"

Her mother's sad desperation faded away and was replaced by a glow of comforting nostalgia. "And you were born the following May. You brought such joy to our lives. You know that, don't you, Caroline?"

"Yes, Mom. Of course."

Her mother quickly got up from her chair and hugged Caroline from behind, pressing her ear against the side of her daughter's head. "I don't want anything bad to happen to you. I don't mind if it happens to me, but it shouldn't happen to you. It shouldn't happen to you."

Caroline slowly rose from her chair and wrapped her mother in her arms. Pressed against Caroline's belly, her mother got tearful again. Then suddenly she started to laugh. "I can already feel him kicking."

"I told you," Caroline said, feeling a bit teary herself, "he's gotta' grow up to be a dancer if he's kicking that much now."

"Or a runner, I suppose." Her mother broke the hug first but gently rested her hand on Caroline's belly.

Caroline saw her mother smile, and it felt like whatever dark cloud her mother had been perceiving had passed. "Can you help me up the stairs, Mom? I think I'm going to turn in early."

"Sure. I'll bring you more pillows. I remember when I was pregnant with you. I could never have enough pillows."

The following morning, Caroline rose after her father, Thomas, was already busy cooking breakfast in the kitchen. The smell of pork sausages frying almost tempted her out of her vegetarian diet. They had a good breakfast, and Zelda had either forgotten her panic from the night before or was hiding it really well. The three of them stopped by the newer of the two restaurants for lunch, and they ate so much there, they only snacked a bit more when dinnertime arrived. Since she was showing, Caroline had a couple of uncomfortable moments when neighbors and friends asked about the baby's father. But Caroline confidently told them the father would arrive soon, and she went to bed that night thinking how great it was going to be for the new grandparents to have a baby in the house again.

The morning after that, right around sunrise, Caroline was awakened by her mother shrieking loud and long in the master bedroom. She pulled on a robe, and hurried in. It looked like her father was sleeping through all the caterwauling, even with her mother's head on his chest. Caroline started to say, "What's going on?" but she never finished. She rushed to check her father's pulse. His hand was cold. *He must have died in the middle of the night*, she thought.

"He went so quietly," her mother keened somewhat softer. "He was already cold when I woke up."

Caroline finally felt herself tearing up as well as the realization that the man lying before her suddenly was unexpectedly out of her life. She pulled a tissue from the box beside their bed to dry her eyes. She fought the urge to wail. She decided she needed to be strong for her mother. "I guess it wasn't painful. He looks peaceful. He might not even have been awake."

"The time went so quickly," her mother whispered between sobs. "He was only forty-seven."

"I know. He seemed really healthy."

The injustice of losing someone they loved at such a young age finally broke both women's composure. They allowed themselves to cry and wail for almost two hours. Then Caroline called the medical examiner to take her father's body away. The official cause of death was ruled a cardiac arrest, though the coroner had difficulty in finding any occlusions or damage that might have caused it. Caroline tried to manage the funeral arrangements, but her mother and her Uncle Horst took over. The funeral was held at a small chapel on the north side her father's sister had suggested.

Caroline noticed an older woman she didn't know near the back of the chapel as she was processing out behind the casket with her mother. She saw her again at the interment in the cemetery. She wore a green dress so dark it was almost black, and her face was deformed. One eye was lower than the other, and the nose was askew. The woman grinned when she realized Caroline was staring at her.

"Who is that woman over there in the dark green dress?" she whispered to her mother.

Zelda followed Caroline's finger toward the strange woman, and a look of revulsion formed on her face. She leaned in toward Caroline and whispered back, "Don't go anywhere near her."

Caroline tried to ask who the woman was as they were being driven home, but her mother refused to respond.

The weeks and months passed in a fog for the two of them. Neither Caroline nor her mother bothered to watch Neil Armstrong walk on the moon. Caroline turned down an invitation from her old roommates to attend Woodstock. The wristwatch her mother had bought remained wrapped and tied with a bow on the highest shelf in the dining room. Her mother drove her to doctor appointments, and they rarely communicated beyond small talk and nostalgic recollections of life before her father's death. Her due date was right around Christmas, and she hoped it would not fall on the twenty-fifth.

By the beginning of December, she could no longer reach Fred. She left messages with anyone who knew them both, but he never called. He never wrote. Caroline imagined him hospitalized or dead. Zelda had to talk her out of heading back to San Francisco, weeks from delivering a baby, to hunt Fred down.

Her Uncle Horst had convinced them to decorate a tree to bring a little brightness back into the house. Caroline found it difficult to be comfortable in any position, lying, sitting, or standing. When contractions started on Christmas Eve, she cried through most of them. Her mother assumed that her hormones were at fault, but Caroline knew it was because the two men she thought would be there for her had disappeared.

The baby boy appeared at eight-thirty Christmas morning after eleven exhausting hours of labor. Amid Christmas carols being played over the hospital's intercom system, the doctor proclaimed that the baby was exceptionally healthy. His cry was unusually loud, so they let Caroline and little Rupert sleep separately that first night. She finally got some peace and quiet to sleep knowing her son was attended by the maternity ward nurses that first night. She assumed her mother had gone home to sleep.

In the morning, the nurse brought her breakfast, and before she had finished it, her mother reappeared with another even older woman in tow. This woman wore a patchwork coat and had graying red hair and green eyes. Her ears seemed kind of pointed at the tip and kind of long. "I brought an old friend who wanted to meet you," her mother explained.

As the other woman sat down in the chair beside her bed, Caroline set her tray to the side and said, "Maybe it would be better if we met after I'm discharged? I was in the middle of breakfast."

The woman turned to look at her mother and spoke in a strong Irish accent. "I can come back, m'dear, but you won't want to wait too long."

"Honestly, Caroline, just listen to her!" her mother cajoled.

Before Caroline could protest, the older woman unbuttoned her coat and leaned in toward Caroline. "I heard your father died suddenly, and your baby's father disappeared. I'm so sorry for your misfortune, cailín."

"It's been a . . . difficult few months," Caroline conceded.

"And I'm afraid it's going to get more difficult for either you or your baby very soon," the woman said softly.

Caroline was suddenly more alert. She wasn't sure if this was a threat. It was delivered in a way that seemed sincerely conciliatory. "Wait a second. Who are you? Do you know something I don't know?"

"It's a very long story," her mother offered. "My friend here, to put it simply, is in a position to help you or your baby . . ."

". . . but I can't help both of you," the woman finished.

Caroline wondered what sort of assistance couldn't be shared between her and her baby. "Are we talking about money or something else?"

"Imagine," the woman said and then paused, "that I have one gift to give, and I can only give it to one person. Would you prefer I give it to you or to your baby?"

"It depends on what the gift is," Caroline replied.

"Let's just say that it would be helpful in counteracting the sort of bad luck you've been having lately."

Caroline tried to think of what could have possibly prevented her father's death and Fred abandoning her. "Are we talking about some sort of experimental drug . . .?"

"Think of it as if it were medicine," her mother offered. "Would you prefer to give the only dose to your son, or take it for yourself?"

Caroline looked critically at her mother. She wondered why this meeting was so important to her that it had to take place while she was still in the hospital recovering from her first baby's birth. "If you're asking me if I value my life or my baby's more, I guess I would prefer to give him the extra help. Is there something you think you can do . . . really?"

"You have a point there, cailín," the woman said as she rocked back in her chair. "It would be a lot harder on the little nipper than on you to deal with this rubbish. So if I'm able to make someone's life a bit easier, you'd prefer I concentrate on your son?"

Caroline was thinking about what would get this crazy woman out of her hospital room. It seemed like a positive answer might do it. "Yes," she said. "I'd take a harder life if it meant an easier life for my son. I think that's the definition of motherhood, wouldn't you say, Mom?"

Her mother rushed to the other side of her bed and held Caroline's hand. "I think you're right, Caroline."

The woman got up from her chair and started rebuttoning her coat. "I guess we're done here then, Zelda." She took her mother by the arm and led her out of the room. She could hear the woman in the hallway tell her mother, "Now I need to get a look at your grandson."

15

CHAPTER 3: YOUNG RUPERT

Rupert's mother often remarked what a quiet baby Rupert had been. He seemed really easy to take care of from the moment she was reunited with him at the hospital. The nurses gave her a Polaroid of her baby lying in the nursery with a little Santa cap on his nearly bald head, because he had been born on Christmas morning in 1969. She stuffed it in the army-surplus backpack she was using as an overnight bag along with a copy of the bill she would have to discuss with her mother. Most of the time, a bottle or a pacifier would keep little Rupert quiet, even initially on the ride home in his grandmother's Impala.

"Uh-oh," Caroline said as she glanced over at her baby in the back seat beside her. "I think we need to change his diaper."

"You're probably right," her mother Zelda said without taking her eyes off the road, "but we'll be home in about five minutes. Let's just do it there."

The cry that rose from the infant carrier a minute later hurt both women's ears, and Zelda immediately pulled over to let her daughter change the diaper.

"Oh my gosh!" Zelda shouted over the baby's wailing. "I've never heard a newborn with such a loud cry."

Caroline was removing the diaper and wiping the baby down, so the decibel level started to drop quickly. "The nurses were mentioning that he had some really well-developed lungs, but I didn't realize what they meant until now."

In the following days, one of the two of them was always steps away from little Rupert. The memory of his ear-splitting cry remained fresh in their memories, so it was easy to be prepared with whatever the baby needed—formula bottle, fresh diaper, rocking, warmth—because it seemed so obvious each time. Caroline assumed that it was because she was attuned to very small signals from the baby

16

so she didn't talk about it with her mother. Zelda assumed that she was just lucky in guessing what her grandson needed, and she didn't want to brag about her success rate, so she didn't mention it to Caroline.

For the entire first year, until that next Christmas, it was amazing that the baby only cried when they were forced to delay responding to him. If they were only steps away, they managed to, on occasion deal with some fairly complex needs. At one point, the two women hung a mobile over his crib and slowly customized it with bits of tin foil and things with interesting smells, like a cinnamon stick and an orange wedge.

Zelda's savings slowly disappeared over that first year, so they had a very small, tabletop tree for Christmas, and the baby seemed to like the colored lights on the little tree. On Christmas morning, both women were awakened by little Rupert's mammoth wail and appeared in the nursery at the same time with, for the first time ever, no idea what the baby wanted.

The baby was standing in his crib holding onto the railing and shaking it as he cried. "I'll check his diaper," Caroline ordered her mother. "You get him crackers."

When Zelda returned without the crackers, Caroline had already changed the soiled diaper, but Rupert was still bawling. "Where are the crackers?" she demanded loudly.

"How do we know it's crackers and not apple sauce?" her mother asked loudly over the wailing. "It could be anything or no food at all. I'm really not sure. Try holding him in the meantime."

As soon as Caroline picked him up out of his crib and stood upright, the baby burped and left a splatter of spittle on her shoulder. Wordlessly, Zelda reached for a nearby towel and cleaned off the baby's face and the shoulder of Caroline's nightgown. As she folded the towel and set it aside again, Rupert was already quieting down. "Diaper change and gas," Zelda summarized. "I'll go grab the crackers and apple sauce from the kitchen in case we need it eventually."

Zelda returned to her memories of raising Caroline, and the two women transitioned into the more common strategy of trying several things before hitting on the right element or combination of elements to quiet the baby's crying or fussing. Rupert started standing and eventually walking without a handhold a few days later, and the women were slightly relieved that they would no longer have to carry him everywhere, but quickly distressed at how rapidly the toddler moved and how he toddled almost as much as he stayed in one place. They discovered he liked music because he smiled and swayed whenever it was played.

By the spring, when the weather was warm enough, Caroline worked part-time as a waitress at one of the family's restaurants to compensate for a couple of workers quitting. Zelda was on Rupert duty alone during those times. He was endlessly fascinated with finding things to come show her when they were in the front- or backyard of the house, so Zelda didn't pay as much attention to where he went, because he usually returned seconds later with some new treasure.

But when that rhythm stopped, it took Zelda a moment to figure out where Rupert had gone. She saw him toddling at full speed toward the street, and then he stopped right at the curb. A second later, a delivery truck zipped past.

Zelda felt like her heart had stopped, and she realized she had been holding her breath and gasped for air. She ran toward her grandson. He started to slowly turn around, and she knelt in front of him and hugged him tightly. "Ka!" Rupert declared.

Zelda released him to arm's length to look at him. "What did you say, Rupert?"

Rupert pointed in the direction the truck had sped off and repeated, "Ka!"

Zelda sighed heavily. "You scared me, Rupert. You mustn't go into the street!"

Rupert pointed at the pavement behind himself. "Tee!"

Zelda realized his baby talk was finally starting to evolve into meaningful words. He had indentified *car* and *street*. And somehow, he had managed to stop himself from running toward an oncoming truck, he couldn't possibly have seen. He wasn't tall enough to see over the parked cars. "Yes, stay out of the street," she repeated.

Over the course of Rupert's second year, his ability to avoid danger was successfully tested several times. Once, he suddenly got up and ran from the spot where he was picking dandelions near the sidewalk and took refuge on the front stoop next to Zelda. A few seconds later, someone with a medium-sized dog on a leash walked past, and the dog barked at the two of them until it was out of sight.

Another time, Caroline took him to the city pool to get him used to being in water. Rupert insisted she put his water wings back on him even though they were getting ready to leave, and seconds after she conceded and fitted them back over him, a teenager goofing around knocked both Rupert and Caroline into the pool. When Caroline resurfaced, she frantically looked for Rupert. He was happily bobbing along nearby with the aid of the wings.

And in the most spectacular example of Rupert's prescience, Rupert was a little frightened during an autumn thunderstorm at night. Caroline frequently got up to check on him and comfort him. At one point, she was awakened by a cry so loud it made her ears ring afterward. She rushed in and Rupert was trying unsuccessfully to climb out of his crib and wailing louder than she'd ever heard him before. She picked him up and held him close. He stopped crying and repeated, "Appy, appy, appy, appy..."

Caroline wondered why he had such an urgent hunger for apple sauce, but she carried him out of the nursery intending to take him to the kitchen for a late-night snack. Once she was in the hallway, the house shook with a huge rumbling crash and the sound of shattered glass. Caroline could hear the sound of the wind and rain as if she were outside, and as she stepped back into the nursery, she almost choked when she saw it.

The oak tree in the backyard, between the saturated ground and the high winds, had fallen against the house, breaking through the wall and window, smashing the changing table in the corner and the crib Rupert had been trying to escape only a minute before. The wind howled and the rain poured in in sheets, and Rupert still in Caroline's trembling arms, calmly reported, "Tree faw!"

After Rupert turned three, his ability to avoid accidents disappeared, and he got lots of bruises, scrapes, cuts, and a dislocated shoulder at one point. Remarkably every injury seemed to heal in less than a day. Even the dislocated shoulder had already gone back into place by the time Zelda drove him to the hospital.

Singing and dancing became one of Rupert's favorite pastimes. He would put on little shows for Zelda when she was babysitting him. Caroline was away more because she had to help manage one of the two restaurants. Zelda decided to sell one of them to consolidate their dwindling staffs and give her daughter more time with her son. Whenever Caroline brought him to the restaurant, Rupert always wanted to climb up onto the little raised platform in the back to perform. The customers seemed to love seeing the little boy sing and dance and generously applauded and cooed. The manager said that tips increased when Rupert was there, so Caroline decided to bring him around more often.

Early in Rupert's third year, it became evident that Rupert could no longer heal quickly. He developed an itchy rash on his forearms that remained for months, and his bruises remained black and blue for weeks.

But Rupert's popularity turned around the slow business at the restaurant. Whether or not Rupert performed onstage, customers cheered just to see that he had arrived. When he performed, even if he fell while dancing or forgot part of the song, the applause would be immediate, and it frequently involved customers giving him a standing ovation. When Caroline would take Rupert out in his stroller, people would rush up and ask if this was the little boy who performed at her restaurant. Caroline would suggest they stop by that night for dinner, because there was a possibility he might perform. Rupert became a local celebrity, and gossip seemed to elevate the speaker who had managed to see Rupert most recently.

Zelda took Rupert out in the stroller to the nearby park on a summer afternoon when he was three-and-a-half years old. Rupert liked to watch the ducks on the river. Zelda liked to replay her memories of walks along the river with Thomas, and she would smile for awhile until she thought about how he was missing the birth and growth of his grandson, and how proud he would be of Rupert. That brought a tear to her eye.

"Gramma, why are you crying?" The little boy had returned from communing with the ducks.

Zelda got a handkerchief out of her purse and dabbed her eyes. "I was remembering your grandpa and I walking here before you were born. It made me sad that he's not here anymore."

"He died," Rupert summarized. "I never met him. Mama showed me pictures and said he died. That means he's not coming back again. Where did he go?"

Zelda was a little shocked that Caroline had broached the topic of death with him at such a young age. She recovered enough to come up with a reasonable explanation. "His spirit went up to heaven, and we buried his body under the ground," she explained.

"You buried him?" Rupert seemed a little shocked.

"When someone dies, the part that is them doesn't live in the body anymore." She held Rupert's hand and led him to a bench near where she'd parked the stroller. She lifted him onto the bench and then sat down beside him. "The part we remember goes up into the clouds and travels among the stars."

"That would be cool," he declared.

"You'll have to wait a long, long time before you can take that trip, Rupert."

"Don't get his hopes up," a female voice said from behind the bench.

Zelda didn't need to turn to know who it was, even after so many years. "I didn't think we'd run into you again so soon, Grogoch."

The old woman sauntered around to the other side of the bench and sat down next to Rupert. The boy wanted to touch all the different fabrics that made up her coat. Zelda tried to pull him back. "Don't bother the lady," she scolded him.

"It's okay," the Grogoch said as she pulled Rupert up next to herself. She turned her gaze back toward Zelda. "You both seem healthy."

"We've had some tight scrapes and some hard times, but things are starting to look up a little," Zelda reported. "I was curious to see what your blessing would look like, and Rupert has manifested some amazing abilities."

"He will get a new one on his birthday every year," the older woman said. "What have you noticed lately?"

Rupert stood up on the bench and became fixated on the woman's large ears.

21

Zelda reached over to pull the boy away, but the Grogoch gently pushed her hand away. "It's okay." she said.

"He was anticipating harm just before an accident happened," Zelda narrated. "Then he could heal very fast. I'm not sure what it is this year. He seems very popular in town; I guess it's because Caroline takes him down to the restaurant to perform for customers sometimes."

The Grogoch chuckled and set Rupert down on his bottom again on the bench. She tickled him a bit in the belly, and Rupert let out a string of giggles. "This is the year of Rupert's charisma," she announced. "I was wondering what drew me here so soon again. I wasn't planning to visit again until he became an adult."

Zelda allowed herself to laugh as well. The explanation made sense to her, because all the attention Rupert got lately was well out of proportion to his charms and talents, she felt. "This is finally a gift that has been a benefit to more than just Rupert. He's bringing back customers to the restaurant, and we're making money again."

"Ohhh," the Grogoch intoned. "M'dear, I'm sure his previous gifts saved you a lot of money you would have paid to hospitals and doctors. Am I right?"

"I suppose that's true." Zelda had accumulated a number of questions she had wanted to ask the Grogoch when she met her again, and she tried to recall them. "So, if your blessing only lasts twenty-five years again, what will happen to Rupert on his twenty-fifth birthday?"

"I have only limited experience blessing babies," the old woman confided. "I don't think the good luck vanishes all at once, as it did for you. I think it takes a while to dissipate."

"So does that mean I'll live another . . . twenty-one-and-a-half years?"

"Oh. You're talking about the other part of the Pooka's curse now," the Grogoch said. She smiled at Rupert, who seemed to be content to watch the ducks from a distance. "Well, the intention behind the curse, if I remember correctly, was to make sure your bloodline died with you. That can be open to interpretation, now that the blessing is interacting with your family as well. Rupert can absolutely not die before he turns twenty-five, and since my blessing is stronger than the Pooka's curse, it should allow you to see him turn twenty-five. But after that, I don't know how soon or how strongly the curse will take hold again."

"I thought you told me that the curse would keep everyone in my family from marrying." Zelda remembered another theory she had developed over the years. "But since I married Thomas, didn't that break the curse?"

The Grogoch sighed. "I've been trying to offset my sister's curses for centuries. They are like an avalanche that picks up speed and volume as it tumbles down the mountainside. It was still gathering power when you and Thomas married. Your daughter has not married, correct?"

"No," Zelda admitted. "She was engaged to marry Rupert's father, I think."

"Then Rupert will never marry either, and your bloodline will end with him. There's nothing I can do about that. There's nothing you, or Caroline, or Rupert, or anyone else can do about that, I'm afraid."

Zelda saw the Grogoch scooting forward on the bench as if about to stand up. "Before you go," she called out as she pulled Rupert closer to herself. "What other kinds of abilities might Rupert manifest?"

The old woman stood and scratched the pointed ear Rupert had been playing with. "You'll have to wait and see. It's never the same with anyone."

The woman turned and started to walk away. "Will I see you again?" she called out after her.

The Grogoch just waved her hand in a vague dismissive gesture without turning around and kept on walking.

"Gramma, was that lady your friend?" Rupert asked as he pointed in the direction the Grogoch had gone.

"I'm not sure," she replied. "I guess so."

"I liked her coat. It was pretty. And she had funny ears. I hope we see her again."

"It's quite possible," she admitted.

Not long after that, Rupert climbed into his stroller and started to nap, so Zelda pushed him over the grass and back up to the path. As she was leaving the park, the Pooka who had shown up at Thomas's funeral was waiting for her. She was wearing the same dark green dress and the same demented grin that made her look even more wild and maniacal than her off-kilter eyes and nose alone. "Griselda Kellerman, née Becker," she called out as Zelda approached, "we need to talk."

"I have nothing to say to you," Zelda spat in her direction as she steered the stroller wide of the Pooka.

"My sister has interfered with my curse . . . again! And my lovely protégé Patricia is unhappy that you have not yet suffered as much as I promised you would. I'm not sure how she's continuing to thwart me. Her blessing should have stopped working after twenty-five years."

"Maybe your curse is already broken," Zelda tossed over her shoulder as she passed the woman with the deformed face.

"No, I would know that." the Pooka snarled. "It has just been suppressed. I will figure out what is causing that, and then you will suffer again."

Zelda started trotting and pushing the stroller faster to get away quicker. She heard the Pooka call out from behind her, "I will find out how my sister is still helping you, and then you will suffer!"

CHAPTER 4: RUPERT'S FOURTH BIRTHDAY

After a year of dealing with the constant barrage of her son's well-wishers and fans, Caroline told her mother not to answer the phone or the door for the several days leading up to Christmas in 1973. She unplugged the television as well, because it seemed to be mostly commercials for Christmas shopping or the Watergate hearings. She didn't go into the restaurant except to pass out paychecks and Christmas bonuses. Before going to bed each night, she cleared a stack of the gifts that accumulated each day on the front stoop.

As she brought in the second armful on Christmas Eve, however, she felt gratitude that Rupert's fifth ability was going to be gone by morning. Her mother had finally confirmed what she had suspected since she had met the Irish woman in the patchwork coat in the hospital after Rupert's birth. There was a rhythm to the odd and miraculous things happening to Rupert, and they always seemed to change on his birthday, Christmas morning. Everything that happened to Rupert seemed to be well intentioned. She hoped that would continue.

At first, the townsfolk and others from as far away as Milwaukee and Green Bay had been content to catch a glimpse of Rupert on the street, going to or from nursery school; at the grocery store, bank, restaurant, or doctor's office; and in their front yard. They relished his performances at the restaurant. By about June, after the *Milwaukee Journal* had featured Rupert's cult following in Sheboygan, the phone started ringing to bring Rupert to various morning TV shows around the state. Caroline had declined further publicity for her son, but by the end of November, people weren't willing to wait for Rupert's next appearance. They started ringing the Kellermans' doorbell.

There was no more space for the last load of gifts under their tree. Or within two feet of it, so she just placed the last five on the dining room table next to the stack of unopened Christmas and birthday cards Caroline had also left to accumulate. She climbed the stairs and checked on Rupert first. He was fast asleep on his little bed, surrounded by a few of the birthday gifts from her aunts and uncles she had let him open early.

When she entered her own bedroom for the first time since the morning, she remembered the daffodils Mike had given her sitting in their vase on her nightstand. Mike had been a patron at her family's restaurant, and he appeared there so regularly, Caroline went up to introduce herself. She intended to thank him with a small token gift after the server had seated him on that Friday evening in October. He brightened as she approached his table. He was a handsome man only a few years older than her with a brilliant smile. "You're Caroline Kellerman . . . the owner." He offered his hand. "I've seen you around here before."

Caroline shook his hand. She had been used to her son stealing the spotlight, so she chuckled in embarrassment at being singled out. "Actually, my mother is the owner, but I help her out here. I wanted to thank you for being such a regular customer. Can I ask your server to bring you a complimentary bottle of wine?"

"I occasionally indulge," he replied, "but that's really not necessary tonight. I heard a rumor that your son might be performing. Is that true?"

Her moment of feeling special vanished. "I'm not sure if my mother is bringing him around tonight or not." She paused for a moment to stand straighter and reaffix a smile on her face. "If you aren't interested in wine, perhaps I could comp your dessert tonight?"

"I hope I'm not being too forward," he said tentatively, "but if you really want to reward my patronage, joining me for dinner would make me the happiest."

Caroline had been so unaccustomed to attention from men since her father had died and Rupert was born, she shivered, and her face felt warm. "I will have to deal with emergencies soon, I'm sure." She didn't step away.

He immediately got up and pulled out the chair across from his. "My name is Mike Stanton, and you are free to get up and do your work, but I hope you will keep coming back to join me when you have the time. I eat alone often, as you know, but it isn't my preference."

He wore a white shirt under the light blue leisure suit, and it was open enough at the collar to see that Mike had a hairy chest, which always got her attention. She sat down across from him. "You can call me Caroline," she said. "And it would be my pleasure to entertain such a handsome and considerate man."

They had continued to meet and talk at the restaurant for a couple of weeks before he offered to take her to a movie. He had suggested *The Way We Were*, and she wondered why he had chosen to take her to such a depressing love story on their first date, but it drew her in, and she cried on his shoulder for most of the last half-hour. He had to travel for weeks at a time, but when he was back in Sheboygan, he would immediately call her for a date.

Mike had entrusted the daffodil delivery to her mother on the morning before Christmas while she was taking Rupert in for a doctor's appointment. Caroline repositioned them in the vase so none of the blooms were obscured. She leaned in and smelled their scent again, which reminded her of mushrooms and freshly cut grass. *He is so considerate,* she mused. *He remembered the one time I had mentioned daffodils weeks ago!*

She washed her face and brushed her teeth and put on her nightgown. When she was done and turning down the covers on her bed, Caroline heard a gentle rap on her bedroom door. Without waiting for her to respond, her mother pushed the door ajar and whispered, "Caroline, are you awake still?"

"Come in, Mom," Caroline whispered back. "I was just about to get into bed." She slid her feet under the downturned sheets and blankets and pulled them up to her waist.

"I know we talked a bit about how special Rupert is." Zelda slowly approached her.

"Yes, but I should tell you I'm still a bit doubtful that this is all an Irish blessing from some fairy. I'm thinking it could all be a coincidence. Nothing has really been that out of the ordinary, right? I mean, he hasn't gotten the power of invisibility or flight. They've all been kind of ordinary things that just happened more often than usual."

Zelda sat on a corner of the bed. "The woman I brought when Rupert was born was named the Grogoch. And I don't know if we can rule out more dramatic abilities than the ones we've seen so far."

"I was sorry to see the rapid healing go," Caroline admitted. "I'm not going to miss his year of being freakishly popular though."

"Well, it's helped the restaurant and brought Mike into your life," Zelda observed. "It hasn't been a total nightmare." She chuckled at her own hyperbole.

"True. I'm glad we're not just barely scraping by anymore."

Zelda pointed at the flowers on her nightstand. "And you have a handsome gentleman calling on you regularly."

"Also true, Mom." Caroline smiled. "But I was under the impression you had something specific to tell me."

Zelda swallowed hard. "Well, I told you we had one fairy blessing our family. We also have another fairy cursing us."

"Are you serious? What does that mean?" Caroline's mind reeled with images of what turf wars between ancient Irish sprites might look like.

"I told you about the troubles I went through when your father was away in England," Zelda began. "It started with that. A girl named Patricia who dated your father for a while in high school got so jealous of me that she made a deal with a fairy called the Pooka. A few weeks later, I met the Grogoch, her sister, and she promised to use her influence to alter my luck for twenty-five years. That blessing ended the night your father died. You remember how hard it was again for us right after that until Rupert was born? The Grogoch blessed Rupert in the hospital, and her blessing should protect him until he's at least twenty-five."

"And then what?" Caroline was frantic at the prospect. "Rupert is going to die on his twenty-fifth birthday?"

"Calm down," Zelda whispered. "I'll try to pass along what the Grogoch told me, but even she can't be too certain because Rupert received her blessing when only a few hours old, and the interaction with the Pooka curse is a little unpredictable. She said Rupert's blessing would continue until he's twenty-five

28

at least, and then it might start to fade away. Since you and I weren't directly blessed, things are likely to get worse for us in twenty years. How much worse, no one knows yet."

"And you believe that there is a Pooka cursing our family?" Caroline felt this was a particularly bad story to tell her right before falling asleep.

"I've met the Pooka too," Zelda said. "You saw her at your father's funeral. She was the deformed woman in the dark green dress."

"That was her?"

"Yes, and a few months ago, she confronted Rupert and me in the park. She's trying to find a way around Rupert's blessing to make me suffer, so you have to make sure you never talk to her. Don't go anywhere near her, and be careful not to talk about this with anyone else who might talk to her unknowingly. She could use any information she gets against us."

"And she's trying to ruin us because some girl you went to high school with got jealous of you and Dad?"

"I get the impression that the Pooka doesn't need much urging to inflict a curse. I don't know what Patricia did to convince her to hurt us." Zelda turned further toward her daughter and put her hand on her knee beneath the blankets. "And there is one other part of the curse I've also debated telling you about."

Caroline squeezed Zelda's hand. "Mom, before you go on, I need to tell you that your story holds together, but it is totally out there." She took a deep breath and sat up straighter. "I was willing to go along with the fairy blessing Rupert because it was a convenient way to think about Rupert's year of healing, his year of avoiding danger, and this past year of his popularity, but I talked about this with the doctor this morning. Frankly, it was a little embarrassing, but he said that sometimes kids get sensitized to danger because they hear things adults cannot, and immune systems work better or worse depending on how stressed someone is."

"You weren't there when he dislocated his shoulder, Caroline," Zelda argued. "That poor boy had to hold his arm up because it was completely dislocated. I drove him to the hospital immediately, and by the time we got to the triage nurse, she thought we were wasting her time, because it was already back in place."

"Maybe Rupert did something . . ."

"And no matter what he heard the night of that storm, how could he have known several minutes in advance that he had to get out of his crib?"

"He was scared," Caroline argued. "That might have been just a coincidence. He wanted to be held."

"That storm lasted for hours, Caroline. Seriously, you think he would start getting upset about it finally just before the oak tree crashed into the nursery?"

"I don't know!" Caroline pounded the mattress with both hands. Zelda sat silent for a full minute, waiting for her to go on. "I will admit that Dad dying just short of your twenty-fifth anniversary is really weird. And I will admit that those two women you're talking about *looked* and *sounded* very bizarre."

"The Grogoch knew things I had never told anyone other than your father. She knew about Patricia and how spiteful she was that your father ended up with me instead of her. And the Pooka showed up right after my blessing ended, at Thomas's funeral . . . to gloat because she was winning again."

Caroline sighed heavily. She knew Mike would be back in a couple of days. Being in his arms always comforted her. "I'm tired, Mom. Can we at least get through tomorrow without discussing this?"

Zelda patted Caroline's knee and got up from the bed. "Of course, dear. Sleep well, and we'll wake up to a glorious Christmas tomorrow."

Caroline waited until her mother had left and closed the bedroom door. She turned off the lamp on her nightstand and slid down under the covers. "Let this just be a normal year," she whispered to herself.

But after the three Kellermans descended to open gifts, at one point, Rupert picked up a present wrapped in gold foil paper with a fancy red-and-white ribbon around it. There was no tag or envelope attached to say who had delivered it. Rupert was on the verge of tears. "I don't want to open this one, Mommy."

Caroline took the package from Rupert's hands and placed it on the dining room table. When she came back to the living room, she knelt down in front of the little boy and hugged him. "What's wrong, Rupert?"

"I don't like what's in that box," Rupert said more defiantly.

Caroline turned her head to look at her mother. They were both dumbfounded. After a moment, Zelda said, "What do you think is in the box, sweetie?"

Rupert looked at both his mother and grandmother warily. "Dead mouse."

Caroline got up from the floor and crossed to the dining room. She picked up the gold-wrapped box again. She shook it gently for the first time. Something small and soft seemed to flop around, and she entertained the idea that her son was correct.

She grabbed scissors from the drawer in the dining room and then carried them and the gift in question into the kitchen. She set the box in the kitchen sink and carefully cut away the ribbon, the paper, and the tape holding the box closed. The smell reached Caroline's nostrils even before she was clear what lay in the bottom of the box. It was a rat, not a mouse, and there was a tag tied with a string around the creature's mid-section that had her mother's name written on it.

She sighed and set down the scissors on the countertop. She walked through the dining room to where her mother and son waited in the living room, not wanting to look up at them until she had come to a stop. "Mom," she said softly, "I think it was intended for you."

Without another word, Caroline sat down next to her mother on the sofa staring blankly out at the Christmas tree and the sizable number of gifts still beneath it. Zelda looked at her for a moment and wondered what had so traumatized her daughter. She got up and went to the kitchen. She came back walking slowly too. She took her seat on the sofa again and whispered to her daughter, "It has to be Patricia."

Caroline looked at her with obvious distress. "Has she ever done anything like this before?"

Zelda was looking at Rupert sitting on the living room floor surrounded by his gifts. He was staring up at them bewildered. "Pick another gift to open, sweetie," she called out. As the boy was searching through the agglomeration, she whispered back to Caroline, "After hearing from the Pooka this summer, I think perhaps Patricia was complaining that she wasn't doing enough to make me suffer. Perhaps this is Patricia taking things into her own hands."

Caroline was watching her son reach over other gifts to slide one out from near the back. "Just take one that's easier to reach, Rupert."

"I want to open this one next. I've been wanting a transistor radio."

Caroline saw one of the two presents she had bought and wrapped for her son appear in his hands when he emerged from beneath the tree. It was indeed the little AM radio he had asked for back in August. She waited for him to rip off the paper to ask him, "So how did you know what it was and what box it was in, Rupert?"

Rupert set down on the floor the radio he had been examining. "It needs a battery," he announced.

"We'll get you one after lunch. Can you answer Mommy's question? How did you know which box had the radio? Were you shaking them like I told you not to?"

"No, Mommy. I just knew it like I already opened it. I saw it."

"Has this ever happened before, sweetie?" Zelda prompted.

Rupert shook his head. "Just today." He started pointing at the various still-wrapped gifts near him. "That's a pair of mittens. That's chocolate. That's a book. That's just a piece of paper with some writing on it . . ."

"Okay, Rupert," his mother interrupted. "Open the box with the mittens next then. Let's see them."

As Rupert grabbed the box and started tearing at the wrapping paper, Zelda whispered to Caroline, "I think this may be Rupert's new gift. He's clairvoyant."

Caroline waited until her son pulled the blue-and-pink, hand-knitted mittens out of the box before replying. She had introduced Mike and Rupert at Thanksgiving a month before. "You remember Mike, don't you, Rupert?"

"Sure." He put on the mittens and reached for the box he thought held chocolate.

"Do you know where Mike is right now?" she asked.

"Somewhere where it's raining," Rupert said rather casually. "No snow on the ground."

"Where is he?" Zelda whispered.

"Are there any tall buildings where he is?" Caroline prompted further.

"There are lots of buildings." Rupert took off the mittens and focused on stacking the chocolate bars on the carpet before finding another gift to open.

"What does the tallest one look like?" Caroline knew Rupert had never been where Mike had gone the day before, even if he'd overheard the name of the city.

"Like a flying saucer on top of some curvy legs."

"Mike's in Seattle," Caroline whispered to her mother. "I never told Rupert that, and he's never been there."

"Maybe he's seen pictures of the Space Needle?" Zelda suggested.

"Do you know the name of the city where Mike is?" Caroline leaned closer to her son.

"I don't know." Rupert was still focused on opening presents. "It's far away and has lots of water."

Suddenly, Caroline's mother got up from the sofa and scurried toward the kitchen. Caroline could hear her clomping down the basement steps and a few minutes later clomping back up. When she returned, she was holding an old high school yearbook. From the cover she could see it was one from 1941. "This was your father's, when he was a senior at Central High," Zelda narrated as she sat down and started paging through the book.

Zelda landed on a page filled with black-and-white photos of young men in suits and ties and young women in dresses with large white collars. She pointed to one with the name Patricia Connor beneath it. "That's Patricia," she whispered. "She's the one who enlisted the Pooka to curse us. She's the one who probably sent us that dead rat too."

"She still lives in Sheboygan?" Caroline whispered back.

"I heard she finally quit Kohler and moved out to Sheboygan Falls, but I don't know where. I'd really like to return her gift."

"How are you going to find her?"

"Rupert," Zelda called out. "Could you come over here for a minute?"

Rupert put down the Big Jim action figure he had just unwrapped and sat down next to his grandmother. "You see this woman here, sweetie?"

Rupert looked down at the photo. "Uh huh."

"Her name was Patricia Connor, and I'm really trying to find out where she lives now. Do you have any ideas where we should look?"

"She's old now like you, Grandma," Rupert explained. "She lives in a little white house on stilts."

"We think she lives in Sheboygan Falls." Caroline decided to see how helpful her son's new gift could be. "We went through that town on the way to your great-aunt Ingrid's house in Fond du Lac, remember?"

"Yeah."

Caroline leaned forward. "Do you know if there's a number on her house?"

"One, two, zero, . . . in black letters, next to the front door. Can I go open more presents now?"

"In just a minute, sweetie," Zelda told him. "Last question: Do you know the name of the street the house is on?"

"He's just starting to read, Mom," Caroline whispered. "He can't help you there."

"It's a really long name," he replied. "Can I open more presents now?"

"Go ahead," Caroline told him. She whispered to her mother, "Until he learns to read, this gift isn't going to help us much."

Rupert got up to continue opening gifts, and Zelda got up to go to the dining room. She rummaged through one of the drawers in the dining room for a bit and then returned with a map of Sheboygan Falls. "Help me look for the longer street names," she asked Caroline.

Caroline sighed. "They are all about the same length."

"Down here," Zelda pointed. "Fairway Meadows Lane. I think that's the longest." She called out to Rupert, "When you saw that white house on stilts, sweetie, was it across the road from a golf course?"

Rupert looked up at the top of the Christmas tree for a moment. "I think so."

In the afternoon after all fifty-one gifts were opened, Zelda and Caroline took armloads of food and toys to the kitchen and Rupert's room, respectively. On one

34

of the trips to clear out the living room, Caroline finally asked her mother, "Are you thinking of going to Sheboygan Falls to confront Patricia, Mom?"

"I'm doing more than thinking of it. I'm planning on it."

"Mom! What if she gets violent?"

"She's fifty years old. What is she going to do? Stab me? Shoot me?"

"She could!" Caroline argued.

"If she's resorting to Irish fairies and dead rodents to get back at me, I don't think that's likely. Besides, she probably won't be there. I'll just return her gift . . . leave it on *her* doorstep."

"I'm going with you," Caroline declared.

"That's not practical, dear. Someone's got to watch Rupert, and don't even think of bringing him along."

Caroline eventually conceded and promised to come looking for her if she wasn't back by six o'clock. Zelda took off in the family Impala with the dead rat in the trunk.

It was almost sunset by the time Zelda turned into the golf course entrance and then onto Fairway Meadows Lane. There were only three houses on the road, near the end, partially shrouded by leafless trees and heaped with snow. The nearest one was marked 120 and was indeed on stilts. Zelda parked on the road across from it. She got the box out of the trunk and carried it toward the house.

Peeling stickers on the long, black, metal mailbox spelled out CONNOR. Zelda held the box against her side and rapped on the wooden door. She took a deep breath when she heard movement inside and a light came on.

The woman who opened the door had more gray hairs than she did. Her posture was worse. Her makeup made her saggy, wrinkled skin almost a uniform, unnatural white, but a few of the larger freckles were visible through the clumsy concealment. She wore a light-green terrycloth bath robe over a white turtleneck, and her green eyes widened with wonder and then immediately narrowed with hatred when she realized who was at her door. "You didn't need to bring me a Christmas gift, Zelda. I thought we decided to forgo that decades ago."

"I thought we had as well, Patricia, which is why I came to return the dead

35

pet you left on our doorstep." Zelda thrust the box with the dead rat toward her.

"I have no idea what you're talking about, Zelda. I've never been to your new house." Patricia set the box down on her porch floor and opened her front door wider. "If you'd like to chat for a bit before you head back to town, please come in out of the cold."

Zelda couldn't decide if she wanted to just leave the hateful woman behind or pump her for information. She finally told herself that it would be better to keep it all in one unpleasant episode rather than to risk tracking her down again. "Just for a couple of minutes," she said as she walked past Patricia and into her home.

After closing the door and leading her through a hallway and living room filled with paper grocery bags full of magazines and newspapers, Patricia sat down on a maroon loveseat with at least six throw pillows on it. The only other open piece of furniture was a high-backed, armless, upholstered chair, and Zelda pretended to brush dust off the seat with her glove before sitting down. "I gather you haven't married," Zelda observed.

"And you are no longer married." Patricia sneered. "But you had a good twenty-five years together."

"We did." Zelda decided not to add anything else catty, because it was the subject most likely to set Patricia off. "I can't complain. My life is good."

"And why is that, I wonder." The question was unsuccessfully casual.

"Clean, honest living."

"And you've still been in contact with an Irish fairy, I hear." Patricia started playing with her pillows.

Patricia didn't look up at her. "As have you . . . I hear."

"Yours can only bless someone once, I'm told," Patricia said as she finally turned back toward Zelda. "And the magic only lasts twenty-five years. The Pooka promised me she would curse your entire family. So, what's protecting you now, thirty years later? Did you find another fairy to protect you?"

Zelda knew not to answer that question. "If you truly loved Thomas, why did ⁊gree to a curse that would kill him at such a young age?"

'₁ve for him died when he told me he never wanted to see me again, and

36

then I found out he had been seeing you in the summers. He told me he couldn't see me in the summers because he had to work in Milwaukee."

Zelda hadn't known what Thomas had told Patricia to keep himself available in the summers. She regretted that he had resorted to a lie. "I'm sorry that he lied to you, Patricia, but I have to think he was just trying to keep you from feeling slighted." Zelda stood up. "And I think that's all I want to share with you now. Please don't leave any more 'gifts' on our doorstep, Patricia, or I will call the police next time."

As Zelda wound her way along the narrow path between the paper bags, Patricia called after her, "Oh, don't go so soon! The Pooka always comes to visit me on Christmas night, and I'm sure she'd love to see you again!"

Zelda marched out the front door without closing it and down the steps. She glanced back at the house when she had the key in the ignition, and Patricia had finally closed the door. She drove back through the gathering darkness toward home, hoping she would not encounter the Pooka along the way.

CHAPTER 5: RUPERT'S FIFTEENTH BIRTHDAY

Rupert eventually learned to control the sea of images of things hidden and things distant his clairvoyance offered him, but it was not until weeks before he turned five that his insights stopped causing shock and embarrassment for the adults around him. His nursery school teacher was angry that he accused her of mistreating her pets at home. She denied it, but as the gossip spread, the county humane society stepped in and investigated. His teacher was suspended, and her cats and dogs taken to a shelter. Caroline had to forbid him from looking into the lives of adults after that. She imagined him looking in on her and Mike having sex, and she didn't want to explain that to a four-year-old.

On the plus side, Rupert was able to disarm bullies rather easily by making their private shame public. And in one case, it was Rupert's tip to the sheriff's office that helped locate a kidnapped girl where her uncle was holding her in a cabin near Shawano.

On Rupert's fifth birthday, his new ability was amusing at first. Zelda and Caroline found almost everything he did and said funny. But it soon became exhausting to be laughing so frequently, and Rupert was getting resentful that he wasn't being taken seriously anymore. Zelda found that taking Rupert out into public was the only respite from her nearly constant giggling. When other people were around and laughing, she finally felt she could relax, even though it made Rupert even more upset that strangers were laughing at him. Caroline tried to get her son to keep performing his song-and-dance routine at the family restaurant, and he eventually gave in and tried to frame the audience laughter as appreciation of his performance. Within days, he developed a list of jokes and funny stories to tell people, so he could imagine that they were laughing at his wit. And most people, including his mother and grandmother, learned to tone down their laughter when Rupert was around to chortles and snickering they tried to hide from Rupert.

Over the ensuing ten years, once Rupert started going to school, most of his new gifts were helpful. Caroline and Zelda agreed that his next gift after the exhausting year of laughter was a calmer and gentler inspiration. Until Rupert turned seven, people frequently got small epiphanies or new ideas in his presence. Caroline said she had never been so efficient. Rupert was glad that people felt happy to see him, but they often left quickly to pursue whatever new thing he had inspired in them. He was glad when the bicentennial celebration was over in July, because far too many of his inspirations were being wasted on red-white-and-blue decorations and American-history-themed parties.

After Rupert turned seven on Christmas morning in 1976, people stopped becoming joyfully inspired in his presence and frequently resented him. With his family, most of the time, his newly honed empathy just helped him be more sensitive. At school, at the restaurant, and elsewhere out in the world, it became difficult for him to reconcile people's words with the subtext he was more keenly aware of. Several times, he lashed out in anger when someone was trying to hide their contempt or jealousy behind compliments. Caroline finally had to counsel him to use his gift to find more honest people and not to worry about or spend time with dishonest people. A girl named Haley and a boy named Trevor became his best friends that year, because they had absolutely no guile. They just liked hanging out with Rupert.

It took a while after Rupert turned eight to figure out what his next blessing was. To him it just built on a tendency he already had to imagine the histories of people and objects he saw. In that year, his imaginary stories ended up being true. His third-grade teacher picked up on his amazing insights and would bring uncommon objects to class and always call on Rupert last to explain where it came from or what its function was. Some of his prouder identifications included a bismuth crystal, a crab's pincer from Japan, and a U.S. Army Medal of Honor he knew had been given by mistake to one of Abraham Lincoln's pallbearers.

His fourth-grade teacher was not as impressed with Rupert's "knowledge of trivia," as he put it. So Rupert kept his fantasies to himself, unless he was with family who loved to test his ability more than his third-grade teacher had and cheered him when he was right. He did his class work and his first real homework without complaint, though he struggled more with science and math.

But when he came back from Christmas vacation, he did his schoolwork in record time, and his hand always went up first. He always knew the answer when his teacher asked questions. Having the town's minor song-and-dance celebrity repeatedly stealing the spotlight started to get under his teacher's skin. The man would push Rupert with ever-more-obscure questions, and Rupert was always right.

Because that was the gift of Rupert's ninth birthday blessing. He felt his intelligence was pretty average most of the time, but for most of 1978, the answer to any question posed to him always popped into his head at that moment. His mother and grandmother made a game out of it and learned that Rupert's omniscience reached far further than the objective facts in books. They used him to check in on distant relatives and to predict the next day's weather. They mutually agreed not to ask Rupert about winning numbers in the Illinois Lottery. And Rupert found he could not get accurate information unless someone else requested the information without his prompting.

On Christmas Eve that year, during dinner at home, just before he turned ten, Rupert's mother asked him what the next year's ability would be. He answered, "Invisibility." At first, he looked curious and confused. Then he looked angry. "That sucks!"

"That would be interesting to see," Caroline commented.

"Actually," Rupert said, "you won't be able to see me, and that could be a big problem."

"I don't think that's possible," Zelda argued. "The blessing only changes your luck, not the laws of physics."

"I asked him, Mom," Caroline said. "It was my question, not his. He's always right . . . for one more day at least. You know that."

"It might not be literal invisibility," Zelda said.

"And the rapid healing when he was two was against the laws of physics," Caroline continued.

"I had rapid healing?" Rupert asked. "That would have been great to have now with all the bruises and strained muscles I've been getting in dance class."

"Sweetie," Zelda said, "you just have to get to class on time so you have more time to stretch."

"I'm just sayin' . . ." Rupert began and then never finished his thought.

The next morning, Caroline went to find Rupert to start opening Christmas and birthday presents, but she couldn't find him seemingly anywhere in the house. She rushed back to the kitchen where her mother was mixing pancake batter. "Mom! Mom! I've looked everywhere. I can't find Rupert!"

"Maybe he's just become invisible, but he's still here." Zelda set the bowl down on the countertop and wandered into the dining room. "Rupert? Rupert? Where are you?"

Caroline scurried after her. "Or he left the house before we got up! We have to go find him!"

"Rupert? Rupert?" Zelda continued to call as she walked past the tree in the living room. "Are you here, sweetie?"

Caroline tried to pull on Zelda's shoulder. "Mom, he's not here."

Zelda was unperturbed. She continued up to the second floor. "Rupert? Rupert?"

They looked again in both bathrooms, in Zelda's bedroom and Caroline's bedroom—even under the beds and in their closets. They eventually opened the linen closet door, even though there was nowhere in there for a ten-year-old to hide. Zelda stood for a few moments in the upstairs hallway calling Rupert's name.

Suddenly both women heard the sound of a nearby door being opened. "I'm right here, Grandma."

Both women turned in the direction of Rupert's voice, and he was standing in a doorway in his pajamas, looking up at them a bit sleepy and confused. "Where

41

have you been?" his mother asked. "We've been searching the whole house for you."

"We didn't check the basement," Zelda observed.

"And you didn't check my room." He looked upset. "I was in bed . . . asleep."

"I thought I did," Caroline said.

"I thought we did too," Zelda agreed. "Maybe we can look at Rupert and not see him unless he speaks."

Caroline turned around at the mention of her son's name, suddenly unsure where he was.

"I'm still over here, Mom!" Rupert shouted. "I haven't moved."

"He's right, dear." Zelda put her arm around Rupert's shoulders. "You just looked in the wrong direction."

"Ugh!" Rupert grumbled. "This is going to be as bad as the year of everyone laughing at me." He sighed. "I'm going to shower and get dressed. I'll be downstairs in a few minutes."

For most of the year, his teachers didn't call on him when he raised his hand, it would take people a while to notice that he was in a room, and when people were looking for him, they seemed to avoid where he was until he found them. His spring report card said he was absent five days, and he was actually only out one day with stomach flu. He also got poor marks for class participation in three of his subjects. Haley and Trevor didn't seek him out to do things after school or on weekends anymore, and when he called them up to propose getting together, they seemed to have forgotten about him until that moment. He had to find them first when they met, or they would never see him.

By the fall, Rupert had gotten used to making his presence known frequently so that people would not think he had disappeared. He found he had to call out the teacher's name to respond to a question in class. His fall report card was more acceptable.

When he turned eleven, he developed the ability to understand and speak every foreign language he heard. Zelda took advantage of the blessing to give him practice in German.

It was difficult to figure out the new blessing when Rupert turned twelve. For most of that year, he was just very sensitive to loud noises. Sometimes it took him a while to fall asleep, because he could hear from his bedroom in the back of the house the sound of cars silently passing on the street in front of the house. It seemed to improve his dancing slightly.

His most distressing ability slowly became clear when he turned thirteen. He had already started his first growth spurt and getting body hair, not a sex object by any means, and yet adults and children of both genders seemed to frequently find excuses to hug Rupert and/or kiss him on the cheek. It was not too out of the ordinary for his mother and grandmother, though the frequency seemed abnormally high. The most confusing attention was from his mother's boyfriend, Mike. He would find excuses to use the bathroom when Rupert was showering and to visit Rupert when he was already in bed for the night. And he always gave him a long, tight hug when he left to go to his home on the south side of town.

When Rupert came back from Christmas vacation during his last year at junior high, he found himself hanging out more often in the weight room at the school gym. He started lifting weights just to see what it was like, and it seemed pretty simple and easy, and he liked the way it made him feel. By the summer, when he went with Trevor and Haley to the city pool, Rupert had already developed a fairly muscular chest and arms. He started adding lap swimming to his exercise routine. And in the fall he added running around the park near his home, and his lower body developed more as well. Trevor agreed to be Rupert's workout partner after school to spot him on his chest presses and tricep dips.

Trevor was a few months older than Rupert and a little thinner. Rupert promised to help him put on more muscle, and the two of them started spending more time together without Haley. Trevor's family decided to go to Florida for Christmas vacation, and Trevor said he didn't want to go. He asked Rupert if he could stay at his house as they had a few times for sleepovers when they were younger. Rupert enjoyed Trevor's easy way of talking and his sense of humor, so he agreed to ask his mother.

Caroline balked for a moment at the idea of two fifteen-year-old boys sleeping in the same room together, but she volunteered the family's air mattress and told Rupert it was fine. Trevor was a little on the shy side, so he would always get ready for bed first and be in a sleeping bag on the air mattress on the floor of Rupert's bedroom before Rupert had finished brushing his teeth. They would talk for a while before going to sleep. Rupert started fantasizing about sliding into the sleeping bag next to Trevor, but he was too afraid to try it.

Christmas Day and Rupert's birthday came and went without much of a hiccup. Rupert noticed that people seemed to enjoy talking to him more than they had previously. He started to think about putting together a new act to perform at the family restaurant as his mother had been suggesting for months.

On Christmas night, Trevor and Rupert took turns using the bathroom before going to Rupert's bedroom to sleep. When Rupert turned off the light and got into bed, Trevor wished him a happy birthday again and started a conversation that lasted a lot longer than their previous hypnagogic talks. After it went on for over a half-hour with Trevor's need for conversation showing no sign of slowing or stopping, Rupert interrupted him to whisper, "Is there something bothering you, Trevor?"

"I'm nervous."

"What are you nervous about?"

Trevor paused. He sighed. He paused again. "I'm nervous about telling you how I feel."

Rupert had no idea if this was leading to something good or something very disappointing. He imagined Trevor was uncomfortable staying with him but had nowhere else to go until his family returned. He finally summoned the courage to ask another follow-up question. "How do you feel, Trevor? Does it have something to do with me?"

"Y-y-yes," Trevor stuttered.

"Are you cold?" Rupert asked. "I can get you another blanket."

"No, I'm okay." Trevor paused. "Just nervous."

"So, am I making you nervous?"

"Yes. It's not your fault though."

"Oh." Rupert tried to think of the most direct way to get Trevor to reveal his feelings. "How do you feel about me, Trevor?"

"I like you. I like you a lot. I think you have a really hot body. I can't believe I said that. I hope you don't think I'm being creepy."

"No, no. I like you too, Trevor. I've been dreaming about getting out of bed and joining you in your sleeping bag." Rupert paused. "I hope that doesn't freak you out."

"In a good way," Trevor assured him.

"Okay." Rupert wasn't sure if that was an invitation. "Do you want me to join you there?"

After a brief pause, in the softest of whispers, Trevor breathed, "Yes."

Trevor kept his arms tightly pressed to his sides as Rupert slid into the sleeping bag with him. He maintained that position when Rupert threw one arm over Trevor's chest. He felt Trevor's heart beating rapidly and his crotch was pressed up against Trevor's leg, so there was no ambiguity about his excitement.

They lay that way for about five minutes. Trevor broke the silence first. "I don't think I'm ready for this."

Rupert brought his arm back and started shimmying out of the sleeping bag. "Okay," he whispered back.

Rupert didn't fall asleep for two hours after getting back into bed. He just listened to Trevor breathing and waited for his erection to go away.

Breakfast the next morning with his grandma, mother, Mike, and Trevor was very quiet and subdued at first. Rupert broke the tension first. "Why is everybody so quiet this morning?"

His grandmother replied, "I guess I'm waiting to find out what your new blessing is, sweetie. It wasn't very clear yesterday."

"I was worried," his mother answered, "that Mike and I were making too much noise last night and woke you up. You slept so much later today."

"I have a dozen questions," Mike said, "and I don't know if I can or should ask any of them."

Rupert put the three adults' candor together with Trevor's late-night revelation and started to develop a theory. It had something to do with honesty, but he wasn't quite sure how it worked. He didn't find out for sure until two days later, when Trevor's family returned from Florida.

Trevor declined a ride home from Rupert's grandmother, so Rupert volunteered to walk Trevor home. Snow was still falling. There weren't many cars out on the roads, and most of the sidewalks hadn't been shoveled yet, so they walked in the street. As they walked through the silent snow and approached the first intersection at the end of the block, Rupert finally got the courage to ask the question: "So are you attracted to guys, or do you just feel close to me?" When Trevor didn't answer immediately, Rupert went on. "I mean, it doesn't matter to me. I like you a lot. I've known you forever, and I thought what we did two nights ago was really exciting."

Trevor kept trudging alongside Rupert through the snow. The only sounds were the crunching of the snow beneath their boots as they walked through the tire tracks, the distant echo of an ambulance siren, and their breath as it came out in puffs of ice crystals. "I'm not sure," Trevor said softly. "I do feel close to you, and yeah, eight years feels like forever to me too." He walked a few more steps, waited for a car to pass, and then continued. "You're really an attractive guy, and watching you work out at the gym has been a dream for me. I can't believe how strong you've gotten in the past year. You're pressing over a hundred pounds now!"

"I know." Rupert ran forward a bit to try to see Trevor's expression that was partially hidden by his hood. "Have you been attracted to other guys?"

"Yeah," Trevor admitted. "Sometimes."

Rupert waited a few seconds before continuing. "I'm surprised we're only having this discussion now. Have you felt this way for a while?"

"Yeah," Trevor said immediately. "I only started feeling comfortable telling you in the past three days—since Christmas morning."

"Okay," Rupert said as he strode next to Trevor again. "Do you want to explore more when we can find some privacy?"

"Yeah," Trevor said. Then he stopped. Rupert moved to face Trevor. "I can't believe I'm telling you all this!" Trevor almost shouted.

"Okay, okay." Rupert put his mittened hands on Trevor's shoulders. "Let's just drop the subject for now, okay?"

"Thank you."

Trevor started walking again, and Rupert fell in beside him again. "What are you thanking me for?"

"It's such a relief to tell you," Trevor said. He patted Rupert on the shoulder. "I really thought you would hate me if I told you, and I never expected you'd feel the same."

"I do," Rupert said softly. "I want to see where this goes."

"Yeah? Cool."

Rupert gave Trevor a big hug when they arrived in front of Trevor's house. Trevor skipped up the drive and in through the garage entrance. Even though he knew Trevor couldn't see it, he waved goodbye to him.

Walking back to his own house, Rupert noticed one of the only other pedestrians he had seen out that night standing in a thick wool coat and wearing fuzzy yellow earmuffs. He felt drawn to check on this older woman standing on the corner. As he got closer, he noticed that her eyes and nose didn't seem symmetric. She grinned widely as he approached. "Are you in any trouble, ma'am?" he called out as he took the last couple of steps toward her.

She turned to face him more directly, and Rupert could see a small V of a dark green dress she wore beneath the wool coat. "You're that Kellerman boy everyone talks about," she proclaimed.

"Yes, ma'am. I'm Rupert Kellerman. Are you waiting for someone to pick you up? There aren't any buses that stop near here."

The woman cursed under her breath toward her feet and then looked up again at Rupert with a creepy smile. "No, I was just waiting for you to come along. I would rather not have told you that, but I can feel you are charmed. I cannot lie to you."

"Why would you be waiting for me?" Rupert asked.

"I needed to figure out who was protecting your grandmother, Griselda

47

Kellerman," the strange woman practically snarled. "Now I know. It's you, Rupert Kellerman. You've been blessed."

"How do you know that?" Rupert demanded.

"Because your family has had such a charmed life for the past fifteen years. You must be about fifteen now, aren't you, Rupert?"

"I am. What do you know about me?"

"Now that's a question I would love to answer for you. Walk with me."

As she took a slow pace through the snow on the sidewalk, Rupert followed along near the edge of the road. "I know that you received an interesting ability this week. I know that if you ask someone a direct question, they will feel little hesitation in giving you a truthful answer. I know that you're thinking about coming out to your mother as a homosexual, and I would very much advise against that. She will not want to hear that bit of truth from you, because she does not want it to be true. I know that the man she has been dating for the past ten years will never marry her, and because of that he will very soon leave your mother broken-hearted. And I am certain that one of the abilities you receive in the next year or two will convince you that you need to be away from your family to be free to love who you want and pursue a career as a performer, which you certainly cannot do here in . . . Sheboygan."

She pronounced the name of his hometown like it was distasteful to her. His mind was reeling with all the information she had given him, and he wondered if it were true. But then he knew his new gift would make it easy to verify what she had said. He could just ask them, and they would have to tell him the truth, just as this strange woman must have been telling him the truth.

He became so focused on getting the answers from his family and from Mike, he started jogging through the snowy street, leaving the odd woman behind. His concern for her evaporated when he realized she was a dangerous woman because of what she knew.

That night, when he got home and started asking his questions, Mike left and never returned. His mother and grandmother cried and tried to convince him that he couldn't know his sexuality yet. He shut himself in his room and pulled from his backpack a brochure from the Interlochen Arts Academy he had picked up at the dance studio. He needed to get away. He felt like this opportunity would be a good start.

CHAPTER 6: RUPERT AT TWENTY-FIVE

Rupert had made it a tradition after he graduated from Julliard in New York City: He spent most of his birthday feeding the homeless at a church in Chelsea. His pager started going off just before noon, and he ignored it, assuming it was the choreographer wanting another individual rehearsal for the February performance in D.C. He told himself he would call him back when his shift was over. He couldn't want to schedule anything on Christmas Day, so he would call him back later when he got home to his studio on the Upper West Side.

Then the pager went off again, and he wondered if it was someone else or the choreographer again. He decided even two pages could wait until he was done serving meals.

When the fourth page came in, Rupert excused himself from the serving line for a moment and scrolled through the numbers on his pager. One was from his father, and the other three all had 920 area codes and numbers he didn't recognize, but it was an area that covered much of Wisconsin north of Milwaukee. It was the area code for Sheboygan, the hometown he had left shortly after his sixteenth birthday.

While he was holding the pager, it vibrated with another number, one he knew well–the home phone number he shared with his roommate Danny. It couldn't just be people wanting to wish him a happy birthday. Only his immediate family and Trevor knew his birthday was on Christmas; he hadn't told anyone in New York. Danny didn't even know. People paging him to wish him a merry Christmas, perhaps?

The cook who was supervising Rupert was named Bert, and Bert noticed

Rupert staring at his pager. "Is there some emergency, Rupert? Do you need to go?"

"I don't know yet, Bert." Rupert said as apologetically as he could. "I've gotten four pages." His pager buzzed again. "Five pages in the past twenty minutes. It wouldn't be leaving you high and dry?"

"No, it's cool, bro'," Bert replied. "Jesse and Connie can handle the serving. You go, and have a very merry Christmas, Rupert."

Rupert grabbed his backpack and jacket. "Thanks, Bert. Same to you."

Rupert jogged up Ninth Avenue and cut over to Eighth to catch the first of two trains home from Penn Station. Once the doors closed on his subway car, he unclipped the pager from his belt again to look at the fifth page. It was his father's number in San Francisco again. That had to be an emergency, Rupert decided. He dashed up the stairs when the train let him off at 66th Street. When he got to his building, Rupert took the stairs two at a time to get to his apartment and unlock the door.

When he opened the door, he saw Danny in a tank top and sweatpants pacing back and forth near the telephone and answering machine on the table. Rupert watched him for almost a minute, surprised that he hadn't seen or heard him open the apartment door. All of a sudden, Danny grabbed his down jacket and walked through Rupert and disappeared down the stairs.

When Rupert had turned twenty-four, he had started seeing afterimages of people that had been there recently. Living in New York, it hadn't bothered him much because he was almost always surrounded by people. If the emotional imprint was weaker, the images were transparent and ghostly. The stronger emotional imprints were hard to distinguish from reality. There were never any sounds. It was always like a pantomime.

He wondered why Danny had left so upset. His afterimage seemed so solid. He threw his backpack onto his bed, shucked off his jacket on a chair, and pushed the play button next to the blinking red light of his answering machine.

The first message was a straightforward one from his father to call him immediately. The second message was from his father stressing how important it was that Rupert call right away. The third message was a call from Deena, a girl in his dance company, wishing Rupert a merry Christmas. The fourth and final message was again his father, and he revealed he had news about a tragedy.

Rupert was breathing hard and fast, and his hand was shaking so much, he had to try twice to correctly punch in his father's phone number. "Hello, Fred?" Rupert said loud and insistently into the receiver.

"Rupert, I'm so glad you called." His father did seem glad to hear from him, but there was something weighing on him that magnified during the time he paused. "Britney took the call from your great-aunt Ingrid, because it was before I got up this morning. I called her back to get more details. Are you sitting down, son?"

Rupert pushed his jacket onto the floor and sat in the chair. "Yes. You're freaking me out, Fred. Just tell me what happened. Did somebody die?"

"Your grandmother Zelda passed away at nine-thirty this morning."

Rupert's eyes started to tear up. His breathing got rapid again. Even though he hadn't seen her in the nine and a half years since he'd left Wisconsin, most of his memories of Grandma were pleasant ones. It was only that night when he came out and Mike left when she had ever expressed any disappointment in him. He had only spoken with her once over the phone a few months later when she told him his mother wasn't going to contest Fred's petition for sole guardianship. Rupert wished he had said goodbye to her. "Do you know how Mom is taking it?" Rupert asked at last.

"She didn't take it very well," Fred said. He paused for several seconds. "She died a few minutes later."

"What? That's not possible!"

"Do you have anyone who can stay with you, son?"

"They're *both* dead? *This* morning? Both of them?" Rupert's eyes overflowed with tears.

"I know it's a rotten thing to happen on your birthday, Rupert. Your great-aunt Ingrid is your grandma's executor, so you'll need to call her when you're ready to get the funeral information." He paused for a few seconds listening to

52

Rupert's sobbing. "I know you didn't get along with your mom the past few years, but I know that she loved you. She worried about you all the time."

"How do you know?" Rupert worried that his question came out too much like an accusation, but he decided it didn't matter if he was suddenly the last surviving Kellerman.

"Your mom called me to find out how you were doing once you moved to New York. A few times a year. I didn't tell her the name you were using or give her any contact information like you requested. She just wanted to know you were okay."

Rupert had changed his name when he was emancipated at seventeen from Kellerman. Everyone from Julliard and the companies he'd danced with knew him as Rupert Rocket. "I have some other calls I have to make, Fred."

"You're welcome to come back here and stay for a while, if you want, Rupert."

"I've got an out-of-town performance coming up at the end of February. I've got a solo and a pas de deux."

"At least try to make it to Sheboygan for the funeral," Fred pleaded. "You're going to hate yourself later if you don't go."

Rupert sniffled. "I'll think about it." He finally gained some composure. "I should call these other numbers . . ."

"I'm here when you need me, son. Call me anytime."

"Thanks, Dad. I love you."

Rupert heaved a big sigh and then started another crying and sobbing jag. He couldn't get out of his mind the idea that he had caused the deaths. If he hadn't left them so angry and full of spite, either one of them might have lived another twenty years or more, he told himself.

For some reason, the song his grandmother used to sing in German from *Cabaret* popped into his head. Something about a fairytale castle and gray skies turning blue. It was about how life changes when you get married, and it always brought a tear to his grandma's eye by the time she finished.

He looked at his pager again. He decided that all of the 920 numbers had to be family from Wisconsin calling about the deaths of his grandma and mother. He called back each number, taking a half-hour between each to pace, cry, and rest.

The first call was his great-aunt Ingrid, and she seemed overjoyed to hear from Rupert. She couldn't talk long because she was getting ready to move into his old house to take care of final arrangements. She urged Rupert to call her back at his old home number in the evening once she was settled in.

The second call was his childhood friend Trevor, whom he hadn't seen in the two years since he'd come to New York on his honeymoon with his new bride Samantha. She answered the phone first but quickly passed the receiver to Trevor. He told Rupert that his mother had discovered Rupert's mother still alive grieving over Zelda's death when she had gone Christmas morning to check on them. His mother had only been away in the bathroom for a couple of minutes, and in that time, Caroline had passed away as well. The paramedics had been called, but neither of them could be resuscitated. It had been too long. Trevor had gone through Caroline's phone book to call Fred in San Francisco and to get Rupert's pager and phone numbers. After that he'd called Rupert's great-aunt Ingrid and his great-uncle Horst and paged him. Trevor wished him a happy birthday, considering the circumstances, and he left it at that. He begged Rupert to come back to Sheboygan for the funeral at least. He said Samantha wanted to see him again too.

He skipped calling Deena back.

The fourth call was the Sheboygan County Sheriff's Office who wanted to let him know they had notified the coroner and transported the two women's bodies to the hospital for autopsies, because the coroner was unable to determine the causes of death. They asked Rupert as the next of kin if he was able to come in and sign a release to the funeral director, and Rupert said his great-aunt Ingrid would claim the bodies and told them she would be arriving at the house imminently.

As soon as he hung up with the sheriff's deputy, the phone rang. It was the funeral director, whom he also referred to his great-aunt. As he was hanging up that call, Danny came in still dressed as he had seen him in his afterimage.

"I'm so glad you're home!" He gave Rupert a hug before he took off his jacket.

"I guess you heard," Rupert said as he pulled out of the hug.

"I was here when your dad called the third time. That's when I paged you. You didn't call, so I headed down to the church to see if I could find you. They told me you'd already left. Are you okay?"

"My mom and my grandma both died this morning."

"On Christmas? That sucks big time!" Danny hugged him again, still with his jacket on. He took off his jacket and sat on his bed to take his sneakers off as well. "You never talked much about your mom. Just your dad. I figured the two of you weren't very close."

Rupert sighed. It all seemed so trivial all of a sudden. There were gay pride parades in New York and San Francisco in June, National Coming Out Day in October, and the AIDS quilt was bringing gay men's health into the spotlight finally. Denmark and Norway allowed same-sex couples to enter civil unions. President Carter had mentioned equal rights for gays. The world had moved on since that emotional Christmas when he was fifteen. Why hadn't he?

Ingrid had faxed him the funeral announcement and the death certificates so he could get a reduced-fare flight to Milwaukee two days later. It wasn't until he was waiting in the terminal for a bus to Sheboygan and watching the ghosts of previous passengers rushing to their ghost buses that it hit him. A birthday had come and gone, but the previous year's ability had persisted. He wondered if this was one that would stay with him the rest of his life. He fantasized if instead he'd ended up with the strength of his fifteenth year, or the rapid healing or charisma he had when he was very young. Seeing afterimages of what had transpired before was already messing with his sense of reality a little too much. And now the only two people who knew his secret were dead. And he couldn't talk to anyone else about it. They would think he was crazy.

Rupert saw his bus pull up and start to disgorge passengers, and what he was seeing seemed real, so he stood up and carried his suitcase over to the side of the bus to be loaded. As he was waiting, he turned around and saw a familiar-looking woman standing a few feet behind him. She wore a long, wool coat and fuzzy yellow earmuffs, and one eye was lower than the other. And her nose looked

55

crooked. She just stood there with a self-satisfied smirk on her face. She was looking directly at him, haughty and amused, and then she faded into empty air.

Another afterimage, Rupert thought. He stayed there looking at where the woman had been. He was trying to recall where he might have seen her before. That she was there in the bus terminal in Milwaukee didn't help him, because he had spent so little time there. He concluded it was someone he'd seen in New York or on one of his touring productions—perhaps when he was hired to dance in Stravinsky's *Les Noces* in Chicago a couple of years before. He gave his suitcase to the driver and boarded the bus.

During the bus ride, Rupert reviewed his contract and the choreographer's notes for his featured part in the debut ballet for the Washington Ballet. The choreographer had seen Rupert dance with the San Francisco Ballet and remembered his name when reviewing New York dancers for his next performance. After spending a year in his teens virtually invisible, he knew the value of standing out, and he knew Rupert Rocket was a name you didn't easily forget. Even though he wasn't part of a company anymore, he was picking up more than enough guest performer jobs to afford his modest apartment near Lincoln Center.

Rupert got excited for a moment when he saw the familiar Chevy Impala parked outside the terminal in Sheboygan. But then he remembered it was his great-aunt Ingrid, who had agreed to pick him up. He collected his suitcase and trudged through the slushy snow and across the street to where she'd parked. He slid his suitcase into the back seat and took his seat in the front next to Ingrid.

"Good day!" she said to him in German. "It's so good to see you. How do you feel?"

"I feel like I'm walking in a dream," he replied in German. "I know intellectually that things have changed, but they don't have the feel of reality yet."

"I know what you mean." She started the car and pulled onto the street. "I'll take you to the house first to drop off your suitcase, and then I promised Roger I would bring you to the restaurant."

"What does Roger want?"

"The restaurant belongs to you now. They're anxious to know what you want to do with it."

"Grandma left me the restaurant?" Rupert had already assumed that the restaurant would go to Roger or one of her surviving siblings after the heartache he'd caused her when he was fifteen.

"And the house, and the car," Ingrid replied. "I just went through her will this morning with her lawyer, and there are only small gifts left to other family and friends. Almost everything was bequeathed to you."

Ingrid seemed to be holding up well after the death of her younger sister and her niece. There was the suggestion of grieving beneath a brave and practical exterior—probably like his own state of mind. "I really appreciate you doing all this work to settle things."

"My parents were very tired of raising children when Zelda came along—their seventh child," Ingrid mused. "They expected me to take care of her as she was growing up. It was easy to do—I'm not complaining. She was very smart, and never really got into trouble. She fit in here a lot better than the rest of us. I always tried to speak English with her."

"I never bothered to find out much about her past," Rupert admitted.

"Oh, I can tell you stories if you want." Ingrid pulled the car into his old driveway. "Your mother didn't have a will, so the lawyer said it will be up to you to settle her estate. It isn't that much, and I can help you with it."

Rupert knew his great-aunt was eighty-eight and a bit frail, so he ran around the car to open her car door and the back door to the house for her before grabbing his suitcase and following. The house was pretty much like he remembered it. Nine years only seemed to change what was posted on the refrigerator in the kitchen.

When he entered the dining room, he saw his mother and grandmother, much older than he remembered, sitting at the dining room table eating and not looking up or talking to each other. Ingrid ambled by the dining room table without noticing anything out of the ordinary. "There are still unopened gifts beneath the tree," she pointed out as they passed through the living room.

"You can put your things in your old bedroom, if you want," Ingrid said as she slowly mounted the stairs. A fairly opaque image of Trevor's mother hurried up the stairs and passed through her to beat her to the top and disappear.

He suddenly worried that he might have to watch his mother and grandmother die if he were not careful. "Ingrid," Trevor called in English. "Were you told where the bodies were found?"

"I believe they were both found in the master bedroom," Ingrid replied as they got to the upstairs hall.

Confirming what she had said, Rupert saw Trevor's mom rush through the closed door of the master bedroom down the hall. "I'd like to avoid going there for now," he announced.

"I understand. I felt similarly, so I'm staying in Caroline's room . . . your mom's room." She opened the door to his mother's bedroom. "I'm going to lie down for a bit, but come get me around four to take you to the restaurant."

"I can drive myself there, Ingrid," Rupert explained. "You can just rest, if you need to."

"Roger is probably there already, if you want to go now. If you want to eat dinner there, you can just bring me back a salad or something light." She left the door open after she went in.

Rupert left his suitcase in his old room. Some boxes and old lamps and tables had been moved in since he left it nine years before, but it was otherwise unchanged. He used the bathroom he had shared with his mother and noticed all the pill bottles, makeup, and hair products his mother had accumulated over the past few years. As he was getting ready to leave, Trevor's mother appeared at the sink and rushed out through him and then through the hallway door.

He kept his eyes looking at the carpet all the way down the stairs. He looked up when he got to the bottom of the stairs, though. He saw Trevor standing in the living room on the telephone with a hand on his mother's shoulder, who was sitting in a nearby chair crying. He kept looking down until he got to the kitchen. He grabbed the keys off the counter and headed out the back door.

Rupert had only driven once before in the past year, and he had been consciously avoiding it. He had been driving down Central Park West, and he had to go so slow to be sure he was plowing through afterimages and not real, live people and cars. He was constantly hearing car horns behind. Sheboygan, thankfully, seemed less loaded with emotionally charged pedestrians and drivers, so he made it to the restaurant at a reasonable speed.

Roger had become the general manager when he was a teenager, after Sylvia and Angelo retired. He must have seen Rupert approaching because he opened the door for him and gave him a big hug. "Rupie!" he said as he gripped Rupert tighter. "You're all growed up now!"

Rupert slid out from his arms and clasped him on the shoulder. "I've moved on to bigger stages."

Roger led him between the tables and past the other staff quickly. "Follow me back to the office for a bit, and then we'll get you some food."

There was only enough room in the small office off the kitchen for the two of them to sit down on either side of a wooden desk piled high with papers and ledger books. "Ingrid tells me I'm the new owner here," Rupert said preemptively.

"She phoned me and told me the same." He indicated the seat closer to the door for Rupert and then sat as well. "I asked to speak with you as soon as possible. The staff has been nervous, since you live in New York, that you wouldn't want to keep the restaurant open, and I've had to reassure them about every two hours or so for the past two days."

"Well, I don't think I can manage things from so far away, and I'm on the road a lot . . ."

"I can manage operations," Roger interrupted. "We just need to have somebody to deal with insurance and banks. I can handle staff and suppliers and advertising. I thought maybe we could find you someone local to buy half of your interest and handle that and some oversight."

Rupert was somewhat distracted by images of Sylvia superimposing themselves over Roger as he spoke. "If someone were willing to do the onsite stuff," he volunteered, "he or she wouldn't have to pay me."

"We could work out a deal where he'd get sweat equity over time," Roger

59

suggested. "We could divide the value into shares and give him a certain percentage each year."

"That's fine," Rupert said. He rocked in his chair, a bit antsy to get his first real food since an early breakfast at LaGuardia. "You let me know when you find someone interested and send me the paperwork."

Roger extended his hand across the desk and Rupert shook it. "A pleasure doing business with you, Rupie!"

As they exited the office, Roger flagged down a server and told him to comp whatever Rupert wanted. Rupert pointed at an empty table near the little raised platform where he used to perform, and the server nodded and handed him a menu.

Rupert immediately decided what he wanted and was starting to look for something to order to-go for Ingrid when he saw a familiar man enter the restaurant. He had a little less hair on his head, but it was definitely him. Mike Stanton had been like a stepfather to him for most of his childhood, and he hadn't seen him since that awful night ten years before when he was fifteen. He had come out as gay and forced Mike to admit that he was never going to marry his mom and wanted to break up with her. Rupert wanted to hide, but he kept his menu on his table and only sneaked glances occasionally.

The server took his order, and when he looked over at Mike's table, he was no longer there. The familiar voice spoke above and behind him. "Oh my god. I should have known you'd come back for the funerals."

Rupert turned to face him. "Hi, Mike. I just got back today."

Mike sighed and shifted his weight from one foot to the other. "I wouldn't fault you if you hated me."

Rupert smiled. "I don't hate you. You were in my life for ten years. I'm glad to see you're doing okay."

"Do you mind if I join you?"

"Uh, that's fine," Rupert replied.

As Mike sat down, he said, "I had heard you left to live with your dad in San Francisco."

"I did," Rupert confirmed. "I finished my GED at seventeen and got a full scholarship to study dance at Julliard in New York. I've been a professional dancer since then, still living in Manhattan."

"That's great. Congratulations." Mike looked around to make sure no one was close enough to overhear and whispered, "Are you still getting those strange abilities on your birthday?"

"You knew about that?" Rupert whispered back.

"How could I not?" Mike laughed. "I was practically living there with you for over nine years. That was some pretty strange stuff you could do."

Rupert was shocked and relieved at the same time. There *was* still someone he could talk to about the blessings. "I've had the same one two years in a row now. That's never happened to me before."

"Hmm," Mike hummed. "Maybe I should hook you up with the Grogoch then."

CHAPTER 7: RUPERT AT TWENTY-SIX

Mike had been introduced to the Grogoch one weekend when Rupert was ten and off with Haley and Trevor. The Grogoch, as he described it, was the Irish fairy who had blessed Rupert on the day he was born for twenty-five years. Once Rupert's twenty-five years were up, she had moved on and blessed Mike a few days earlier. His business immediately picked up, and he got a promotion. He volunteered to help Rupert out, and Rupert remembered what Roger had told him. After eating, the three men went back into the restaurant's tiny office to work out the language of their partnership.

Rupert met with Ingrid several times before the double funeral. She helped him go through his mother's things. He told her to sell or give away most of his mother's possessions except the journals she had kept religiously from her teen years. He studied those journal entries and some letters between his grandparents he found in the dining room to slowly piece together the story of the Grogoch and the Pooka. His grandfather had died when his grandmother's twenty-five-year blessing had run out, and his mother and grandmother died when his own blessing ran out.

The troubling, niggling fact that he was still coming upon ghostly and solid-seeming images of the past didn't make sense. If his blessing had run out on his twenty-fifth birthday, why did he still have such an extraordinary ability?

On the morning of the funeral, Rupert decided he was ready to enter the master bedroom, and he immediately regretted the decision as soon as the first images took shape. His grandmother looked panicked, lying in bed reaching toward the ceiling with her arms trying to grasp something above her that was just beyond her fingertips. And then clutching at her chest and lying still. His mother entering the bedroom, rushing to the bed, and checking for her mother's pulse was just as heartbreaking. She didn't want to believe it was true. Her expression conveyed the fear of being trapped and alone. She left to let Trevor's mom in, and the two women wept and tried to comfort each other for a while. In the brief time when his mother was again alone, Rupert saw her teeter unsteadily on her feet, and fall to the floor. Rupert decided to back out and close the door, because he couldn't watch any more of it.

At the funeral, Rupert tried to socialize with the restaurant employees and all the cousins, aunts, and uncles who arrived from as far away as Colorado. He knew his father was not going to attend, but he was surprised that Mike showed up. Mike told him that he hadn't seen the Grogoch again since they had talked, but he would pass along Rupert's desire to speak with her. Rupert joined some of his cousins as pallbearers and rode to the cemetery with Ingrid.

When they arrived, a small crowd was already ringing the two graves in a familiar part Rupert's grandmother had taken him to—his grandfather's grave. *All of the Kellermans together again*, Rupert mused. He wondered how long the Pooka's curse would torture him until it finished him off.

As if on cue, he scanned the crowd as the caskets were being lowered into the graves, and standing somewhat off to the side was the short, disfigured woman he remembered seeing both at the bus terminal in Milwaukee and on the street corner on the way home from Trevor's at fifteen. *It has to be the Pooka,* Rupert concluded. His mother's journal had mentioned the short stature, the graying red hair, one eye lower than the other, and the crooked nose. She wore the same wool coat as when he'd first met her, but without the earmuffs, as it was a warm enough day for the snow to start melting, leaving patches of brown grass exposed around the graves. She had a smirk on her face and didn't break eye contact when Rupert stared at her.

He took a couple of steps in her direction, and she started to laugh. He glanced back at the priest who seemed impatient to begin the interment ceremony, so he stepped back and tried to ignore her. After the ceremony was over, the evil fairy had already departed. He caught Mike by the elbow. "Did you see the Pooka here?" he whispered.

"No," Mike replied. "*You* saw her? I don't know what she looks like."

"It's the third time I've seen her," Rupert reported. "She just vanished from the bus terminal while I was waiting to board the bus in Milwaukee to come here. I'd assumed it was just an afterimage, but then I remembered where I'd seen her before. She was the woman I'd met just before New Year's Eve when I was coming back from dropping off Trevor. She was the one who convinced me to ask you and Mom and Grandma all those embarrassing questions."

Mike started walking toward the line of black limousines very slowly. "I regret what I said that evening. I tried to explain to your mom that it was just my doubts, and I was still committed to making it work with her, but she didn't want me 'pretending,' she said. I really miss the time I spent with your family, Rupert."

"I shouldn't have put you on the spot," Rupert said as he came to a stop a few feet from his limo. "And I didn't need to do that to my grandma and mother either."

Mike pulled him into a gentle hug. "Your mom never stopped loving you, Rupert. She was disappointed that you were gay, and your grandma was just sad because she wanted to see you get married some day."

Rupert broke the hug and looked up at the tall earnest man who had been like a father to him for so many years. A new tear formed in each of Mike's eyes. "I've been reading Mom's journals and Grandma's letters. They said there was a woman here in Sheboygan named Patricia Connor who convinced the Pooka to curse our family. The Grogoch told Grandma that it would mean we would have horrible luck and we would never marry, but she shielded Grandma and then me from the curse for twenty-five years. At the end of Grandma's blessing, Grandpa died. At the end of mine, Mom and Grandma died. I . . ."

"I'll take care of the restaurant for you," Mike said as he patted Rupert on the shoulder. "You just do what you need to do and grieve. I'll help Ingrid sell the house; I have some connections. You can call me if you need some company or any money." He started to walk away toward the other cars, but Rupert pulled him into another hug. "Are you okay?"

"I will be." Rupert choked a bit. "I just hope things don't get any worse."

Mike just nodded and walked away. Rupert got into the limo where Ingrid was already waiting. "You could have invited him back to the house," Ingrid softly suggested.

Rupert closed the door and scooted further in. "I have to give him that throw pillow Mom wanted him to have. I'll see him again then or at the restaurant before I go."

The limousine took off from the curb. Ingrid looked a bit confused. "The one Caroline embroidered with your name and birth date?"

"She wanted him to remember my birthday for some reason."

Ingrid extracted a handkerchief from her purse and blew her nose. "You have one of the easiest birthdays to remember. Christmas Day."

"You'd be surprised how many people forget a birthday in the midst of the biggest holiday of the year." Rupert had already stopped telling everyone in New York his birthday, just so he could blame that for its lack of celebration. "Do you know a woman close to Grandma's age named Patricia Connor?"

"I'm not sure," Ingrid replied. "You can check your grandparents' yearbooks. I already boxed them to donate to the library, but you can dig through there when we get back."

Once they were back at the house, Ingrid indicated the sealed box with the tag "LIBRARY" in a corner of the dining room, and Rupert tore into it. He pulled his grandmother's senior yearbook first and sat at the dining table paging through it, but there was no Patricia Connor there. He noticed another yearbook near the top of the stack with the same year. "Ingrid," Rupert called out, "did Grandpa and Grandma go to different high schools? I thought they met in high school."

His great-aunt stepped out of the kitchen for a moment. "They were both at Central until North opened. Your grandpa stayed, but Zelda graduated from North."

Rupert found Patricia quickly. She was an awkward-looking, pale girl with freckles in the freshman photos. He found a photo of his father at seventeen, and he agreed with both women's taste. Grandpa had model good looks when he was young. He found the last yearbook from Central, and there was Patricia Connor again, then a prettier young junior. And Rupert got a feeling of déjà vu. He had seen the photo somewhere before. ⬜Did I ever meet Patricia Connor, Aunt Ingrid?⬜

"I don't think so." Ingrid moved to look at the photo over Rupert's shoulder. "Ah. But I did meet her once when your grandparents were first dating. Your grandpa brought her to the May Day celebration in the park. I think Thomas was just using the girl to fit in. There were a lot of bullies back then that were picking on kids with German accents, and your grandpa had one, stronger than mine."

"Do you know where she's living?" Rupert started developing a plan in which he would somehow force Patricia and the Pooka to drop his family curse.

"Now? I have no idea." Ingrid set her dishtowel down and sat in the chair next to Rupert's. "When you were very young, you helped Zelda find her."

Without knowing how, Rupert suddenly recalled a vision from when he was four years old. "In a white house on stilts near a golf course in Sheboygan Falls."

"She could be anywhere or nowhere, Rupert," Ingrid cautioned. "That was over twenty years ago that your grandmother visited her."

Rupert pushed his chair back and got up from the table. "I have to try," he nearly shouted. "Can I borrow the car for an hour?"

Ingrid called back in German, "It's yours now. You don't need my permission. I wish you much luck." She slid the car keys across the table toward him. "Be careful!"

"Thanks," he called back in German as he headed toward the front door. "See you soon!"

As he drove, Rupert tried to chuckle at his great-aunt's caution. Patricia Connor, if he even found her, would be over eighty, just like his grandma. Then he remembered something he had read in his mother's journal about the Pooka and Patricia. According to his mother's journal, they met up on Christmas night every year. He hoped the Pooka was no longer around, but since he had seen her at the cemetery, he realized he might be walking into a trap. His current ability gave him no defense against an evil fairy.

He made it all the way to the golf course and turned left onto the first road, and he could already see the white house on stilts in the distance. He immediately pulled the car over and stopped. He started to worry that he was indeed doing something dangerous. So far, the Pooka had been satisfied just to taunt him. Who knew what supernatural power she could wield? Maybe it was better to turn back, leave town the next day, and leave behind in Wisconsin all the Irish fairies and their machinations?

A person walked by on the road, right outside his window, and Rupert turned to look who it was. He recognized the wool coat and the red-and-gray hair, and it made him jump up in his seat. It was the Pooka. But she had walked right by the car without looking in, so Rupert started to suspect it was just an afterimage. He pulled the car back onto the road and crept along behind the Pooka image. When it walked up the stairs of the house and vanished, he parked the car across the road. Evidently at least the Pooka thought Patricia Connor still lived there.

Rupert got out of the car and fought an urge to dash around the house to see if he could see if anyone human or fairy were there. Maybe no one was home. He didn't want to look like a freak to any passersby, so he calmly and slowly walked up the stairs to the porch and knocked on the door.

After nearly a minute, when Rupert was about to give up, the door opened, revealing an elderly woman with gray hair, skeletal features covered in white foundation that made her look like a frail little clown in white sweats with yellow racing stripes. "Rupert Rocket!" she called out in a squeaky voice. "I was told you might come calling."

Rupert could feel himself getting angry at her audacity. He was surprised that she not only knew he was coming but knew his new name. Rupert looked at the mailbox beside the door with the peeling name C NNOR on it. "You have to be the bitchy old woman who couldn't handle being dumped by my grandfather, so you had to go curse me and my whole family. My mother and the woman you were so fucking jealous of are dead now. It's time for you to move on and end the curse."

Rupert noticed that the woman looked mildly amused at his attempt at intimidation. "Would you like to come in, Rupert?" she said as she stepped back from the door.

Rupert was completely unprepared for the woman to be cordial. He glanced back at the car and dismissed a fleeting impulse to run away. "I really only came over to ask you to lift the curse."

"It's a bit too cold to be having a conversation on the porch," she said as she rubbed her thin hands together, "so come inside so I can shut the door."

"Are you alone?" Rupert asked sheepishly.

"Not any more," she replied as she stepped behind the door out of sight.

She's just an eighty-year-old woman, Rupert, he told himself. *You can take her if she tries to attack you.* He entered the house and shut the door. Every wall in the house was stacked from floor to ceiling with cardboard boxes. He found Patricia in an adjacent room sitting on a loveseat facing an empty high-backed upholstered chair. She gestured toward the empty chair, and he sat down, feeling mortified that he had ripped into her at first meeting her, and she was being extremely polite.

As he looked up from his fidgeting hands, his eyes were drawn to movement in the next room. He got up from the chair without saying anything and crossed to the dining room on the other side of the front door, where he saw the old woman he had just left in the parlor now wearing a dark turtleneck and blue jeans sucking on the proffered breast of the creature he had come to call the Pooka.

Rupert turned and headed back into the parlor repeating a disgusted "oh-ho-ho-ho-ho" as he walked. The afterimage in Patricia's dining room was also renewing his fear that the Pooka was lurking about. He stopped in the doorway to the parlor. Patricia, once more in her white-and-yellow sweats, looked up confused. "I think I have to be going."

"In answer to your request," Patricia called out before he could even turn to leave, "I find I must decline. The paltry amount of misery your family has endured is insufficient. Now that your blessing has finally worn off, you *will* have to pay for your grandmother's treachery."

68

"Give it up!" Rupert yelled back at her, finding new reserves of courage. "The woman you hated is dead now. Making my life hell isn't going to hurt her anymore!"

"I vowed to end the Kellerman line," she countered. "Once you're gone, it will be erased, because I have been told you can't have any children."

Rupert decided not to correct her. He studied her for a moment more and decided her hatred was too insane to be reasoned with. "I don't know what kinky lesbian sex you've been having with the Pooka, but it's . . . disgusting . . . and you're a bitch!"

He dashed out the front door and didn't close it entirely. He barely avoided colliding with the Pooka approaching the front steps from the other direction. A split-second pivot and sidestep that would have impressed his choreographer back in New York managed to keep contact to a light graze of her wool coat.

"You will feel more of my curse in the coming years, Rupert Rocket, née Kellerman!" she called from behind him.

Rupert pulled the car door open, dove inside, and turned the ignition as he was closing the door. "This was a big mistake," he announced to the empty car.

From that point on, the easy ascendancy of Rupert Rocket in the modern dance and ballet worlds faltered and crashed. When Rupert returned to New York after the funerals and taking care of his mother's few bequests, he was greeted by a letter and six-hundred-dollar check from the Washington Ballet canceling his upcoming debut performance. They were instead mounting a ballet based on Hansel and Gretl, which had been cast while he was in Wisconsin.

He managed to join a touring production, but he twisted his ankle just before the first performance and his contract got bought out again for a pittance. His roommate Danny moved in with a boyfriend, and Rupert had to pay the whole rent for one month before he found a suitable replacement. Once Rupert's ankle healed, he got an offer to teach a class, and he took it, because his savings were rapidly evaporating. In his second week teaching, he was called into the administrator's office and put on leave for allegedly sexually harassing one of the female students. He wrote to Mike for his share of the restaurant's profits, and it didn't arrive for three weeks. When he called Mike to thank him finally, Mike asked him about a personal gift check he had sent the following day, and decided to wire it instead when Rupert told him about his mail delays.

Because it had been too long since Rupert Rocket had been reviewed, his agent dropped him. Rupert leaned on a favor owed him from a friend in a Broadway production, but Rupert wasn't Asian enough for "The King and I" nor black enough for "The Lion King," so all he was offered was a replacement chorus part in a new musical about the Titanic. It became steady work for Rupert for most of that year. But because the set was expensive to maintain, and despite winning best musical, the production company kept making layoffs and cutting pay. He was on a furlough for the entire month of December while they rotated in less experienced dancers, which had never happened to him before.

He considered visiting his relatives in Wisconsin or Fred in San Francisco, but he decided to save his money, because he feared the musical would close soon. He found another agent who could handle musicals as well as his straight dance jobs and he told her to be discreet about shopping his availability during his month-long furlough. Because most of Rupert's friends were with family or on tour, and even Rupert's new roommate was in Europe, Rupert spent his birthday feeding the homeless at the church in Chelsea.

Rupert was relieved that the afterimages that had plagued him for two years were finally gone, but he couldn't tell if he had gained a new ability yet. He took the train down to Chelsea looking around carefully and trying not to engage anyone, but hoping his strange blessings had finally run their course and he was normal for the first time in his life. When he got to the church, everything still seemed normal. He put on his apron and hairnet and took his place behind the steam tables as they opened the front doors to let the diners in.

The initial rush was over after about forty-five minutes, and an older woman in a patchwork coat with reddish-gray hair, large, pointed ears, and a strong Irish accent approached him without a tray. "I was wondering if you might have a wee bit of time for a chat, my dear."

Rupert smiled to match the woman's. "Just make sure to let folks in line through when they come. What can I help you with?"

The old woman winked. "I think maybe it's *you* that needs the help. They call me the Grogoch."

Rupert dropped and unsuccessfully recaught the serving spoon he had been holding. "My grandma's Grogoch?" he whispered.

"Yes, indeed." She stepped back to let a man get served. "Yours as well. I wouldn't be here otherwise."

She stepped back up to the other side of his steam table. "What do you mean?"

"You must have called me." Her tone was very matter-of-fact.

"I don't think I've ever met you," Rupert said. He tried to place her face but could not.

"Well, you were just a wee lad both times," she said with a nostalgic smile. "You have the ability to call someone to you who can help you."

"I *had* that ability. That was two years ago." Rupert remembered the year after his twenty-third birthday when he would accidentally encounter a plumber moments after discovering a leak, someone would sit down next to him on the subway with a book that held needed information, and he never had to wait for a taxi.

"And it's back again." The Grogoch chuckled at his confusion for a moment. "You've got a luck echo."

"What is that?" he asked while serving another diner.

"You've started to experience all of your previous blessings in reverse."

The Grogoch started to walk away from him, and he hurried around the steam table to follow her. "Where are you going?"

"Away," she said without any sarcasm or irony. "I suspect I've given the information you wanted from me."

"Will I see you again?" he called after her.

She stopped for a moment just inside the front door to the church. She looked up at the rose window for a moment and then looked back at Rupert. "One more time, I should think."

71

And with that she skipped out the door and was gone.

Rupert trudged back to his spot in the lunch line trying to piece together the implications of what the Grogoch had told him. He figured he could remember the abilities of the past few years, and his mother's journal would cover most of the rest. He hoped that it meant another twenty-three years of protection from the worst of the Pooka's curse. He had finally managed to keep a mostly absent flight attendant as his roommate, and his chorus job, though not as high-paying and prestigious, was steady.

As he went to the kitchen to refill an empty pan, he looked at the older patrons picking at or gobbling their food, and he wondered what he would be like when he joined their ranks. He stopped walking at just that moment. Rupert emotionally and physically crumpled. He might never reach their age, he feared. He suddenly felt like he had a terminal disease that would kill him when he turned fifty.

CHAPTER 8: RUPERT AT TWENTY-SEVEN

When you know any help you need will reach you fairly quickly, you start making more assumptions about people who come your way. But Rupert had learned three years earlier, when he had first received that particular blessing, he still needed to be careful. Sometimes the help arrived in person, and sometimes it was a referral. Such was the case with his first real boyfriend, Jorge.

His ex-roommate Danny and his boyfriend Max had invited Rupert out to a gay bar in the Village on a Monday night when he didn't have to work. It was a warm spring night, so after a gym workout and a shower, he put on a tank top with the Julliard logo on it and a pair of khaki cargo shorts. He shivered a bit in the chill wind as he headed to the subway station, but he knew the train platform and the bar would be warm, so he endured the chill and hurried along.

Danny and Max weren't there yet when he arrived, so Rupert ordered a rum and Coke and settled into a dark corner of the bar near one of the fire exits. He was approached by a slightly shorter black man with a shaved head and a very muscular body barely contained in a white T-shirt and blue jeans. "Hi." He pointed at Rupert's shirt. "Did you work there or go to school there?"

Rupert had forgotten which shirt he had chosen and looked down to check. "Oh. I graduated from there about four years ago . . . in dance performance."

"Nice," the younger man said as he positioned himself to block Rupert's view of the other patrons. "I graduated from Steinhardt in music composition. My name is Luke." He extended his hand.

Rupert shook it. "I'm Rupert. Nice meeting you."

Luke's eyes got wide and his jaw dropped. "I've seen you perform! You're

Rupert Rocket, aren't you?"

"That's me." Rupert grinned briefly. He had gotten used to his minor celebrity again and knew it was important to curtail any gushing early on. "How about you, Luke? Have you composed anything I might have heard?"

"Um, yeah. Maybe. I did most of the tracks for Tibia." He looked to Rupert for a sign of recognition.

Rupert had no idea what it was other than the formal name of the shin bone. He shook his head and offered a palms-up gesture and a weak smile.

"It's an MMORPG . . . an online role-playing game," Luke explained. He moved in and stood by Rupert's side close enough to brush his arm.

"I have to travel a lot for work," Rupert said apologetically. "I don't usually have time to play video games." He studied Luke's face for some clue of what kind of help he might be giving.

"I guess it's lucky I caught you on a night off," Luke suggested. "Does that mean you're single?"

Rupert remembered that he had been complaining to Danny and to some of the other chorus boys about having a long dry spell in dating. He thought Luke was attractive, and the way Luke was finding opportunities to brush or touch him made him think the attraction was mutual. "For a few months now, yeah," he replied. "I'm supposed to meet some friends here, but maybe I could hang out with you another time?" He pulled out his wallet and handed Luke a business card. "It's just a pager number. I'm not at home very much."

Luke put the card in his back pocket. "Thanks. Are you performing anywhere now?"

Rupert wasn't sure how much information to reveal so early on. "I'm working six to eleven here in town—six nights a week."

Luke studied him for a moment. "If you're awake and hungry by noon, I could meet you for lunch. My schedule is flexible."

Rupert didn't want to seem overly eager. "Sure. Page me later on this week to arrange it."

Luke didn't seem to know whether or not he was being dismissed, his weight shifting back and forth between his feet. He finally decided. "I was going to get a drink. Can I get you anything?"

Rupert smiled and held up his half-full tumbler. "I'm good. I'm waiting for friends to meet me here. They're running late."

Luke nodded slowly and took a tentative step away. "Lunch Thursday maybe?"

Rupert took a sip of his drink. "Sounds good. Have a nice evening, Luke."

Luke took a couple more steps away then looked back at him. "You too, sexy." Then he blended back into the crowd near the bar.

Danny and Max arrived a couple of minutes later, and throughout their first few minutes of conversation, Rupert smiled and nodded a lot. His thoughts were on Luke and how he might be the boyfriend he had been hoping for.

Luke's page came less than twenty-four hours later. They chatted again briefly and made plans to meet near Rupert's place on the Upper West Side for lunch on Thursday. Rupert drew two hearts on the note pad where he had transferred Luke's number from his pager. His blessing finally had brought him something of more lasting value than a spare umbrella when a downpour broke out or a discarded MetroCard with residual value enough to get him where he was going. He had a date with a sexy guy who was also involved in the arts and could meet in his free time on weekday afternoons.

When the appointed time arrived on Thursday, Rupert decided to wear a plain white shirt as Luke had been wearing when he'd met him three days before. Luke was already sitting in a booth inside the diner on 71st at Columbus Rupert had chosen. He wore a denim, short-sleeve shirt and gray basketball shorts Rupert glimpsed when Luke stood up to hug him. "I thought I would get here first," Rupert said. "You had to come all the way from Brooklyn."

"It's okay." Luke pushed one of the menus across the table toward Rupert. "I hate being late, so I'm usually early. You never know if the subway is going to break down."

"I suppose." Rupert looked over the menu, though he was pretty certain he would get a paddy melt and chocolate shake again. "I only had to walk a few blocks, so it was easier to plan. How is your writing going this week?"

The recounting of Luke's leads from a film producer and another game software company lasted well through ordering and the arrival of their food. Rupert studied Luke carefully and convinced himself that Luke had been the help the universe had offered him in his loneliness. By the time the lunch was over, Luke got very bold about keeping eye contact with Rupert. And so, when Rupert made a thinly veiled invitation to Luke to come back to his place, there was a look of hunger in the composer's eyes that belied the full meal he had just eaten.

For Rupert, the sex was great, and he liked that Luke was also a kisser. Luke didn't stay after cleaning up, but he promised to page Rupert again soon as he slid out the apartment door quickly, without another hug or kiss. Their trysts were always sexual and could only happen at Rupert's place, and only when his roommate wasn't home. Rupert tried to gently suggest that they could do some other type of outing, and after much cajoling, Luke relented.

They met for brunch in Chelsea just before a Sunday matinee performance Rupert had to work. The food came quickly, and Luke seemed very distracted. "Is everything going okay?" Rupert asked.

"I'm . . . I'm just a bit worried I'll run into someone I know." Luke focused again on his croque-monsieur.

"I can't imagine you having any enemies," Rupert cooed. He scanned around to see if there was anyone there he recognized.

"I haven't told my friends that I'm seeing you," Luke admitted. "I don't want them to get the wrong impression."

Rupert suddenly wondered what the correct impression would be, but before he could ask, a pair of very skinny, young, black boys came up to their table. "Lukey-baby," the one with the pierced lower lip called out, "you haven't been back here in months. Where ya' been hiding?"

"How is James?" the one wearing the jacket with padded shoulders immediately asked.

"He's . . . fine." Luke seemed to be trying to communicate some instructions to his two friends, and Rupert started to recall that Luke had never revealed the name of the ever-present roommate who made it impossible for them to use Luke's bed in Brooklyn.

"I'm so rude," the pierced-lip boy said as he turned toward Rupert and extended his hand like a duchess. "I'm Chantal."

"I'm Dorian," the other young man announced without offering his hand.

Rupert shook Chantal's hand gently. "I'm Rupert. Did you two want to join us?"

"We need to grab our table before someone else steals it," Dorian explained, as he tried to herd Chantal away.

"We're meeting Jorge, Lukey," Chantal called back. "You should stop by before you go."

"Friends from NYU," Luke offered in a low voice after they left.

"I was kind of hoping you'd introduce me," Rupert admitted. "I was curious how you'd describe me."

"You did fine without me," Luke said without making eye contact.

"So . . ." Rupert began. He waited for Luke to look up. He glanced up for only a moment and then focused on his food again. " . . . I was thinking maybe we were moving toward being boyfriends."

"Um, I like you a lot, Rupert," Luke began, still only occasionally looking up at him, "but I kind of already have a boyfriend."

"James, I gather." Rupert sighed. He started to wonder why his blessing had only brought him more sex when he was clear that he wanted love.

"We've been together six years," Luke said as he finished his food and pushed his plate away.

"Oh."

"I don't think I can see you again."

Rupert's jaw dropped at the suddenness of the announcement.

"It was fun, but I can't risk it getting back to James." Luke grabbed the strap of his backpack as if he were about to get up from the table. He fished his wallet out of one of the pockets and laid a twenty-dollar bill on the table between them. He stowed the wallet, zipped the pocket shut again, and started to rise as he spoke. "If anyone sees me out with you again, I'm afraid it will get back to him, and that would make me feel too guilty."

Rupert stayed seated, teetering between anger and sorrow. Finally, a tear appeared in one eye, and he dabbed it with his napkin. He sat there silently staring at the place Luke had vacated and his twenty-dollar bill. He eventually started picking at his omelet again, but he didn't feel very hungry.

He wasn't sure how long after that he felt a gentle warm hand on his shoulder. Rupert dabbed his eyes again before turning. It was Chantal. "You need to pay your bill here, and join us at our table," he said very softly.

Rupert coughed. "I'm okay."

"No, honey," Chantal said as he slid into the seat across from Rupert. "You need to join us at our table. If I'm reading the interpersonal dynamics right, Lukey just dumped you. He's done this before."

The temptation to take refuge in the younger friends of Luke's who seemed so sympathetic was strong. "I guess I could come over for a few minutes."

Chantal got up and offered his hand to Rupert. When Rupert grasped it, Chantal pulled him up to standing, grabbed the twenty-dollar bill Luke had left, and pushed him toward a booth on the upper level of the restaurant. Chantal stopped a waiter and pointed at the table below where Rupert had been eating. "We're paying for that empty table, so ask the waiter to bring that bill up to our booth."

Chantal slid into the booth next to Dorian and gestured toward the open seat next to a slim and handsome Latino man with the wisp of a goatee around his mouth. His blue eyes seemed to light up when he looked up at Rupert. "I'm Rupert," he said as he offered his hand to the new man.

"I'm Jorge," the new man replied. "Wait. Are you Rupert Rocket?"

"You know him?" Dorian called from across the table.

"Yes, that's my name." Rupert grinned at his good fortune of another handsome, sexy man who knew who he was.

As Rupert sat down next to him, Jorge explained, "Luke had told me he was going to fix me up with you."

"Really?" Rupert tried to imagine when that might have happened.

"A couple of months ago. I kept bugging him to follow through. I saw you dance at Lincoln Center two years ago. You were amazing!"

"You're a dancer?" Chantal asked.

"And a singer now," Rupert replied. "I'm in the chorus of *Titanic*, the musical, and I have to show up there in forty-five minutes."

"Rupert Rocket." Jorge stared at him in amazement. "Can you get us tickets to your show?"

"Jorge, that's way too forward," Dorian chided as he poured a tall glass from their pitcher of mimosas and set it in front of Rupert. "We just met him."

Rupert pushed the goblet away. "I can't drink right before a performance," he apologized. He fished his wallet out of his back pocket. He put two twenties in the middle of the table and a business card in front of Jorge. "This has my pager number. Check with me later in the week, and I'll see what I can work out with the box office."

Jorge grabbed his knee under the table. "I will."

After several minutes of laughs and conversation when Rupert couldn't wait any longer to get to the theatre, Jorge slid out and stood up right after Rupert did. He gave Rupert a big hug and said, "Break a leg, Rupert!"

Rupert grinned broadly and waved goodbye again at all three of them as he dashed down the steps and out the door. He stopped by the box office on his way to the dressing room and asked the cashier if there were any orchestra seats open in the next few nights. He was told there was nothing yet, but he'd hold an unclaimed will-call ticket for him, if he wanted.

Once he had finished applying his makeup and started getting into his costume he got a page from a new local number, and he wondered who it was, but he was only a couple of minutes from a brush-up rehearsal and resolved to return it after the matinee.

The producers provided a Chinese takeout dinner for the cast between shows, and while everyone was finishing eating, Rupert took advantage of the payphone at the stage door to return the page. He heard the voice answer "Hola," and he knew immediately who it must be. "Jorge," he replied, "I didn't expect you to contact me so soon. How are you doing?"

"I'm at Dorian's, and I wanted to find out when you are usually done with work for the night," Jorge replied. "I could meet you at the stage door for a few minutes at least tonight."

Before Rupert could respond, the stage manager passed by handing him an envelope with his name on it. "Hold on a moment," he told Jorge. Inside was a note from the box office manager:

> I heard you were looking for an orchestra seat for tonight. This
> guy wanted me to give away his ticket, because he couldn't
> make it to the theatre tonight.

Rupert didn't pause long enough to figure out how the miscommunication had worked out in his favor. He knew his blessing had come through for him again. "I'm back. How would you like to see me perform tonight?"

Rupert left the ticket in the will-call again under Jorge's name, and after the evening performance, he changed clothes and washed up in record time. Jorge was there wearing a *Titanic* baseball cap when he exited the theatre. Jorge said he was hungry, and so was Rupert, so they stopped at Joe Allen for food and cheesecake, and when they finally agreed to stop talking and leave so that Jorge could get enough sleep before work the next day, it was almost one in the morning. They hugged and kissed and made plans to meet again for dinner the next night when Jorge got off work.

He put Jorge in the cab that had just disgorged a passenger at the curb next to them and decided to walk home along the Hudson. There was just enough haze to make the high-rises on the Jersey shore look like palaces. The wind carried the smell of the river up to where Rupert was walking. When he looked up higher in the sky, he saw a shooting star arching overhead. Rupert felt like his life was finally starting to turn around.

Every date with Jorge seemed to go perfectly. When they wanted to see a movie, there were always good seats left. When they went out to dinner, they were always seated immediately. And just when Rupert didn't think he could wait any longer, Jorge invited him back to his studio on the Lower East Side, and Rupert stayed the whole night waking up every few hours to have alternately tender and awe-inspiring sex with Jorge.

Jorge seemed to tell Rupert everything about his life. But Rupert couldn't be quite so forthcoming when Jorge asked him how he managed to be so lucky all the time. Jorge introduced him to more of his friends than Dorian and Chantal, and Rupert invited Jorge to meet Danny and Max. When Jorge started making plans to spend Christmas Day with Rupert after his festivities with his family and Rupert's volunteering at the soup kitchen, Rupert paused. He knew if he told Jorge his birthday after the fact, he might get upset. Jorge hated being blind-sided. It was the one common theme when Jorge described his interactions at work and with his family.

But he also knew that his next blessing would arrive shortly before they met, and he had had enough difficulty dealing with it at twenty-two when he was single. He couldn't imagine how Jorge would deal with a year of people constantly thrusting cash in Rupert's direction. The wealth blessing tended to make onlookers wonder what Rupert had done to earn the remuneration or gift.

On the Christmas Eve before Rupert turned twenty-seven, he stared at the phone knowing he couldn't put off the call to Jorge any longer. He had come up with plans to meet Jorge only at places where they could be alone, to make excuses when Jorge wanted to meet with other people around, and to lead Jorge on with phone calls, claiming he was on tour for a year. None of them seemed satisfactory. They would all make Jorge suspicious. He finally picked up the phone and dialed.

"How is my favorite performer doing?" Jorge answered. He had caller ID on his home phone.

"I have been a bit nervous about something happening tomorrow," Rupert carefully relayed.

"You mean us meeting at four o'clock? That's making you nervous?"

"Tomorrow is my birthday," Rupert blurted out. "I get a little weird about that sometimes."

"Hey, papi. It's okay. We can find some place to celebrate tomorrow. You should have told me sooner. I could've set up a party for you."

Rupert sighed. He felt like he was in a no-win situation. If he told the truth, he would sound crazy. If he lied or made excuses, it would make Jorge feel betrayed.

Jorge interrupted his manic contemplation. "Can you hang on one minute, Rupert?"

"Sure."

When Jorge came back on the line, he was curt and emotional. "I'm sorry, sweetie. We have to take my mama to the hospital. I'll call you when things settle down."

Before Rupert could respond, he heard a dial tone.

The next day, volunteering at the soup kitchen was too ridiculous to be a server. Even the homeless people started offering him whatever spare change they had on them. Bert agreed to put Rupert in the kitchen, and once the rest of the kitchen staff got it out of their systems to give him a few dollars, he was able to dice vegetables in peace.

On the way home from the church, Rupert politely declined and ran away when strangers approached him holding out money. When he got to his apartment, there was a Christmas card lying alone on the dining room table. His roommate had included a fifty-dollar bill and the scrawled greeting:

Merry Christmas to the cleanest, quietest roommate ever!

Rupert put the fifty in his wallet and sighed. It was going to be a lucrative but exhausting year. He set his pager down next to the phone and called Mike to wish him a merry Christmas. Mike promised to get a birthday gift and a profit-sharing check out to him in the next day's mail.

"I don't know what I'm going to do," he told Mike. "I've been dating a really great guy the past few months, and I feel like this next blessing is going to make him run."

"What is it?" Mike asked.

"Everybody I meet—all year—wants to give me money."

"Hmm," Mike hummed. "I guess I can see good and bad sides to that. Is it still okay if I send you the checks tomorrow?"

"Yeah, it's fine," Rupert replied. "Have you seen the Grogoch at all lately?"

"Not in a few months. Hey, I got promoted again, and now I have use of the private jet."

"Congrats, Mike." Rupert finally smiled. At least Mike's blessing wasn't twisted by freakish abilities like his was. He heard a beep on the line. "Call waiting, hold on."

Rupert tapped the cradle to switch calls. "Baby, I'm so sorry!"

"What is it, Jorge?"

"I wanted to give you a big birthday and Christmas gift today, but I'm still stuck at the hospital with my mama. They're saying that her kidneys are not working right, and she has to start dialysis. I met with the social worker, and I applied for assistance, but I don't know if we'll get it for the transportation and supplies, and she'll need someone to do her chores for her. . ."

"I understand," Rupert interrupted. "Let me know how it goes. I have another call I have to get back to."

"Oh, okay, papi. Happy birthday, and I'll see if I can get away to give you your gift tomorrow."

"Get some rest, Jorge."

"I promise. Good night, sweetie."

Rupert clicked back to the call with Mike. "Still there?"

"Yup," Mike replied. "It gave me a chance to address an envelope for your checks tomorrow."

"My boyfriend called to tell me his mother is becoming an invalid," Rupert reported. "I suspect between his job and caring for her, I won't be able to see him anymore."

Mike sighed. "Tough break, kiddo."

"One parting gift from my last blessing, I guess."

"What do you mean?"

"I was looking for a way to keep Jorge from witnessing my wealth blessing this year, and it looks like he won't now."

"Get some rest tonight," Mike advised. "Look for those checks in the mail later this week."

"Thanks, Mike."

After he hung up the phone, Rupert pulled out his bulging wallet and emptied it onto the floor between his feet. He looked down at all the coins and bills he had accumulated during the day. He sighed. He sighed again. And then he started sobbing because the bliss he had felt with Jorge the past few months had abruptly come to an end.

CHAPTER 9: RUPERT AT TWENTY-EIGHT

The one time Rupert saw Jorge again was a little over a month and a half later. They had traded a couple of phone messages in the intervening time, and in both, Jorge had promised to let Rupert know when he had some free time and Rupert had suggested that his schedule was also full. In truth, he had spent a lot of time between performances hiding out in his bedroom. Every time he went out, strangers kept coming up to him and offering him money. He rarely accepted any more, but in cases where he had just paid a bunch of bills or the donor was especially persistent, like his business partner Mike or his roommate, he relented and thanked them for their generosity.

He found it difficult to hang out with Dorian and Chantal, because that raised chances of running into Jorge or Luke. Spending time with Danny and Max also became difficult because it was a constant reminder of what he had lost with Jorge. On a particularly warm night in February after a performance, he decided to break out of his cloistered routine and head to a gay bar in Midtown near the theatre.

The snow had almost all melted except for the formerly tallest drifts dotting the curbs, and the sidewalks were slick with the runoff. Rupert kept his head down, because the wind was strong and brisk, and direct eye contact seemed to embolden people to stop him to hand him cash. He knew that Luke, Dorian, and Chantal favored bars in the Village, so he was surprised when he pushed through a crowd and nearly toppled into Chantal holding court on a couch near the back of the bar.

He hoped he could anonymously back away, but Chantal immediately called out, "Rupert dearest, where have you been hiding yourself all winter?"

Rupert turned back with an apologetic grin. Chantal had frosted his hair with blond highlights and wore fake eyelashes. "Don't just stand there, honey." He patted the couch beside himself.

"Nice to see you, Chantal," he said as he sat down next to him.

Chantal glanced briefly at a drawstring bag decorated with sequins on his lap and then looked back at Rupert. "You look absolutely destitute. I don't have any cash on me, but if you care to stay a bit, I can get some from my ATM."

"I'm doing okay right now actually," Rupert said holding his hands up in discouragement. "But thank you. How are you doing?"

Before Chantal answered, he had to swat away the young man sitting next to him who whispered in his ear and held up a ten-dollar bill. "I'm . . . holding up. Dorian is talking about moving back to Baltimore, and Jorge is a mess."

"What's going on with Jorge?" Rupert regretted asking only after the words got out. "He and I have been playing phone tag a lot lately. Is his mother doing okay?"

"She's at home now, and he spends most of his nights and weekends with her when the nurse is off duty." Chantal sighed. "Between work and taking care of her, I haven't seen him much either. He said he would try to sneak out tonight after she went to sleep. So you might be in luck."

Chantal sat there with a big smile as if he had revealed a pleasant surprise, but it made Rupert anxious. He had gone from spending several nights a week with Jorge to no contact at all during the past six weeks, and he wondered if Jorge still carried a torch for him. He started to hope that something might still be salvageable. He rationalized that he could explain to Jorge all the people wanting to give him money as an unfortunate side effect of his celebrity. He wanted to stay to find out, and he wanted to run away immediately.

Before too much time passed, Chantal waved toward the crowd in the front of the bar and said, "There's our boy now."

Rupert turned to look, and he almost didn't recognize Jorge at first. He had shaved off his goatee and his hair was cut much shorter than he'd ever seen it. His

86

bright blue eyes seemed troubled until he saw Chantal and Rupert on the couch. Then he smiled. Chantal asked the young man on his other side to vacate his spot so the three of them could sit together, and Jorge sat down between them. He turned to Chantal first, "I didn't know Rupert was going to be here too."

Rupert wasn't sure how to interpret that statement. His first impulse was to get angry that Jorge didn't want him there. He tried to calm down enough to allow for the possibility that it was a pleasant surprise. He settled on a compromise. "I hope I'm not crashing your plans." He smiled to make it seem a tease and not the serious concern it was.

Jorge quickly turned back to face Rupert. "Oh, no. I'm happy to see you."

Chantal touched him on his shoulder. "Rupert just showed up unexpectedly, sweetie. I'm glad you could get away. You look exhausted."

"Your new look is nice," Rupert added.

Jorge smiled briefly in Rupert's direction and immediately turned back to Chantal. "Thank you for meeting me, Chantal. It's been so crazy. She's finally sleeping through the night, so I feel better about leaving the house late like this."

"We can always meet closer to your place, if that makes it easier," Chantal offered.

"No, I needed to get away—into the city."

Rupert got up from the couch. "I really feel like a third wheel right now, so I think I'll head out."

He only got two steps away before Jorge was up also and catching him by the elbow. "Don't go yet. I need to talk to you too."

Rupert felt confused. Jorge was treating him like he wasn't there, and now he wanted to talk just to him. "We can talk some other time if you want." He took another step away. He had a sense that this was a conversation he wanted to put off.

Jorge scooted in front of him and put his hand on Rupert's chest. "No, I wanted to apologize for not seeing you on your birthday."

Rupert folded his arms, and Jorge withdrew his hand. "I know you had to take your mom to the hospital."

"I wanted to take you out to dinner and buy you a gift. Can I at least give you some cash to make up for it?"

Rupert huffed, somewhere between annoyance and disgust. "No, thank you, Jorge. I should get going."

He pushed through the crowd at a steady pace, leaving Jorge behind. But moments after he was out the front door, Jorge was again beside him. "Don't be mad at me, Rupert. It's just that I've been really busy with work and taking care of my mama."

Rupert saw smokers outside the bar apparently listening in. "I know that Jorge," he whispered back.

"Did I do something wrong?" Jorge didn't seem to care as much about being overheard.

Rupert herded Jorge further from the smokers. "I wonder why you were able to arrange to meet Chantal, but not me."

"He reached out to me."

Rupert sighed. "I called you too."

This time Jorge sighed. "I've known Chantal for years. You and I only met seven months ago. Meeting you . . . is more complication than I wanted right now."

Rupert looked into those blue eyes that had so frequently caused him to melt, and he saw fear and pain. "You want to break up with me, I guess. If seeing me has become complicated."

Jorge just stood there with his mouth open. Rupert saw one of the smokers from in front of the bar approaching him with cash in his hand, and he started to walk away.

Jorge caught up to him again. "It sounds like you don't want to see *me* anymore. You keep walking away from me."

Rupert came to a halt. "Listen, you've got your job and taking care of your mom. I've got the show six nights a week. I think it's just not practical right now. I'm only free after eleven o'clock at night or on Monday evenings."

"Maybe when things calm down a bit for me . . ."

"Fine." Rupert took off again without him. "Let me know."

Rupert didn't look back, and Jorge stopped chasing him. A couple getting out of a taxi near him started fishing cash out of a wallet and a purse, and Rupert started running. He finally stopped when he got to 60th Street, and walked the last few blocks with his hood pulled up and his gaze down. He started thinking, *My blessing is really a curse too. Or maybe the curse is turning it into something bad.* He resolved to call Mike when he got home.

As soon as he got in the apartment, he shucked off his jacket and sat down next to the phone. The message light on the answering machine was flashing, so he played the two messages, one from his stage manager and one for his roommate. He picked up the phone and dialed Mike's cell phone, because he was rarely at home anymore.

"Hey, Rupert," the familiar voice began. "I'm driving back to Sheboygan from Milwaukee right now, so I have you on speaker. Let me know if you have trouble hearing me."

"Hi, Mike. I don't want to disturb you if you're driving."

"It's okay. It's just like I'm talking to someone in the car. I have both hands on the wheel, and my eyes on the road. How are you doing?"

"I just broke up with Jorge."

"I thought that happened back in December. Are you okay?"

Rupert cradled the phone against his shoulder and moved to the kitchen to fix himself a peanut butter sandwich. "It probably did. We just made it official tonight. I just got so angry. But I don't think I was really angry at Jorge. I am getting fed up with being a battleground for two Irish fairies. Every time I get something nice happening in my life, it gets ruined—usually by one of my 'gifts.' If I were face to face with either one of them now, I would be tempted to strangle them."

Mike chuckled. "Now, now. The Grogoch has been very good to me. This has been the luckiest two years of my life so far. I have lots of friends, my job and the restaurant are doing really well, I've got a company car and use of the company airplane and a company cell phone . . ."

89

"This isn't helping, Mike," Rupert interrupted.

"Sorry. . . . You were saying you felt angry."

"Don't you ever feel like getting too much good luck is oppressive?"

"Me? I am enjoying it, but I know your blessing keeps getting warped by your family curse. I mentioned that to the Grogoch the last time I saw her."

"What did she say?"

Mike chuckled again. "In your case, she said that the bad luck would start overwhelming the good luck as time went on. But I have to tell you, Rupert, . . . normal people go through breakups, lose jobs. It's part of life. You just think you've got it worse because your first twenty-five years were so lucky."

"They weren't that lucky either," Rupert retorted. "I had to keep dealing with people not noticing me, laughing at me, fawning over me, sexualizing me, . . . for a year at a time. I could hear people's thoughts, see images of traumatic events everywhere I went, and I generally felt like a freak all the time!"

"Some of them worked out pretty well in your favor. You had a year where you healed really quickly. One year, your blessing gave you straight A's. And when you were a teen, you got really muscular really fast."

There was a crackling noise on the phone, and when Mike's voice came back it was much softer. "I'm losing the charge on my phone. Do you want me to call me when I get home?"

"I'll probably be in bed. You can try me tomorrow night late if you're not busy."

"I'll try to make it . . . " There was silence, then a dial tone.

Rupert hung up the phone and went back into the kitchen to eat his sandwich. "What would happen if I were able to kill the Pooka?" Rupert wondered aloud. He fantasized that his life would get nicer again. He might be able to get back into a dance company and do solos again. He might be able to afford a nicer apartment and have a boyfriend with a similar schedule. He brushed his teeth, did some calisthenics, and headed to bed with hope for a better future.

A month later, during a Sunday matinee, though, Rupert twisted his ankle onstage and had to limp offstage and let a swing replacement take over. The doctor at the emergency room that night said it was severe, fitted him with a brace to help immobilize the ankle, and gave him a cane. He tried and failed to get his laundry to the laundromat the next day. He tried and almost failed to get groceries home from the store while leaning heavily on the cane. On Tuesday afternoon, he hobbled to the 1 train, cursing all the staircases New York City required its commuters to climb and descend. At a city office in Harlem, he filled out the forms to start his workers comp claim.

But within six weeks, after only two payments, the producers at the theatre canceled their workers comp insurance and fired him. Rupert met with his union rep to see about contesting the termination and the withdrawal of funds, but he warned Rupert any settlement he might negotiate could be months away and not very substantial. Rupert tried to apply for unemployment benefits, but he had to declare his periodic payments from his family's restaurant in Sheboygan, and that made him ineligible.

At Danny's urging, Rupert finally relented during his lonely convalescence and got a laptop computer and a subscription to AOL. Within a week of logging on, he had seven of his friends emailing and instant messaging with him almost daily, including Dorian and Chantal.

Dorian forwarded an email from Luke and suggested that he might want to bury the hatchet. Luke was inviting friends to attend a benefit at BAM in Brooklyn where he was going to be deejaying. Dorian said he would accompany Rupert and play peacemaker, if necessary. Rupert said he would think about it, but when the night came, he found himself hobbling onto a 2 train bound for Brooklyn in a nice shirt and tie.

When he climbed up out of the subway, Dorian was waiting for him wearing a bluish-gray wool coat and carrying a paper bag from some deli. "You look like you've just arrived in a foreign country, Rupert. It's just Brooklyn," he teased.

"What's in the bag?" Rupert asked as he retied his scarf around his neck and followed Dorian across the busy street.

"A bagel with cream cheese," Dorian explained as he lifted the paper bag. "Luke always forgets to take time to eat when he's working a party like this. I

91

know you are out of work. Do you need some cash to get by?"

"I'm okay for now," Rupert lied. "I get checks from my stepfather every month."

There was a steady increase in foot traffic as they approached the opera house that housed the Brooklyn Academy of Music. As some of the other patrons noticed Rupert, they tried to get his attention, but he pretended to ignore them and joked to Dorian, "The panhandlers here are better dressed than the ones in Manhattan!"

Rupert managed to get in the doors surreptitiously accepting and pocketing a couple of donations when Dorian wasn't looking. As Dorian gave their names at the will-call table, Rupert dug into his pocket to examine the bills he'd so quickly stuffed out of sight. He held seventy dollars. *I should hang out around rich people more often,* Rupert mused.

He let Dorian check both their coats because he knew it would be awkward when the coat check attendants tried to pay *him* for watching his coat. He wandered into the theatre. The logo for the Elton John AIDS Foundation was projected onto a screen, and the music was the electronic bebop he knew Luke favored.

Dorian rejoined Rupert just inside the entrance wearing a pink jacket with fringed, gold epaulets he'd seen once before. He flicked a couple of the cords dangling from the epaulets and smirked. Dorian raised his eyebrows and whispered back, "I wore this for Elton. I'm sure he would approve."

While Dorian went up to the booth to deliver Luke's snack, Rupert circulated around the floor, smiling and introducing himself to whomever he could. After thanking them, he helped them rationalize their donations by telling them he was out of work and had medical expenses. When he caught the eye of an Arab-looking man in his forties and his Asian wife accepting champagne from a waiter, he noticed the familiar look of someone who was trying to place where they had seen him before.

"You're Rupert Rocket!" he declared as he extended an open hand in Rupert's direction.

Rupert transferred his cane to his other hand, shook the man's hand, and nodded toward his wife. "Yes, I know," he teased. "And whom do I have the pleasure of meeting?"

"My name is Hakim. This is my wife, Azami." He gestured toward the waiter who had just departed. "Can I help you get some refreshment?"

"I'm fine for now," Rupert said.

Someone else tapped him on the shoulder, and he turned to see a man in a tuxedo slip a hundred-dollar bill into his breast pocket and gesture toward his cane. "I hope this can help you with your medical expenses," the man whispered before winding his way back into the crowd.

"I saw you dance at the American Ballet Theatre two years ago," Hakim continued. "You were amazing, but I haven't seen you anywhere since then."

Hakim's wife pulled him aside to whisper something Rupert couldn't hear. "My wife reminds me you are injured, so of course, you haven't been performing lately. Are you doing okay financially? Could you use some extra cash?"

Rupert decided that when someone knew who he was, it was risky to accept cash from them, because of the reputation he might start to get. "I'm doing all right with that as well," Rupert lied. He was only just getting by with the funds his current blessing provided. "What brings you out tonight?"

Before Hakim could answer, an older woman in a ball gown handed Rupert a check and said, "I hope you recover quickly and can perform again soon."

"I'm sorry about the interruption." He looked at the amount on the check—one thousand dollars—and his eyes widened in shock.

"I see I'm not your only fan here." Hakim's wife whispered in his ear again and took off into the crowd. "I've seen you take in two donations in the past two minutes without even soliciting them. That is some amazing fundraising skill you have. I'm on the board of a nonprofit ballet company here in Brooklyn, and we need someone on staff to start managing our income. Would you have any interest in becoming their development director? They can pay a base salary and bonuses based on your results."

"I really don't have any experience," Rupert said.

Hakim put his hand gently on Rupert's back. "You seem like a natural, and you know the industry."

Rupert smiled. "When would I start?"

Hakim patted him on the back. "We can start you tonight. Walk with me."

For the next two hours, between intermittent check-ins from Dorian, Hakim led Rupert around the benefit venue introducing him to a couple dozen attendees. Some wrote out checks to the ballet company on the spot, and others received a business card from Hakim for later follow-up. Rupert was surprised that his wealth blessing was so transferable, but as he watched each of the new donors approach, their expressions seemed to show pleasure in handing him money, no matter where it would later end up. As Hakim gathered his wife to leave, he passed a card to Rupert as well and asked him to call the following day to arrange an introduction to the ballet staff and company.

Dorian found him moments later. "So, who was that man leading you around all night, Rupert?"

"I think I have a new job."

"That's good," Dorian quipped. "You were getting too mopey."

By September, Rupert didn't have to wear the brace or use the cane anymore. He was regularly making visits to corporations and foundations during the day and going to other benefits several nights a week. It was at a benefit for the Alvin Ailey American Dance Theater's South African residency that Rupert met Arthur. He was a shy, slim, athletic Chinese-American man a few years younger than Rupert. Rupert wasn't sure if Arthur naturally was drawn to him or if he were assigned to escort him, but they were never more than two or three feet apart the whole evening. They talked about Princess Diana, the Hale-Bopp comet, the Mars rover, the return of Hong Kong to the Chinese, cloned sheep, the cheaper neighborhoods in Manhattan, and just about every other topic besides dance. About halfway through the evening, Rupert got a sense that Arthur was there to distract him and keep him from poaching the other dance company's donors.

"You know who I am, don't you?" Rupert finally asked him.

"You said your name was Rupert," the intern replied as innocently as he could muster.

"Come on. You knew who I was when I walked in the door."

"No, really," Arthur protested. "They just told me to follow you around and talk to you while you were here. Are you a really big donor for the Theater?"

"I'm the development director for another dance company in Brooklyn," Rupert revealed. "I'm just seeing who is here that I might not know."

"You must be really good at your job," Arthur admitted. "I'm flat broke. I have no money on me at all. And I've been trying to figure out how to get you some money all night. I almost asked my supervisor for a loan!"

Rupert chuckled. "Don't do that. Here's my card." He handed Arthur one of his brand new business cards. "Feel free to call or email me if you'd like a chance to see how our ballet company operates."

Arthur studied the card. "Thank you, Mr. Rocket. I might just take you up on that, if you're sure it's okay."

"It would be my pleasure, Arthur."

Rupert left the building wondering if the previous year's blessing were still holding on. He had wanted to hire an assistant, and that would definitely be a step up for the young man he met tonight.

Arthur took the job the second time Rupert offered it in November. Through the end of the year, the younger man was in a constant state of amazement that a 27-year-old like Rupert could quadruple the company's budget in just a few months. There had been a slight suggestion of flirtation between them. Arthur told him he was dating someone but made sure he knew it was a white man like Rupert.

By the time his twenty-eighth birthday rolled around, Rupert was more than ready to let go of his wealth blessing. On Christmas Eve, he sat at his computer in his bedroom trying to remember what his next blessing would be. He realized it was either the dominance blessing or that obscure one that had something to do with growing. He decided he needed to make a list so he would have a better sense of what was to come.

He gave up on it halfway through and got ready for bed. He realized whether it was the dominance or the growth blessing, both would be easier to deal with than the wealth one had been.

In the morning, as he was getting ready to go volunteer at the church, he found his roommate in the kitchen cooking breakfast. "You hardly ever cook when you're home," Rupert observed.

"I wanted to do something nice for you for Christmas," she said as she offered him a plate of pancakes and sausage. "Here you go."

"That's sweet of you," he said as he set the plate down on the table and started toward the refrigerator to pour himself some juice.

His roommate snatched a glass from the cupboard and set it next to his plate. "I can pour that for you."

"I can handle it. Thanks."

As he sat down to eat the breakfast, someone buzzed to be let in. "I'll get it," his roommate shouted as she dashed toward the intercom.

A minute later, she returned escorting Arthur, his assistant, in. "Hello, Mr. Rocket."

Rupert had tried with limited success to get him to call him Rupert. "Merry Christmas, Arthur. What brings you here for the first time ever?"

"I wanted to see if there was anything I could do to help you," he said a bit more meekly than usual.

"I wasn't expecting to see you until Monday, Arthur."

"I can help you too," his roommate volunteered.

It was suddenly clear which blessing was revisiting him. He pointed at Arthur. "You." He pointed toward his open bedroom door. "Go wait for me on my bed." He pointed at his roommate. "You go to your room and stay there for the next fifteen minutes."

They both stared at him for a moment and then simultaneously said, "Yes, sir," and took off down the hall.

When Rupert had been twenty-one, he hadn't really taken full advantage of the dominance blessing. He accepted others' help as graciously as he could and made his own requests minimal. This time he decided to play the role with more commitment. After he finished eating the breakfast his roommate had prepared, he left the dishes in the sink and sauntered back to his bedroom. Arthur was perched nervously and expectantly on the edge of Rupert's bed.

"Take all your clothes off," Rupert ordered.

Rupert closed the door to his bedroom as Arthur began disrobing. He decided to skip volunteering at the church and celebrate his birthday a bit differently this year.

CHAPTER 10: RUPERT TURNS TWENTY-ONE

Early in the morning on December 26, 1997, through the dim light escaping around his bedroom window shade, Rupert looked over at the sleeping form of the younger Asian man still asleep next to him. He was his assistant, who had responded to a baffling need to check in on Christmas morning at the home of his boss and do whatever he asked of him. Rupert thought back to the last time he received this particular blessing, when he had turned twenty-one. He tried to remember what had made him decide to back off and avoid using it to his advantage.

Friends from Julliard had taken him out drinking on Christmas night 1990. He was surprised that everyone he invited to join in bar hopping had been eager to do so on such short notice, and he decided to volunteer at a church feeding the homeless. He figured it would be a safe, anonymous place where he could start to deal with the next blessing, and it would keep his mind occupied with no family to visit except a birth father in California and a stepfather in Wisconsin.

And it felt like a bit of penance for the debauchery to come that night. Now that he was finally legally able to buy alcohol, his younger friends wanted him to buy rounds for them, and he'd agreed. They would meet at the World at nine o'clock for dancing first, and then move on to the West Village. That gave Rupert plenty of time to eat dinner and change into his club attire after volunteering.

He arrived at the church on Ninth Avenue in Chelsea early to get orientation and training with a couple of other new volunteers. The manager was an older black man named Bert who got such a kick out of pronouncing Rupert's name, he used it often. He asked Bert if he could work on the serving line, and Bert agreed immediately. Everyone at the church seemed so eager to defer to Rupert or help him, he started to wonder if his new blessing was going to allow him to get his way for a year.

Rupert had received many blessings that eventually got annoying and wore out their welcome, so as he served the lunches, he tried to imagine what could possibly go wrong with winning every argument and getting preferential treatment. Maybe people would avoid giving him negative feedback? Maybe it would be harder to figure out what someone else wanted or liked if they were always deferring to him?

He decided those consequences didn't seem too bad, and he looked forward to a more helpful blessing than the past year's odd blessing. The only extraordinary thing he noticed happening was that his friend Danny's spider plant seemed to become much healthier and larger after he watered it during Danny's summer vacation.

Shortly after the kitchen staff started refusing to refill the food trays on the steam table, Bert said Rupert could take off, that the others would handle the cleanup. It was below freezing, so he jogged over to Eighth Avenue to catch the first of two trains back home. The salt on the sidewalks was not doing enough to clear them, and he barely grabbed the railing in time to keep from slipping and falling as he descended the stairs into the subway station. The few other commuters there all rushed to his aid, but he assured them he was fine and didn't need their help.

His pager went off as he was exiting the subway at Lincoln Center, and he recognized the number as his father's. Rupert jogged the rest of the way to his apartment and was so glad to get out of the cold and into his building. As he rode up in the elevator with a woman he'd seen a couple of times before, she smiled at him and asked him if there was anything he needed. Rupert smiled back and said, "No, I'm good."

When he got to his tiny studio, he closed the door and dove onto his bed to turn up the radiator next to it. As he took off his boots and jacket, he started to warm up again and dialed his father's number. "Merry Christmas, Fred," he said.

"Merry Christmas and happy birthday, son," his birth father said. "Did you have a good day? Is there anything you need?"

"I volunteered to feed lunch to some homeless people, and some friends are taking me out drinking tonight."

"That's right," Fred said. "You're legal now. We already had the talk about responsible drinking, didn't we?"

"Yup. I'm gonna' make sure I stop drinking before it impairs my ability to get home safely." Rupert chuckled a little at his own paraphrasing of Fred's advice.

"Britney and I missed you this year. Are you going to be able to visit before you start rehearsals again in January?"

"I'll be there in April for the San Francisco Ballet audition," Rupert reported. "I'll send you the dates when I reserve my flight."

"If they hire you, would you move back out here?" Fred seemed excited at the prospect.

"Unlikely," Rupert replied. "They're planning to perform here in New York. I'd just be subbing for one of the dancers who can't travel."

"Well, it might be a foot in the door. You never know."

"That's true. Fred, were you just calling to wish me a happy birthday? Or did you have some news?"

There was a silent pause before Fred spoke. "I've been talking to your mom . . ."

"Fred, I told you," Rupert interrupted. "I don't want to hear about it."

"Okay. Whatever you want. Would you like to continue talking?"

Rupert paused for a moment. It was an unusual question for his father to ask. Fred was friendly toward him, but he didn't like talking on the phone for too long. "We can end if you have other stuff you need to do."

"I'm here for you. It's your day. Hey, maybe I could take some time off and come out and visit you for once. I haven't been to New York City since I was a teenager. I could help you get settled into your new place and do things with you when you're free."

Rupert glanced around his tiny studio and wondered where a second person would even stand, much less sleep. "I'm pretty settled in already, I've been in New York for over four years now, and there isn't even enough floor space for you to stay with me."

"If you tell me to come, I'll be on the next plane."

Rupert felt strange. He wanted to hang up on Fred as quickly as he could. The dynamic was getting weirder the longer they spoke. "You really don't have to do that."

"Let me know if you need me to be there for you."

"I will. Merry Christmas, Fred, and thanks for the talk."

Rupert disconnected the call and dropped the receiver into the cradle as if it had suddenly become disgusting, covered with slime or cobwebs or mildew. "Ugh!" he said as he dropped it.

After a bit of leftover pizza and salad, Rupert showered and shaved and changed into a pair of black pants, a white button-down shirt to catch the black lights at the club, a striped bowtie, and a dark green vest woven with gold fibers that sparkled in normal light. As he was adding bits of gel to his hair, his phone rang.

Rupert sighed. He had been out all day, so now everyone would be trying him again. He quickly cleaned off his hands and picked up the receiver. "Rupert Rocket," he announced when the call connected.

"Rupert!" Danny effused. "We're sharing a taxi to World. We should be leaving here in ten minutes and be in front of your building in twenty."

"Thanks, Danny. I could have come to your place. You didn't have to pick me up separately."

"We just wanted to make it easier on you," he explained. "You are going to be buying the first round since you said you're legal now, right?"

"That's right." Rupert took his wallet from his nightstand and counted the cash. He had sixty dollars. "I can help out with cab fare and buy the first round, but then I'll be tapped out."

"If you're low on dough," Danny said, "we can pay for the cab and the drinks. You don't have to spend any of your own money. We want to make sure you're happy."

Rupert paused before responding. The only ones who knew it was his birthday were his family. He hadn't told anyone else today was the day. This too had to be part of his new blessing. "I'm sure we'll all have a good time. I'll see you guys in about twenty minutes."

"Okay. Let us know where you'd most like to go after World, and that's where we'll go, right, guys?"

Rupert could hear Danny and at least three other friends shouting "Right!" in the background.

Again, Rupert quickly disconnected the call and dropped the receiver in the cradle. He shivered at the change he had heard in Danny's demeanor as well. Danny was a good friend and conscientious, but he often argued with Rupert and teased him, and being surrounded with Rupert Rocket fanboys reminded him a little too much of work, and he just wanted to relax. He considered begging off when they arrived, excusing himself with some made-up stomach ailment that had suddenly come on.

He put his hands on the ends of the bowtie but paused before untying it. Even if they didn't know it was his birthday, he could pretend that their deference was in honor of it, and he could handle it for one night. If the effect lasted all year, he'd come up with some way to deal with it.

He finished styling his hair, put his jacket back on, and headed back downstairs to the lobby. After a couple of minutes, he saw the taxi pull up and idle in front of the building. He was tying his scarf tighter and walking toward the taxi when Danny jumped out of the front seat and stood next to it gesturing for Rupert to take his place. Danny wore a gray suit and Gatsby cap he'd never seen him wear before. Rupert looked at the other three of his friends in the back seat and asked Danny, "Where are you going to sit then?"

Danny smiled. "We'll make room. Don't worry about us."

So, with Danny sitting on Theo's lap, they managed to pull up in front of the World night club, a huge banquet hall in the East Village turned into an underground dance bar. They joined the line to get in, and between the early hour and Michaela's acquaintance with the doorman, the five of them were let in with only cursory scans of their IDs.

When they got inside, a pair of very tall male bouncers pointed them toward the table where they had to come up with one hundred and fifty dollars to enter. The five of them counted how much cash they had between them, and they realized they would have too little to buy drinks after paying the cover charge. Rupert held up a finger to indicate they should wait and walked up to the table to talk to the cashier.

She was an Asian woman who looked very hardened and bitter. She only glanced up at Rupert briefly as he approached and then turned her attention back to the chatter on the walkie-talkie lying next to the cash box. "Cash only," she shouted over the heavy bass thumping coming through the double doors to the ballroom. "Thirty each."

He put both hands on the front edge of the table and leaned in. "I'm Rupert Rocket, and this is my entourage. I think you should put us on your comp list and let us in immediately."

When she looked up into Rupert's face again, her expression changed completely. She looked apologetic. "Yes, sir. I'll put you on the comp list now, Mr. Rocket." She dug into a plastic bag and dumped a bunch of yellow poker chips in front of him. "Here are some drink vouchers. Enjoy your time here at the World, and let me know if there's anything else I can do for you."

Rupert gathered up the chips and said, "I'll let you know. You're doing a good job tonight."

"Thank you, sir."

One of the bouncers opened the door to the ballroom for them. They approached, passing the poker chips to each other. "These are each good for a free drink," Rupert tried to explain over the loud music.

Even though it was early, there was already a substantial crowd on the dance floor. Most of the dancers were in vintage and more formal clothing and vogued frequently. Some of the others stood off to the side just freezing in model-like poses. Rupert turned to see if his friends were still with him or if they had wandered off, and all of them were tightly clustered behind him.

"What do you want to do first?" Theo shouted.

"I don't know," Rupert replied. "I'm surprised it's so crowded here on Christmas."

"Would you like to dance first or get drinks?" John asked.

Somewhat out of habit and feeling so good made Rupert forget about his new blessing for a moment. "What would you guys like to do first?"

"Whatever you want," Michaela replied.

"You pick," Danny said.

"Yeah," Theo and John agreed.

Rupert sighed and trudged toward the bar. He imagined the fun teasing and scandalous stories he had enjoyed with the four of them during their time at Julliard had disappeared. He worried that they would never return. They had become his servants, sycophants solely focused on his pleasure. There had to be some way to salvage the coming year. He laid five of the yellow poker chips on the bar, and he tried to recall each of his friends' favorite drinks. "What do you usually drink, John?"

"I'm flexible," John replied.

"I mean, think back," Rupert persisted. "When we've gone out before, what do you usually order as a first drink."

"Just something basic like a rum and Coke," he replied carefully.

"All of you," Rupert said as he turned to the other three. "Michaela, Theo, Danny, step up to the bar and order whatever you would usually order when we've gone out before."

Through a similar process, he managed to get through their first stop barhopping using halting recollections of their previous behavior and insisting that they repeat them. They ended up at the Monster next, and though he had been there before with Theo and Danny, it was Michaela's and John's first time there. Michaela felt immediately at home at a more thoroughly gay venue, but Rupert could see that his straighter friend John was getting uncomfortable being cruised so much.

He took John aside after they'd been downstairs dancing for almost an hour. "You seem like you're not having such a good time," Rupert observed.

"Don't worry about me," John said. "I just want to stay with you. You can tell me to do whatever you want. I actually feel much more open to trying new things tonight."

Rupert had harbored a secret crush on his handsome friend for most of his time at Julliard. In an environment where most of the male dancers were gay, John's aloofness made Rupert curious. He spent time getting to know him, and he listened patiently to all of John's troubles with women. All the while Rupert hoped that John might give up on women entirely and have sex with him finally.

"Where is the bathroom?" Michaela interrupted.

"Upstairs between the bar and the middle staircase," Rupert explained.

"Do you mind if I go now?" she asked.

Rupert sighed. "Not at all. Go now, if you need to."

"I'll be right back," she assured him before heading toward the stairs.

"Could I get you another drink?" John offered.

"Not at the moment," Rupert replied as he lifted his tumbler. "Maybe in a little while."

"Okay," John said. He stood there watching Rupert sip his drink. "Is there anything else I can do for you? Are you hungry? I could run out and bring you back something."

Danny had been listening and leaned in. "If you want, I could get you something to eat too."

"No, no, guys, I'm fine." He looked at the two of them and Theo hovering not far behind Danny.

Before he could continue, Michaela came back. "The line was too long, so I came back. I wanted to see if you needed anything."

Rupert sighed, and Theo approached closer to listen in with a worried look on his face, as if he suddenly realized he had been ignoring his king and master for too long. "I am really happy that all four of you agreed to come out dancing and drinking with me tonight, but I think it might be better if Michaela and John, you two went home. We can try getting together again on New Year's Eve."

Both John and Michaela nodded, looked down, and headed toward the coat check. Theo and Danny watched them leave and then turned back toward Rupert with anxious expressions, hoping they too would not be dismissed.

"Let's dance for a while yet," Rupert suggested to them.

Rupert removed his tie and vest and unbuttoned his shirt completely, exposing his naked torso. The style at this bar was more a combination of disco dancing, with a certain amount of bumping and grinding that could only remotely be called dancing. He told Danny to take off his cap and jacket and unbutton his shirt as well. He told Theo to remove all his clothing above the waist. They heaped their discarded clothing in a corner and reentered the packed crowd dancing very close to each other, frequently rubbing up against each other.

Rupert could tell that Theo and Danny were both really excited, so after a couple of hours, and after Rupert had fought off a dozen other guys who wanted to serve him, the three of them gathered the rest of their clothes, drank a lot of water to replace all the sweat, and headed back to the coat check to leave.

They ended up at Danny's apartment, and Rupert was too drunk to be thinking about consequences. The three of them had sex for several hours. At one point, when Theo got up to use the bathroom, Rupert looked around at the bedroom that was bigger than his whole studio. "I would love to live here," he whispered to Danny.

"Really?" Danny whispered back. "I have a roommate already, but I could probably ask her to move out, if you want."

Rupert changed gears slowly. "I live in a really tiny studio," he commented.

"I can tell her to move out in the morning," Danny volunteered. "Unless you want her out immediately."

"No," Rupert said. "Let's see how much time she needs to find another place."

"That would be great," Danny said. "I could take care of you every day . . . if you want."

Rupert kissed Danny again. "I would like that."

106

Danny's roommate moved out in the first week of January. Rupert continued spending nights in Danny's bed until then, frequently inviting Theo over for another three-way. After Rupert moved his things into the vacated bedroom, he started noticing a subtle change in Danny. He was still lovingly devoted to Rupert, but there were flashes of emotion Rupert noticed when Danny didn't think he was being observed. Danny seemed resentful about sharing Rupert with Theo, and about the loss of the other good friend he had so callously told to get out—with Rupert's help.

Rupert started to worry what would happen on his twenty-second birthday, when the dominance blessing wore off. Would all of Danny's resentments suddenly bubble to the surface? Would he be angry at the way he had let himself be used? Or would a year of being so devoted to Rupert become so familiar that Danny wouldn't even want to break the habit?

When Rupert took stock of all his other relationships since his last birthday, he realized there was a strain on all of them, especially the choreographers and producers who were supposed to be telling him what to do. It gave him opportunities, like winning the audition for the San Francisco Ballet. It saved him money when he could claim special discounts or free goods and services.

He started to notice that people were avoiding him. Except for the people he was closest to who wanted to submit to him whether he was in their presence or not, people begged off meeting him. They sent proxies to deal with him. They kept their interactions short and then disappeared as quickly as they could.

At the end of the year, on his twenty-second birthday, when people stopped wanting to submit to Rupert and instead started thrusting monetary donations in his direction, Rupert felt weary. Except for Danny's unflagging devotion and proclaimed love, he felt lonely and isolated. The desire to give him money seemed more often to grow out of a concern for Rupert's welfare, so he quickly learned he could turn down the cash and continue a fairly normal exchange at last.

But Danny showed up at the stage door one night, as he often did for Friday and Saturday night performances, when they resumed on January 3, 1992. It was obvious even in the poor street lighting that Danny had been crying and was still emotional. "I need to talk to you about us," he said as the two of them walked slowly through the crowd toward the river on their walk back to their shared apartment.

"Okay," Rupert said warily.

"I still love you, and I think you're really sexy, Rupert."

"Thanks. I feel the same about you, Danny."

"But I've felt like I'm waking up from a dream this past year since you moved in." Danny sighed twice before he continued almost a minute later. "And it doesn't feel real to me, Rupert. It feels like someone else was living my life and then just handed it back to me on Christmas Day."

Rupert felt guilt at having abused his friend with the previous year's blessing, angry that he had the additional burden in his life of constantly managing extreme circumstances. "I don't know what to say."

"You've treated me really well," Danny maintained. "I can't fault you at all. It's just that . . . I need some time to figure out what I really want from you."

Rupert sighed, and it came out in a huge cloud of tiny ice crystals. "Do you want me to move out?"

"No, no. With you working nights and me working days, I rarely see you at home anymore." Danny stopped walking and looked out at the Hudson River. "I just think we should be friends for now. You sleeping in the other bedroom, and us hanging out just on the weekends."

Rupert came up behind him and hugged him, looking out at the river over his shoulder. "This year, you can call the shots. Let me know when you want me."

Danny turned around in Rupert's embrace and kissed him lightly on the lips. "I want to stop by an ATM on the way home. I think I owe you some money for something."

"I don't recall."

They started walking again. "I don't remember how much it was, but I think it was around forty dollars."

Six years later, Danny had moved out to be with his new boyfriend Max, and now his young assistant Arthur was headed down the same path. Rupert's dominance blessing was reverberating back through his life, and he had much more frequent contact with Arthur during the work week than he ever had with Danny. Rupert couldn't have Arthur avoiding or resenting him.

Rupert pushed the sheets down to admire and stroke Arthur's smooth, athletic torso and butt. Arthur startled awake and turned over. "I must have fallen asleep, sir. Do you need anything?"

Rupert chuckled. "Sleeping is good. I'm sorry if I woke you, Arthur." He lay back down, and Arthur moved partly on top of him to cuddle. "I really enjoyed the time with you tonight, but I think we should think of this as a one-time thing. I don't want you to feel like I'm sexually harassing you."

"I would never accuse you of that, sir. I think you're really sexy, and I loved what we did."

Rupert sighed and tousled Arthur's hair. "Unfortunately, that doesn't matter. If other people around the office started to suspect I was being sexual with you, I could get in trouble."

"What should I do then?"

"Just go back to acting around me the way you did before: thinking for yourself, taking initiative, and learning from other people in the company besides me."

"I can still be your assistant and help you that way?"

"Of course. But as much as I've enjoyed it too, we have to curtail the kissing and the sex. Okay?"

"If that's what you want, I will try, sir."

Rupert chuckled and ruffled Arthur's hair again. "And please, call me Rupert. Not Mister Rocket, and especially not sir. Okay?"

"Okay . . . Rupert . . . sir."

"Keep practicing."

CHAPTER 11: RUPERT TURNS TWENTY-NINE

When Rupert was twenty-eight, he had to usually deny that he needed anything. When he did need something, he tried not to say anything. So at the corner bodega, he would just put his purchases on the counter, and if asked if he needed anything else he would silently nod or shake his head. When someone at work was doing something wrong, he would only fold his arms and shake his head. He found it helpful to pretend he was mute.

When he needed to ask for something, he tried to always phrase it as a question not a request or demand. "Do you have this in a size 10?" at the shoe store. "Could you give me my usual?" at the barber shop. If they followed up with an offer of other assistance, anything at all he might want, Rupert just shook his head and smiled.

The dominance blessing put the heaviest burden on Rupert's closest associates. He could avoid or disappear on his family and friends when they turned up or called wanting to please him. His biggest challenges were with his roommate, because she was in his home, and Arthur. Arthur spent the better part of eight hours a day, five days a week with Rupert, and it was in his job description to assist Rupert.

Rupert tried to evict the roommate, but she cried and begged not to send her away. So, Rupert moved out. His new job and dividends from his restaurant back in Sheboygan made it possible for him to move up to a one-bedroom apartment in a doorman building in Williamsburg. It was a quiet, safe place for Rupert and a shorter commute to work.

Arthur tried hard to act like a normal employee. Rupert tried hard to send

Arthur tasks to do via email. Occasionally, Arthur lapsed and had to be asked to get up off his knees—and/or stop calling Rupert sir. For a few weeks, Rupert relented, and allowed Arthur to follow him home on a Friday night, but by March, his resolve returned. Arthur was not to enter Rupert's new apartment.

One male friend from the chorus of *Titanic*, a very handsome bisexual man named Charlie, who had put him off when they were working together became a regular fuckbuddy for most of the rest of the dominance blessing. Rupert enjoyed finally being able to bend the stud's will.

By October, though, the guy stopped returning Rupert's calls. He realized that the effects of his dominance blessing were often like an addiction that many people could only shake by going cold turkey.

Arthur, however, showed no signs that his devotion to Rupert was waning, only kept at bay when they were both in the office. Rupert insisted that Arthur not close his office door when they were conversing, and Rupert demanded that Arthur leave immediately if he showed up unannounced at one of Rupert's appointments. Arthur's unflagging devotion tugged Rupert toward fantasizing whether the gay couples suing to marry in Hawaii might some day give him and Arthur the option.

By the end of the year, when Rupert was about to turn twenty-nine and get a new blessing, Arthur seemed to be abiding by all of Rupert's rules. Rupert wished Arthur a good Christmas on Friday night and then got on a plane to Minneapolis the next morning.

He had made arrangements to spend his birthday and Christmas with Trevor and Samantha, who had moved to Wausau from Sheboygan months before. He took a bus from the airport to a private bus depot on the north side of town. Trevor was in the waiting room at the depot when Rupert disembarked. He smiled and spread his arms wide for a hug when he saw Rupert enter the building. Rupert set down his suitcase and entered into the hug. "Thanks so much for the invitation, Trevor."

"I'd do anything for you, Rupert."

While still in the hug, Rupert became concerned that he had to be on guard

111

around his childhood friend for the next three days until his blessing changed. What Trevor said could be innocent friendship, or it could be a newly awakened desire to submit to him. He decided it was safest to distract Trevor. "So where is Samantha?" he asked as he finally stepped out of the hug and sat down on one of the plastic chairs.

Trevor sat down next to him and put his hand on Rupert's closer knee. He had put on some muscle and lost a little of his dark brown hair, but Rupert still remembered the first guy he'd ever had sex with, smiled, and let the hand remain. "She's spending the weekend at her mom's in Green Bay and won't be back until Monday. So, in the meantime, we can do whatever you want. I'm totally open. What would you like to do?"

Trevor's hand was still on his knee. "I haven't eaten since I left LaGuardia. Maybe you could suggest a good restaurant? It would be my treat."

"You're my guest," Trevor insisted, "so it's *my* treat. Do you feel like burgers?"

"Sounds good. Do you have a suggestion of where to go?"

"Wiggly Field. Sam's friends took us there back in October, and the food was great." Trevor got up and grabbed the handle of Rupert's suitcase and took a step toward the door before realizing he'd forgotten something. He turned back and asked, "Are you ready to go?"

Rupert nodded and followed Trevor to a dark-blue SUV. It was like so many of the oversized cars that were starting to proliferate in New York City streets. Trevor put the suitcase in the cargo area in back and then opened the passenger-side door. Rupert studied Trevor's face for a moment while he knocked the slush off his shoes and slowly pulled his legs in. Trevor looked right back at him, his blue eyes and his smile reading no differently than a reunion with a long-time friend.

Rupert tried to stay quiet during the drive to the restaurant. There wasn't much car traffic on the freeway. It was mostly semi trucks, several without trailers attached. White smoke billowed out of the tall smokestacks of the nearby paper mill. High above the tree line on the other side of the road, Rupert saw the lighted downhill ski slopes of Rib Mountain. When Trevor periodically broke the silence, he seemed to be testing the waters, and he wondered if his old friend was slowly sliding into a more submissive role with him:

"I don't have to go to work on Monday, so we can stay up late tomorrow night, if you'd like."

"If there's anything you forgot to pack, we can stop on the way home and get it, . . . if I don't already have it."

"Samantha made up the guest room for you, Rupert, but I can switch with you and sleep there, if it's not comfortable for you."

The restaurant seemed like a sports bar. Their walls were covered with photos of various softball and volleyball teams the restaurant had sponsored. During dinner, Trevor seemed to divide his focus between the sportscast on the TV over the bar and Rupert. When Trevor looked his way, Trevor always broke into a brief smile before he spoke. Rupert was content to answer Trevor's questions about life in New York and listen to Trevor's stories about the move from Sheboygan halfway across the state. Rupert started to get the impression that Trevor too was feeling the pull of his dominance blessing, but as with his father and stepfather, it was always filtered through language that was ostensibly friendly or loving. He both wanted to test what he could get Trevor to do and was afraid that he would either immediately or eventually feel ashamed of what he'd agreed to do for Rupert. Would he be like Arthur, and it would register as a new, authentic emotion reserved for Rupert? Or would he register the difference with his past behavior and reject the new Trevor?

He decided to test the waters. Rupert knew that the wrong choice could ruin one of the last friendships from his childhood among a plethora of others he had let lapse since leaving Wisconsin. "So, I'd sort of like to sleep in the same room with you like we used to as kids. Does that sound crazy?"

"No, not at all . . . for the next two nights at least until Sam gets back. I'd really like that. I remember how much fun it used to be, talking to you until we both fell asleep. Sam and I took a weekend workshop in massage. Maybe I can work your muscles a bit before we go to bed tonight. Would you like that?"

Rupert just smiled and took another bite of his burger. Trevor smiled back, so it seemed it was decided. All through the rest of their time at the restaurant and during the entire car ride to Trevor's new home in the suburb of Schofield, Rupert's mind was like a mustang he was trying to break and domesticate. He kept alternating between being a good friend and being a selfish dom. Trevor rushed around the back of the SUV once it was parked in his driveway to open Rupert's door before he could do it himself. He circled back to unload Rupert's suitcase and then took the cement steps up to the front door of his tri-level home two at a time carrying it. He stood at the door waiting for Rupert to catch up.

"Your new place in Brooklyn is probably nicer than this," Trevor apologized as Rupert climbed the last two steps. He inserted a key into the lock and beckoned for him to enter first.

Rupert slipped out of his wet shoes from the melting snow in Trevor's driveway. The house was actually very spacious. A short staircase to the left seemed to lead up to a family room with several doors off of it. The space to the right over the garage was a dining room and an open doorway into a kitchen. The few furnishings there looked new. Rupert ran his hand along the leather-covered cushions of one of the dining room chairs.

"Sam insisted we get all new furniture when we moved," Trevor announced as he entered. He slammed the front door shut, slipped out of his own slush-covered boots, and set the suitcase down on the landing between the steps down to the garage and those up to the family room. "Can I get you anything to drink?"

Rupert turned and faced him. "Do you have any vodka or rum?"

Trevor looked sheepish. "Sam doesn't let me keep hard alcohol here at home. I can get you a beer or some wine. . ."

"A beer is fine," Rupert interrupted before Trevor could suggest a late-night liquor run.

Trevor indicated the steps up. "Just go up and make yourself comfortable. I'll bring a couple of beers up in a second."

Rupert settled into a tan suede recliner that faced the big flat-screen TV next to a smaller straight-back chair upholstered with a floral-print fabric. A small white end table was barely noticeable between the two chairs. Trevor eventually passed by, set two open bottles of beer (a Point and a Miller Light) on the end table, and carried Rupert's suitcase off somewhere behind. "Which one is for me?" Rupert called over the back of his chair.

Trevor returned and picked up both beers. "You can pick. I like them both."

Rupert chuckled. "I haven't seen a Point in over three years, but I should probably stick to the Light. I'm still single, so I can't afford too many calories."

Trevor smiled, perched on the edge of the other chair, and handed the bottle with the gold label to Rupert. "You're still in great shape, Rupert. Cheers!"

Rupert clinked bottles with Trevor. "Cheers. And thanks, buddy."

"I'm so glad you're here." Trevor took a first swig of beer.

Rupert took a sip from his bottle as well. "It's good to see you too, Trevor."

What Trevor was saying and doing was a bit confusing to Rupert. It seemed at times to be purely friendly, and at other times, it seemed Trevor was about to get on his knees and call him sir. He wondered if his dominance blessing was already wearing off three days early. Maybe Trevor's reaction was going to be a bit different, like Mike's and Fred's was. That seemed like the best assumption, and Rupert put aside the fantasy of renewing their sexual relationship. This was really what Rupert had been hoping for: a birthday with friends who would be easier to not dominate.

Trevor popped popcorn and turned on ESPN to fill the times when they weren't talking. As soon as Rupert started to yawn, Trevor showed him the guest bedroom where he had stowed the suitcase. "We don't have a bed yet for in here, so I inflated the air mattress and made it up." Trevor stared at the air mattress for a moment more. "I'll sleep here. You can take our bedroom until Sam gets back at least."

Rupert felt so much more relaxed because he assumed Trevor wasn't going to turn submissive on him after all. "Maybe we could move it into the other bedroom . . ."

"I forgot we decided that." Trevor started dragging the air mattress toward the doorway. "You wanted to talk until you fall asleep like we used to when we were kids."

Trevor stopped when he got to the doorway, because all the sheets would fall off when he tilted the mattress to get it through the doorway. "I'm not sure there would be much room to walk around in there if we brought this in."

"It's okay . . ." Rupert began.

Trevor looked like he was debating with himself for a moment as he waited for Rupert to continue. Finally, he said, "Would you like to at least come into the other room and get a massage before bed?"

Rupert was feeling a little buzzed from the wine at dinner and the beer afterward. "Sure. Sounds good."

He followed Rupert past the open bathroom door to the master bedroom. It was a bigger room, but it had two dressers, two nightstands, a king-size bed, and a vanity table and chair. Trevor immediately moved to the picture window and drew the curtains closed. "Just . . . get undressed and lie on your stomach," Trevor suggested.

Rupert had never been shy about his body. He was out of his sweater, shirt, T-shirt, pants, socks, and underwear in a half-minute. "Which way should I lay?"

Trevor seemed to be fighting with himself about whether to look at Rupert naked or look away. "Just lie across." Trevor gestured vaguely to indicate Rupert's feet could hang off the side of the bed.

Once he was lying down, Rupert turned his head to see what Trevor would do next. Trevor took off only his sweater, shirt, and pants, leaving his T-shirt, socks, and boxers on. He pulled a tube of something out of one of the nightstand drawers. "We got this at the workshop," Trevor explained. "It's supposed to stay slick for a bit and then it evaporates."

"Very fancy," Rupert commented.

Trevor sat down next to Rupert and started smearing the gel on Rupert's back. He performed some light strokes at first, and then he moved to straddle Rupert and started digging in deeper. Rupert couldn't help but moan after spending most of the day traveling and fighting crowds. He noticed he was getting hard, and he wondered what he would have to say about that if Trevor asked him to turn over.

"Am I doing okay?" Trevor moved down to massage Rupert's glutes.

"Uh-huh. Feels good."

Trevor slid down to work on Rupert's hamstrings. "You know . . . I would do anything you wanted."

Rupert propped himself up on his elbows. "Really? Like what?"

"Anything."

Rupert had assumed he didn't have to worry about Trevor wanting to submit, but here was the familiar entry point again. He decided to test his theory. "Stand up over there," Rupert gestured toward the vanity, "and take off your T-shirt."

Trevor moved off the bed, stood where Rupert had indicated, and took off his T-shirt.

"Take off your socks," Rupert added.

Trevor pulled off one sock, and then the other. Rupert could tell that Trevor was aroused too.

"Would 'anything' include having sex with me?"

"Whatever you want, Rupert." Trevor was smiling, but his eyes had a faraway stare, as if he were sleepwalking.

Suddenly a vision of Trevor having to explain this to his wife flashed into Rupert's head. He realized he was one step away from ruining his longest friendship—two decades. "No, Trevor. I'm a little tired." Rupert got up from the bed and gathered up his clothes. "I'm just going to go right to sleep in the guest room on that air mattress. You just get a good night's sleep here, and I'll see you in the morning."

"Are you sure?" Trevor took a couple of steps toward Rupert.

"I'll see you in the morning, buddy." Rupert dashed into the guest bedroom, centered the air mattress in the middle of the empty carpet, and closed the door.

In the middle of the night, Rupert got up to use the bathroom. As he opened the bathroom door to go back to bed, he found Trevor standing naked just outside it. Rupert was also naked but too sleepy to figure out why Trevor was standing naked in front of him. "Did I wake you?" Rupert tried.

"I woke up and needed to use the bathroom too," Trevor whispered.

Rupert tried to sidle past Trevor without touching him. "It's all yours."

Once back in the guest bedroom, Rupert realized he was breathing heavily, as if he had narrowly escaped some danger. He wondered how he was going to get through these last two days.

The following day and a half, Trevor continued to offer Rupert whatever he wanted, and he arranged other opportunities when both of them were naked. Rupert had to bite his lip to remind himself not to take advantage of what Trevor seemed to so desperately want to offer him.

As soon as Samantha arrived back on the afternoon of Christmas Eve, she also wanted to make sure Rupert got whatever he wanted. Rupert fell back into the habit of denying that he needed anything and pretending he was mute.

On Christmas morning, Rupert stayed in the guest bedroom until he was pretty sure his blessing had shifted from dominance to that odd one about growing things. When he emerged finally, around eleven in the morning, Samantha and Trevor wished him a happy birthday, gave him gifts, and made him breakfast like good hosts, not the urgency of submissive slaves.

"Do you have any indoor plants here?" Rupert asked.

"Sam has a little cactus on the kitchen window ledge," Trevor replied.

"Does it need water?"

"I usually only water it on Wednesdays," Samantha replied.

"Could I water it today?"

"I suppose a day early wouldn't hurt it." Samantha led Rupert into her kitchen where a tiny button cactus was indeed perched on the window ledge next to the stove. She poured a small amount of water into a mug. "It only needs a few drops—enough just to wet the top of the sand."

Rupert took extreme care not to overwater the cactus. He set the mug back down on the counter and looked at the cactus again.

"You look like you're expecting something to happen."

"Just hoping, I guess." Rupert was looking for some sort of proof that the dominance blessing was gone.

When Boxing Day came on the twenty-sixth of December, Rupert packed his suitcase, and Trevor carried it out to the SUV. He waited in the foyer for Samantha to come say goodbye, and she rushed into the hallway. "Come into the kitchen," she urged.

When he entered, Samantha pointed him toward the cactus on the window ledge. It had almost doubled in size and sprouted bright red fruit. Rupert sighed. The year of people serving him was finally over.

"Isn't that amazing?" Samantha asked.

"It's a beautiful sight," Rupert agreed.

CHAPTER 12: RUPERT IN 1999

The following year was 1999. Millennial fever was everywhere. Rupert was glad that he had a nice low-key blessing while everyone around him was freaking out. It had been the twentieth century for so long, most data systems were not very forward thinking and only included two of the four digits in the year, so programmers were scrambling to keep systems from thinking it was 1900 when it became 2000.

The IT department at the ballet company where Rupert and Arthur worked had already changed over all their databases and templates by March and sent reminders to all their vendors and donors by April.

Rupert's stepfather Mike visited from Wisconsin about the same time, and Rupert showed him around. Among the sites Mike wanted to see was the Brooklyn Botanic Garden. The snow had all melted weeks before, and the daytime temperatures had only started to break sixty degrees for a couple of days, so Rupert knew there would be very little in bloom. The Botanic Garden was hyping its cherry blossom festival, but no exact starting date had been announced yet.

When they made the rounds, a few flower beds had blooms, but many plants still had closed buds, including the cherry trees. "It looks like they'll be in bloom in one more week," Mike observed as they passed by the trees. "I can see little bits of pink in some of the buds. I should have come a week later."

Rupert backtracked slightly, blowing on and touching leaves and branches of the cherry trees they had passed. He continued to stroke and blow on them as he and Mike proceeded along the pathway. When they circled around to the entrance again, there was a lot of commotion. People were rushing in carrying cameras. Mike convinced Rupert to head back in where they had begun to see what the excitement was about.

In the hour since Rupert had passed by the cherry trees, they were now all bearing large pink blossoms. "Did you do that?" Mike asked with a knowing grin.

Rupert just nodded at first, also smiling.

"That's a great blessing."

"I've sort of perfected it since I last got it at twenty," Rupert said as he stepped back to let other visitors appreciate the newly and suddenly opened cherry blossoms. "Back then I wasn't sure how to work it."

Mike stepped back a bit as well. "We should get you to Wisconsin this summer to help the farms that sell to our restaurants."

"My job keeps me pretty busy now," Rupert said as he clasped Mike on the shoulder and urged him back toward the entrance.

"You don't think you're going to get back into dancing?"

"I don't know." Rupert had thought about it at every dance performance he had been to over the past two years. "I'm a little out of shape, and I'm getting a bit too old."

Mike almost choked on the bottle of water he was drinking. "What? You're twenty-nine and in great shape. What do you mean?"

"Most dancers retire at thirty-five . . . or earlier."

"You've got six more years then. Is there some other reason you don't want to perform any more. You've got such fantastic talent."

Every time Rupert thought about auditioning again, two thoughts came up immediately. First, he liked the steady hours during the day, the steady paycheck, and the relatively easy tasks that his job required. Second, he remembered how his last job had ended, with a physical injury. "I worry that that sort of work is so physically demanding, it's easy for me to get injured."

As they continued to walk down the boulevard toward the public library, Mike still looked puzzled. "Maybe I don't understand performance work then. I thought that you practiced and rehearsed so that you don't get injured, and if you do accidentally get injured, they still pay you until you're ready to return, right?"

"When I twisted my ankle at a performance for *The Titanic,* I only got disability checks for a month, and then they cut me off and fired me."

"That can't be legal," Mike said. He patted Rupert on the back as if to comfort him.

"It's not, but I'm still waiting for the union to fight the producers, and I had very little to gain."

"That was really bad luck."

"Exactly," Rupert agreed. They stopped at the curb waiting for the light to change to cross the boulevard.

Mike seemed to be silently processing the news until they were almost across. "You're worried that your family curse is more likely to hurt you when you're performing?"

Rupert sighed. He had to admit that his potential for bad luck was a deterrent. "I haven't had any real sickness or injury since I left that life behind. I don't want to push my luck."

Rupert had finally finished a list of all the blessings he was likely to get again for the next twenty years. "I could always consider becoming a stand-up comedian when I get the laughter blessing," he mused.

"You're getting them in reverse order?" Mike asked.

"So far, yeah."

"Your grandma said you were a rapid healer as a toddler."

Rupert tried to recall the list he had posted above his computer at home. "I think that was when I was two, so I'll get that again when I'm forty-seven."

"Maybe you could try dancing then? When you don't have to worry about injuries?"

Rupert wasn't sure if he was serious. "Restart my dancing career at forty-seven? I don't think so."

They walked back mostly in silence. Rupert appreciated the greater number of trees in Brooklyn compared to his old life in Manhattan. He had started touching a small tree on his block every morning on his way to work, and he decided to stop, because others were frequently gathering around it and pointing at its phenomenal growth, and he didn't want news crews clogging his quiet street.

At one point, Mike noticed Rupert exchanging smiles with another young man passing by. "Are you seeing anyone now, Rupert?" he asked.

"You mean romantically?"

Mike chuckled. "I forgot you young guys considered that only one of several options."

"There is a guy named Charlie I've seen. We used to work together. He has a girlfriend now."

"That doesn't sound like it's going anywhere," Mike observed.

"And there is a guy who is crazy about me at work . . ."

"That doesn't sound like a good possibility either," Mike interrupted. "Are you really not meeting any available guys?"

"I don't know." Rupert remembered Trevor and Danny and Luke and Jorge and Arthur—all caught up oddly in his blessings. "I think I'm not really a good candidate right now. My life keeps taking such bizarre turns, I don't think anyone could deal with it all."

Mike stopped walking and caught Rupert's arm to stop him as well. "You can't let the Pooka's curse ruin your life, Rupert. Maybe you have to work a little harder to gather up a little happiness and security, but you can't just give up. You're a smart, talented, attractive young man, and . . . there are thousands of men out there who would want that . . . and hundreds of them who wouldn't mind the odd little things your blessings and curse dish up."

"Well, oddly enough, I haven't met any of them yet."

"That guy you smiled at back there—Would you have stopped him to talk if I weren't here?"

"Some random guy on the street?"

"I don't think you're even allowing for the possibility of a boyfriend, Rupert." Mike put his hand on Rupert's shoulder. "You keep focusing on guys who are unavailable, like the guy with a girlfriend, or the guy at work. I hear Match dot com is allowing same-sex matches now. You could try there."

Rupert chuckled and took a step away. "Computer dating? Come on, Mike.

No one takes that seriously."

"I do. I've met some great women there." He started walking past Rupert.

Rupert fell in next to Mike as they walked again. "That's not where gay men my age go. They hang out at bars and volunteer at Housing Works . . ."

"What's that?"

"It's a charity for homeless homosexuals," Rupert clarified. "I have my job. It's challenging, and I'm becoming friends with some of the dancers there. I get invited to benefits several times a month, and I go out with my friends every weekend. I'm going to rent a bungalow in Fire Island with them this summer, and I'm sure to meet guys there."

"You're the last person I'd expect to become a monk, so I'm glad you're putting yourself out there a little bit."

"I am. Don't worry about me, Mike."

"I had one other thing I wanted to discuss with you."

Rupert waited a moment. "So, what is it?"

"Maybe we should wait and discuss it during dinner tonight."

"Is it bad news?" Rupert walked a bit ahead so he could see Mike's expression better. He looked serious. "You have to tell me now. It it's bad news it's going to ruin my appetite, so I'd rather hear it now."

"It's not horrible, especially now that you've got a steady paycheck coming in."

"Is something wrong with the restaurants? Is that what this is about?"

Mike sighed. "Roger and I have been meeting once a month to go over the books for the restaurant. He's been keeping track of my hours and my ownership percentage over the past four years, and according to the terms of our partnership agreement, I've bought out your stake in the restaurants."

"Oh."

"I plan on keeping them both operating, and Roger is going to stay on as general manager . . ."

"So, you wanted to let me know I wouldn't be getting any more checks?"

"If you are in trouble, you can always ask me for a loan," Mike said, "but yeah, I worked off my last purchase of your interest last month. You're no longer an owner. I thought that was what you wanted."

"That was our agreement," Rupert confirmed. "I'm just surprised the transition is already over."

"Hey, if you want to reinvest, I can make you a decent offer for up to ten percent."

"I'll think about it, Mike. Thanks."

Rupert's mind ranged through all they had talked about, and he found himself coming back to the blinders he'd donned when it came to dating prospects. He regularly turned down nice guys who talked to him. And now it was clearer that he was already picturing the breakup when one or more of his blessings or his curse would rear their heads.

And he had forgotten that Mike had been donating his time for years in exchange for Rupert's shares in the restaurant, and the familiar monthly checks were going to stop. He didn't need the money that much anymore, but it was a regular reminder of the family restaurant and life back in Sheboygan that he would miss. The connection to Wisconsin would wither to occasional Christmas cards from Trevor, Mike, and his cousins. The memory of his mother and grandmother in their final minutes—a scene that replayed regularly in his nightmares—would become his stronger connection to them than walks along the river, family dinners, and performing at his family's restaurant . . . which no longer belonged to his family now.

Even though he and Mike usually got along very well, and he valued the one person in the world that knew about his simultaneous curse and blessing, Rupert sighed in relief as he waved goodbye to his unofficial stepfather at his departure gate at JFK. Mike had become a symbol of everything Rupert had lost: his family, his family's business, his hometown, and the optimism and excitement about life that the older man had in abundance, and which Rupert had already forsaken at twenty-nine.

Rupert's happiness came in very small injections. Seeing Arthur's smiling, handsome face every morning when he arrived at the office was one. Lurking outside the studio door, watching the dancers rehearse through the narrow glass pane was another. And lately, provoking trees to bud and flowers to bloom was a simple joy as well, but none of these endured more than a few seconds. And then he felt depressed, like he was just enduring his life.

By June, Rupert had stayed at a rental cottage on Fire Island with Danny and Max and Dorian two weekends in a row, met handsome, sexy, friendly guys at the beach during the day and at the clubs at night, but he still couldn't follow through in meeting any of them again. He researched and found a gay therapist in Manhattan near where he used to live. His name was Dr. Lawrence Weston, and he agreed to help Rupert with his depression without resorting to any medications. They just talked. Every Tuesday, Rupert would leave work a few minutes early to get to Dr. Weston's office for his five-thirty appointment.

Dr. Weston suggested several exercises or new behaviors for Rupert to try. Rupert wrote a letter to his mother apologizing for leaving her at sixteen and demanding that she release custody of him to Fred. He drafted an email to Mike apologizing for embarrassing him enough to abandon his mother. He made plans to check in on Jorge. And through it all, as much as Rupert unburdened himself of guilt, he still felt an anger and resentment he couldn't mention, and Dr. Weston noticed.

"I still hear a significant amount of agitation and stress when you describe your life, Rupert. Are you certain there is no one else with whom you have unfinished business?" Dr. Weston removed his glasses and uncrossed his legs, which Rupert had come to know as a signal that his therapist really wanted his attention.

"I've told you about Danny and Theo?"

Dr. Weston flipped back through his notes. "Yes."

"And Charlie, the guy I used to have sex with when I lived near here."

"Yes. Him too."

"And Luke? The guy who dumped me and walked out on me at brunch?"

"I believe so." Dr. Weston set his pad aside on the green leather couch where he sat across from Rupert in an easy chair. "I suspect there is someone you have deliberately decided not to share with me. It's most likely someone who's been in your life for a long time."

"I told you about Trevor, I know."

"Perhaps someone like that, yes," Dr. Weston continued. "Maybe it's another relative, someone outside your immediate family?"

"I was close to my Uncle Horst and Aunt Ingrid, but they were always good to me. I don't resent them at all." Even as he said it, Rupert realized his anger about his curse and blessing were often personified in the two Irish fairies who had cast them—the Pooka and the Grogoch. Those were probably the two his therapist was fishing for.

"I sense an epiphany." This was one of Dr. Weston's favorite phrases.

"Well, . . ." Rupert began, "there are two individuals who really, really messed up my life, but I don't think you would believe they have the influence I attribute to them."

Dr. Weston leaned back, crossed his legs, and combed his short, graying hair with his hand. "Whether someone's influence on you is physical or just symbolic, I take both of them seriously."

Rupert glanced over at the clock on the shelf hopefully. Dr. Weston noticed. "We still have ten minutes, and I can give you an extra five minutes today and more time tomorrow, if you want."

"If I told you what they did to me and my family," Rupert carefully explained, "you would think I was crazy, and that's not a revelation I want my therapist to have."

"I'm afraid you may have already crossed that bridge by telling me your accusation will make you sound crazy." Dr. Weston uncrossed his legs again. "The important thing to keep in mind, Rupert, is that when you describe your relationship with these two people, I may not come to the same conclusions as you, but your conclusions are important for me to know, if I'm going to continue to help you."

Rupert sighed. He needed to test his trust with the therapist he had seen only nine times before. "If I told you Santa Claus was real and I thought he dropped

127

in on me from time to time to terrorize me, you wouldn't be required to commit me?"

Dr. Weston leaned forward and spoke a bit more softly. "I assume this is hypothetical, correct?"

"Correct," Rupert replied. "I don't believe in Santa Claus."

"So, are we talking about a mythological figure then?"

Rupert decided he could stop answering the questions at any point, but this still felt relatively safe. "You could say that," he confirmed.

"I should also remind you that what you say here is completely confidential. I have no reason or obligation to report what you tell me unless I determine you may be a danger to yourself or others. If you are suffering from a delusion, but it isn't driving you to harm anyone, it stays between us . . . and we work on unmasking it."

Rupert realized he had already shared every painful encounter and relationship in his life over the previous sessions. The revelation of his curse and the blessing, even if his therapist didn't believe it was real, could be helpful. If the otherwise unflappable Dr. Weston freaked out, he could always discontinue the therapy with him. "When my grandmother met my grandfather, he was also dating another woman named Patricia Connor. When my grandfather dumped Patricia, she got back at our whole family by making a pact with a supernatural creature to curse us. Not long after that, my grandmother met another supernatural creature and convinced her to bless her for twenty-five years. When that first blessing was over, my grandfather died suddenly and unexplainably. When I was born, I also got blessed for twenty-five years. Every year on my birthday, the blessing affects me differently. And because the blessing and the curse are fighting in my life and making me miserable a lot of the time, I get really angry at those two individuals responsible."

Dr. Weston looked nervously at his clock. "We can continue . . . a . . . another five minutes yet, and before you leave, we should make another appointment in the next three days, okay?"

"Okay," Rupert said tentatively. "What do you think?"

"I'll . . . I'll have to think about it a bit. It's surprisingly detailed for a delusion."

"I'm not going to hurt anyone, Dr. Weston . . . honestly. I have gotten really angry at them, but I've never hurt them, even when I was in their presence and could have."

"You've actually seen these 'supernatural creatures?'"

"Only once or twice that I remember. They are a pair of very odd-looking old sisters who seem to pop into my life every few years."

"They're human?"

"They look human," Rupert clarified. "But they're both a little deformed. One just in the ears, and the other in the eyes and nose. They both have similar Irish accents."

"And they have cursed and blessed your whole family, and you blame them for your grandfather's death?"

Rupert looked at the clock again hopefully. He needed to think more about how to phrase and explain the Pooka and the Grogoch to his therapist so they wouldn't sound quite so impossible. "One cursed us, and the other one blessed us," Rupert clarified. "The curse also killed my mother and grandmother on the morning I turned twenty-five."

Dr. Weston seemed anxious for the session to end as well and stole a glance at the clock again. "We really need to end here today, Rupert. I have another client due in ten minutes, and I have to prepare." He pulled a pocket calendar out of his shirt's breast pocket and opened it to a ribbon bookmark. "I can see you tomorrow at 2:00 or 8:00 p.m. or Thursday at 3:15 p.m. Could you come back at any of those times?"

Rupert had an appointment with a donor in Connecticut Thursday afternoon. "Of those times, it would have to be tomorrow. Eight o'clock is a bit easier for me. Are you sure that's not too late for you?"

"When I encounter a breakthrough like this, I like to take advantage of it, even if it keeps me a bit later than usual." Dr. Weston stood, repocketed his calendar book, and ushered Rupert to the door. "I'll see you at eight tomorrow night."

Before getting on the train back to Williamsburg, Rupert took a slight detour to the flower district on 28th Street and convinced a vendor in the process of closing up his storefront for the night to sell him a crocus bulb. He stole some soil from a neighbor's garden and dumped it in the plastic bag. When he got home, he poked drainage holes in the bottom of a Styrofoam cup and then filled it with bulb and dirt. The bulb had already sprouted a green chute after handling it slightly and since bringing it home on the train, so it was easy for Rupert to know which end of the bulb to point upward. He decided to bring it to his evening appointment the following night in case he needed to demonstrate the reality of his blessing.

CHAPTER 13: RUPERT TURNS THIRTY

Rupert left the Styrofoam cup on the window ledge in his office the next day. Just being in his proximity, the first chute broke the surface of the soil by the end of the day. Arthur pointed at it as he was getting ready to leave and Rupert was studying some spreadsheets. "What have you got there, Rupert?" he asked.

Rupert looked up. He had developed a habit of teasing Arthur with talks of fictional guys he was dating. He continued: "It's a gift for someone I'm seeing tonight." He closed his laptop and grinned tendentiously.

"I keep your calendar, remember?" Arthur chuckled. "You already told me you had another therapy appointment tonight. If you want to get dinner beforehand, you should plan to leave soon too."

"Are you angling for a dinner date with me?" Rupert looked at his assistant. He had started working out during his lunch hours over the previous year, and he was filling out his shirt more, wearing nicer clothes, and trimming his hair a bit shorter. Rupert had seen some of the dancers coming by Arthur's desk to talk to him, and he had to admit it made him a little jealous, despite having turned down Arthur's advances.

"If you'd be eating alone, I'm happy to wait until you're ready to go," Arthur confirmed.

Rupert closed his laptop and stood. "I can finish my reports tomorrow," Rupert announced. "Let's go somewhere in Midtown, okay?"

They rode together on the subway to Grand Central, and Rupert led the way to a Greek restaurant on Lexington. As they were waiting for their food, Rupert finally felt the courage and necessity of asking Arthur the question he'd been holding back for weeks. "So, are you dating anyone?"

Arthur was distracted, looking at the Styrofoam cup on the corner of the table. "It already looks taller and thicker than it was an hour ago when we were in your office." He paused and then looked at Rupert again. "I'm sorry. What did you ask me?"

"It's not important," Rupert said softly. "I've developed a bit of a green thumb this year. I thought I would give it to my therapist as an additional thank-you for helping me the past couple of months."

"Your life seems to be perfect," Arthur argued. "You have a great apartment in Williamsburg, you have a great job, you're in great health . . ."

"I have a lot of anger issues, Arthur."

Arthur's smile faded. "Is this about me?"

"No. You've been a great assistant."

"Are you still angry about leaving your performing career?" Arthur looked sincerely concerned.

"No. Well, a little."

"Should I keep guessing?"

Just then, their waiter brought their food, and both men looked at each other unsure if they should drop the conversation and just eat. Rupert picked up his fork, but he just held it for a moment. "Four-and-a-half years ago, on Christmas morning, both my mother and my grandmother died. My mom was only forty-nine. I blame a person whom I feel is responsible, but who will never come to justice for it. Let's just leave it at that."

"Whoa!" Arthur said softly as he lifted his own fork and started poking at his souvlaki. "Your mom and grandmother were murdered, and the killer is still free? I would still be outraged. I would be . . . crazy if it happened to my family."

Rupert started to tear up remembering the afterimages of their deaths. "There is no proof that she was responsible," he whispered.

"It was a woman? How did they die?"

Rupert put down his fork and dabbed his eyes with his napkin. "I really don't want to go there, Arthur. I hope you understand. I'm sorry I brought it up."

The two of them sighed and silently ate their food. When they were almost done, Arthur was the first to speak. "What kind of plant is it?" He gestured at the cup.

Rupert swallowed a bite of pita. "Crocus."

"You must really like your therapist," Arthur said with a hint of accusation.

Rupert smiled. "If I liked him like that, I'd bring him roses. Crocuses are neutral, aren't they?"

Arthur laughed. "Sure."

At the late-evening session, Dr. Weston accepted the crocus and put it on his desk before taking his usual place on the green leather couch. He wanted more details from Rupert about the two fairies and his encounters with them. He asked how the "blessings" had manifested over the years. After Rupert listed a few of the effects, Dr. Weston stopped him. "Do you have a blessing affecting you now?"

More than things he imagined or how people treated him, the cornucopia blessing he was currently experiencing seemed the most like magic. He knew grasses like bamboo often grew by an inch or two a day, but the trees and flowers he had been affecting for the previous few months were rivaling and perhaps surpassing that rate. "I bought a crocus bulb last night right after our session. I looked it up online this afternoon. Crocuses usually take at least six weeks to grow and bloom from bulbs. . . It got that big in just a day."

"Are you saying that you made it grow faster?" Dr. Weston said as he finished making notes, set his pad aside, and leaned forward.

"I'm saying just watch it over the next few days." Rupert smiled and leaned back in his armchair. "There are no leaves and no bud yet, but I suspect it may bloom before the week is over."

The session continued for a few more minutes while Dr. Weston diverted their conversation to a dance student who had accused Rupert of sexual misconduct years before. Rupert forgot he had mentioned it, and he clarified that the girl had recanted, and he was not formally charged.

Rupert felt oddly guilty as he left the office and walked down Broadway to catch a train back to Brooklyn. He realized that his transient abilities had occasionally allowed him to drag secrets and desires out of people in his life. In reexperiencing some of the blessings over the past five years, he had realized he was not helpless in avoiding a blessing's effects. He had learned to say no or run away during his wealth blessing. He had learned to be careful with his speech during his dominance blessing. He had even learned to avoid plants that didn't need his cornucopia blessing. Rupert was starting to realize that having power and exercising power were not the same thing.

Arthur was already at his desk when Rupert arrived at the ballet company offices the next morning. He wound his way around the various desks slowly and stopped in front of Arthur's. "Could you come into my office for a minute?"

Arthur's smile changed into worried curiosity. "Sure. . . Do I need to bring anything?"

"No." Rupert continued into his office, sat down behind his desk, and opened his laptop.

Arthur was about to sit in one of the two canvas chairs on the other side of the desk, but Rupert stopped him. "Let's close the door this time."

Arthur straightened up and padded over to the door and pushed it closed. He was looking down and moving slowly when he returned to sit in the chair. Rupert waited for him to look up. When he finally did, he seemed frightened. "I'm not going to fire you, Arthur. I really just wanted to talk about some stuff that has been on my mind."

His assistant let out a sigh, and his shoulders collapsed a bit. "You usually insist that I keep the door open."

"I know. That was for a different reason. Some of what I'm about to tell you is personal, and I'd prefer that it stay between us."

"Of course." Arthur seemed more curious than afraid.

"I really respect you, Arthur," Rupert began. "I have been impressed with your ideas and the high quality of your work. You always show up on time, you treat me and everyone else here really well, and most wonderfully, you are a self-starter. I don't feel like I have to supervise you constantly."

Arthur waited a moment and then said, "Thank you. So, is there a *but* coming?"

"Not really." Rupert chuckled. "I mean, it doesn't have to do with you. I realize that by being your boss, there is a certain power dynamic that is implied."

Arthur just nodded his head slowly.

"But really, we just have different tasks to do. I just have to make sure what you're doing helps support what I'm trying to do to reach the goals Hakim and the rest of the board of directors set for me. But other than that, we are more like a team."

"We *are* the development department," Arthur conceded.

"Yes, and I really like you as a person, Arthur. You make me laugh, you are supportive, and you are more generous with your time than anyone expects you to be."

"Thank you . . . Rupert." Arthur crossed his arms and redistributed his weight in his chair. "I like . . . working with you, too. I'm learning a lot."

"That's great." Rupert closed his laptop and leaned on his forearms. "And there is this thing where I stole you from Alvin Ailey and had sex with you several times. The first time was after you told me you were dating someone, and the last two times after I gave you mixed signals and said it was okay again."

Arthur reached across the desk and clasped Rupert's hands. "I was okay with all of that," he whispered.

He withdrew his hands but Rupert grabbed them back. "You are so damn sexy. I've considered firing you just so I wouldn't have to worry about sexual harassment when we got together."

Arthur didn't break out of the embrace. "Seriously?"

Rupert smiled. "Not really. I could never do that to you. You're too good at your job. Thus, my dilemma."

"Well . . . I had sort of been thinking along the same lines." Arthur looked impishly coy.

Rupert squeezed Arthur's hands tighter. "What do you mean?"

Arthur pulled his hands out of Rupert's grasp. "The executive director of another ballet company in New York wants to hire me as an assistant."

Rupert swallowed hard. "That would be a bit of a promotion for you."

"And better pay," he added. "But I haven't given them my answer yet. I had been wanting to get your opinion on it."

Rupert sighed. "I hate the idea that I won't see you every day. I love the prospect that I might be able to see you at night. I am a bit conflicted."

"We would also be in more direct competition," Arthur said. "That is also a concern for me."

"You shouldn't worry about that . . . unless you were going to work for ABT."

Rupert started to chuckle, but when he saw Arthur wasn't joining him in laughter, he stopped. "You're going to work at ABT??"

Arthur disengaged his hands and leaned back in his chair. "I haven't said yes yet. I'm just thinking about it."

Rupert knew that this was a major career move for Arthur, and now was not the time to be selfish. "I think you should take it. It's a great opportunity for you. And I'll manage to find a new assistant, and we won't discuss work when we get together."

"We could still get together?" Arthur's eyebrows were raised, as if he could conceive either answer.

"As often as possible," Rupert said with a grin.

The following Tuesday, Arthur gave Rupert his two-week notice, and Rupert met with the human resources director to process the release and start searching for a replacement. At the end of the day, he gave Arthur a big hug just before leaving for his therapy appointment. When he got to Dr. Weston's office, his eyes were immediately drawn to the Styrofoam cup on his desk. The first stalk was taller and had leaves, and two other shoots were poking out of the soil.

The therapist followed his eyes. "Yes, your flower has grown remarkably fast. I looked up its care, and I just watered it twice. They don't usually bloom in September."

"I expect it will bloom by my next appointment," Rupert said as he moved to sit down in his usual armchair.

Dr. Weston stood in front of the green couch where his notepad was lying. "I . . . I . . . I am not certain what to make of it. My mind went to growth stimulants or faster-growing varieties of crocus, but I realize that it's not important really." He sat down on the couch and continued. "You were trying to prove to me that two older Irish women you met back in Wisconsin were responsible for strange things happening to you, because you thought I wouldn't believe you."

He picked up his notepad, glanced at it, and then put it down again. "I had a female client, older than you, who was from Turkey. She was convinced that a gypsy had put a curse on her. Whether or not the gypsy had any real power, she had symbolic power over my client. It made her physically and emotionally sick. She had to be checked into an emergency room with new-onset ulcerative colitis and an inner-ear infection that caused her vertigo. She stopped therapy with me before I could help her deal with the stress and fear that was affecting her health.

"You seem like you're in good physical health, Rupert, but I know you're dealing with a lot of stress right now. You have managed some significant epiphanies during therapy, but I want to make sure you don't start to get physical symptoms."

"I appreciate that," Rupert said while Dr. Weston took a breath.

"I was wondering if it might be helpful, either with my supervision or on your own, to confront these two women and tell them how their actions have affected your life. I am concerned that such a confrontation may need to be face to face."

"I'm not sure that would do much good," Rupert said. He remembered his one adult contact with the Grogoch at the church and his two contacts with the Pooka back in Wisconsin. "One is kind of aloof, and though she is compassionate, she doesn't believe she can change what is happening to me. The other is just mean and unforgiving and sadistic. She would just laugh at me and belittle me if I faced her again."

"They both sound a bit abusive to me," Dr. Weston volunteered. "I wonder if there isn't some way then to just box them off, partition them in your life, so that they become a separate part of your past. I could suggest visualizations to cut off their influence in your future, so that you could live free of it from now on."

"That would be nice," Rupert admitted. "Some of the things that happen to me, though, are decidedly difficult to see as random. They follow a pattern, a rhythm."

"Try to let go of your expectation of pattern. We've talked about self-fulfilling prophecies . . ."

"I'll get back to you at the end of the year," Rupert joked.

"What do you mean?"

Rupert had gotten into the habit of reviewing his upcoming list of blessings and making plans and strategies for dealing with them every Saturday morning. "The cornucopia blessing will end December 24th. It will be kind of hard to ignore the coincidences for the next one."

"What is the . . . next one?" Dr. Weston leaned forward.

"I'm due to repeat what I call the vanity blessing," Rupert explained. "For an entire year, every person I meet will compliment me on something."

Dr. Weston smiled. "If you are still coming to me then, I will do my best to *not* compliment you then."

"Oooookay," Rupert replied warily. "Make sure you take note. Anytime from Christmas 1999 to Christmas 2000."

Dr. Weston made a note on his pad. "Done. And I see we are done for today. I will be on vacation next week, so I will see you again in two weeks."

Rupert whispered conspiratorially. "Make sure someone waters your crocus!"

Dr. Weston made another note. "I will take care of that, thank you."

In October, the New York Yankees won their twenty-fifth world series, and everyone celebrated, even if they were Mets fans. Rupert finally found a replacement for Arthur to assist him. Arthur was too busy to meet him until the Sunday before Halloween. They met for brunch in Chelsea and Rupert introduced Arthur to Dorian, Chantal, and Danny. After brunch, Arthur followed him back to Williamsburg, and they had sex for several hours, and then Arthur left to get some sleep at his apartment in Harlem.

In November, Arthur and Rupert spent one day or the other every weekend together. Rupert discontinued therapy with Dr. Weston, who told him he had to replant the crocuses, which were still blooming. Five-year-old Cuban refugee Elián Gonzales was rescued in the straits of Florida clinging to an inner tube. Arthur and Rupert attended a drag Thanksgiving celebration at Chantal's, and both of them wore blond wigs and matching white ball gowns.

On Christmas Eve, Arthur stayed overnight and gave Rupert his Christmas gift–a DVD of *The Matrix*.

When Rupert awoke on Christmas morning, Arthur had at some point placed a large, ornately wrapped gift between them on the bed. Arthur kissed him on the cheek and said, "Happy thirtieth birthday, Rupert!"

Rupert sat up in bed and his jaw dropped. "I never told you it was my birthday. How did you find out?"

"You are so adorable!" He kissed Rupert on the lips. "When I had my exit interview with HR back in September, she let it slip that your birthday was December 25th."

"You already got me *The Matrix*."

"I always get separate birthday and Christmas gifts, so you should too," he declared. "Open it!"

Rupert immediately ripped and tore at the wrapping paper and bow. He could smell it even before he opened the box. "This is too much!" he gently scolded as he lifted the black suede jacket out of the box.

"I saw it, and I thought you would look really sexy in it." Arthur kissed him on the lips again.

Arthur left again on Sunday night after more sex and going out dancing. Rupert found a stronger hanger for his new jacket and shoved it into his hall closet. Even though it was lined, it was still a bit too cold to wear it outside. As he was at his home computer, waiting for his email to load, he looked up at the list of blessings and hadn't noticed anyone going out of their way to compliment him all weekend, so he resolved to call Dr. Weston to tell him he thought he might indeed be able to let go of the idea of being cursed and blessed.

Rupert left a message on his old therapist's voice mail with his office number on Monday morning. Around 2:45 that afternoon, his new assistant, Sherry, transferred a call to his desk. "This is Rupert Rocket," he announced as the call connected.

The familiar voice of his therapist said, "It was so good to hear from my most interesting client this year."

Rupert just laughed.

CHAPTER 14: RUPERT TURNS THIRTY-ONE

The Y2K bug everyone had feared never materialized in January 2000. The stock market was still booming from all the business activity in preparing for it, so people had a bit too much nostalgia for a second Bush in the White House, and the election in November was a virtual tie. The electoral votes that would decide the new president were in Florida, where just over five hundred votes separated the two candidates. And according to Florida law, that required a recount.

Much to Rupert and Arthur's dismay, the U.S. Supreme Court ruled that the recount of Florida's votes in the presidential election needed to stop. It was taking too long, they felt, and left the country without a clear successor to President Clinton. That essentially declared George W. Bush the winner over the Democratic candidate who won the popular vote, Al Gore. For a time, though, everyone was fascinated by the term "hanging chads" and the suspicious coincidence that the Governor of Florida at the time, the one overseeing the ballot recount, was the new president's brother.

Rupert cordially accepted all the compliments his vanity blessing brought him. It didn't disrupt his life much. That got him looking forward to the next one coming down the pike. An equally mild blessing would take the stage when Rupert turned thirty-one: the prophecy blessing. He remembered how after his eighteenth birthday he had wondered if he had become normal again, because nothing out of the ordinary seemed to be happening. It wasn't until fairly late that year that he realized in retrospect that he had dreamed of the election win of the first George Bush and an end to the Iran-Iraq war. Persistent dreams of a wall being dismantled and people flooding through it wasn't fully clear until two years later when the Soviets withdrew from the Warsaw Pact countries, the USSR disbanded, and the Berlin wall fell.

In the list of blessings above his computer at home, he had written "big world-shaping events" in a note next to the prophecy blessing entry.

One Friday night in October, Rupert had just finished his shower before going out to dinner with Arthur, and he noticed Arthur was no longer in his bedroom. He wrapped his towel around his waist more tightly and stepped out into his living room, and he saw Arthur sitting at the small computer desk in the corner with the monitor off. He had his glasses and pants on, but no shirt or shoes. "What are you looking at?" Rupert called from a few feet away. He only had two things posted above his computer, and his wall calendar was probably the less interesting of the two. He wondered why he hadn't taken down the list much earlier after Arthur started spending every weekend with him.

"Hey, handsome!" It seemed like that had become Arthur's default greeting to satisfy the demands of the vanity blessing quickly. "I was just looking at this list. I was wondering what you used it for."

"Um, it's a word list. Are you sure you don't want to shower too?"

"You mean like a vocabulary list?" Arthur finally turned in the chair toward him and started putting on the shirt he'd had in his lap.

"I guess you could say that," Rupert replied. He searched for something else to distract him, but Arthur was not easily deterred.

"There are handwritten notes that don't seem to be definitions—'must touch or breathe on' next to *cornucopia*, 'only when asked' next to *omniscience*. And why do the numbers go different directions?"

"What do you mean?" Rupert was stalling to figure out what would finally satisfy Arthur's curiosity about his blessing list.

"They go down zero to 24 on one side and up from 25 to 49 on the other side. And why would you put such easy words like *strength, laughter,* and *wealth* on a vocabulary list?" He pointed at the list as he read from it.

Rupert decided he had to get Arthur away from the list. He dropped his towel, turned the chair away from the wall, and pulled Arthur up into an embrace. "I'm really hungry. Can we talk about this at dinner?"

Arthur smiled and kissed him on the chin. "Sure. Where do you want to go?"

Late that night, after dinner and more sex, when Arthur was asleep, Rupert got up quietly and took the blessing list off the wall above his computer. He transferred his handwritten notes to the original document on his computer and then crumpled up the paper version and put it in the kitchen garbage bag.

When Rupert's distractions from that corner of the living room were insufficient the following evening, he simply told Arthur that he was developing a new vocabulary list with more difficult words.

In November, Rupert's great-uncle Horst died, and at first, Rupert wasn't going to go to the funeral. He made excuses that his final giving drive of the year was in full swing, and he couldn't get away from work. Arthur continued to suggest that he would regret it, and his great-aunt Ingrid could use the comfort of his presence. Eventually, Rupert made plans to go alone, despite Arthur's offer to accompany him.

With his home in Sheboygan sold years before, Rupert had to arrange to stay at a motel. The ride in the single-engine plane up from Milwaukee was bumpy but mercifully short, and Trevor was waiting for him when he entered the small terminal at the small airfield in Fond du Lac. "Rupert!" he called out over other people also getting up from their seats. "Over here!"

"Hi, buddy," Rupert said as he gave his childhood friend a quick hug.

"You seem like you never age! Do you only have one suitcase?" Trevor pointed at the small overnight bag Rupert carried.

"I'm only staying two nights." Rupert admired how handsome and sexy his friend had remained too, even with his hairline receding a bit. "Where is Samantha?"

Trevor ushered him out to the parking lot toward his blue SUV. "She wanted to see her mom in Green Bay since it was easy to drop her there on the way here. I got in just before you landed."

Once they were both in the car and buckling their seatbelts, Rupert said, "You don't have to stay for the funeral. I appreciate you meeting me and taking me to my motel."

Trevor pulled out of the parking space. "I knew your uncle too. My mom sometimes asked me to come along when she visited him and Ingrid in the nursing home. He was a great guy. Very funny."

Rupert thought about the times he had seen his great-uncle Horst before he left Wisconsin and then at his mother's funeral. He had always been supportive, even though he occasionally teased him as a young boy. He came to see him sing and dance at the family restaurant in Sheboygan. His grandmother always told stories about him as a boy after he left to go back to the house he shared with his great-aunt Madeleine in Manitowoc. After she died, he and Ingrid had moved into the same rest home.

"Do we need to get you some food?" The late afternoon sun was low in the sky, and they were driving down a residential street.

"I can wait until you're ready for dinner. I got a snack at Mitchell Field."

A minute later, they turned onto a more commercial street. "It should be somewhere around here." Trevor pulled into a parking lot. "We're here, I think."

Rupert double-checked the slip of paper with his reservation info in his wallet. "Yup. Did you want to come in?"

"Sure. I can hang out until you're ready to go to dinner. It looks like there's a decent selection of places in walking distance."

Rupert held onto the slip of paper, and Trevor carried his suitcase into the motel office. Rupert recited his reservation number, and the older woman called it up on her computer. "Were you wanting double occupancy?" she asked as she looked at the two of them.

"I never asked you where you were staying," Rupert apologized.

"I wanted to see what it was like here before I decided," Trevor said.

Rupert studied his old friend for some clue about what was going on with him. He seemed happy to be there and that was the only thing Rupert could read. "Do you have . . . ?" Trevor began.

Rupert spoke at the same time. "How much would double occupancy be?"

The woman looked at Trevor and then at Rupert. "Twenty-five dollars more per night."

After a pause, Trevor stepped away from the desk and pulled Rupert toward him. He whispered, "I don't want to put you out. I can get another room."

"I don't mind," Rupert whispered back. "It would give us more time to talk, and we could head to the funeral together tomorrow. When are you picking up Sam again?"

"I'll pick her up after I drop you off at the air strip again."

Rupert nodded toward the motel clerk. "So what do I tell the nice woman there?"

"I can pay the extra fifty. I was expecting to pay more than that."

Rupert turned and called to the confused-looking woman behind the desk. "Double occupancy, yes."

Trevor went to restow Rupert's suitcase in his car as the woman ran his credit card. Five minutes later, both of them had keys and were getting out of the car closer to their room. Rupert opened the door and let Trevor enter first. It was just a single queen-size bed, two chairs, a television, and a doorway to the bathroom. "Not too fancy, but fine with me," Trevor announced. He went back out to bring in their suitcases.

Rupert was sitting on a corner of the bed when Trevor reappeared with the bags. He set them down on the floor near the door and sat down fairly close to Rupert. "So . . ." Trevor began.

"Yes?"

"So I really like your suede jacket."

"And . . . ?"

"And Sam and I had a talk after the last time you visited."

Rupert waited a moment. "About what?"

"I told her that you and I . . . had fooled around sexually as kids."

Rupert could feel his heart beating faster. "Oh. How did that go over?"

"Surprisingly well." Trevor paused. "But then she asked me if I was bisexual, and I immediately said yes. I didn't think about it at all. I was afraid she was gonna' ask for a divorce, but she was smiling. I'm sure I looked terrified. She said you seemed like a nice guy, and if I wanted to have a fling with you when you were in town, that was okay with her."

"Wow. No pressure." Rupert collapsed onto his back on the bed. "Why didn't you tell me before?"

Trevor sighed and repositioned himself to more easily look at Rupert's face. "I wanted to wait until I saw you in person. I didn't want to spring it on you over the phone."

Rupert got up on his elbows. "So you were expecting we would have sex again?"

Trevor looked more embarrassed than frightened finally. "Well, just hoping really. I don't know if you're still interested in that with me."

Rupert immediately tried to imagine how Arthur would react to this sort of news. "I have a boyfriend now . . . I think."

"So . . . you're monogamous?" Trevor waited with a hopeful grin.

Rupert and Arthur had never had that talk. They were spending so much of their free time together, it was possible Arthur assumed they were exclusively dating. Rupert rationalized that he couldn't be held to an implicit promise. "I've only been having sex with him lately, but we've never talked about it."

Trevor got up and paced at the foot of the bed. "We are going to have to decide. That bed isn't very wide, and I know you always sleep naked."

Rupert sat up again. "We should think about it a little longer. We can decide after dinner."

After Rupert checked in by phone with Ingrid, they went to dinner at a diner two blocks from the motel. During dinner, Trevor frequently brought up times when they would have sex when they were teenagers. He seemed to finally give himself permission to discuss it. And not only discuss it, but specify things he had enjoyed and things he still wanted to try.

By the time they were back in the motel room after dinner, they were embracing and kissing as soon as the door closed. Three hours later, they were both naked and exhausted, lying on top of the sheets on their backs. Not long after they both cleaned up in the bathroom, they fell asleep spooning.

They managed to transition back into just being friends by the time they got to the funeral home where the ceremony was held the next afternoon. Ingrid wouldn't let go of Rupert's arm during the entire event. She would occasionally ask Rupert questions whispered in German about his life in New York and before that in San Francisco. Then she asked several of the same questions again, and Rupert got a tear in his eye more from the loss of her faculties than from his great-uncle's absence.

Once Ingrid was led into her limo by several of her nieces and nephews, Trevor came up to Rupert and gave him a big hug. And that too evoked more tears. It had been too long since he had been with family and friends outside New York, and he realized, however rootless he liked to consider himself, Wisconsin was still in his blood.

There was an extreme tenderness to Trevor when they were once again back in the motel room that night. And that made Rupert tear up even more. Trevor kissed him all over gently and then started massaging Rupert, taking each piece of clothing off him slowly, one at a time as he worked on him. This time when they got ready to sleep, Trevor held Rupert tightly in his arms for a long time before releasing him and sleeping.

When Trevor drove Rupert back to the small airport the next morning, they rode in silence. Rupert was afraid he would break out crying again. As they pulled into the airport parking lot, Rupert finally said, very quietly, "You're sure Sam is going to be okay with this?"

"I already know," Trevor said as he turned off his car's engine. "Do you think Arthur is going to be okay with this?"

Rupert put his hand on the car door handle, but he didn't open it yet. He was again trying to imagine Arthur's reaction. "I don't know. I might not mention it to him . . . at least not right away."

Arthur was waiting at the gate when he stepped off the last plane at the Newark airport that evening. "Rupert!" he called as he ran toward him. "You look great! Are you okay? How was everything?"

Rupert set down his small suitcase and embraced Arthur. "I got kind of emotional. It's good to see you."

Arthur picked up the suitcase and led the way toward ground transportation. "Did you learn any new vocabulary words?"

"Just one. *Exculpate.*"

"That's a good one," Arthur said. "I don't think I know that one."

Rupert waited a little more than a month–after his birthday–to bring up the topic of monogamy. Arthur quickly announced that he hadn't had sex with anyone other than Rupert since he started his new job at ABT. When Arthur asked Rupert how recently he'd slept with someone else, Rupert felt compelled to tell him that he had done so in the previous month. All Arthur said in response was, "Oh."

By then, Rupert had turned thirty-one and his prophecy blessing had begun. He wished he could predict what would happen between him and Arthur, but all he started to get in his first visions was about double-helix strands of DNA, and every link was labeled with attributes like eye color, hair color, and skin color. By February, the Human Genome Project announced that they had completed the mapping of human DNA.

By February, Arthur decided that he and Rupert should just be friends– at least until Rupert was ready to commit more exclusively to him. Rupert was tempted to lump this bit of bad luck with the effects of his family curse, but he realized it was just a dumb decision on his part to sleep with Trevor. He should have checked with Arthur instead of assuming he was okay with it. Rupert had never thought of Arthur as being that traditional, though he had heard enough clues about his family that it made sense. They met for lunch once after that, and then only exchanged emails.

Rupert didn't try to meet anyone else, for dating or sex, for a while. When he got home each night, he would watch television and do research online for work. On weekends he would just plan outings with Danny, Dorian, or Chantal. His next vision showed him a couple of men getting married in front of a windmill. By April, the Netherlands announced that same-sex couples could get married, and it was the first country in the world to go beyond civil unions for gays. It made being single even more depressing for Rupert, and he wondered if he was ready to tell Arthur he could commit to just him.

Trevor called and discussed the possibility of visiting him in New York, on his own this time. Rupert found he couldn't refuse his friend's request. Arthur would have to wait a bit longer.

By May, a more nightmarish vision dominated Rupert's dreams every night. He saw cataclysmic scenes of people jumping from burning skyscrapers, people burning to death, people dying in plane crashes, people crushed by falling debris. Eventually he saw jets crashing into the World Trade Center, the Pentagon, and the U.S. Capitol. The nightmare seemed so real, it made it hard to concentrate on his work for the ballet company. He told Trevor not to fly to New York anytime soon. He felt like he needed to do something more.

In June, he resolved to warn the authorities of some horrific air disasters in New York and D.C. He decided that the FAA and the FBI were the best agencies to receive his concerns. He worded careful emails to the intake addresses at both to put them on the alert for what had to be hijacked jets being used by terrorists to destroy major buildings.

Two weeks later, two white men in dark suits and ties showed up at his office and asked him to accompany them for some questions. He assumed they were responding to his emails, and he followed them out through the incredulous stares of his coworkers. They opened the back door of an unmarked, dark blue car, and he got in. He noticed there were no handles on the insides of the doors, as in a police car, and the glass was tinted enough that he had trouble following where they were taking him.

Rupert was ushered into a nondescript building downtown somewhere with scaffolding obscuring the ground floor and second floor. They continued to lead him with grips on his upper arms through a marble lobby and down an elevator. He ended up in a brightly lit room where a long, narrow table was surrounded by four metal chairs, and there was a video camera on a tripod plugged in in one corner.

One of the men pulled out a chair on the far side of the table and said, "Have a seat."

The other man turned on the video camera, produced a folder, and opened it on the table. He slid out printouts of Rupert's emails to the FBI and FAA. "Rupert Rocket, we received this email from you, and we want to know where you got your information."

CHAPTER 15: RUPERT IN CUSTODY

By late June 2001, the Italian and German Intelligence Services, the *Bundesnachrichtendienst* and the *Servizio per le Informazioni e la Sicurezza Militare*, had provided the Bush administration with intel that al-Qaeda was planning an attack inside the United States. Indeed, a wiretap of an al-Qaeda cell in Milan specifically revealed a plan to strike the United States using jet aircrafts.

Therefore, when Rupert's email started circulating at FBI headquarters, it set off multiple alarm bells. They checked all of his emails and started checking his phone calls for any sign he was an Islamic jihadist operative or sympathizer. That Rupert seemed to have knowledge of classified international intelligence made him "a person of interest." Rupert seemed to have information about specific targets that no one outside of al-Qaeda leadership seemed to know yet.

At Rupert's first interrogation, the two interrogators were so similar in appearance, he distinguished them by the only obvious differences between them. One had longer sideburns. One wore a tie with diagonal stripes.

"Have you had any contact with employees of domestic or foreign intelligence services?" Stripes continued.

Before Rupert could answer, Sideburns told Stripes, "Let's establish that we have the right person." He turned to Rupert. "Your birth name was Rupert Kellerman, correct?"

Rupert swallowed hard from Stripes' preview of their eventual line of questioning. "Yes. I changed my name legally at age seventeen when I started . . ."

Stripes interrupted. "When we ask a yes-or-no question, please just answer yes or no, or we're going to be here all night."

Rupert remembered that it had been after three o'clock when he was escorted out of the ballet company's offices, and he wondered why they thought it would take so many hours to clear him of complicity. He was a boring gay man working for a small ballet company. He knew some influential people whom he canvassed for donations, but he doubted any of *them* had terrorist contacts. He was about to respond to Stripes, but then he decided that would just antagonize him further, so he waited for the next question.

Stripes sat on a corner of the table. "And you reside at 242 South Second Street in Williamsburg?"

"Yes."

Stripes seemed to be reading off another printout in the folder. "Mother deceased. Father living in San Francisco. No siblings or offspring."

Rupert didn't notice a question, so he waited silently.

"Are those details correct?" Sideburns clarified.

"Yes." He decided to risk a clarification. "My birth father lives in San Francisco."

"You have more than one?" Sideburns asked.

"One birth father, one unofficial stepfather. Mike Stanton lived with us until I was fifteen. I lived with my birth father when I turned sixteen."

Stripes got up from the table and began writing notes on a notepad he had produced from somewhere. Sideburns sat down in the chair across from him. "You work as the development director for the Brooklyn Ballet Company and School, correct?"

"Yes."

"And in that capacity you have contact with a . . ." Sideburns looked at a list in the folder again. "Hakim Noor, one of your board members, correct?"

"Yes." Rupert started to worry that his attempt to warn the government might implicate innocent people like Hakim.

Stripes approached from the side with his notepad held out in front of himself. "Did you ever meet or hear him speak of a cousin named Ramzi bin al-Shibh? He

152

is a Yemeni seeking asylum in Hamburg."

"No. May I add further clarification?"

Stripes looked at Sideburns and nodded. "Go ahead," Stripes said.

"I see Hakim maybe twice a year or so at ballet functions," Rupert said, turning to face Stripes. "The only member of his family I've met or heard of is his wife, Azami." He hoped this would close down that particular line of questioning.

"In your email," Stripes continued as he pulled the document out of his folder, "you state that you can't be sure of the source of your information. So, you haven't had any contact with employees of any domestic or foreign intelligence services?"

"Not that I know of," Rupert clarified.

"Have you ever been to Hamburg, Germany?" Sideburns asked.

"No."

"But you have been to Germany?" Sideburns said.

"I was there for two weeks in Frankfurt for a dance performance." Rupert was sure they had that much information on him already if they knew so much about Hakim. They were probably trying to get him to lie to cover his tracks, so to speak, so they would know where to start digging.

"And you've been to Italy?" Sideburns continued.

"A week in Rome with short side trips to Venice and Milan."

Stripes moved to stand behind Sideburns and almost shouted over the end of Rupert's answer, "Have you ever been to Iran, Afghanistan, or Pakistan?"

"No."

After a pause, Sideburns took over again. "Your maternal grandparents were born in Germany. Do you still have relatives there?"

"Third or fourth cousins, I suppose." Rupert wondered where they were going with all the mentions of Germany. "I don't know."

"Why did you change your name from Kellerman to Rocket?" Sideburns continued.

"I was trained as a performer. It was catchier. I was seventeen at the time."

Suddenly, Stripes left the room, but he didn't turn off the camera. Its red light still shone in the corner.

Sideburns loosened his tie a bit and put his elbows on the table and leaned in toward Rupert. He spoke a bit softer. "Try to help us out a bit here."

"I'm trying," Rupert said. "I did contact you, remember?"

Still in his soft voice, Sideburns explained further. "We got your email, and it matched some intel we received from foreign intelligence services, but the CIA has been unable to independently verify any of it. If you send us the same intel about planes being used to destroy buildings in the U.S., we are stuck with trying to figure out if you made a lucky guess, or you know more than you're telling us. We get hundreds of email tips a day at that email address you wrote to. We checked you out. We couldn't figure out where you might have heard about these planned terrorist attacks. You can't just make detailed claims like that and expect us to believe you have nothing to do with it."

Rupert sighed, and Sideburns stopped talking. He understood why people were not eager to provide tips of criminal activity. Their first worry is that you're an accomplice. "I thought about whether to write to you guys for a couple of weeks before I sent the email. I finally decided it would be better that somebody checked out my . . . hunch . . . before something really horrible happened. I thought that by coming forward and telling you, it would become clear that I wasn't involved. If I were, it wouldn't be in my best interests . . ."

"And I understand that," Sideburns interrupted. "So, you're going to stick with your story that you don't remember where you heard about the attacks?"

Rupert stayed silent for nearly a minute. If they thought he was a crackpot, at least they might start to pay more attention to his claims—as more evidence accumulated. "Just be on the lookout. If you see anyone suspicious getting onto a jet plane . . ."

Sideburns got a little louder as he interrupted again. "There are thousands of flights passing through U.S. airspace every day. I'm afraid that's not very helpful advice. If we knew who was organizing the attack, or even what date they had set, that would help us a lot."

Rupert realized he couldn't narrow his predictions down much. Some happened a couple of weeks after he dreamed them, and one when he was eighteen had taken almost two years to come true. "Maybe the targets I mentioned could help?"

"How certain are you of them?" Sideburns calmed down a bit.

"I . . . didn't get the impression there were more than . . . those three, but I guess there could be."

At that point, Stripes stepped halfway in the room and gestured at Sideburns. He was pointing at his wrist. "Wait here for a bit," Sideburns said as he followed Stripes out.

What could easily have been an hour later, an older Latin man in a short-sleeve, white shirt and black tie ducked in and announced, "You're free to go. Follow me."

As they walked toward the elevator, the new man handed Rupert a plastic bag with the contents of his pockets, a piece of paper, and a pen. "Just sign this release form to acknowledge return of your possessions." He called the elevator.

Rupert signed on the line by holding the paper up against the wall. He handed the form and pen back just as the elevator arrived.

On the ground floor, the man pointed Rupert across the marble lobby toward the main entrance. "There will be a blue car waiting to take you back," the man said. When Rupert turned to thank him, he was already turned around and headed back to the elevator.

A blue sedan was indeed idling at the curb right outside the entrance, and Rupert got in the back seat. He noticed that his driver was a man considerably younger than he. "Can you take me to Williamsburg?"

The young driver glanced briefly over his shoulder at Rupert. "I have to return you to where we picked you up, on Schermerhorn. Sorry."

It was after seven o'clock when Rupert got dropped off in front of the ballet's offices. It was still hot out, so he unbuttoned his shirt, rolled up his sleeves, and headed toward the G train home. After he got off the train in his neighborhood, he smiled when he got to the maple tree on the corner that had been just a sapling two years before during his cornucopia blessing. Now it had branches that reached halfway across the street and up above many rooftops.

The doorman looked gravely at Rupert when he entered the lobby of his building. "What's wrong?" Rupert asked.

"They had notices signed by a judge," the doorman started to apologize.

Rupert didn't want to wait for the elevator. He took the stairs two at a time. When he got to his apartment door, he was breathing heavily, but started to calm down a bit. The door was closed and locked.

When he opened it, however, there was a piece of paper lying on the floor just inside the doorway. It was some sort of receipt from the FBI. Rupert picked it up and only got through reading the first couple of items before he dashed into his living room. His computer was missing. His desk drawers were open and empty. The cushions on his couch were askew. His rug had been pushed up against a wall. The blinds were raised. And his dining table was loaded with almost everything that had been in his kitchen.

Rupert walked into his bedroom, and the pillows and mattress were against a wall, with slashes down their sides and leaking stuffing. All the clothes in his dresser and closet were lying in heaps on the floor. His bike was on its rack on the wall, but the seat had been removed and was lying on the floor.

He walked toward the phone and set the receipt down on the table where his answering machine would have been. He picked up the phone and dialed Mike's number by memory. After four rings, it went to his answering service, and Rupert left a message for Mike to call. Rupert called Dorian next. He answered on the second ring.

Dorian was chuckling when the call connected. "Hello, stranger."

"Hey, Dorian. I'm sorry I haven't called you all week. Are you busy right now?"

"I'm just finishing dinner," Dorian replied. "What's up, sweet cakes?"

"I gave a tip to the FBI a couple of weeks ago, they brought me in for questioning, and while I was there, they ransacked my apartment. I just don't want to be alone right now."

"Soooo," Dorian began. "Am I to understand that you and that little Asian boy had a fight?"

"Arthur and I are . . . on a break."

"Sweet cakes, do not quote *Friends* to me," Dorian teased. "I don't have the patience to be reminded of that white-washed cast."

"Sorry. Can you come now?"

Dorian arrived forty-five minutes later. His hands stayed on his cheeks for the first couple of minutes as he slowly entered each room and gasped.

"I don't know where to begin," Rupert said as he surveyed his disorderly bedroom with Dorian.

Dorian stood by his side and put an arm around Rupert's shoulders. "Are you more likely to eat or sleep next?"

Rupert turned to face Dorian. He was wearing one of his trademark jackets with huge shoulder pads—this one embroidered in yellow with circles made of dragons. "I haven't had dinner yet."

Dorian pushed Rupert out of his bedroom. "Then let's get you fed." Rupert started to gesture toward his kitchen as they moved, but Dorian shook his head. "No, honey. You need a break from all this before we tackle putting anything back together. I'm taking you somewhere nice. Where is nice in this part of Brooklyn?"

They ended up at an all-night diner near Rupert's subway stop. Dorian ordered tea while Rupert downed a Caesar salad. Eventually, Dorian brought the conversation back to the reason his place had been searched. "So do you know what the FBI was looking for?"

Rupert sighed and spoke softly. "I contacted the FBI a couple of weeks ago about a potential terrorist attack." He wondered after he said it if he could explain it any more clearly to Dorian than he had to Stripes and Sideburns.

Dorian leaned forward and grabbed Rupert's hand that wasn't holding his fork. Rupert wasn't sure if he was angry or teasing. "No, no, no no! I can't believe how trusting you white people are toward law enforcement. What did you think they were going to do when you told them? Thank you and leave you alone??"

Rupert decided he was definitely being shamed. "I didn't think that much about it, to tell you the truth. The thought of thousands of people dying wiped any consideration of personal consequences away, I guess."

Dorian sighed and calmed down a bit. "It's not your job to save the world, Rupert."

Do I have a god complex? Rupert asked himself. His blessings certainly had the potential for influencing significant parts of destiny—for a lot of people. It was the FBI's job to protect Americans, but that was such a big job. They probably needed help like his.

Then he remembered his fourth grade teacher quoting Sophocles' *Antigone:* "No one loves the bearer of bad tidings." He remembered how much trouble he had gotten into as a young boy with his clairvoyance, empathy, and omniscience blessings. No one ever thanked him for revealing a secret. He realized that without solid corroborating evidence his intuition had as much potential to heighten awareness of an attack as it did to trivialize it.

"I will try to keep that in mind," he told Dorian.

They returned to Rupert's apartment after eating and spent two hours rehanging and folding clothes, rebuilding and making his bed, putting everything back in the kitchen cupboards and drawers, and straightening out the couch and rug in the living room. Dorian put his fancy jacket back on and hugged Rupert lightly before departing around ten o'clock.

Rupert showered and got into bed early. He was more weary than tired, and he wasn't looking forward to more dreams about people dying horrible deaths. But they came again, and this time, there were some changes. The U.S. Capitol was no longer destroyed by a jet. And he saw Dorian more clearly as one of the victims crushed to death in the collapse of the World Trade Center.

When he got to work the next day, Rupert told Sherry not to disturb him for a few minutes and closed his office door. He tried to reach Dorian, but the call just went to voice mail. He sent Dorian an email asking him to call him when he could.

When Rupert looked up again, Sherry was standing at the glass door to his office waving with an apologetic look on her face. He gestured for her to enter.

"I'm sorry, Mr. Rocket," she began when she stood in front of Rupert's desk. "Selina in HR asked me to be the one to tell you, since I was here when it happened."

"When what happened, Sherry?"

"Well . . . after those two men led you out yesterday, two other men showed up with a search warrant to copy all the files and emails on your computer."

"Oh." Rupert had expected the FBI would be that thorough.

"You're . . . not upset?" She seemed shocked at his nonchalance.

"At least they left my laptop here," Rupert explained. "They confiscated my home one."

"Um," Sherry began and then paused. "Are you . . . are you in some kind of trouble, Mr. Rocket?"

Rupert sighed and forced a smile. "Not really. They just had some questions for me. I wasn't arrested."

"You . . . should probably let Selina and the Board know, so they don't get the wrong idea," she suggested.

"Good point." Rupert leaned back in his chair. "I'll work on those emails next."

By the end of July, Rupert received his laptop and paper records back from the FBI. Dorian took Rupert's advice to heart and said he would make sure he left his building immediately at the first sign of an emergency. His nightmares continued every night, and he noticed the addition of images of a plane just crashing in a field. And he more clearly saw an image of the twin towers of the World Trade Center smoking after their impacts.

Two weeks later, Sideburns and Stripes showed up at Rupert's office again. Instead of waiting for them to come get him, this time he went and met them in the lobby at the receptionist's desk. He hoped it appeared he was just leaving for an early lunch.

They took him to the same nondescript building in downtown Brooklyn, but this time, they took him up in the elevator and into a room with a high ceiling and a one-way mirror along one wall. They sat him down in the chair behind a small desk-like table and took positions on either side of him facing the mirror.

There was a microphone on the desk with a cord extending behind him to the wall opposite the mirror. While Rupert waited for the interrogation to begin, he glanced over at each of the two men and noticed both Stripes and Sideburns had guns in holsters.

An older woman's voice came from a speaker high above the mirror: "Mr. Rocket, we are following up on an email you sent to us back in June. We finished going through the evidence seized from your home and office, and there were letters between your grandparents and a journal from your mother among them." The sound of shuffling papers came from the speaker, and then she continued. "We wanted you to explain references in those documents to two Irish women code-named Grogoch and Pooka. In your own dealings with these two individuals, what sorts of things did they give you?"

Rupert's jaw dropped. The last thing he expected was that the FBI would think his family's fairies were Irish terrorists. He squinted to see if he could see who was on the other side of the glass, but he couldn't. "They were acquaintances of my grandmother. I only met them a couple of times. It was always coincidental, never planned."

"Do you know their real names?" the woman asked.

Rupert smiled but then thought better of it and looked more serious. "I do not."

"The journal in particular talks about them giving you gifts on your birthday every year. Are you saying they did not deliver them in person?"

"That's correct." Rupert wondered what criminal activity they were imagining he was undertaking with the two fairies.

A new man's voice came from the speaker. "In your email you specify that you were worried planes would be hijacked and crashed into the World Trade Center in Manhattan and the Pentagon and U.S. Capitol in D.C. We want to know . . ."

"I think their plans have changed," Rupert interrupted. "They're not going after the Capitol anymore."

In the silence that followed, Rupert realized the grave error he had just made. He had given the FBI reason to believe he was still in contact with the terrorists.

"What I was about to say," the man continued, "is that we need you to explain again where you are getting your information."

CHAPTER 16: RUPERT ARRAIGNED

The Bush administration chose to ignore multiple warnings that al-Qaeda, headed by Osama bin Laden, was planning to imminently attack the U.S. As early as 1998, the CIA had heard al-Qaeda was planning an attack that involved hijacking airplanes. At an address before the European Parliament in April 2001, a witness testified that a large-scale attack on U.S. soil was planned. Almost every month from then on, the CIA reported to the president that terrorists already in the U.S. were about to attack using airplanes.

The main advisor to Bush on the matter was his National Security Advisor, Condoleezza Rice. She was dubious that any attack with planes or ground troops could last more than a matter of minutes against the repelling forces of the U.S. military. Without a specific date or target, she brushed off each report because it had no "specific threat information."

By the time of Rupert's second interrogation by the FBI in mid-August, they were getting desperate to prove to Rice that countermeasures needed to be implemented immediately. Rupert had specific targets that the FBI needed to corroborate to elevate the threat level of their gathered intelligence.

They kept him in the same room for hours, as a variety of faceless voices asked questions trying to break Rupert's insistence that he wasn't sure where he'd gotten his information. Finally, the older woman who had started the interrogation and to whom a lot of the other speakers seemed to defer got back to the microphone in their dark control room behind the one-way mirror:

"Mr. Rocket, I feel certain after spending the past few hours with you today . . . and watching the video of your previous interrogation, that you really are trying to help us. I do appreciate that. But as interesting and potentially useful as your theory is about jets being used as missiles against buildings, it is ultimately just *your* story. Without some validated corroborating evidence, we cannot act on your warning. It would be irresponsible of us to panic the country based on a single person's story."

Rupert sighed. He wondered if they had agents studying new applications for jet piloting licenses and poring over lists of suspects from al-Qaeda territory recently arrived in the U.S. Were they following up his tip and trying to corroborate it on their own? "I have to assume you have tried to verify my . . . hunch . . . and haven't been able to. If you knew the source of my information, it wouldn't help you at all."

One of the many male voices took over. "Please just let us decide that. We all want to be done with this as much as you do, I'm sure. . . Where did you hear that the World Trade Center, the Pentagon, and . . . now a farmer's field in Pennsylvania were the targets of the attacks?"

Rupert took a swallow from the paper cup of water they had finally refilled for him a few minutes before. He leaned forward to speak closer to his microphone. "I have a pretty good record for my predictions. I accurately predicted the completion of the Human Genome Project and the passage of same-sex marriage in Holland."

The same voice sighed, said something away from the mic and then addressed Rupert: "The progress of the Genome Project could easily be followed from journal articles and news reports, and the Dutch parliament had been debating same-sex marriage for almost two years before it passed. Neither of those events approach the serious consequences and huge leap of faith of your 'hunch.'"

As Rupert tried to come up with a rational retort, the woman's voice came back on. "I am tempted to close this investigation as inconclusive. Mr. Rocket, I am feeling charitable and choosing to see you as a well-meaning, lucky guesser. I will, however, be more inclined to pursue charges against you if you waste the Bureau's resources on another unsubstantiated piece of information." She paused for a moment. Sideburns and Stripes shifted their stances and seemed uncomfortable. "I hope I have made our position clear. Would you agree, Mr. Rocket?"

"Yes, ma'am," Rupert replied.

"Then you are free to go. Gentlemen, please escort Mr. Rocket out of the building."

Rupert noticed that Stripes and Sideburns treated him much more delicately on his last exit from the FBI field office in Brooklyn. There was no car waiting for him this time, so he checked his wristwatch and decided there wasn't any point in going back to work for less than an hour, so he searched for a subway station that might eventually get him home to Williamsburg.

Very early on Tuesday morning, September 11, nineteen Arab men checked in with their cell leaders by phone and were assured of a fantastic afterlife for their holy sacrifice. They reported to their respective airports in Newark, Boston, and D.C., boarded their airplanes without incident, and proceeded to hijack their respective planes and crash them into symbols of America's evil empire.

United Airlines Flight 93 out of Newark bound for San Francisco turned around over Ohio. That maneuver and phone calls passengers and crew received in flight convinced passengers their flight was doomed to crash as those already down in New York and D.C. They managed to get the cockpit door open, but during the struggle to regain control of the airplane from the terrorists, the plane crashed in a field near Indian Lake and Shanksville, Pennsylvania. All forty-four aboard the plane died. Thousands more Americans died that day or from injuries and inhaled dust in the weeks and years that followed.

Al-Qaeda leaders later claimed Flight 93 was supposed to target the U.S. Capitol.

Rupert was at work that Tuesday morning in September. He was still groggy from little sleep. It had been interrupted every hour or two with more detailed images of people trapped, crushed, incinerated, and eviscerated. He had only been in his office at the ballet company for a half-hour when the first of the planes hit the North Tower of the World Trade Center in downtown Manhattan. He heard cell phones and office phones ringing in a chorus right around nine o'clock.

Everyone watched coverage of the attacks on their computers or on the television in the dancers' lounge while periodically trying to call friends and loved ones who worked downtown. With millions of people around the city and the world trying to do the same, there were often delays in connecting, which made everybody panic even more.

Despite Dorian appearing regularly in his nightmares, Rupert maintained the hope that he was wrong. He hoped that as with the change of his prediction about the U.S. Capitol's destruction, Dorian might be spared in some last-minute change of fate.

Chantal got through to Rupert that evening. Rupert had considered going down to volunteer with the medical and triage centers set up in Riverside Park and elsewhere, but he decided he needed to be home to receive phone calls from friends and relatives in other parts of the country that had no idea that Brooklyn, where he lived and worked, was miles away from the fallen towers. Chantal had gone over to Dorian's apartment at ten-thirty, and his roommates said he had never arrived home.

By Friday afternoon, Chantal was able to get a list of their unaccounted-for employees from the firm where Dorian had worked. And Dorian was presumed dead, not scheduled to be out of the office or coming in late that day.

Just before eleven on Friday night, Danny called. He asked if it was too late or whether Rupert wanted to come by for an impromptu memorial for their friends who had died on the tragic day they were starting to call 9/11. Rupert didn't pause a moment. It took him a couple transfers and quite a bit of walking, but he was able to eventually make it to Danny and Max's place on the Upper East Side just after midnight. He spent the night on their couch. He managed to only wake up once, and his dreams were less insistent, but still dark.

Waking on Saturday morning in Danny's living room still in the clothes he'd put on twenty-four hours before, Rupert just lay there for a few minutes with his eyes open, staring at the ceiling. He had seen Dorian's death so vividly in his dreams for so many weeks, it still had the feeling of not being real. He tried to imagine Fire Island without Dorian. Chantal had been an emotional wreck. He and Dorian had been best friends for years. He wondered if Jorge knew. Chantal had probably called him as well. He wondered if he should tell Arthur. He and Dorian had gotten along pretty well the few times they had met.

Max, Danny's thin but athletic Eastern European boyfriend, was the next to rouse and rise. He broke Rupert out of his reverie when he appeared in the doorway to the bedroom where Danny still dozed wearing just boxers. "How are you doing, Rupert?" Max whispered as he took a few steps closer to the couch where Rupert was just beginning to sit up.

"It's just starting to hit me," Rupert reported. He scooted over to make room for Max to sit down.

"My friend Anna's sister was rescued from the rubble," Max said as he sat down, "but she had lost too much blood and was too dehydrated. She died in the hospital yesterday."

"I didn't know you'd lost someone too."

Max offered Rupert a half-smile and then looked toward the closed bedroom door. "I had only met her sister once. It is just hard for Anna. They were very close." After a pause, Max continued. "I will probably be most heartbroken about Dorian. He was always such a great guy. Really nice and kind."

"I'll miss him too." Rupert had cried a lot the first two days, but four days out, he couldn't even summon more tears if he wanted to. He just sighed a long heavy sigh.

"Theo left after you passed out," Max reported. "I hope we didn't wake you."

"No, it was fine. I'm sorry I couldn't stay awake to say goodbye."

After nearly a minute, Max turned back to look at Rupert. "Danny said you had a premonition this was all going to happen. The planes, the towers, and Dorian."

Rupert had forgotten he had let that particular secret out to Danny months ago when the visions had started and he hadn't grasped their significance entirely yet. He looked warily at Max, wondering if he was just curious or if an incrimination was coming.

"Did you tell Dorian?"

Rupert sighed again, and he did manage to tear up slightly at the suggestion that he might not have done enough to save his friend. "I advised him to be observant and to leave work at the first sign of trouble. That's all I could do. He was on the sixty-first floor of the South Tower. Too many people thought the first strike in the other tower was just an accident, and they didn't evacuate."

Max's tone was immediately conciliatory. "I heard that too."

"If I had known what day it would happen, I could've . . ." Rupert broke into a full weep.

Max put his arm around Rupert. "I'm sorry. Maybe I shouldn't have brought it up again."

Rupert just continued to cry softly, sniffling occasionally. Danny showed up in the bedroom doorway in tank top and boxers. He rushed to the other side of Rupert and sat down saying, "Are you okay, Rupert? What did you tell him, Max?"

"I . . . I just mentioned that you told me about his premonition."

"It's okay, Danny," Rupert managed to say. He wiped his eyes with his sleeve and stood up. "I should probably head home. Where's my jacket?"

Danny immediately stood as well. "You don't have to go right away!" He hugged Rupert and didn't let go.

Rupert extricated himself and stepped back. "I appreciate that, but I have laundry and dishes piling up at my apartment."

Max dashed back into the bedroom and returned with Rupert's jacket. "Thanks," Rupert said as he accepted it. He took a few steps toward the door to leave.

Danny followed Rupert to the door. "Call me later today and let me know how you're doing, okay?"

"I will."

Rupert walked slowly down the hall, down the stairs, through the lobby, and out onto the sidewalk. It took him a lot less time to get home than it had to get there eight hours earlier. He got to the corner and looked up at the tree he had helped with his cornucopia blessing. The leaves were just starting to yellow for the fall.

Somewhere in the back of his mind, Rupert registered the two police cars parked across the street from his building, but he was so focused on getting home and just cocooning all weekend, he continued plodding down the sidewalk as if everything were fine.

When he got to within forty feet of his building, the doors to both police cars opened, and officers met him at the front door to his building. The two men and one woman all looked very tough and not at all sympathetic. "Are you Rupert Rocket?" one of the male officers asked as he grabbed the hand about to unlock the front door.

"I am," Rupert said as he turned to face them. "What's going on?"

"Please turn around and put your hands behind your back," the officer replied. "You are under arrest for violating Title 18, chapter 113B of Federal Code. You will be remanded to the custody of the U.S. Marshal where you will await trial . . ."

At that point, Rupert felt himself dissociating from his body. He didn't hear anything else the officer said. He didn't recall feeling the handcuffs placed on himself. He kept thinking that this wasn't really happening.

"Do you understand these rights?" the officer repeated more loudly.

Rupert managed to say yes eventually. He tried to remember what he was agreeing to, but it didn't occur to him. The ride to the prison in Manhattan, the handoff to the U.S. Marshal and the new handcuffs, the bagging of his personal possessions, the photographing, changing into his orange coverall, and being led into a briefing room all passed in a haze for him.

Rupert was informed that a judge had agreed to hold him over the weekend until a Monday morning grand jury hearing. He was asked if he wished to place a phone call and reminded that he needed to let them know if he wanted a public defender. Rupert didn't recall exactly what he'd said, but eventually they sat him down in front of a phone, and he called Mike.

The call connected on the second ring, but it took Mike a few seconds to say hello. Rupert realized it was even earlier on a Saturday morning in Wisconsin.

"It's Rupert. I need your help."

"What can I do for you, Rupert?" Mike sounded cheerful but concerned.

"I've been arrested. I think I need a lawyer. I don't have a lawyer."

"Let me get some paper to take notes, Rupert. Give me just a second. Okay. Where are you being held?"

"Federal prison in Manhattan." The marshal who was watching him make the call didn't seem very sympathetic, so he didn't ask him for more specifics. "I think there's only one."

"Do you know what you've been charged with?" Mike didn't sound upset or judgmental, which Rupert really appreciated.

"All I remember is title eighteen."

"I don't think that's specific enough," Mike said, still very patient and calm.

"I think they think I had something to do with 9/11."

Mike paused. When he spoke again, he sounded surprised and a little panicked. "Rupert, listen to me very carefully. You need to make sure you don't say anything more where any of the marshals can hear you. I'll try to hire a lawyer for you, but I'm going to have to do some research, so I might not have anyone there until tonight. You need to refuse the public defender and request that you not be questioned until your lawyer arrives. If they bug you for his or her name, just tell them they will report in before the end of the day. I don't know what they do out there in New York. Did they say anything about a grand jury?"

"I'm going before them Monday morning."

Mike paused again. "Just trying to get everything down. So you haven't been indicted yet?"

"I don't think so," Rupert replied. "They just brought me to the jail and told me I had to stay here over the weekend until my hearing Monday morning."

"Hmm. I'm not a lawyer, but if they don't have an indictment yet, it would seem unusual that they took you into custody. I suppose they thought you were a flight risk."

"They said something about a criminal complaint."

"Okay, okay. Was there anything else I need to tell the lawyer?"

169

"Well, I don't know how you're going to tell the lawyer, but I think this is a result of my current . . ." Rupert whispered the last word: *blessing*.

"Got it," Mike said. "Hang tight. I'll see if I can get a flight out there today, but for sure by tomorrow. Try not to worry, Rupert."

"Thank you so much for your help, Mike. I don't know what I'd do without you."

Rupert's cell was like a narrow college dormitory room, with a toilet in the corner, a narrow cot along one wall, and a chair and small writing desk opposite the cot. When the steel door slid shut and was locked, Rupert felt very alone.

Rupert was given a lunch and dinner that reminded him of frozen dinners he'd bought at the local bodega when he was at Julliard. He was escorted back to the same briefing room in the evening. A woman in a gray suit and skirt and white ruffle blouse got up from her chair when he entered. She extended her hand. "Mr. Rocket, Mike Stanton retained me to be your lawyer. My name is Loretta Freiberg. Please have a seat."

She indicated the metal chair across the table from her. "Please wait outside," she told the guard who had brought Rupert there.

When Rupert sat down and the guard closed the door, Loretta continued. "I'm sorry I couldn't get here sooner. I didn't check my messages very early today, and then it took me a while to track down the criminal complaint and review it."

Rupert sighed. "Thank you for taking the case. I already feel better that you're here."

"Good," Loretta said, and then again, "good. I have to tell you there is good and bad news about your case, but I have worked in federal court before, and I think I can help you." She pulled a small stack of papers from her brown leather valise. "If you feel up to it, it would be good if you could read the complaint and let me know if there's anything in it I can clarify for you."

Over the course of the interview, Rupert got the sense that the judge had agreed that the connection to Hakim's cousin was the most likely source of his information about the 9/11 attacks. Loretta clarified that most of the information was circumstantial–that Rupert had been in Germany at the same time as Hakim's

170

cousin, bin al-Shibh; that one of the ballet company's donors had ties to al-Qaeda as well; and that Rupert had foreknowledge of most of the details of the attacks. One thing that looked worse was a call allegedly placed to Rupert's home phone from the terrorist cell in Hamburg where the hijackers had received their orders. And the most damning was a security photo from the Newark airport showing two of the hijackers talking to Rupert.

"They were just asking me for directions!" Rupert shouted when he read that part of the complaint. "I was on my way to Wisconsin for my great-uncle's funeral!"

"Was there anyone traveling with you who could corroborate that?" Loretta asked as she furiously scribbled more notes on her yellow legal pad.

Rupert reminded himself that Arthur had volunteered to go with him to the funeral. If he hadn't insisted on going alone, Arthur could have vouched for Rupert's story and kept him from having sex with Trevor again. And then they'd still be together. And he might not be in jail. He wondered if Mike still thought his family curse was not so bad. "No," Rupert reported. "I can prove that I was on my way to a funeral, though. I didn't go there to meet with those guys."

"The timing of the call from Germany and your subsequent meeting with the hijackers is going to sound suspicious to the grand jury on Monday." Loretta looked up from her notes to gauge Rupert's reaction. "That in combination with your videotaped admission knowing details about the attack is likely to get you indicted and arraigned."

Rupert groaned. "What do I do now?"

"Just try to remember anything that might help us refute the call and the meeting at the airport," Loretta advised. "I will work my butt off tomorrow to try to prepare for your grand jury Monday morning. I'll try to get some time to talk with you before the hearing starts so we can exchange information. Mr. Stanton informs me that he will pay bail if I can get the judge to agree to it, but there is already a ruling against you for being a flight risk, so it might be high."

But on Monday morning, Rupert was out of ideas, and Loretta was only able to get bail set at $875,000. The prosecutor had subpoenaed Rupert's bank records and saw all the payments from Mike over the previous six years and advised the judge to take both men's assets into consideration when setting bail. Mike couldn't afford so much, so Rupert remained in jail. His trial wasn't set until February.

Mike showed up outside the court room as Rupert was being escorted back to jail. Rupert could only shout "Hey, Mike!" before he was led away. He turned to Loretta, who was walking beside him. "Tell Mike I think my next blessing is going to make this all go away!"

CHAPTER 17: RUPERT TURNS THIRTY-TWO

By the first week of October, Mike managed to pay Rupert's overdue rent and utilities, explain to his employer that he was not coming back for at least four months, and contact Rupert's friends to let them know where he was. Arthur was the first one to visit Rupert in prison. He was sitting in a chair on the opposite side of the clear acrylic window with little air holes when Rupert was led into the reception room.

"Rupert!" he heard the familiar voice shout as he pulled the chair away from the low wall to sit down.

"I was so surprised to hear you were here," Rupert said with a smile. "How have you been, Arthur?"

"I got a call from your stepfather two days ago. I would have been here sooner, but it took forever for someone to let me know how to arrange a visit."

Rupert was happier than he expected to see his former-and-potentially-future boyfriend. "How are things at ABT?"

"My boss keeps me busy, but I like it," Arthur said somewhat off-handedly. "Mike said you were being charged with international terrorism. How is that even possible?"

"I can't really talk about the case," Rupert said gesturing with his elbow toward the guard standing next to the door behind him. "My trial isn't until February, and they set my bail too high, so I'll have to stay in here until then."

"You poor guy!" Arthur said as he leaned closer to the partition. "You have a good lawyer?"

"Yeah," Rupert said. "She's great. I'm optimistic that I'll be found not guilty."

"I hope so." At that point, Arthur's smile and enthusiasm disappeared. "I have some potentially bad news for you, and I thought you'd rather know about it before it's too late to do something about it."

Rupert couldn't imagine how his life could already have gotten worse. He waited for Arthur to continue.

"I just took a call earlier today for my boss. Your boss was calling her asking for potential candidates for a newly open position. Yours."

All the air escaped from Rupert's lungs at once. After he inhaled some back, he said, "Whoa! That was fast."

"You have to look at it from their perspective," Arthur explained. "It doesn't look good to their donors if the development director is in jail."

"I understand, but one, I'm not guilty, and two, that was pretty fucking fast to boot me without telling me."

"Well, if you are found not guilty, you should be able to get another job," Arthur offered. "Eventually."

"I've had a lot of time on my hands, as you can imagine, so I've been stretching and working out more. I may give performing another shot."

"You look great." Arthur stood up to see Rupert's lower body. "That jump suit is really not very flattering, though."

"It's all they had in my size," Rupert joked.

Arthur laughed. "I keep imagining that you're having sex in here all the time."

"Not at all." Rupert leaned back in his chair and folded his arms. "I keep to myself when they let us out for exercise . . . and I'm not allowed to have sleepovers."

Arthur laughed again. "Well, I guess you're doing pretty well if you're able to joke about it."

"Well, we're only at week four out of twenty-one, so check back with me in a few weeks."

The guard on Arthur's side came up to warn him that his time was up. "I'll try to get away again next week, if I can." He pushed his chair back and blew a kiss at Rupert.

"Thanks for coming, Arthur! It was great seeing you!"

The following week, Mike came by for a visit. He was on a mobile phone talking when Rupert was led into the reception room. Mike glanced up briefly as Rupert was sitting down and said, "I will get it all straightened out when I'm back. I am in New York right now, and I'll be home tomorrow night. We'll talk then." Mike disconnected the call, sighed, let the small phone fall into the pocket of his tweed jacket, and looked up at Rupert again. He seemed tired and worried and more than a little distracted. "I'm sorry, Rupert. I don't feel like I have any free time anymore."

Rupert grinned. "You still think the Grogoch's blessing is a blessing then?"

Mike leaned in and whispered, "You shouldn't be talking about that where they can hear you."

"I'm sure it means nothing to them. How are things going?"

Mike pulled a notepad out of another pocket and flipped pages for a moment. "I met with Loretta last night after I got to town, and she's been asking me to help her understand the evidence the U.S. Attorney's Office collected. She's concerned that your mom's journal makes her look crazy and you like an antisocial rebel. And she thinks the prosecution will try to make a case that you were radicalized from a young age by two older Irish-American women with ties to the IRA."

Rupert sighed. "That's like so much of their case. It's all inferences and circumstantial evidence."

Mike flipped a couple more pages in his notes. "It's going to be hard to get around the call three years ago from the hijackers' cell in Hamburg and the video showing you talking to two of them."

"It was three years ago?" Rupert asked. "Did Loretta tell you that?"

"Yes, she said they had evidence that you spoke on the phone . . . one minute and thirty-seven seconds with someone at the number in Hamburg."

Rupert got excited that he had found a defense. "Three years ago I had a roommate. She might have been the one to answer the call. It might not be me."

"I don't know if that can be ruled out or not," Mike said. "They wouldn't have listed it as evidence if it weren't more airtight than that, right?"

"And they can't possibly know who on the other end . . . oh, maybe the CIA or the BND had a wiretap on their phone by then."

"I don't know. You'll have to mention that to Loretta. Are they treating you okay in here?"

"A little rough sometimes, but generally okay, yes. I wouldn't recommend it. Two stars tops." Rupert grinned, but Mike didn't seem to register his wit. "Other than helping with my defense, is then anything else going on that I should know about?"

"No, no," Mike said finally looking more directly at Rupert. "Some tax stuff I'm dealing with. I'm dating a woman long-distance. She lives in Chicago, and she's been up to Sheboygan a couple of times. Funny thing. She asked about you."

Rupert laughed. "How did I come up?"

"Laura and I were down in the basement den at my new place, and she noticed the pillow your mom made with your name and birthdate on it: 12-25-1969."

Rupert remembered that the pillow had been the one gift his mother had bequeathed to Mike. He still wondered what she was thinking. Perhaps it was to try to keep him in his life. "Ah. Are you two serious yet?"

"Not too. We're taking it slow. We only see each other once or twice a month." Mike's mobile phone started buzzing. He fished it out of his pocket. "Stanton here. Okay. Let me call you back in twenty minutes." He disconnected the call and dumped it back in his jacket pocket. "I have to get going. Is there anything you want or need that I can try to get in there to you?"

"I go through reading material really fast, and the library here is from another century."

Mike was already getting up from his chair on the other side of the partition when he replied. "I will see what I can do on that." He was scribbling something on his notepad when the guard on the other side let him out.

176

Rupert passed the monotony of his incarceration with meals, exercise, reading, and a small amount of television. The memories of civilians dying on 9/11 were quickly replaced with visions of President Bush ordering troops to Afghanistan, which he did a week later. Now there was a focus in his visions of President Bush so gleefully happy about his results in Afghanistan that he and his advisers and buddies started eyeing the oilfields of Iraq. Rupert found this ridiculous because Iraq played no part in 9/11 and had actually denounced the attack. But the dreams persisted with more details over time of the multiplicity of lies Bush's team came up with to justify invading the country. And a team of fixers muzzling the objections of the intelligence community.

Rupert was on his cot mulling over the phrase "weapons of mass destruction" when a guard came by, waking him by banging on his cell door with his baton. "Visitor, Rocket," the man barked.

Rupert put on his shoes while the guard unlocked his door. He was led past his neighbors' cells, down the stairs, and across the atrium to the reception room. He could see Danny on the other side of the partition as soon as he got there. He rushed forward and sat down. "Hey, Danny! Thanks for visiting!" Rupert called out.

"I'm sorry it took me a couple of weeks," Danny said with just the barest suggestion of a smile. "I had to ask for time off."

"I know it's a hassle that they don't allow evening visitors. How have you been? How is Max?"

"We're both doing fine," Danny reported. "He's got a big freelance project for one of his clients, so he hasn't had much free time to spend with me. Do you have any idea when you'll be out of here?"

Rupert sighed. He thought about all the years he and Danny had been friends, even through the semi-boyfriend stage of his dominance blessing. He looked a little lonely and isolated, like Rupert had been the first person he'd spoken with in days. "My trial isn't until February, and it's more likely that it will be delayed than earlier, my lawyer says. But we both agree that the prosecution's case against me is pretty flimsy, so we think we can win it. The toughest are a video of me talking to two of the 9/11 hijackers in the Newark airport, and . . ."

"Did you know them?" Danny interrupted.

"No, they were just asking me for directions. And there was a phone call to our old place after you moved in with Max. Some call from the terrorists' headquarters in Hamburg, Germany, they say I took."

"A wrong number maybe?"

"I don't know," Rupert replied. "They claim I talked to them for around a minute and a half, so that makes it sound like an intentional call, not a wrong number."

"Bummer. And you have no idea who it was or why they called?"

"I don't even remember the call. It was three years ago."

Danny leaned forward closer to the partition and talked softer. "Chantal is really taking Dorian's death hard. He quit his job, and he doesn't answer phone calls or emails very often. Max thinks he may be a suicide risk, and we don't know what to do about it."

"There's not much I can do from in here," Rupert said. He remembered how distraught Chantal was at the impromptu memorial the night before his arrest. "I might be able to get Arthur to check on him too, if you think that will help."

"Sure," Danny said, brightening slightly as he leaned back in his chair. "The more people he sees, the less alone he'll feel. Oh. I guess that applies to you too. Are you getting enough visitors?"

Rupert sighed. He realized his friends had busy lives, and he had tons more free time than they did. "My lawyer stopped by once, and Mike, and Arthur. And now you. I guess four visits in five or six weeks isn't too bad."

"I'll try to come by again in a week or two," Danny promised. "I miss you . . . Max and I both miss you. And Theo and Jorge were asking 'bout you."

"*Jorge* was asking about me?" It had been almost three years since he and Jorge had had any contact. They had managed to avoid each other pretty successfully despite having friends in common, including at Dorian's memorial the previous month. "I haven't heard from him in a long time."

"He's still taking care of his mom," Danny said. "We just saw him out one night last month. I think Max mentioned that you were in prison."

"Great." Rupert didn't even try to remove the sarcasm from his voice. "That's bound to increase his respect for me."

"Yeah, no. He did say something kind of catty I won't repeat."

"I didn't think I hurt him that much," Rupert mentioned. He noticed the guard on Danny's side lurking directly behind Danny. He pointed toward him. "I think our time may be up. Thanks for coming by."

Danny looked startled to finally notice the guard standing behind him. "Oh. Okay. I'll try to come back soon."

As Danny was led out, he seemed uncertain where he was going. Rupert realized there was stress among his friends because he was in jail too.

Arthur made it back to visit just before Halloween and told him of a new department ABT was opening in 2002. He said the newly forming Collaborations Office would need a director-level administrator, and the position would be open from February 1 to March 31 for applicants. Arthur said he would recommend Rupert for the job if he were out of prison and cleared of charges by then.

On November 1, Danny came back for another visit as well. He brought Rupert some news magazines to read. And he had some good news: "Max remembers being there when you got that call from Germany!"

"What?" Rupert sat down across the partition at the same time as Danny. "Is he sure?"

Danny still seemed almost out of breath. "I told him about the phone call from the hijackers' cell in Hamburg, and he remembered one night when the three of us were at your place getting ready to go out, and you took a phone call. We assumed it was one of your relatives back in Wisconsin, because you were speaking German. When you got off the phone, you said it was a wrong number. Someone from Hamburg."

"That's incredible!" Rupert said. "And can he figure out what day it was?"

"We'll have to see if we can figure it out somehow."

Rupert wondered if Loretta could use Max as an eyewitness to prove that the call was accidental, just like the meeting at the Newark airport. "I'll check with

179

my lawyer, Danny. She may want to talk to Max, so ask him if that's okay."

As winter came on, Rupert's cell started feeling drafty and cold at night, so he started wearing his prison uniform to bed to add to the sheet and thin blanket on his cot. Although he had managed to lay low and stay out of arguments in the TV room and exercise areas, there were occasionally new guys who tried to prove how tough they were. One was a short but beefy Puerto Rican gang member named Juan. Because Rupert was one of the few white men in his cell block, Juan assumed he was going to easily back down for him.

Juan came up to him as he was finishing a bench press in the gym. "*Blanquito!*" he called.

Rupert sat up slowly. He gave the new prisoner an icy stare and said nothing.

"Hey, *blanquito*. I'm talking to you." He pointed directly at Rupert.

Rupert slowly got up from the bench and stood beside it, looking at the man with the headband and lots of scraggly facial hair. He noticed several of the other prisoners gathering behind Juan expecting a fight. "If you're looking to work in, go right ahead. Do you want me to take off some of the plates so it won't be so heavy?"

The prisoners behind Juan started chuckling at him. "I heard you helped those Arabs who brought down the Trade Center," he said. "I knew people that died that day."

Rupert had been careful not to talk about his case with anyone in the prison, and the guards were forbidden from revealing that sort of information too. "If that was your idea of a pickup line, I should tell you right now, you're not my type."

The prisoners surrounding the weight bench and the two of them started laughing raucously. Juan turned on them and pointed back at Rupert. "This guy helped kill thousands of people!" he insisted.

Rupert moved in very close to Juan, so that when he turned around again, his nose was only inches from Rupert's chest. Rupert whispered, "If you walk away now, I'll leave you alone. But if you persist, *muchacho, haré tu vida un infierno!*"

"*¿Como harás eso?*" Juan drew the words out slowly and softly without backing away from Rupert.

Rupert turned to his audience and shouted, "No, no. I already told you, dude! You're not my type! Find someone else to suck your . . . *pinga*."

Rupert turned around and lay down on the bench and launched into another set just as the crowd howled. He glanced up between lifts and saw his challenger retreat from the laughter and taunting of the other prisoners. If there was one thing Rupert had learned in life, it was how to work a crowd.

No one visited for a couple of weeks, and Rupert started to wonder if Chantal was going to host another drag Thanksgiving dinner. When Rupert finally got another visitor, he was surprised to see Hakim sitting in the chair on the other side of the partition when Rupert entered the reception area. "I didn't expect to see you here . . . at least on *that* side of the partition."

"Rupert," the older Arab man began, "I . . . "

"So, you're looking for absolution maybe? For not testifying on my behalf? For getting me fired from my job?"

He seemed calm and subdued. He wasn't rising to meet Rupert's anger. "You have to let me explain, Rupert."

"No, I don't." Rupert pointed behind himself. "I can walk right back out that door now."

"I tried to keep your job open for you, Rupert. I was outvoted."

Rupert didn't say anything. He stewed about the possibility that Hakim was telling the truth and not covering his ass.

"And I couldn't testify on your behalf," Hakim continued. "If I had, they would have just gone searching for a new scapegoat, and that would likely be me."

"So, you decided to just throw me under the bus?"

Hakim only raised his volume slightly, and he didn't look Rupert in the eye. "My cousin helped plan the attacks. You are in a much better position to fight the accusations than I. I have a wife and a son now who I have to consider. They were threatening to extradite me back to Yemen."

Rupert took a deep breath. His visions of the current administration's deceptions and the hysteria for retribution probably had infected the U.S. Attorneys Office as well, especially in the Southern District of New York. It was

181

not unreasonable that they had threatened Hakim to keep him from testifying. "I didn't know they were blackmailing you. I'm sorry. You probably feel like I brought this all on you."

"I don't blame you at all, Rupert." Hakim got out a handkerchief and dabbed at his eyes. "Everyone is demanding retribution for the attacks, and until they catch Osama bin Laden, that's likely to be convenient targets like you and me."

"You're probably right."

"And if you need a recommendation for any job when you get out of here, you can count on me, Rupert."

The rest of the visit involved small talk about Hakim's family and the ballet company, and Rupert got Hakim to agree to be an anonymous source, if Loretta needed information he might have.

The nightly visions of Bush's trumped-up war against Iraq continued all the way through December. But on Christmas Eve, Rupert slept the whole night through, with the certainty that in the morning, when he awakened as a thirty-two-year-old man, the nightmares would disappear, and the new blessing would arrive.

When Rupert arrived in the dining hall, he took his tray and sat next to the biggest, meanest man in his cell block—a mob hit man named Frankie. "It's my birthday today, Frankie."

"Scram, Rocket," he hissed back.

"I think you want to give me your apple crisp, because it's my birthday."

Frankie looked at him like he was crazy. "Are you for real?"

"The realest," Rupert said with a smile. "Give me your apple crisp."

Frankie turned back to his tray, lifted the saucer that held his dessert, and set it gently down on Rupert's tray. He looked down at his remaining food again and whispered to Rupert, "Just get out of here now, okay?"

"Sure thing," Rupert said as he rose to find a new seat. "Thanks."

He scanned the room holding his tray. His gaze landed on the guard who most frequently had the responsibility of locking Rupert in his cell at night. The blessing he had received on his seventeenth birthday that had allowed him to sail effortlessly through transferring his guardianship to Fred and emancipating himself to gain early admission to Julliard was back. And Rupert started to imagine what concessions he could win from the guard with the aid of his intimidation blessing.

CHAPTER 18: RUPERT'S TRIAL

Rupert hadn't seen Loretta, his attorney, in eight weeks when he was informed that she was back to talk to him. He wondered if she was busy with other cases or the discovery of the prosecution's evidence. By then she would have looked through all of Rupert's possessions that had been seized and whatever records the prosecutor had obtained from banks and telephone companies.

She was already settled in with her valise unloaded of laptop computer and stacks of paper. She looked up briefly as Rupert entered the briefing room. "Come in and sit down."

"Hello, Loretta," Rupert said carefully as he sat down across the table from her.

She looked embarrassed for a moment. "Oh, yes. Hello, Rupert. We have a lot to go over, so just let me finish getting organized, and then I have some announcements and some questions."

"Okay. I have some news too, when you're ready for it."

"Good, good. Let me start while I have everything still in mind." Loretta did something on her computer, huffed out a big breath, and then continued. "I have finished going through discovery and deposing their witnesses. Most of their witnesses are just tech people to verify their surveillance evidence, but one of their witnesses you may know. He was a board member at the ballet company you worked at, Hakim Noor."

"He came to visit me," Rupert interrupted. "He said he would try to help us, as long as his help remained anonymous."

Loretta smiled. "I guess that makes sense. They categorized him as a hostile witness. I'll try to set up a meeting with him."

"And I have another witness you can call for us," Rupert added. "My friend Max remembers being with me when the call from the Hamburg terrorist cell came in and can verify that I reported it as a wrong number."

"So, he heard your side of the conversation and can confirm what you said on the call?" Loretta asked. She was looking down at a yellow legal pad where she was taking notes.

Rupert's shoulders slumped. He finally saw the problem. Max couldn't help exonerate him. "Oh. Yes, he heard me speaking, but the conversation was in German, so I don't think he knows what I was saying to the caller."

Loretta looked up and paused for a moment studying Rupert. "Hmm. Let me think if just verifying your reporting at the time would be helpful. You do understand that you could have told him anything to cover your intent, and he wouldn't know the difference, right?"

"I see that now. I'm sorry I brought it up."

"No, no. Don't ever hold back any information that pertains to your case," Loretta said as she put down her pen. "Something you might consider insignificant could be the break I was looking for."

"Got it." Rupert tried to remember if he had heard anything else in the past eight weeks that would help his case.

"The stuff they seized from you is mostly okay, except for your mother's journal."

Rupert leaned forward. He never knew how people would react to her stories of his blessings and the two fairies influencing his family's fate. "What did you think?"

"Seems like a red herring to me," Loretta said as she set some paper she had been scanning down. She looked Rupert in the eyes. "She seemed intelligent, but a little detached from reality. A lot of it reads like fantasy, so I don't think the prosecution is going to want to touch it."

"Okay."

"We also need to ask Mike for financial records from his restaurants,"

185

Loretta continued as she reviewed her notes again. "They're going to try to prove that he was laundering money for al-Qaeda and sending it to you under the guise of profit sharing."

"Yikes," Rupert said. "Was there anything else?"

"The prosecution has also come back to me twice with plea bargains," she continued to report. "The first one was ridiculous, so I rejected it out of hand. The second one I need to run by you just in case you have become more willing to change your not-guilty plea." She scrolled through something on her computer screen. "They won't budge on the charge—conspiracy to commit a felony—but they are willing to reduce the class from A to B, and to reduce your prison sentence from life to ten years, eligible for parole in five."

"I still don't see how they can claim I was a co-conspirator," Rupert almost shouted. "I didn't do anything."

"Well . . . the prosecution is building a case around your volunteering information to the FBI," Loretta explained. "They are going to try to sell the jury on the idea that your reporting of al-Qaeda's plans to the FBI in advance was designed to sound too crazy to be believable, and thereby throw investigators off the possibility."

"Wow." Rupert couldn't believe how much trouble his desire to avert the disasters was getting him into.

"I know it's verkakte," Loretta commented. "But the judge might allow it, and the jury might buy it. I'm going to need your help to try to refute that narrative."

Rupert sighed. "Okay. I have no idea what . . . well, one of the FBI people in my second interrogation, a woman, when she was dismissing me, she said I seemed like I had good intentions in coming forward."

"I'll check for that," Loretta said as she pawed through the many papers she had laid out. "I was thinking we might want to schedule some character witnesses. No offense, but you look so white bread, it shouldn't take much praise and support of you to sway the jury. Depending on the racial balance of the jury, of course."

"What do you mean?" He wondered what race of people would be more or less likely to acquit him.

"It's some technical stuff. I may be hiring a jury profiler to help me this time. Nothing for you to worry about. The main thing for you to consider is if you lose, I will, of course, argue for leniency, because you have a clean record outside of that sexual harassment charge . . ."

"She recanted." Rupert was so tired of having to defend himself from that old bogus accusation. "I'm gay. She was just trying to get me fired, so I couldn't give her a bad grade."

"The school expunged it, but the police report is still on your record," Loretta said. "Anyway, the maximum sentence is life if you don't take the plea bargain, and it's unlikely we can get that reduced beyond twenty-five years, if we lose."

"We're not going to lose," Rupert declared. "You just have to let me do the closing summary at the end of the trial."

Most of the time, Loretta seemed completely unflappable. This request made her visibly confused. "Huh? Why would you want to do that?"

Rupert knew that his intimidation blessing usually only kicked in after the target had had a chance to object. "I'm not sure if it's my looks or my performance background or my celebrity, but I can often win over a crowd if I can make direct eye contact with them. Please just grant this one request, Loretta."

Loretta looked wary but resigned. "All right, but we should discuss what you're going to say in advance."

"That's fine." Rupert folded his arms and smiled.

Two weeks later, Rupert got his first letter. He took it back to his cell to read on his cot. It was from Danny, and it had been opened, but he could see it had originally been sealed with two red, foil, heart stickers. Danny had written it by hand on both sides of a sheet of theme paper instead of typing it on a computer and printing it out. Rupert wondered why he had made so much extra effort instead of coming for a visit. As he read the letter, it became clearer:

I hope you're doing better, Rupert. It doesn't look like I'll be able to see you any more before the trial next month. I have to sign a letter that I won't have any more contact with you until after the trial because I'm gonna' be . . . a character witness for you! Your lawyer interviewed me, and then gave me the news yesterday. It felt like I'd passed a test or won an audition. I hope I can help you win your case. I have to meet with your lawyer one more time before the trial to coach me on what sort of things to mention. Max was sad to hear that he could not be a witness about your phone call. Chantal finally emerged and said she will come visit you before the trial. (Yes, she wants us to call her she now instead of he.) Theo and Arthur and Max are going to see if they can get off work to come watch at least part of your trial. I'm a little nervous about it, but I'll be okay if it helps you win. Everybody misses you—especially Arthur. He can't visit any more either because he's gonna' be a witness for you too. I hope you're doing well and that you get out next month.

Love,
Danny

Rupert was initially glad that his two closest friends would be speaking on his behalf at his trial. But then he realized that they had both had sex with him during his domination blessing, so that might be a problem for their objectivity if the prosecution went there. He made a mental note to discuss it with Loretta and started imagining what he would say to the jury.

Three days later, late in the afternoon, a guard stepped into Rupert's cell where the door was left open most of the day now, at Rupert's request. He announced that Rupert had a visitor, but visiting hours were about to close.

"I would hate to have one of my friends turned away," Rupert explained. "You don't mind extending your shift a couple of minutes to allow the visit, right?"

"Well, we're not supposed to, because then we also have to let the guard at the gate know." This particular guard had already acquiesced to Rupert so many times in the preceding eight weeks, he didn't put up much resistance anymore.

"Please do that for me."

"I'll be right back," the guard promised.

Two minutes later, the guard returned and gestured for Rupert to follow him. "It's all set up. You'll have reception to yourself. Take as long as you need."

Rupert followed him out into the hall and down the stairs before he responded. "I'm sure we won't need more than ten minutes. Thank you."

Chantal was already waiting in the chair on the other side of the partition when Rupert got to the reception area. For once, all the other chairs on both sides were empty of other prisoners and visitors. Chantal wore a women's black wig with straightish hair that came to a severe flip in the front. She wore a diaphanous kaftan of blues and greens, and Rupert could see that she wore green, slick-looking, fake nails with a sequin glued onto each one. She wore false eyelashes, maroon lipstick, and a large silver stud in her lower-lip piercing.

Rupert's jaw dropped as he sat down across the partition from her and took in the new appearance. "You look amazing, Chantal."

"I am thinking about changing my name to Phoenix to more completely change my identity," she reported. "I'm sorry it's taken me so long to visit. I was going through . . . a bit of drama in my life, but I think I've landed in a solid place, sweetie."

"I'm so glad to see you," Rupert gushed. "I was worried about you."

"Oh, don't worry about me," Chantal advised. "I will always bounce back. You should know that about me by now."

"Okay, I'm not sure of the protocol: I was wondering if you were embracing the idea of cross-dressing, or if you felt more transsexual now."

"I'm not sure," Chantal replied. "I'm trying this out, but it seems like I'm on the right path. How are they treating you in there?" She leaned closer toward the partition. "Are you getting beat up? You don't look like you've acquired any

189

scars or bruises."

"I'm fine." Rupert laughed. "My trial is in a couple of weeks. Arthur and Danny are going to be testifying for me."

"I heard. I am praying the jury can recognize your innocence, sweetie." Chantal crossed her legs and displayed her sparkling fingernails. "Do you like these, or do you think they're too much?"

"It's a nice touch," Rupert replied. He remembered all the times he had admired Chantal's wardrobe choices as being daring, but clearly she had just been flirting with androgyny. Now she looked feminine but of the glamour-punk variety. "I'm really sorry I wasn't around to help you through the grief of losing Dorian."

"Oh, please, Peaches." She brushed his apology away like it was an overly exuberant puppy. "You were jailed the day after his memorial. And it wouldn't have mattered. It was something I had to go through alone. Is it always this deserted in here? All those empty chairs?"

"I called in a favor with the guards to see you," Rupert said very close to the partition. "Visiting hours just ended."

"Oh." Chantal stood up as gracefully as a helicopter lifting off. "I won't keep you then. I just wanted to make sure you were all right and wish you good luck at your trial."

Rupert stood as well. "Thank you for coming. It is such a load off my mind seeing you healthy and thriving."

Chantal tried to hide her embarrassment behind her hand. "You are too sweet, honey!"

Mike managed to sneak in one more visit the day before the trial began. He said it was to help bolster Rupert's spirits, and he stuck around for the first two days of the trial, which began, auspiciously or not, on Valentine's Day in 2002. Rupert was given a gray suit and black tie to wear and transported by van to the courthouse right after breakfast in time to have a brief meeting with his lawyer before the trial began. Loretta was wearing the same skirt, jacket, and ruffled blouse as when Rupert had first met her. She wore more makeup. She was accompanied by a fairly young, thin man with short, black hair and wearing glasses. Loretta introduced him only as Fenton. Rupert shook his hand and sat down across the table from the two of them.

"We're just going to be listening to the U.S. Attorney's case all day today, probably—and objecting a lot," Loretta advised. She slid a pen and a pad of yellow Post-It notes across the table toward Rupert. "So we will have to pay close attention. Use those to pass any questions or comments to Fenton during the trial. We can talk more freely again during any recesses."

"Got it," Rupert said. He put the pad and pen in the pocket of his orange coveralls.

"Stay cool," Fenton added. "The prosecutor will try to rattle you to make you look like an angry person to the jury. Don't fall for it."

"Don't stare at the jury or the judge or the prosecutor unless they're the only one speaking," Loretta continued. "Try to stay neutral—no big smile or frown. Go for a look of sedate curiosity."

"I'm a trained performer. Should be a piece of cake for me."

"And are you still wanting to give the closing summary?" she asked. "It will be our last chance to appeal to the jury before they go into deliberations."

"I know," Rupert inserted.

"And they are more likely to view you favorably if I'm the one talking about your innocence and the holes in the prosecution's case. People pleading on their own behalf are viewed with more suspicion."

"I understand. I'm certain it's the right play."

The courtroom was medium-sized. Rupert could see Mike and his friends in the nearly full gallery as he followed Loretta and Fenton to their table in the front. The prosecution's table was already occupied by a balding older man also in a gray suit and a maroon tie and a younger Latina woman in a light blue pant suit. Both of them had their noses buried in papers when Rupert sat down.

The bailiff opened a door on one side, and twelve middle-aged people—six white, two Asian, and four black—and evenly divided between women and men filed into the seats in the jury box. They were definitely more diverse and older than his more heavily white grand jury, and Rupert wondered if that was the result of Loretta's profiler.

The judge was a somewhat overweight, mature black woman, and she entered with a veneer of detached intellectualism. Rupert stood with everyone else until she took her chair at her desk at the bench. After giving instructions to the jury, she invited the prosecutor to offer his opening remarks.

The story he told was what Loretta had warned him about. He described Rupert as the son of an unstable, single parent whose behavior became so erratic and rebellious, she allowed him to go live with his otherwise absent father and his mistress in San Francisco. He completely left out any references to the Grogoch and the Pooka. He intended to prove beyond reasonable doubt that Rupert had been recruited by al-Qaeda while in Germany and agreed to warn the FBI about the 9/11 attacks in such an outlandish way, it eroded confidence in other intelligence sources claiming the same things, leaving the country open to attacks that could otherwise have been prevented.

Loretta's story was starkly different. She painted a picture of a happy well-adjusted child with a loving mother, stepfather, and grandmother taking care of him in a small town in Wisconsin. In her narrative, Rupert had chosen to live with Fred and Britney to get a chance to know his father and explore living in a larger city where it was easier to pursue his passion, dance. Germany was only one of many international destinations where Rupert performed as briefly as a few days or as long as a month, with grueling schedules that left little or no time to socialize outside the performance venue. She intended to prove that Rupert's approach to the FBI was out of a sincere desire to prevent the tragic deaths of 9/11, and that the meeting for a few seconds with two Arab men in the Newark airport was simply to direct them to the United ticket counter, as they requested.

Rupert felt Loretta got much more useful information out of Hakim than the prosecutor did. He established for her that his cousin and Rupert had never been in the same city and that he had never introduced the two of them.

Loretta scored her greatest victory in cross-examining the FBI agent Rupert had nicknamed Sideburns. He had just finished testifying to the accuracy of the interrogation video in evidence where Rupert described al-Qaeda's upcoming targets as the World Trade Center, the Pentagon, and the U.S. Capitol. At the judge's invitation, Loretta got very close to the box where Sideburns sat. "Were you shocked when you heard my client describe targets terrorists were intending to ram with jets?"

"At that point, no," Sideburns replied. "I had already read those claims in his email weeks before."

Loretta moved still closer to him. "Was the U.S. Capitol indeed destroyed?"

"Of course not." Sideburns started to laugh, completely unaware that she was in the process of setting him up.

Loretta stepped back and looked at the jury. "So how about during the next interrogation you attended—when my client said the U.S. Capitol was safe, and instead that plane would crash in a field in Pennsylvania?"

"Actually, my first thought was that he was still in communication with the other terrorists."

Loretta turned back to face the witness stand. "But United flight 93 did indeed crash in a field in Pennsylvania, did it not?"

"Yes." It started to dawn on Sideburns that he needed to be more careful in his answers.

"The passengers and crew tried to wrestle control of the plane from the terrorists, and it never made it to its intended target, somewhere in Washington, D.C., correct?"

"Objection!" the prosecutor shouted. "Defense is asking for verification outside witness's personal knowledge."

"Counselor?" the judge asked in Loretta's direction. "You are approaching a point with this line of questioning?"

Loretta bowed her head slightly in the judge's direction. "Very quickly, your honor."

"Overruled. Continue, counselor."

"So, Mr. Davidson," Loretta continued, facing Sideburns, whose name Rupert finally learned, "as one of the agents assigned to conduct and review my client's testimony, what is your explanation of my client's accurate prediction that one plane would crash in a Pennsylvania field?"

"I . . . well, he was . . ." Davidson mumbled.

"I withdraw the question," Loretta interrupted. "In your experience interrogating informants, Mr. Davidson, if someone accurately predicts an unexpected failure in part of the plan, is it likely that he was trying to, as the prosecutor seems to think, discredit the potential for the attack?"

"Objection!" the prosecutor shouted again. "Defense is trying to confuse the witness."

"Sustained," the judge agreed. "I'm not sure I follow your question either, counselor. Please rephrase."

"My apologies, your honor," Loretta said. "I'm trying to get the expert witness to explain why someone who contacts the FBI to warn of an attack, and then accurately predicts the results of that attack, how he is working *with* the attackers." She turned to Davidson again. "It would make more sense to try to lead you astray, wouldn't it, Mr. Davidson?"

"Objection . . ." the prosecutor began.

"No, I can answer this," Davidson interrupted. "The defendant described the 9/11 attacks, but with no corroboration, so we couldn't take it seriously."

"I'm sorry, Mr. Davidson," Loretta interrupted. "But if the FBI and CIA had multiple pieces of evidence going back to 1998 that suggested a terrorist attack on U.S. soil was imminent, how did my client's warning email invalidate all of your previous intel and not bolster it?"

"It was too unbelievable to take seriously," Davidson argued.

"Yes, who would ever think to hijack planes and crash them into buildings?" Loretta said with heavy sarcasm. "No further questions, your honor."

Rupert allowed himself a brief smile when he noticed Davidson leaving the witness box a bit dazed, followed by the concerned and questioning looks of several jurors.

Rupert was glad when six days of the prosecutor's case were over. Loretta finally called Arthur and Danny up to testify. They both did really well, even when the prosecutor tried to imply they were tainted because they had had sexual relationships with Rupert. Arthur had put it best: "My personal life does not affect my judgment. When I was Mr. Rocket's assistant, I was privy to most of his dealings with our donors and board, and he always conducted himself with a high degree of ethics and responsibility. He was so well liked, giving to the ballet company increased over four-hundred percent in the year after he became development director."

In the recess before closing arguments, Fenton and Loretta switched chairs so that Loretta could whisper directly to Rupert: "So when you go up there, try to focus on the things that the prosecution was unable to prove. The content and purpose of the call from Hamburg. The content and the preparation for the meeting in the Newark airport. And they didn't prove you did anything to assist the hijackers beyond directing them to a ticket counter. Try to sound confident and friendly, and don't bring up your race, your sexuality, or any other details about yourself. Let Danny and Arthur's testimony do that."

"I will do my best," Rupert assured her.

The prosecutor's remarks characterized Danny and Arthur as Rupert's "buddies." He again painted Rupert as a rebellious individual with a criminal record who had multiple direct and indirect contacts with al-Qaeda leadership. And he concluded that Rupert's accurate prediction of the attacks could only be the result of contact with and cooperation with the terrorists who carried them out.

The judge was leaning toward disallowing Rupert's closing remarks, but once she asked if Rupert felt dissatisfied with his representation, it gave Rupert an opportunity to speak to the judge directly, and with the aid of his intimidation blessing, the judge quickly allowed Loretta's petition. Rupert took his time getting up from his chair at the table and crossing to the jury box. Over the course of the three weeks of the trial, Rupert had had plenty of opportunities to snatch glances and observe the various jurors. He felt four were already on his side. He focused more on the other eight as he spoke:

"You've heard two different stories of why I wrote to the FBI and the FAA to warn them about an attack that eventually happened exactly the way I said it would. The prosecution at one point tried to suggest I was just a lucky guesser. That's what the FBI said during my second interrogation, and it's probably true.

"I know it looks bad when you see me talking to two of the hijackers on a video, but you remember how short the conversation was. About the amount of time to offer quick directions. Not enough time to pass along instructions or updates, as the prosecution would like you to believe.

"The prosecution doesn't know what happened in the phone call from the terrorist cell in Hamburg. The length of the interchange in German was longer, because I couldn't understand the guy's accent very well, so it took longer to realize he had dialed the wrong number. I was with friends who remembered me describing it as a wrong number at the time. And the prosecution was unable to find other calls from that number to suggest otherwise.

"I think all of that evokes more than reasonable doubt. I hope you agree with me and return a verdict of not guilty. Thank you for your time and patience."

Rupert scanned all of the jurors' faces one by one, and some of them immediately started nodding, and the rest still seemed to be taking in his words. He took that as a positive sign, and he was grinning as he turned and approached the defense table to sit down again.

During the judge's final instructions to the jury, Fenton and Loretta switched seats again. "Not too bad," Loretta commented in a whisper. "I saw some nodding heads. That's good."

"Thanks," Rupert whispered back. "I feel pretty confident."

As the jury was being led out of the court room, Rupert's guards accompanied him, Fenton, and Loretta back to their briefing room just down the hall from the court room. They passed the time with sandwiches Fenton went out to pick up and recounting stories of moments in the trial. Both Fenton and Loretta were surprised when one of the guards ducked his head in forty-five minutes later to tell them everyone was expected back in the court room.

As Rupert walked back through the court room, he looked out at the gallery. Theo and Arthur were gone, but Danny was still there, and some new reporters had arrived to cover the verdict.

"This is one of the shorter deliberations I've seen," Loretta commented as they took their seats at the table in the front again.

"Is that usually a good thing or a bad thing?" Rupert asked.

"Hmm," Loretta intoned. "In most cases, I would consider it a bad thing. But in this case, it could be a good thing."

"When the judge comes back in again," Fenton whispered, "and when they read the verdict, make sure you stand and face her. If you're guilty, you'll have to wait for your sentencing hearing. If they find you not guilty, you'll have to go back to the prison to check out there, but then you'll be free."

"Whatever happens," Rupert whispered back, "I want to thank you both for doing such a great job on my case."

The bailiff suddenly shouted, "All rise!"

Rupert stood up and noticed for the first time that the jury was already back in their box. The judge sat in her chair, everyone sat down again, and then she paused several seconds before asking the jury forewoman about the verdict. Rupert found himself thinking, *If there were ever a time I needed a blessing instead of a curse, it's now.*

CHAPTER 19: RUPERT TURNS THIRTY-THREE

Fenton and Loretta just stared at the jury for a few seconds. Then they turned to each other and shook hands. Rupert couldn't hear what they said to each other. Fenton patted Rupert on the back. Rupert turned around and saw Danny making his way to the front of the gallery, and when he got there Rupert stood up and hugged him over the railing. A guard came up and pulled the two of them apart and led Rupert out of the court room. Fenton and Loretta didn't follow him out this time. They remained packing up their books and papers.

Reporters in the hallway took photos and shoved recorders and microphones in Rupert's direction as soon as he was out in the hallway. He ignored them and followed the familiar path down the stairs to the van at the delivery entrance that would take him back to the prison. Rupert and the single guard were the only ones in the back of the van as it pulled away for the brief ride. When the doors opened, the guard took him by the upper arm and exited the van, walked up to the gate, waited for it to open, and walked through.

He was told to go into his cell and handed a white, plastic garbage bag. After six-and-a-half months there, he didn't have much to gather up: a few books, some papers, and Danny's letter. Next, Rupert was led to the intake area and given a large, clear, plastic bag of clothes and a smaller, clear, plastic bag holding his pager, his wallet, his keys, some coins, his wristwatch, and a pair of sunglasses. Rupert returned the suit they had lent him for the trial and stripped down to his underwear. He pulled the clothes out of the bag one piece at a time and put them on: a sock, a T-shirt, another sock, slacks, shoes, an Oxford shirt, and a light blue jacket. They looked familiar but odd to Rupert.

Rupert clipped the pager to his belt, slipped his watch over his wrist, and pocketed the other items from the smaller bag. He looked back at the orange coverall and boots he had changed out of that morning, lying on the cement floor next to the bench. They looked familiar but odd also.

The guard led Rupert back out to the main gate, shook Rupert's hand and patted him on the shoulder. He mumbled something about luck and missing him and then turned and walked back toward the prison.

Rupert stood in the street next to the curb for about five minutes. It was chilly in the light jacket he had chosen to wear back in September, and he shivered. A cold late-winter wind was blowing Rupert's hair and making his whiskers and the hairs on the back of his neck stand up. He had to step back up onto the curb when a yellow taxi pulled up next to him. The rear door nearest Rupert opened, and Danny stepped out and gave him a long, tight hug. Rupert continued to stand with his arms down while he was being hugged.

Danny stepped back out of the hug. He hadn't aged much since they had met fifteen years before at Julliard. He still had the lean, athletic physique he'd had as a teenager, but he had gained a little more weight, most of it muscle. He looked up at Rupert with eyes that were tearing up and a smile that was rapidly disappearing. "What's wrong, Rupert? You don't seem happy to be free."

"My life got interrupted," Rupert observed. He stared at the taxi, wondering if they should be getting into it, but Danny was standing in front of the rear door closest to them. He decided to wait.

"You still have your apartment," Danny said.

"I do?"

"Yes. Mike's been paying your rent and utilities. I was going to take you there now."

"Oh. Okay."

"Max phoned me and said he's arranging to meet everyone for dinner at Joe Allen tonight," Danny announced.

"When?"

"When did he call or when are we meeting for dinner?"

"When did he call?" Rupert clarified. "You were just at the courthouse, and now you're here."

"Oh!" Danny said. He grinned and pulled a mobile phone like Mike's out of his pocket. "Max and I finally got cell phones while you were locked up. We should get you one too." He pointed at the pager.

Just then, the taxi driver lowered the window near them and asked them if they were waiting for someone else. Danny said no and climbed back into the back seat and waited for Rupert to follow.

Rupert stood there for a moment. He took inventory of what sort of life he was stepping back into. His friends were still there, except for Dorian. His apartment was still there, Danny said. His job was gone, according to Arthur and Hakim. And he had been just an observer from the sidelines for more than a half a year, trying every day to entertain and manipulate the guards and other prisoners into leaving him alone and not hassling him. He realized he had become accustomed to seeing everyone and every new environment he entered as a potential threat.

He decided to pretend he was back in his old life. He had been a performer, an actor at times. He could do it. He ducked down and sat in the back seat next to Danny. He pulled the door shut. The cab drove off toward the Brooklyn Bridge. Danny still looked a little wary. Rupert put his hand on Danny's knee and smiled, and then Danny smiled too.

When the cab pulled up in front of Rupert's building, Rupert opened the car door and was about to step out when Danny said, "Do you want company or to be alone?"

Rupert smiled and grabbed Danny by the shoulder. "Company. I've had enough alone time to last me about a decade."

The older, short doorman rushed up to Rupert as he entered the lobby. "So good to see you again, Mr. Rocket!" he said as he grasped Rupert's hand in both of his gloved hands. When he released the hand, the man turned and headed toward the mailboxes and called from over his shoulder, "I've been saving your mail."

Rupert had no idea how much mail he got in five months, but the box turned

200

out to be not so big, but filled two-thirds full with envelopes of various sizes. He put the box under his arm before taking a closer look at its contents and headed toward the elevator. Danny stepped into it after him and said, "I think I'll just hang out with you until I hear from Max when we're meeting everybody, okay?"

"Sure." Danny seemed happy to see him, but something about the way he was acting was making Danny concerned. He pushed the button for his floor, and the door closed. "I'm fine. I still have the feeling that I'm dreaming I'm free from prison, or prison was a nightmare I'm just waking up from."

"I can understand that," Danny said. He patted Rupert on the back, and then followed him out the open elevator door.

Rupert took a moment to remember which was his apartment door key. Once the door was open, he set the box down just inside and walked in. He took his jacket off as he entered the living room and draped it over the back of an easy chair. He heard Danny close the door behind him as he stalked toward the flashing red light of the answering machine, imagining it had run out of tape or couldn't count past ninety-nine messages.

"Yeah," Danny called out as he entered the room, "you probably have a lot of messages."

Rupert looked at the number and wasn't sure what he felt. The number nine was displayed, and he wasn't sure how quickly news of his incarceration had spread nor whether so few he knew missed him much. "There are only nine," he reported.

"Oh," Danny called out as he came up to stand beside Rupert, looking down at the answering machine, "Mike must have played all the messages when he got in here. Those must just be the ones since he called everybody back in October."

Rupert pushed the button, and it took a couple of minutes for the tape to rewind. He didn't care that Danny was right there listening. By the time all eighteen messages played, he had listened to two messages each from Danny, from Trevor, and from Charlie the dancer he used to have sex with during the dominance blessing. Individual messages were from his assistant Sherry (wondering why he wasn't at work), Chantal (wondering how he was doing after the memorial), his landlord (wanting the overdue October rent), Arthur (proposing a lunch together), and Denise, John, Michaela, and surprisingly Luke all calling to find out why they hadn't heard from him in so long. His stepfather, Fred, had called four times, increasingly upset by Rupert's silence.

"Is there anything I can do for you while you're getting settled?" Danny asked.

Rupert turned in a circle to survey the room while he thought. He probably had email messages backed up as well. "Maybe you could sort my mail from that box into stuff I do and don't want to see?"

"Sure," Danny said. He took off for the front hall. He came back and set the box on Rupert's dining table to start sorting.

"I'd better call Fred back," Rupert told him. "I think Mike forgot to let him know I was in jail." He was surprised he still remembered the number after not dialing it for so long.

When the call connected, Rupert said, "Hi, Fred."

"Oh," Fred's girlfriend Britney said. "Fred's not here right now. Is this Rupert?"

"Yeah, Britney. Could you tell Fred I'm sorry, but I was in prison for five months, and Mike was supposed to let him know that."

"We were worried sick," she said. "I'll have him call you back as soon as he gets home. Why were you in prison?"

Rupert sighed. "It was a misunderstanding. My trial ended today, and I was declared innocent."

"You're really, truly okay, Rupert?" She sounded like she was getting emotional.

"I'm fine, Britney. Just make sure you let my dad know that I wasn't ignoring him."

"I will."

Rupert hung up the phone, and then regretted that he had not told Britney goodbye. He'd just hung up on her. Maybe there was something wrong. "Danny, how would you say I've changed since I was arrested?"

Danny stopped sorting and turned in his chair to face Rupert. "You're more muscular, I think. Shoulders and chest for sure, maybe arms . . ."

Rupert interrupted. "I meant emotionally, I guess."

Danny stood up and crossed to Rupert where he was standing in the middle of the living room. He put his hand lightly on Rupert's forearm. "Well, you seem quieter. I'm sure you're stressed out by the sudden change. You seem kind of like you're in shock."

That response was more serious than Rupert expected. While he thought about it, he walked over to look at the two stacks Danny had made on the dining room table. On the top of one stack was a letter from the Brooklyn Ballet and School, probably his termination notice. He moved it to the side and started looking at the letters and postcards beneath it. There were dues notices from Equity and AGMA, utility bills, a third notice on the hospital bill he assumed he was still paying off, a hand-addressed letter from Mike, and two Christmas cards. It looked like Danny had correctly chosen junk mail for the other stack.

"I was surprised to hear the message from Luke," he said as he turned to face Danny.

"Chantal said he wanted to make amends with you," Danny reported. "He asked Max if it was okay to show up at your coming-home party tonight. If it would be too awkward, I can call . . ."

"No, it's okay," Rupert interrupted. "After all that's happened, I shouldn't hold a grudge against Luke just because he wasn't what I wanted." After a pause, Rupert moved to the chair at his desk and turned on his computer. "Did Chantal say anything about Jorge?"

Danny sat down on the couch. "I didn't ask. I think I told you how he responded when we told him you were in jail."

"Not in detail, but I get the point."

"So right now," Danny said, "I think we're planning on you, me, Max, Chantal, Denise, Michaela, John, Theo . . . Luke . . . and Arthur."

Rupert was focused on downloading his email. "Okay," he mumbled. "It will be nice to see Denise again, . . . and Arthur."

"Did he visit you in jail?" Danny asked.

"Arthur? Yeah, a couple of times."

Rupert saw only fifteen emails scroll onto his screen. The first ten were from late September and early October, the last five dribbling in during November and December. Luke wrote a long apology for not being upfront about being in a relationship. Most of the rest were friends trying a second route to determining his whereabouts. Surprisingly, the school he taught at for a couple of weeks before he was dismissed for alleged sexual harassment was letting him know they needed instructors again. A choreographer he had worked with wondered if he was available to dance. And Julliard wanted donations.

Rupert showered and changed clothes and dug a warmer jacket out of his hall closet, the suede one Arthur had given him. Max called Danny first to tell him Joe Allen couldn't seat their party until eight-thirty, so Danny suggested the Gramercy Tavern and confirmed it was okay to invite Luke. He called a second time to tell Danny they had reservations for seven o'clock and that Theo would arrive a few minutes late.

Danny seemed surprised that Rupert wanted to take public transit into Manhattan. Rupert explained that they had plenty of time before their reservation and he wanted to be around people, on the subway and on the street. They ended up hanging out in Washington Square Park for almost an hour before heading to the restaurant.

Chantal had just arrived when Rupert and Danny did. She was wearing a short, curly, blond wig; a tight, zebra-print, knee-length dress; and huge gold hoops for earrings. Danny pushed past the crowd near the entrance to go give Max a hug and a kiss. Chantal and Rupert slowly followed Max and Danny into the side dining area.

Already sitting at the joined tables in the back on the left where Danny and Max took two open seats beside each other were Denise, Michaela, John, Arthur, Luke, and a blond man with a moustache sitting next to Luke Rupert didn't know. "Who is that?" Rupert whispered to Chantal.

Chantal slid her arm around Rupert's waist to keep him from moving any closer to the table. "Oh, come on, sweetie. Take a guess."

Rupert noticed the man's shoulder touching Luke's and with his hand on Luke's thigh. He remembered that Luke stopped seeing him because he didn't want his friends to see Rupert with him, so this had to be the mythical boyfriend. "James?"

"Bingo."

"That's pretty ballsy to bring him to my welcome-home party . . . from federal prison!"

"The only way for you and Luke to be friends is to introduce you to James." Chantal pointed at three of his dancer friends. "Who are the two women and the man to their left?"

Rupert whispered more directly into Chantal's ear. "From left to right, Michaela and I graduated Julliard at the same time, Denise and I met at a dance performance in the Poconos, and John was the only straight male ballet dancer in my classes at Julliard. Michaela and John are both friends of Danny's as well."

"I feel sorry for Johnny. He's the only straight person here."

Rupert snickered. "What about Michaela and Denise?"

Chantal turned to more directly whisper into Rupert's ear. "I have a strong hunch those two will be cohabiting by the end of the night."

Rupert's snicker exploded into a full giggle, and finally Chantal giggled as well. Luke, James, and John all looked over to try to figure out why the two of them were laughing and not yet joining them at the table. At that moment, both Rupert and Chantal felt hands on their shoulders from behind.

"What are we waiting for?" Theo said. He slid into the room between them pecking each on the cheek.

Once all eleven of them were seated, Rupert between Chantal and Theo, Rupert reflected on where he had had breakfast that morning before heading to the court room for final statements in his trial. He had eaten a breakfast of really bad oatmeal and fruit in the cafeteria of Manhattan's federal penitentiary. He looked again at the menu and the fantastic, creative dishes he could order. He assumed there was still money in his bank account unless Mike had somehow gained access to it to pay his bills. *No, he must have paid out of his own funds,* Rupert thought. *I still have money.*

Rupert looked at the empty seat at the other end of the table between Arthur and Max. He whispered to Chantal, "Why is there a twelfth seat. Was Jorge invited too?"

Chantal replied in a low voice, "You'd have to ask Max; he was doing the inviting. But I believe Jorge's last word on you was that he would meet you one-on-one before he would ever meet in a group again."

Chantal's words seemed to be prophetic. The next day, Rupert got an email from Michaela confirming that Denise had gone home with her after the dinner. And two days later, Rupert got a call from Jorge.

"Luke told me you got out," Jorge began.

"Two days ago," Rupert confirmed. "The jury acquitted me."

"Congratulations."

Rupert paused to check the time. He was expecting a phone interview with Arthur's boss about a new job. "How is your mom?"

"She's into a routine now with the dialysis appointments," Jorge reported, "and my sister moved back, so we can split helping mama on nights and weekends after the nurse leaves."

Rupert smiled. He had never really wished ill on Jorge. He was his first boyfriend. He was glad he was getting some of his free time back. "So, would you like to meet in person some time? I have to get off the phone for a job interview in a couple of minutes."

"I'll have to see what my schedule ends up being in the next two weeks," Jorge said.

Rupert decided to use his intimidation blessing because he was in a hurry and Jorge was just equivocating because he was scared. "You should meet me for lunch on Monday."

"I'm not sure what the workload will be like . . ." Jorge began.

Rupert interrupted. "I'll plan to drop by your office at 1:00 Monday."

"Okay."

"I'll confirm with you that morning. Bye for now."

After Rupert hung up from the phone call with Jorge, he only had time for a quick bathroom break before the phone rang again. It was the executive director of the American Ballet Theatre. She mentioned receiving recommendations from both Arthur and Hakim, and she spent some time laying out her vision for the new collaborations office. Rupert had to admit that he had never worked in a booking office, but he felt his years of experience in dance and theatre domestically and abroad gave him lots of ideas for and contacts with potential collaborators for ABT. At the end, she said that since the position would be directly supervised by the general manager, Rupert would need one other interview. The HR department would coordinate schedules to set it up.

Immediately afterward, Rupert's phone rang again. "Rupert! How did it go?"

"Hello, Arthur. You mean you weren't listening in?"

"I don't do that," Arthur said. "Did she put you off or tell you your next step?"

"I'm not sure," Rupert confided. "She said HR would contact me . . . to set up a meeting with the general manager."

"Oh! That's good then!"

"It is?" Rupert trusted Arthur's intuition or inside knowledge, but he wanted to hear the confirmation again.

"Yes. If the GM likes you, they may make an offer. There's only one other person still in the running."

"Thanks for the inside scoop." Rupert chuckled. "I'll let you know if I hear anything."

"Great. I'll do the same."

The following Monday was April 1, and Rupert awoke in a goofy mood, his first since before 9/11 and his arrest. Even before he got dressed, he went into the living room, checked his phone directory, and called Jorge at his office. When Jorge answered, he almost shouted, "I'm completely naked!"

Jorge sounded flustered for a moment and then asked, "Is this Rupert?"

"Yup," Rupert replied. "Are you still free for a one o'clock lunch near your office?"

"Yes, I think I can swing that. Just meet me in front of my building." Jorge paused for a moment. "You will be wearing clothes, won't you?"

Rupert smirked. "You know how Chantal has started cross-dressing? I think I'm going to do the same."

"You are??" Jorge was incredulous.

"April fool!" he shouted into the phone and continued a bit softer. "I would make an ugly drag queen, I'm sure."

"Probably true. See you in three hours."

They ordered food for takeout from a deli and carried it a couple of blocks to Bryant Park, because spring had arrived early, and it was already over sixty degrees out. They managed to grab one of the small metal café tables and two empty chairs in the shade. Rupert just sat and looked across the park as he slowly chewed a bite of his sandwich. He was slowly starting to appreciate the longer views when they were available in New York City. So much of the time, he felt like he was just moving from one tall, block-long box to another, the sky above it more like a ceiling—just a small strip of blue or white color.

Jorge seemed to read his mind. "How does it feel to be out in the world again?"

Rupert had spent the entire winter principally shuttling between his cell, the showers, the cafeteria, the lounge, the laundry room where he worked, and the gym—six rooms—and he was rarely outside because it had been a cold and snowy winter. Now he could go to restaurants, parks, bars, friends' homes, or travel to other cities or countries like he had before. But it still felt like boxes to him, and it hadn't before. "I'm not sure I've made the adjustment yet," he finally said. "Going home alone to my apartment still feels like heading back to my cell in prison. At least the food is better." He smiled trying to lighten the mood a bit.

"It may take a while to adjust," Jorge offered. "You've only been out a couple of weeks now?"

"Only nine days," Rupert corrected him. "How does it feel to have your sister's help in caring for your mom now?"

208

"I'm sure it's not the same," Jorge said as he brushed breadcrumbs off his hands and lap, "but I kind of feel like I was given my old life back, too. I don't rush home from work anymore, hoping that I get there not long after the nurse leaves. I don't rush home from a grocery run any more, hoping that she hasn't fallen, or gone into shock, or wandered off. I don't have to apologize for being late to work because the nurse arrived late or some crisis is happening. Once I put in my eight hours, I can usually forget about mama for a while, see friends, see a movie, go out to dinner . . ."

"Or to lunch," Rupert interrupted.

"I was kind of afraid of meeting you, because I still had this feeling you were mad at me." Jorge stopped to take a sip of his soda. "At the same time, I thought you might be crazy or at least have anger issues, because you just ran away from me that night."

"Jorge, you were my first boyfriend. I loved the time we spent together, but when your mom got sick, I never saw you anymore. And that was kind of all right with me, because I was going through some stuff too."

"We both stopped trying to make it work," Jorge summarized.

Rupert thought about it for a moment. He had just given up on Jorge, because Jorge would've flipped out over the wealth blessing, and certainly a lot of others that had followed it. He wondered if there was any point in salvaging the relationship now, over five years later. He thought of Arthur, and what he had said about wanting a monogamous relationship. It would be so easy to manipulate Jorge into dating him again using his intimidation blessing, but that wasn't the person he wanted to be any more. He decided he needed to prove to himself that Arthur was going to be enough for him, and that meant not trying to hook up with Jorge or Charlie or John or Theo, even if they wanted it. "We should at least try to be friends now," Rupert finally said. "It's driving our friends nuts trying to figure out which of us to invite to their events."

"Okay," Jorge agreed. "Any chance I'll see you dancing again?"

"Perhaps. It depends. I might give it a shot again if I don't get this job I'm applying for."

Jorge finally smiled when he looked at Rupert. "I hope you get it . . . even though I'd love to see you dance again."

Two days later, Rupert got dressed in a suit jacket and tie and arrived ten minutes early at ABT's offices not far from where his welcome-home dinner had been two weeks before. Security issued him a pass, and the ballet's general manager, Rick Kassel, approached him from the ABT reception desk as soon as he got off the elevator. He shook Rupert's hand. "Rachel tells me promising things, and I've looked at your letters of recommendation and vita. Come this way."

Kassel ushered him into a small conference room off the lobby with glass walls and big picture windows. "Thank you, Mr. Kassel. I was actually hired as a dancer here once several years ago."

"Please call me Rick," he said as he sat at the glass-top conference table and laid out some papers on it. "I noted that on your resume, and I actually saw you perform, I think—I remember your Wolf in *Peter and the Wolf*—ten years ago, right?"

"That's correct." Rupert smiled, hoping the connection would work in his favor.

"Hard to forget a name like Rupert Rocket," he commented.

Luke had confessed to him at first that he thought Rupert worked part-time as a porn actor. He wondered if the sour face Rick made when he mentioned his name was echoing the same sentiment. "I legally changed my name when I was seventeen," Rupert explained. "I'm kind of stuck with it now."

Rick scanned through Rupert's resume again. "You certainly have a long and varied career in dance and theatre," he commented. "And you have no desire to dance professionally again?"

"I'm sure I could." Rupert tried to make light of the suggestion that he was too much of a butterfly to stay at one job. "I've been working in development for the past four years, and I have settled into having my evenings and weekends free and sleeping in my own bed."

"The job you're applying for may require you to work overtime on occasion, and there could be travel," Rick advised. His air of concern seemed to be changing into one of disappointment.

"I'm sure I could handle it," Rupert said quickly. "I am excited about the possibility of arranging special events for ABT."

Rick looked at his resume again—as if he were searching for something he had missed. "I don't see any experience with event planning or booking agencies in your background."

"I was frequently in charge of event planning for the Brooklyn Ballet," Rupert insisted. "Benefits and galas."

"And you haven't toured, or even performed in several years . . ."

It sounded like Rick was trying to come up with excuses not to hire him. Rupert had already decided that he needed this job, and he would use his blessing to clinch it. "I've had a background in both performance and arts administration, which is what your job description said you wanted for the director of collaborations. I can start immediately. I think you should just go ahead and offer me the job."

"Well, we do have one more candidate to interview, and . . ."

Rupert was used to being insistent with the intimidation blessing. "You know I'm the right one. Offer me the job."

Rick sighed. "You're probably right, Rupert." He stood up from his chair and reached his hand out toward Rupert. "The job is yours." As Rupert stood and shook hands, Rick continued. "Arthur will forward the offer letter to you, and when you've signed it and returned it, we'll let you know your first day to report."

Through the end of the year, trying to get other artists and groups to collaborate with ABT was initially easy with his intimidation blessing to fall back on. But Rupert found that over the months between the initial agreement and the first rehearsal, and even between the first rehearsal and performance, things often fell apart. A soloist would fall sick. A musical group would get a better booking. A filmmaker would miss a deadline. Rupert wondered if the Pooka's curse was taking hold of his fate again.

But on his thirty-third birthday, Rupert was revisited by the blessing he had received at sixteen—the one that showed him the consequences of every decision he was contemplating, often years into the future. His list on his computer called it the consequence blessing. It had been the one that had tempted him to leave his mother and grandmother for the greater freedom and success he envisioned having if he moved to San Francisco to live with Fred. And it would be the one that could finally give him the success in his new job that had been eluding him, and the clarity he needed about Arthur.

CHAPTER 20: RUPERT TURNS THIRTY-FOUR

In the last eight months of 2002, Rupert's boss at the American Ballet Theatre, Rick, was getting more and more concerned about the new director of collaborations' effectiveness. He stopped by Rupert's desk several times a week to get updates on his progress with various initiatives. Rupert confided in Arthur that the stress of not yet announcing any collaborative performances was getting to him. Arthur suggested that Rupert take advantage of ABT's discounted ballet studio time to work off some of the stress in the middle of his workday. Rupert was surprised that it took Arthur's suggestion to get him to consider adding dance back into his life incrementally.

Rick had set mid-January 2003 as the time for Rupert's first review, and he wanted very much to have good news to share with him before the review. By the time he was back from the end-of-year holidays, he only had two weeks to go. But he also had a new blessing. He called Mike, the only person he could reliably get on the phone who knew about his curse and blessings, to discuss a strategy.

"This is Mike Stanton." His stepfather sounded very official when he answered Rupert's call.

"Hi, Mike. It's Rupert." Rupert was calling from his bedroom on a Saturday morning.

"Rupert," Mike acknowledged. "Did you get a new phone number?"

"Oh, yeah," Rupert said. "I'm calling you from my new mobile phone. Max and Danny got it for me for Christmas."

"Did my birthday check arrive okay?" Mike asked. "I checked yesterday, and you hadn't cashed it yet."

"Yes, it did. Thank you. I haven't been able to get to my credit union yet."

"You're at a credit union now?" Mike had gone through Rupert's finances while he had been in jail, so he knew this too was new.

"Yeah," Rupert confirmed. "That was a suggestion from Arthur. I'm still getting used to having to go to a single outlet to deposit money. I really liked all the ATMs before, but not the fees."

"Are there any other changes you've made in the past few months?"

Rupert thought back to their last conversation. It had been in May, just after he'd started the new job at ABT. "The new job isn't going so well, and I need to do something about it in the next couple of weeks, or I'm likely to be out of work again. I have a new blessing, but it takes some initiative to make it work, and I am not sure about the best thing to try."

"What is it?" Mike asked.

"I call it my consequence blessing, the same one I had at sixteen. I used it to make contact with Fred, and I started to see how that would lead to more personal and career freedom. It's sort of like a slide show in my head. As soon as I start to investigate a new possibility, I get flashes of things that are likely to happen if I pursue it. Back then, I saw all the way into the future to getting into Julliard a year and a half later. As I started to dial your number this morning, I got flashes of keeping and excelling at my job. So, I think I'm doing the right thing. But I don't know what to try. I keep failing to convince other artists to collaborate with ABT. And they're a really good, world-renowned ballet company!"

"You're counting on me to help you?" Mike sounded a bit depleted. "I have no clue about all sorts of things you are trying to do. I don't know your relationship with your boss. I don't have a clear idea of how much you have to commit to something before your blessing kicks in. I run the sales division for an aircraft manufacturer and two restaurants in Sheboygan. That's it. Arts administration is not in my bag of tricks. That's your expertise, Rupert."

"I really don't have the hang of how to activate this blessing yet," Rupert explained. "When I was in my teens, I wasn't trying to learn how to use them; I was trying to avoid them. Maybe you could send the Grogoch my way next time you see her?"

"I haven't seen her in almost two years." Mike seemed flustered now, running out of patience. "I doubt she'll be any use to you even if I do encounter her soon again."

"Okay. I'll see if I can work it out on my own." Rupert paused to decide if he should change the subject or just end the call. "I was just so sure that your help was going to be what I needed to succeed."

"Well, like you said, you're not clear on how the blessing works yet, so maybe my advice isn't what makes a difference," Mike suggested.

Rupert sighed. "You may be right. I'll try to call again in the next two weeks and let you know how it goes."

"Keep plugging away at it, Rupert. You'll figure it out."

"Have a good weekend, Mike."

Rupert finally got out of bed and showered. While he was showering, he tried to replay in his mind what had happened. He had made the call, and the visions of the future had started, while the phone was ringing. And he had seen successes in his work that allowed him to keep his job. He tried to recall if there were specific collaborations in the visions that were responsible for his new success, but he couldn't recall any details like that. Had Mike's call really been a dead end, or was he missing something?

Rupert got out of the shower and toweled off. Mike seemed to think that his relationship with Rick was important. He also wasn't sure how artistic collaborations started, or how far he had to go into it to see if it was going to work out. Before the consequence blessing, Rupert had called or written to artists to feel them out—how they felt about ABT, how open their schedule was, whether they saw any publicity value in partnering with ABT. Perhaps that was the point at which his blessing would kick in and guide him. He decided to attack the task of digging up new, outside-of-the-box possibilities on Monday instead of just babysitting the foundering ones he had managed to cobble together.

He met Arthur and Chantal for brunch on Sunday, and he used it as a brainstorming session. He asked them, "What would be a surprising and newsworthy person or group to work with ABT?"

Chantal lifted her nearly empty flute of mimosa. "George Fucking-W Bush."

"Not happening!" Rupert and Arthur said almost simultaneously from similarly half-full mouths.

Chantal set her glass down again. "Norah Jones. Justin Timberlake. The Dixie Chicks. I don't know."

Rupert paused while he swallowed his food. "I'm unlikely to get an A-list celebrity, Chantal."

Chantal refilled her glass from the pitcher in the center of their small round table in the corner. "You said you wanted to think outside-the-box, Rupert."

"How about the Minneapolis Sculpture Garden?" Arthur suggested. "It doesn't need to be an artist collaboration. It could just be a unique space."

"Hmm," Rupert hummed. "Like that opera company we saw performing at the brew pub in Brooklyn."

"Or just staging a really big ballet by joining with another ballet company," Chantal suggested. "Like that one you boys used to work at."

"The artistic director has been insisting we do more single-narrative pieces," Rupert recalled.

"The Lincoln Center management has been asking if we might work jointly with the Philharmonic," Arthur recalled.

"Maybe you could get a jazz or blues group to work with one of your choreographers," Chantal suggested.

"Or even just some other producing organization in St. Louis or Los Angeles or even at a university," Arthur mentioned. "It could be just a single performance or an annual tradition."

Rupert started writing down all the ideas on a couple of napkins and continued onto a third before the pitcher was empty and the plates were clean. He said his goodbyes on the sidewalk outside the café and headed into the subway. When he got home, he rushed to his computer and copied down all the ideas into an email he sent to his work email. The next day when he got to work, he kept putting Rick off as he contacted new potential partners. With each phone call, he started to see visions of referrals to other artists, timelines by which a group might be ready, specific pieces to focus on with collaborator targets. In just one case, Rupert started talking to a theatre producer and imagined repeatedly calling the man and getting no response. *I'm not going to waste my time there,* Rupert smugly observed.

By the time his review came on January 17, 2003, Rupert had already reported on two contracts and three verbal agreements for collaborations with ABT in the next two years. Rick complimented his creativity and industriousness and gave Rupert praise as well for his attitude and his improved effectiveness in his job. Rupert reiterated his desire to help the ABT grow, and he immediately saw flashes of great reviews and a bonus at the end of the year. He smiled, believing that 2003 was going to be one of his better years.

He called Mike and Danny with the good news and then grabbed his athletic bag and headed over to the ballet studio to stretch and take another class. When he returned, he stopped by Arthur's desk and asked him to dinner that night to celebrate. Rupert suggested a very fancy Italian restaurant in Midtown.

On his way there, Rupert paused in front of a bodega with flowers for sale and had a vision of spoiling Arthur with surprises and gifts until he finally agreed to take him back. He settled on a pink rose after staring at a bucket full of red ones for a couple of minutes. He carried it carefully into the restaurant, down the stairs to the lobby and waited with the rose behind his back, watching other patrons enter.

When Arthur appeared on the stairs to meet him, the light from above made him look like an angel descending through the clouds. Rupert whipped the rose out in front of himself and held it out for Arthur as he approached. "You didn't have to do that." Arthur smelled the rose and smiled before giving Rupert a hug. "Congratulations on doing so well at your job, you get to keep it!"

When they broke out of the hug, Rupert kept a hand on Arthur's shoulder. "Thank you so much for helping me get the job *and* keep it. I owe you."

The maître d' led the two of them past the live jazz band and the artificial waterfall to a large corner booth farthest from the entrance. The two of them scooted in from opposite sides and sat very close together in the middle. Arthur laid his rose down on the table and looked up at Rupert. "It was my selfish pleasure . . . to keep you employed, so you could take me out to expensive restaurants and buy me flowers." He chuckled.

"You were also," Rupert added, "instrumental in the defense strategy that freed me from prison. I'm not forgetting that either."

"Your lawyer thought it was a good idea," Arthur explained. "I agreed. I was happy to help."

"I was thinking about what you told me." Rupert stopped and opened his menu. He was trying to remember how long ago it had been. Everything before his incarceration was blending together into one collage.

"Any particular thing?" Arthur asked as he opened his menu as well.

"About wanting to wait until I could date you exclusively."

"I was kidding about that." Arthur put down his menu.

"You were?" Rupert put down his menu too.

"You're a hot, young guy," Arthur explained. "I really don't expect you to want to settle down anytime soon."

"Hmm." Rupert wasn't sure how to respond. As a performer, he had long ago gotten used to being objectified for his looks. It felt more hurtful this time that someone he cared about was assuming he was superficial, that the time they had spent dating meant nothing to him. "What would you say if I told you I have decided, this year, to be celibate until you believe that I am really ready to commit to monogamy?"

There was silence for at least half a minute. Their waitress saw their menus down as a signal and came over to take their orders. Once she left, Arthur stared at the patch of tablecloth before him where the menu had been, just to the left of his rose. He continued to stare at it silently for almost two minutes. Rupert waited.

"I was kind of hurt when you came back from your great-uncle's funeral and told me about Trevor," Arthur began. He paused for a moment before continuing. "I didn't have any right to be. We had never talked about monogamy."

"It was a reasonable assumption," Rupert argued.

"It was . . . eye-opening for me." Arthur finally turned to look at Rupert. "I often let my feelings get ahead of the reality of my relationships. I have a very active fantasy life."

Rupert wasn't sure if he had finished his thought. "Okay."

At that point, the waitress came and poured a splash of wine into Rupert's glass. He swirled it, smelled it, and tasted it like a sommelier would. He nodded, and the waitress poured glasses for both of them, set the bottle on the table, and left again. Rupert took another sip of the wine.

Arthur ignored the wine and looked over at his rose again. "I guess what I'm trying to say is that I'm concerned it's unrealistic and unreasonable of me to expect anyone . . . to only have sex with me."

"I suspect," Rupert said as he grabbed Arthur's closer hand under the tabletop, "that desire can occur to anyone. The trick is just getting it to happen for both guys at the same time."

"Yeah?" Arthur turned to look at Rupert again.

"I think I'm getting there," Rupert announced. "I haven't had sex with anyone since my birthday."

"Three weeks," Arthur teased sarcastically. "That's impressive."

"And there hasn't been anyone but you or that one slip with Trevor since the birthday before that."

Arthur squeezed Rupert's thigh under the table. "Not even while you were in prison?"

"A prison is not a very sexy environment, despite what you may have heard." Rupert moved Arthur's hand off his leg and scooted out around the table. "I have to go pee. I'll be right back."

Rupert wound his way around the tables and the waterfall and past the jazz band to the rest room. It was pretty empty, and only one other gentleman entered once he was done at the urinal and washing his hands. He dried them and headed back out into the dining area. By the time he got around the waterfall, he could see someone sitting on the edge of his booth near Arthur. Within seconds, the

219

short stature, the short reddish-gray hair, and the dark-green, full-length dress all came together, and he rushed the rest of the way back.

When he was standing over her, Rupert tried to keep his tone to an insistent whisper. "What the hell are you doing here?"

The Pooka turned her head slowly to look up at Rupert. The disfigurement of her eyes and nose was etched into his memory. "I was here dining with a friend, and I saw you were here, but you got up to leave as I was approaching. Your charming dinner companion here offered to let me wait here for your return."

"She says she's a family friend visiting from Wisconsin," Arthur offered.

"Yes, Rupert and I go back many, many years," she called back to Arthur.

Rupert looked around at all the well-dressed patrons around them. Some were already starting to stare. "I think you should leave . . . now!"

She ignored his demand and smiled back at Arthur. "I was telling Arthur here, how amazing it was that you managed to be acquitted of charges brought by the FBI. It's too bad you had to spend so many months in jail before your trial."

"Arthur," Rupert whispered. "She is not a family friend. Don't listen to anything she tells you."

"Oh, Rupert!" The Pooka pretended to be hurt by his accusation. "I just wanted to pass along news from my protégé Patricia. She is so looking forward to you getting everything you deserve."

"She's still alive?" Rupert asked.

"Oh, yes." the Pooka continued to taunt. "She is excited about an even more dramatic change in your fortunes due any day now. You won't be relying on that old gift from my sister anymore." She rose and stood next to Rupert and continued soft enough for only Rupert to hear. "As with Zelda and your mother, your luck will eventually . . . run out."

She quickly walked away and was lost behind the waterfall before Rupert turned back to look at Arthur.

"I'm a little confused," Arthur said.

Rupert quickly took his seat again.

"You say she's not really a family friend. So how does she know so much about you?"

Rupert tried to think of an excuse that would keep Arthur from taking what she had said seriously. "She's one of my crazier fans. She even showed up at my mother's funeral."

"Do you know her name?" Arthur asked.

Rupert decided that the less Arthur knew about the Pooka, the better. "I don't really."

"Do you know her sister . . . the one she said who gave you a gift?" Arthur looked innocently curious, as if it were just a matter of having kooky relatives.

"She was a friend of my grandmother's from when I was a young boy," Rupert admitted. "I've only seen her once since then."

"She also said something about someone named Patricia, and you seemed surprised she was still alive."

"Uh, Patricia has . . . dementia, so I don't put much stock in anything she says. She has to be over eighty by now. The woman you were talking to takes care of her back in Sheboygan, I think."

"Well, it was nice that she came over to say hello," Arthur suggested. "I think she meant well, even if she was intruding."

Rupert decided not to indulge Arthur's curiosity about the Pooka. It would only scare Arthur. By the time their food came, the topic of conversation had shifted back to weekend plans. Arthur was getting together with friends from Alvin Ailey on Saturday, so Rupert proposed meeting for a Sunday matinee movie.

"That sounds nice," Arthur said. "Just you and me. Like a date?"

"Like a platonic date, yes," Rupert corrected.

"What movie are we going to see?"

"Let me surprise you," Rupert requested.

Over the course of the spring, Rupert continued to ask his younger friend out on social dates, a process that they described to their baffled friends as courting. Luke, Danny, Michaela, Denise, Jorge, and Theo thought it was quirky but sweet. Everyone else thought they were crazy, especially because they had been intimate before. "We are starting over," Rupert would explain. "I'm hoping

221

it becomes more intimate soon, but I'm willing to wait."

By the middle of summer, when Rupert invited Arthur to drive with him to a rental cabin in the Finger Lakes resort area in upstate New York, a moonlight swim had been the turning point. And from then until the end of the year, Arthur and Rupert spent two to five nights a week together and most of their weekends.

A court in Massachusetts had declared that same-sex couples in the state could get married, but Rupert took little comfort in the news. There were too many states still scrambling to outlaw gay marriage, and the wrong political wind could easily abolish the right in Massachusetts as well.

As predicted, Rick offered Rupert the bonus in November to be paid in January. Since the Pooka had managed to identify Arthur, Rupert occasionally checked with Arthur. He wanted to know if she might have cornered him somewhere and put a bug in his ear.

On the morning of December 25th, Arthur stole out to the living room where his coat was lying to fetch two envelopes. He hopped back under the covers with them and handed them one by one to Rupert. "This one is for Christmas, and this one is for your thirty-fourth birthday, old man!"

The Christmas envelope was decorated with candy-cane, holly, and little snowman stickers, and Rupert pulled out a pair of tickets to go see *Wicked* on Broadway in March. "I got those discounted since Denise is in the show."

Rupert laughed and held Arthur tighter. "Thank you so much, Arthur."

"Open the other one."

The birthday envelope had heart and birthday-cake and gift-box stickers on it. Rupert pulled a folder out that said it was from Atlantis Events. Inside it was a reservation for a stateroom portside for two on a gay February cruise around the Caribbean. Rupert kissed Arthur hard on the lips. He turned to glance at his alarm clock. It was five after nine o'clock. It was difficult finding the exact moment when his blessings switched, but he decided to ask any way.

"Arthur," he said as he pulled away slightly, "do you love me?"

Arthur got an impish grin that bordered on embarrassment. "I guess I do."

Rupert kissed him again. He didn't care whether his next blessing had kicked in yet or not.

CHAPTER 21: RUPERT TURNS THIRTY-SIX

Throughout the year of Rupert's honesty blessing, it was clear to Rupert, just by asking, that Arthur wanted to spend as much time as possible with him. Both had demanding jobs at ABT, but Rupert still had to frequently remind Arthur that he should be at his desk to help his boss, Rachel, not hanging out at Rupert's desk.

In their free time, they went to Broadway shows; they walked in Central, Prospect, or Riverside Park; they went to dance performances, comedy and improv shows, piano recitals, movies, and even theme parks in New Jersey. And over the course of those outings, they ended up at night either at Rupert's apartment in Williamsburg or Arthur's apartment in Harlem, about forty-five minutes and two train lines apart.

As with many new couples, Arthur and Rupert found that pragmatism had pushed them toward living together. Arthur had started wearing contacts instead of glasses, and he was always leaving his case or his cleaning supplies at the other apartment. Rupert was most frustrated that Arthur only had one umbrella, for those sudden showers when he'd left his own umbrella in Williamsburg. Arthur ran out of Rupert's soy milk. Rupert didn't remember to make ice cubes until after he'd arrived there with an overheated Arthur craving them. Because they were so different in height, nothing that fit one fit the other except for socks. Arthur ended up taking his loofah, his contact supplies, his iPod, a change of clothes, his umbrella, his phone charger, the silicon lube he preferred, and an apple in his backpack when they would go out. Rupert tried to cram his briefcase with a small bottle of his soy milk, his supplements, his charger, a change or two of clothes, his swimsuit and workout towel, his ballet shoes and tights, and whatever book he was reading.

"We look like refugees!" Rupert shouted in exasperation when he and Arthur met for ABT's performance at Lincoln Center one night in October. His briefcase was almost bursting at the seams and was heavy. He also had a bag of groceries because the grocery stores in both their neighborhoods would be closed after the performance.

Arthur had on a suit and tie, carried a stuffed briefcase with his laptop and reports to review overnight, and shouldered a very full backpack of supplies for after the performance and the following morning. "We can just leave everything at the coat check." This had become Arthur's standard response to Rupert's ongoing frustration.

"Okay. I'll buy you a second loofah to keep at my place."

"It's not practical to duplicate half our possessions to keep at the other apartment," Arthur finally conceded.

Rupert was generally pretty careful about what he asked people during the year of his honesty blessing, but he was so exasperated, he just blurted out, "What do you think we should do about it?"

As Arthur turned away to craft a response, Rupert immediately regretted his impulsive use of his honesty blessing. "Well, we have to either learn to live without certain things, or we really need to consider living together."

"Is that something you really want to do?" Rupert knew that follow-up questions like that often revealed more ambivalence.

"I . . . I'm not sure," Arthur said slowly. "It is a big step, but we're practically living together now any way."

Rupert decided, despite his best efforts, he was still leaning too heavily on his blessings. Every time he invoked the honesty blessing, for example, *he* got all the information on which to base a decision. At that moment, Arthur was probably afraid to be more definitive, because he didn't know how Rupert felt. "I love spending time with you, Arthur. I love you, and I want you to be happy. The only thing about sharing the same home with you that concerns me is having time to myself, to meet with my friends, or even just to be alone."

Arthur smiled. "I want the same thing. We can work that out. You've already done that with me. When you had an early meeting last week and wanted to go to bed early, for example."

Rupert hugged him. "Whether we've used it very often or not, we've still had our own domain to retreat to. Just the idea of that possibility takes some pressure off."

"We won't be able to get further apart than a room apart when we're both home," Arthur argued, still holding tightly to Rupert. "You can still leave, if you need more separation, and I can always move out temporarily or forever, if we decide it's not working. It's not a permanent decision."

At that point in 2004, countries all over the world had started decriminalizing homosexual sex, and the U.S. Supreme Court (in Lawrence v. Texas) struck down the last remaining U.S. sodomy laws. Countries had started prohibiting discrimination based on sexual orientation. The U.S. Census Bureau reported that there were gay heads-of-household in over ninety-three percent of the country's counties. Belgium and several Canadian provinces joined the Netherlands in allowing same-sex couples to marry. The City of San Francisco married thousands of gay couples. Some countries and states were at least allowing separate-but-equal accommodation in the form of civil unions or domestic partnerships.

And then the California Supreme Court voided all the same-sex marriage licenses. And several states passed laws explicitly banning same-sex marriage. At this point in time, the United States still seemed pretty hostile to two gay men marrying.

Rupert took in what Arthur said. Living together was the pinnacle of commitment in gay relationships that started with a new toothbrush on the bathroom sink, and he wasn't sure if he was ready. It had so much weight to it. He knew couples like Trevor and Samantha who had entered into cohabitation with no worries, no drama. It was not "the big step" for them. Marriage was.

His grandmother Zelda had always called marriage, *eine Verbindung,* a joining or binding. To her it had been an irrevocable decision that, however lightly it was entered, paid massive dividends. It was the reason, on that fateful night when he was fifteen, that she had decided to reject his announcement of being gay. She claimed it was tantamount to admitting that her grandson would never know joy or security.

When Danny and Max had moved in together, Rupert's friends all organized a party to celebrate the commitment. They had brought them gifts. They had dressed up. Max had even bought them matching rings to wear. It was the impulse of marriage, even without the legal recognition.

And he remembered reading in his mother's journal, in the years Rupert had been living in San Francisco and then going to Julliard, her periodic returns to one particular aspect of the Pooka's curse. She blamed it for Fred getting cold feet. She blamed it for her son turning out gay. At Patricia Connor's urging, the Pooka had set forces in motion that would let no other Kellermans marry. Rupert was the last survivor and would remain the last.

It took a couple of weeks, two phone calls with Mike, and the advice of almost all of his friends for Rupert to agree to let Arthur move into his apartment. As the boxes started arriving in his living room, Rupert glanced over at his computer. Arthur didn't want to keep lugging his laptop home from work, so Rupert had agreed to let him use his home computer after the move. And that was the computer where he kept his list of blessings. Whether or not he was successful in hiding it under an innocuous file name, Rupert knew in time, it was only fair to tell Arthur about the Grogoch and the blessings and warn him about the Pooka and her curse.

Twice while Rupert was watching Arthur unpack boxes and offering advice about where to put things, he started to bring up his blessings and curses. He tried by starting with meeting with the Pooka at the Italian restaurant, but then he backed down. He tried drawing Arthur's attention to how he couldn't lie to him (due to his honesty blessing), and Arthur laughed it off saying, "Why would I?"

Once Arthur took a break from packing to rest in their bed, Rupert pulled up his blessing list on his computer. He started looking at what he could expect in the coming years, and he started to believe he could minimize the coincidences of all of the next ten years, but after those, the laughter blessing would be hard to avoid explaining. He had plenty of time to find the right time to reveal that secret. He closed the file, turned off the computer, and headed into the bedroom to cuddle his new domestic partner.

In December, Rupert's great-aunt Ingrid was checked into the hospital with jaundice, and by January, she died of liver failure. His second cousins, children of Ingrid's older siblings, invited Rupert to come for a memorial service, but since Rupert didn't know any of the other attendees well, and going would put him too geographically close to Trevor and his willing temptation, he ordered a floral arrangement and sent his regrets.

By January, Rupert's job was going well, he and Arthur were getting along well, and he felt his performance at ballet classes would improve if he got in better shape. As a result, he started going to the gym more often, and for longer workouts. He took a second dance class, in jazz and modern styles. and he swam laps more often. Rupert had boundless energy, thanks to the return of his strength blessing, and within a couple of months, he wasn't fitting into some of his shirts, jackets, and pants.

Arthur watched Rupert pull clothes for spring out of their closet, hold them up or occasionally try them on, and then usually throw them into a growing heap on the bedroom floor. "Maybe you need to tone down your workouts," Arthur gently suggested. "You're getting so big, we're going to have to get you an entirely new wardrobe."

Rupert stopped sorting for a moment and looked at himself in the full-length mirror. He remembered this happening when he was fourteen–starting out thinking he would just get in a little bit better shape, and then overdoing it and getting the proportions and definition of a competitive bodybuilder. He started to get concerned that bulking up had reduced his flexibility, but he stretched and realized that dance and swimming had kept him limber. Maybe closer to a really buff Olympic gymnast. "You think I'm getting too big?"

Arthur chuckled. "I love you, sweetie, in whatever size you come in. I don't mind that people ogle you wherever we go."

Over the course of the spring and early summer, Rupert worked hard at trimming down a little and eating less. He was able to drop twenty pounds and increase the definition of his muscles still more. Arthur admitted this look was sexier to him, so Rupert fought the urge to bulk up even harder and usually succeeded. The two of them went to Fire Island once with Max and Danny, and Rupert was getting hit on several times per hour. Arthur just laughed at it. Rupert was glad he wasn't getting jealous.

Their apartment was full of their friends when their one-year cohabitation anniversary came up in December. In addition to celebrating "one year without breaking up," as Chantal put it, the celebrants were happy that all of Canada, Spain, and California had made it legal for same-sex couples to marry. Denise and Michaela, who had also moved in together in the past year, were talking about going to California to get married.

When Rupert heard that, he pulled Arthur aside and asked, "You heard about Denise and Michaela going to California?"

"Yes." Arthur seemed confused about why Rupert was asking.

"Is that something that you . . .?" Rupert had trouble finishing the question. It started to seem desperate or insincere to suggest just because it was possible.

Arthur hugged Rupert. "I'm very happy the way we are, Rupert. I don't need a license to validate our relationship. You're really good to me, and I love you."

"I love you too," Rupert echoed. "There was something else I wanted to bring up."

Arthur remained in his embrace. "You want to go somewhere for your birthday?"

"It's possible," Rupert admitted, "but I wanted to let you know about something that is likely to happen next year."

"Does this have to do with work?" He had told Arthur about upcoming work trips to meet with more arts groups, so that too would change his schedule and availability starting in 2006. Arthur pulled out of the hug and looked up at Rupert. "This doesn't have anything to do with that family thing, does it?"

Rupert's jaw dropped. "I'm not sure what you mean. What family thing?"

"Those two crazy old ladies," Arthur replied. "One of them ran into us two years ago at that restaurant in Midtown, remember?"

"No, I'm thinking about turning my job at ABT into a part-time job, so I can pursue performing, maybe modeling."

"Well, you've certainly got the looks and the body now," Arthur commented. "You're not concerned about the decrease in income."

"I think next year will be good for my income, if I can get in front of more people."

Rupert was anticipating his hypersexuality blessing, where, after he turned thirty-six, everyone he met would feel attracted to him, even if they weren't usually attracted to men. It had been a bit overwhelming when he was thirteen, because he didn't know how to manage other people's (especially adults') expectations. Mike had been especially drawn to him. At least his mother's and grandmother's approaches were more affectionate, with frequent kissing. That had been the first time he had noticed Trevor's attraction to him. But back then Trevor was so timid, it was easy enough to ignore his overly subtle advances.

Rupert was developing a plan that he could use his new, sexier body and his sexual blessing to try to expand the Rupert Rocket brand from dance to modeling. He had learned at thirteen that the blessing worked with images of him as well as in-person encounters. He had started to research photographers and modeling agencies in New York, and he was planning to do a portfolio shoot in the first week of January.

On Christmas morning, Rupert and Arthur opened gifts together and begged off all family and friend invitations at Rupert's request. He said he just wanted to have a quiet holiday, but it was also an opportunity to gauge Arthur's tolerance for all the sexual advances he might receive in his presence.

It was a brisk but sunny day in New York City on December 31, 2005. Both Arthur and Rupert dressed warmly in layers. They had spent the previous week holed up in their apartment, and Rupert finally agreed to go out on New Year's Eve. They went to the epicenter of the celebration in Times Square in the early afternoon and managed to get a spot on 46th Street with a good view of the ball.

On the way there, Rupert found that the easiest way to keep from emboldening people to approach him was to keep his head down and not make eye contact with them. This didn't necessarily stop everyone, but social conditioning made it hard for many people to ingratiate themselves to a stranger while others were watching. Having Arthur along to kiss and hold also seemed to be a deterrent for the bolder strangers.

By six o'clock, it was dark, and the effects of his sexual blessing seemed to hold members of the nearby crowd to admiring looks. He and Arthur were able to eat the sandwiches they had brought for dinner without being disturbed. Rupert watched Arthur as he scanned the crowd around them.

Arthur finished chewing and then set his sandwich down in his lap. "Is it my imagination, or are more people staring at you than usual?"

"Give me a kiss," Rupert suggested.

"You don't have to ask me twice." Arthur gave him a long, lingering kiss.

When Rupert pulled out of it, he turned Arthur's head to look out at the crowd. "See. They're not staring right now. You just give me a kiss or a hug if you think I'm getting too much attention, and they'll back off."

Arthur took advantage of Rupert's advice many times before midnight and the ball drop. Even the most die-hard admirers were reduced to infrequent furtive glances in Rupert's direction. During the count down, everyone was looking up at the ball. Rupert cuddled closer to Arthur for warmth. Another long kiss right at midnight lasted almost a full minute.

"Happy 2006, sexy!" Arthur shouted over the noisemakers and horns and shouts.

"Happy new year!" Rupert shouted back. "Let's head to the subway!"

Once they fought through the huge throng in the square and on the subway platform, they eventually got on a train home to Brooklyn. The subway car was also fairly noisy, but the two of them could speak without shouting.

Rupert ducked down slightly to look directly into Arthur's eyes. "So you were okay with all the attention and propositions I was getting today?"

Arthur turned to kiss Rupert on the cheek. "If I know you're coming home with me," he replied slowly, "I don't care how many people throw themselves at you."

They stayed quiet until they got out to change trains. Rupert couldn't stop smiling at Arthur, because he felt so lucky to have a lover who didn't get jealous.

"What are you smiling at?"

"My smart, sexy, wonderful boyfriend," Rupert said with a goofy tone and expression. "Can't you tell?"

"You're serious about launching a career as a model at thirty-six?" Arthur asked. "Most guys start in their teens."

Rupert tousled Arthur's hair and gave him a one-armed hug. "I have a good feeling about it. If it doesn't work out, at least I'll have some good photos to show for it."

When back at ABT after the holidays, Rupert's boss, Rick, said Rupert could cut down his hours as long as he achieved his target goals. Rupert called a fashion photographer named Horst like his great-uncle, and they talked about Germany and working in theatre, and Rupert booked him for a three-hour photo shoot the following Saturday afternoon. Arthur volunteered to go with him as a consultant on Rupert's wardrobe, hairstyles, and makeup.

Horst's loft was in downtown Manhattan in the meatpacking district on West 13th Street. Rupert and Arthur walked by the non-descript entrance several times before determining they had the right one. They were buzzed in and climbed the creaking wooden stairs to the second floor. They knocked on a metal door set into a brick wall. A lean athletic man close to Arthur's age with blue eyes and a light-brown moustache opened the door.

"Beautiful greetings!" Horst called out in German. "It is a great pleasure to meet the very honored Rupert Rocket!" He gestured for the two of them to enter.

"I don't recall giving you my surname," Rupert said carefully in English.

"Ah," Horst said as he switched to English, "I looked up your phone number on the Internet, and then I looked at reviews of your performance work in a Web browser."

Arthur was familiar with more of the online computer applications, so he told Horst, "I've been trying to get him to use his mobile phone more."

"That would be harder to identify," Horst conceded. "Follow me, please."

They walked through a small foyer with a tiny refrigerator, a wooden folding chair, and a sofa from the 1970s and into a huge room. It was brightly lit with spotlights and floodlights, and there were interesting pieces of furniture scattered around, including an armoire with one of its doors open. There was a vanity with a mirror. There was a motorcycle. And there was a huge roll of white paper or screen that unrolled from a huge roller attached to the high ceiling and spread out covering several feet of gray, cement flooring. Donna Summers' disco music blared from a raised room in the rear accessible from a catwalk ringing the room on three sides.

"You can put your bags and your changes of clothings over there." Horst gestured toward a pink-upholstered divan.

As soon as they had set down everything they were carrying, Horst pulled Rupert away by the arm toward the white backdrop. "Don't you want me to put on makeup or get changed?" Rupert protested.

"No," Horst said very curtly as he continued to haul Rupert over. "We will start with no makeup, and your usual, ordinary clothings."

Rupert tried to at least smooth his hair down as he walked. Horst let go, turned on some additional lights, and stepped behind a small camera on a tripod. He gestured for Rupert to back up. "Two steps more," he indicated.

"Do you want me to pose?" Rupert asked when he came to a halt. "I've never done this before."

"Just be your sexy self for now," Horst advised. "I am trying to decide how much to expose you."

Rupert leaned forward to try to squint through the glaring lights to see Horst. "You're going to do what to me?"

"Oh." Horst stepped out from behind the camera. "I meant that I need to adjust the film exposure. Some of the English phrases still confuse me." He switched to German. "Is it okay if I just give you directions in German?"

"That's satisfactory," Rupert answered in German.

Over the course of nearly four hours there, Horst shot Rupert from dozens of angles, in varying states of undress, draped over or otherwise posing with the motorcycle and several pieces of furniture. Horst dwelt a bit longer than necessary touching Rupert's face, hair, arms, and crotch, but it seemed to be within common definitions of professionalism.

When they were done, all three men were exhausted. Horst had been standing or dashing about. Rupert had been holding sometimes very precarious poses for several minutes at a time. Arthur helped Horst move the furniture, retouched Rupert's makeup and hair, and brought out sodas from the small refrigerator in the foyer periodically.

"I have a bed upstairs," Horst said in German out of nowhere.

Rupert looked at him suspiciously. "That's good, I guess," he replied in English.

"No," Horst continued. "I was wondering if you and the boy wanted to take some more revealing photos up there . . . on the bed."

"What is he saying?" Arthur whispered.

"I think we can start with just the fashion shots for now, Horst." Rupert started repacking his changes of clothing.

"I will call you when the proof sheets are ready," Horst finally switched to English as well. "Probably in four or maybe five days. I can show them at agencies I work for, yes?"

"Sure," Rupert replied. "That would be fine. Thank you."

Horst switched back to German as Arthur started carrying the suitcase of clothes back toward the foyer. "And if you want the full, sexy, naked shots later, just call me, and we will find time."

Horst kissed Rupert on the lips and then awkwardly patted him on the back. Rupert picked up Arthur's backpack and followed Arthur out. "I'll wait for your call about the proofs," he called back over his shoulder.

When Arthur and Rupert arrived home after work three days later, there was a message from Horst. He asked Rupert to come see the proofs at a different address than the one on 13th Street, at ten-thirty the following morning. It was an ordinary office building near Times Square, and when the elevator doors opened, Rupert stepped into a lobby crowded with younger models dwarfed by huge posters of other models on the walls. Everyone turned to stare at Rupert when he arrived.

Horst appeared from a hallway off to one side. "Rupert Rocket, follow me please!" he called as he gestured awkwardly with his hand.

Horst led him back into a dark office lit only by a candelabrum and a desk lamp. "This is him," Horst announced as they took seats in front of the desk.

"You were right," a woman with a very deep voice commented from behind the desk. When she leaned forward and caught the light, Rupert saw a very attractive woman in her forties with nicely understated makeup wearing a solid cream blouse. "He is even more tasty in person."

Rupert noticed proof sheets filled with his photos spread out on the woman's desk. "Hello," he said.

She turned to address Horst. "I've circled the ones I want you to print, but I want to be there for the next shoot, and I may want to bring one of our fashion clients too."

"He can do editorial," Horst offered. "He was a dancer and an actor."

She was leaning on her forearms on the proofs and looked up briefly at Rupert. "How tall?"

"Six-two," Rupert replied.

"And that sexy voice too," the woman commented. "He could do film!"

"I'm sorry," Rupert said. "I appreciate the compliments, but who are you?"

The woman cackled, and Horst joined her in laughter. "That's Margot," Horst finally explained. "She wants to be your agent, and you won't find anyone better, so just sign the damn contract."

CHAPTER 22: RUPERT TURNS THIRTY-EIGHT

Rupert had already, with only a cursory understanding of what was going on at thirteen and with three weeks interacting with people at ABT and on the street, understood something important about his hypersexuality blessing: People reacted differently to being in the presence of someone sexually attractive. The range of reactions broadened considerably when it fought against a long-standing sexual orientation or committed, monogamous relationship. The single gay and bi men (more than half the men Rupert met) would proposition him, with varying degrees of persistence. Those who were in relationships would want to hang around him, touch him casually, and encourage going away alone with him without saying specifically why. Lifelong lesbians were about the only women who could ignore Rupert after a casual glance. Others would "accidentally" brush up against him, compliment him repeatedly, demand a hug or a kiss, or even describe out loud what they would like to do to him.

Margot, the modeling agent Horst had taken Rupert to meet, was more of a voyeur. Both in Rupert's initial go-see with Horst and at Rupert's second photo shoot with Horst, Margot always kept her distance, always asking an assistant to take his measurements, fix his hair or makeup, or give him a new outfit to put on. Margot's attention rarely waivered from watching Rupert, even when she was talking to Horst, an assistant, or her client, Shannon Baxter. Shannon was a promotion director for an international line of leisurewear, and Rupert guessed she was married, because she limited herself to stroking the fabric of Rupert's clothing (only while he was in it), purportedly to assess the garment's composition.

When the shoot was finally over after two hours, Rupert shook hands with Margot and Shannon and couldn't escape a hug from Horst. He shouldered the backpack and left. He grabbed a burrito from a taqueria just south of Union Square on his nine-block walk back to ABT. The snow had once again melted, but a cold late-January wind blew, and Rupert wished he had packed earmuffs or a cap. Rupert marveled that there were still diehard chess players waiting for opponents at the outdoor chess tables in the park.

As soon as he arrived back at the office, Rick zipped past saying he was going into a meeting and would check in with him after it. Rupert hung his coat on the coat rack and stowed his backpack in the empty bottom drawer of his desk. He sat down and turned on his computer monitor, and before his desktop lit up, Arthur was already at his desk. "How did the shoot go, sexy?"

Rupert grinned. "You can't keep abandoning Rachel," he chided.

"She's in a meeting," Arthur maintained. "So, what happened?"

Rupert chuckled. "They took more pictures. I did one in a tuxedo, one in this one-piece thing they called a romper, and all the others were in shorts or swimsuits."

"Who was there?" Arthur sat on the corner of Rupert's desk.

"Just Horst, Margot, two assistants I'd never met, a makeup artist, a hairstylist, a set decorator, and one of Margot's clients. Someone named Shannon. I'm supposed to go over to her office for a screen test at some point next week."

Arthur's jaw dropped. He looked surprised and then slowly more elated. "You already booked work?"

"It's essentially an audition," Rupert explained. "I don't even know what it's for yet. Her company does leisurewear and . . . evidently, swimwear."

Arthur leaned in closer and started whispering. "They're meeting now to discuss your Storm King Art Center proposal."

"I should be in there to pitch it," Rupert pleaded.

Arthur shook his head and whispered, "Rachel said it's too distracting having you in review meetings. She wants the proposal to speak for itself."

As with Rupert's dominance blessing, the hypersexuality blessing also had as much of a tendency to drive people away from him as to attract them. In subway cars, in work meetings, at restaurants with Arthur, and on the street, there were a minority of people who reacted by turning away or running away. The idea that they found Rupert sexy caused them too much distress to stay in his presence.

Rick did stop by after the review meeting. He pulled up a chair next to Rupert's desk. He seemed to be working a little too hard at smiling. "Rupert. Rupert. I should let you know first, that we decided to give you the green light to negotiate a collaboration contract with the Storm King Art Center."

"That's great," Rupert inserted as Rick continued to talk.

"And we tabled discussion of the proposal for the Tennessee Performing Arts Center. I've got notes of other information we want you to gather that I'll email you about."

"Okay," Rupert inserted in the brief pause Rick took to breathe.

"And, we are going ahead with plans to increase our administrative staff. Because you are just here twenty hours a week now, we were hoping we might encourage you to work remotely from now on—from home. You work pretty independently already, and it would save you a commute."

Rupert liked the idea of coming into the office regularly. He appreciated all the familiar faces of the staff and dancers at ABT. He had gotten used to eating his lunch at some of the places just south of there in Union Square. He had only ever heard of the extraordinary circumstance of working remotely when someone with unique expertise had kids or lived too far to commute. He was single and could get to the office from Brooklyn in thirty-five minutes usually. "My commute is fine, and I don't have a photocopier at home," Rupert argued.

Rick leaned in and lowered his tone. "I'm sorry, Rupert. We need this space for new hires. You can email me anything you need photocopied, and we can print it out and copy it here. I.T. will set you up with a log-on so you can access your work email at home, and we can send any packages or letters that come for you here home with Arthur every day."

Rupert finally conceded and agreed to say his semi-goodbyes that Friday, starting to work from home the following Monday. It became a bit hard to watch

Arthur leave for work in the mornings and to then shave and sit down at his computer.

Fortunately, his mostly unintentional exile was broken up with calls from Margot and urgent requests that he show up somewhere, sometimes at her office in Times Square, or at clients' elsewhere in Manhattan or Queens. He successfully booked a shoot for a men's jewelry catalog. Shannon used Rupert on some sale flyers and then offered to book him for the whole season. In between commercials and photo shoots and store appearances for her, he also worked for a real estate brokerage, medical education videos, and a perfume commercial (in which he danced in tights). As Fashion Week approached, Margot was sending him out to various designers' studios almost every day either for a go-see or a fitting. Three of them ended up using him, and Margot and one of her other agents spent hours the weekend before the show training him to walk on a runway the correct way.

In the makeup and changing rooms at Fashion Week was the first time he had worked with more than one model. And they were all sexy and gorgeous. And they were often wearing nothing but a dance belt when they were changing. And as soon as the show was over, they lined up to talk to Rupert. He excused himself after the second runway show and called Arthur on his cell phone, but it went to his voicemail. "Arthur, I just want you to know that there is a crowd of nearly naked male fashion models surrounding me right now, and I am looking forward to seeing you tonight."

One with an Australian accent sat in his lap as soon as he ended the call. "I haven't seen you around before." He offered his hand. "I'm Ian."

Rupert shook his hand. "Hi, Ian. I'm Rupert. It was nice working with you. I have to finish changing, so . . ."

Ian got up immediately. "No problem, mate. Maybe we can go get a drink when you're changed."

Another young, tall, muscular man still wearing only the swimsuit he had worn in the final promenade squatted down beside Rupert's stool. "I'm staying at a penthouse overlooking the harbor," he said in a British accent as he put his hand on Rupert's knee.

"That's great," Rupert commented as he tried to put on his socks.

"We could have it all to ourselves," the model continued.

"You have an amazing body!" another of the models called out.

"Thank you." Rupert struggled to put on his shoes without looking up at all the men crowding around. "I have a boyfriend."

"You can bring him along," the British model insisted.

Another model elbowed his way in front of Rupert. "I want you all to myself."

A fourth model called over his shoulder, "You are so sexy. Why are you covering up with all those clothes?"

"Sorry, guys." Rupert got up and started pushing his way through his new fans. "I have to get going, but maybe I'll see some of you at one of the other shows."

As he made his way out of the tent, he heard one of the male models shout, "Which other shows are you working?"

By the end of the year, Rupert had signed a twelve-month spokesmodel contract, had shot a series of commercials for a telecom company, and appeared in a plethora of catalogs. He had been sent off to Italy, Spain, France, and England for photo shoots and fashion shows. Margot was even starting to get interest from production companies in Hollywood. Rupert worried that they wouldn't be so interested in him once the hypersexuality blessing ended on Christmas morning. On Christmas Eve, as they were getting into bed, Rupert told Arthur that even if being a model and actor had made him crazy rich, he was considering retiring and going back to working at ABT.

Arthur climbed onto Rupert straddling him and put his hands on Rupert's shoulders and shook them. "Are you insane?" Arthur shouted with a small amount of sarcasm. "You are making tons of money, your name is known all over the world, you get to travel, and it's even helping your work at ABT. Why in the world would you want to give all that up?"

"Hmm." Rupert just looked up at Arthur for a few seconds. "I would like to bow out before I get kicked out. I want to leave gracefully, while they're still wanting more."

"Seriously?" Arthur straightened up but stayed straddling him. "Your celebrity career is definitely still on the rise. There is absolutely no evidence that you have hit a plateau. You're going to be in movies!"

"That's not for certain yet," Rupert cautioned.

"It's inevitable, Rupert." Arthur finally climbed off and Rupert rolled over and hugged him from behind. "I'm really proud of you. I've told you before. I'm not jealous at all."

"You've been fantastic about all this," Rupert said as he stroked Arthur's hair.

"I love you, Rupert. I only want what's best for you."

"I love you too, Arthur." Rupert paused before he continued. He had been already concerned that he had been spending too much time away from Arthur with all his travel. "I'm thinking of giving up my job at ABT next month. I'm getting enough income from modeling and acting now. I think I might have enough clout to start bringing you with me when I have to travel."

"I have my job working for Rachel," Arthur argued. "I can't keep taking vacation days to travel with you."

Rupert hugged him closer. "I'd rather have you with me. I'm making enough money for both of us now. Maybe you could quit your job?"

"They're not going to let you bring me." Arthur rotated to face Rupert.

"I don't mind making that an absolute condition," Rupert volunteered. "I won't take a job unless you can come."

"How will you explain me tagging along?" Arthur joked. "They're not going to believe I'm your brother . . . or your wife."

"Maybe as my assistant?"

"I like my job working at ABT," Arthur replied. "I don't think I'd be happy just accompanying you for your work. I need work of my own."

"I've been working remotely for most of this year." Rupert propped himself up on his elbow and looked down at Arthur. "You could apply for my job, and you could do it from wherever we are. You don't have to be with me every moment, but it would be nice to keep seeing you at the end of each day."

"I'll think about it." Arthur kissed Rupert lightly on the lips and lay back down. "It was kind of lonely when you were gone for most of last month."

"I think you'd be great at my job," Rupert encouraged.

The following morning, as Rupert knew it would, the year of hypersexuality ended and the year of hyperacusis, as his doctor had diagnosed it when Rupert had been twelve, began. It didn't hit him until around nine-thirty on Christmas morning, as Arthur was preparing to serve him breakfast in bed. Every thud when Arthur let a cupboard door fall closed, every clink when Arthur picked up a metal spoon, the grating of the spatula against the fry pan—all of it sounded like it was happening an eighth of an inch from Rupert's ear. The sounds from their kitchen, including the scuffing of Arthur's slippers on the tile flooring and the wheezing from the slight congestion in Arthur's sinuses competed with the roar of cars going by outside the window, the intense shouting of their neighbors above and below them, and the sonorous clang of the elevator down the hall arriving at his floor. Rupert lurched for his bedside table where he had placed a brand-new package of earplugs just as Arthur arrived carrying a tray of food.

"What's wrong?" Arthur seemed to scream. He calmly thudded the tray down on a corner of the bed and crossed to where Rupert was in a panic to open the packaging for the earplugs. "Are you okay?"

Rupert dropped the package and put his hand over Arthur's mouth for a moment. With his other hand, he gestured with his index finger against his lips to encourage Arthur not to speak again until the earplugs were in place. He winced at the sound of the plastic cover separating from the cardboard back, and quickly stuffed one of them into each ear. The whorl of sound around him faded to a dull background cacophony, and Rupert let out a sigh.

"My hearing is a little sensitive today," Rupert explained. "I will try to get it checked out next Tuesday, if I can get an appointment."

"Your birthday always seems to be a little weird for you," Arthur observed. "Maybe you should ask about that when you go."

When Rupert continued to wear the earplugs day and night, Arthur expressed his concern. Rupert tried to tell him it had happened to him when he was a boy, and it went away after a year, as he expected this auditory sensitivity would as well. Quitting his job at ABT also gave him fewer reasons to go out into the oppressively loud city of New York, and Rupert wore noise-canceling headphones over his earplugs so he could relax at last after Arthur left for work.

It was two weeks later when Rupert had a meeting with some film producers that he could start to see where this particular blessing could ruin his new celebrity. At first the producers started to ask Rupert if the earplugs he wore indicated that there was a problem with his health. Rupert assured him that he was temporarily a bit more sensitive to sound, and it wouldn't affect his work.

"But a movie set is a loud environment between takes," the other producer said. "You would have to take them out to work. We can't have them in the shots."

Rupert replied quickly. "If I can take them out just before we shoot, I'm sure I'll be okay."

"And you can hear us okay while you've got them in?" She gestured at the earplugs Rupert had worn throughout the meeting.

"You could even talk softer," Rupert advised. "I hope you don't mind making this small concession."

"I think we can work with it," the male producer said. "We've seen how your YouTube presence has ballooned in the past year. Your face seems to be everywhere."

"Thank you," Rupert acknowledged. "I have one other small concession. I think Margot may have mentioned it."

"What is it?" the woman asked.

"I spoke with her about providing space for your . . . partner," the other producer mentioned. "I can't have him on set, if he's not legitimately on payroll, though."

"No," Rupert assured. "He can stay with me wherever you put me up, but he's fine on his own. He'll take care of his own food and transportation."

"We will also want you to be discreet about that relationship," the woman warned. "I know it sounds stupid, but most of our anticipated audience won't buy a gay actor in a heterosexual role."

"I'm afraid that ship had already sailed." Rupert chortled. "I've already been seen in the tabloids with him here in New York."

"As far as the rest of the world knows for sure," the woman continued, "he is just a friend of yours. They don't have to know what you do in bed."

"Okay," Rupert said somewhat tentatively. He could imagine them wanting him to butch it up, appear in public with a woman, but he decided to cross that bridge when he came to it.

"Did you have a lawyer we should send the contracts to?" the man asked.

Rupert wondered if he should mention Loretta, his criminal defense attorney, but then he realized he should consult her first before sending her an entertainment contract. "Just send it to Margot, my agent, for now," he advised.

And in April of 2007, Rupert and Arthur said goodbye to their apartment and furniture in Williamsburg, Brooklyn and headed to JFK. When they landed at LAX, they were met by a limo driver carrying a sign with Arthur's surname, Shu. His assistant for the film, a young man named Derrick, had warned him about using his real name anywhere outside the set, for hotel reservations, for restaurant reservations, and for arranging limousine service.

From the day of the first table read until the last reshoot in November, Arthur and Rupert followed the same routine. Rupert would wake before Arthur, because his makeup calls were rarely later than seven or eight in the morning. He would put on his disguise of hoodie and goggles and jog through the streets of the expensive neighborhood near their bungalow, come back for a shower, wake Arthur with a kiss about the time Derrick arrived, and ride back to the sound stage or to a new location. Arthur would then rise, go to the gym, shower, eat a late breakfast, and open his laptop to work on collaborative projects for the American Ballet Theatre back in New York. Except on night shoots, Arthur and Rupert usually met for dinner at one of the tonier restaurants in Beverly Hills or Malibu, just because they only had to take the precaution of entering separately to throw the paparazzi off their scent. The patrons were unlikely to rat them out, because most of them also had something to lose at the hands of anyone's indiscretion.

On days when Rupert wasn't called to set to portray his character in the science fiction film production that had hired him for a seven-figure income, Rupert tried to treat Arthur to something special. A hike and a planetarium visit in Griffith Park. A weekend away on the island of Catalina. A beach day at a fellow star's home in Malibu. A trek through the poppy reserves of Antelope Valley.

And Derrick suggested and helped planned outings to the more traditional places Arthur wanted to see, since it was his first time in L.A.: Grauman's Chinese Theatre, the Walk of Fame, Disneyland, the Santa Monica boardwalk, and Universal Studios. Arthur also watched from the audience when Rupert was at a convention or doing a TV interview. After a few too many interviewers and fans called attention to his earplugs, Rupert took a rare day off to order custom-made earplugs that would be less noticeable.

Even though it was chilly, Arthur and Rupert opened all the windows to let in fresh air when they returned to Williamsburg the Sunday before Thanksgiving. In addition to all their suitcases from eight months in California, Arthur had to go back down to the lobby several times to carry all the packages and mail that had accumulated. Rupert joined him on the last load.

"Mr. Rocket," the doorman said as he reentered the lobby, "I wonder if I might have a word with you."

"Certainly," Rupert replied.

Arthur took off toward the open door to the mailroom again. "I'll be right back."

The doorman, a very kind, older man who had been working days since Arthur had moved in years before, took his arm and led him toward the front door. "The management company and I in particular have really enjoyed having you as a tenant the past few years. You've always been kind and generous to me and the rest of the staff. But your celebrity over the past year has put quite a burden on us. We have had to put additional security on call, because some of your fans won't leave the premises after a simple request."

"I'm so sorry," Rupert said. "What can I do?"

"The management company is willing to help you relocate to a property with better security."

"Oh. Let me get back to you on that. I need to talk to Arthur."

"Of course, sir."

Rupert helped get the last two boxes of their mail from the mailroom and rode up in the elevator with them. Rupert looked in and saw how many were fan mail. "I hadn't really gotten a sense of my celebrity while we were in Los Angeles," he told Arthur.

Arthur waited until the doors had opened on their floor to respond as they headed toward their open apartment door. "You were kind of living in a bubble. I did searches for Rupert Rocket online while you were working. You have an official and a couple of unofficial fan clubs. You were listed as one of the sexiest celebrities over thirty, twice."

"Oh." Rupert followed Arthur into their apartment and added his box to the others on the dining room table.

"You've had offers for new representation from the top agencies in the country," Arthur continued.

"I'm sticking with Margot for now," Rupert inserted.

"And she is juggling two other film offers for you before your first one is even in theaters."

"And I was so sure a year ago that I should quit," Rupert admitted.

"Yes," Arthur agreed. "I also got an email back from Chantal last week I forgot to tell you about. She's inviting us to her drag Thanksgiving again."

"I'm only going if we are allowed to skip the drag this year," Rupert moaned. "I have been in so much makeup and in so many costumes these past few months, I think I deserve a break for a couple more months."

"I'll let her know." Arthur chuckled. "I hope we don't have to be so careful being seen together in New York now too." He ducked in to use the bathroom.

When he returned, Rupert began again. "Margot says I shouldn't have to worry about New York paparazzi until closer to the premiere, but that's another reason we might need to take building management up on their offer to relocate us."

"Huh?" Arthur sat down on their couch and gestured for Rupert to join him.

246

"When did this happen?"

Rupert sat down next to him. "Just now in the lobby. If all this is really this crazy already, and it's likely to get worse, we will need a bit more security. Maybe one of those buildings in Battery Park City?"

"Can we hire a chauffeur?" Arthur asked.

Rupert kissed him on the cheek. "At the very least," he confirmed.

Arthur and Rupert rode the subway to Chantal's for Thanksgiving, and Rupert decided to minimally conceal himself with dark glasses. When they arrived at the party sans wigs and dresses, they were initially teased but allowed to eat and drink with the rest of their friends.

Rupert still had to finish out his spokesmodel contract, but that too wound down the week before Christmas, so that Arthur and Rupert had plenty of time together at the end of December. On Christmas Eve, when Arthur was already getting ready for bed, Rupert turned on the Christmas tree lights to look at while he turned on their computer and opened the file that held his list of blessings. When he turned thirty-eight the next morning, he would get the blessing he experienced when he was eleven: the ability to understand and converse in any language he heard.

On Christmas morning, Arthur noticed something he had become accustomed to was different. "You aren't wearing your earplugs."

"I don't think I'm going to need them anymore."

Arthur jumped out of bed and grabbed two of the gifts from beneath their tree. "This one is for your birthday, and this one is for Christmas," he said as he laid the two gifts on the bed.

Rupert smiled and turned to Arthur. "Say something to me in Chinese."

"I'm not fluent in it anymore," Arthur reminded him.

"Whatever you remember," Rupert prompted further.

"*Nǐ gǎnjué hén hǎo ma?*" Arthur asked.

"*Wǒ gǎnjué hén hǎo. Wǒmen zǎocān chī shénme?*" Rupert instantly replied.

"I don't know," Arthur responded. "Maybe eggs and English muffins?"

"*Nàyàng jiù hǎole.*" Rupert laughed. As a boy he had always enjoyed seeing

247

the surprise on people's faces when they realized he could understand languages he'd never studied.

"I thought you just spoke English and German," Arthur said. "This is the first time I've ever heard you speak Chinese."

Rupert realized showing off his new ability was going to draw more attention than the limited times he had used it at eleven. He needed an explanation quickly. "I started studying it and practicing it on the set when I was waiting in my trailer," Rupert lied.

"Okay. And your sensitivity to sound started on Christmas morning last year and ended on Christmas morning this year. You know how strange that sounds, don't you?"

Rupert was out of ideas on how to cover for his blessings. He decided to try distraction. He hugged Arthur and then jumped up and headed toward the kitchen. "This year, *I'm* going to make breakfast."

Arthur followed him into the kitchen. "You shouldn't have to work on your birthday," he argued.

Rupert hugged and kissed him when he arrived in the kitchen. "Before I met you, I used to serve food at a church in Chelsea to homeless people on Christmas Day. I used to look forward to that."

"Did you want to do that again today?" Arthur asked innocently.

Rupert grinned. "I think those days are behind me, but maybe you can at least let me serve you instead."

"Okay," Arthur said as he skipped out of the kitchen. "Make mine sunny-side up."

"Hǎo de," Rupert muttered under his breath. He wondered if there was some activity he could start that would utilize his omnilinguistic blessing.

He went out of the apartment into the hall where there was a window facing Manhattan. He followed the skyline until he found the United Nations building, hugging the river among the skyscrapers. "Hmm," he intoned thoughtfully. "Maybe."

CHAPTER 23: RUPERT GETS RECRUITED

Before the movie's press junket began in February, Rupert specifically refused work during January 2008. He told Margot he needed a break after his first film's grueling production schedule. Arthur had put him in charge of hunting for apartments and interviewing car services and potential chauffeurs. Rupert confessed some small concern that they could afford all of that. He told Arthur he was distressed that all the stocks in which he had invested his newfound wealth were plummeting quickly in value with the promise of a recession. Rupert didn't tell Arthur at first about a side activity he wanted to investigate as well.

Rupert had asked Hakim for a referral, and by the third week of January, Rupert had an informational interview with a director at the United Nations' refugee agency. The woman's name was Jenny Athiambo, and Rupert had done a little research to impress her. When he was shown into her office, he noticed her skin was dark, her hair was trimmed close to her scalp, and she wore a long, yellow skirt and blouse. The black-red-and-green Kenyan flag hung on her wall. He stood in front of her desk smiling.

She stood up as well and indicated one of the two chairs facing her desk. "Please have a seat, Mr. Rocket," she said with a slight British accent.

"Do you speak Swahili?" Rupert asked as he sat down.

"I speak a number of languages," Athiambo said as she moved Rupert's resume to the center of her desk, "and that was a point that confused me on your vita. You write that you are fluent in English and German and 'facile' in forty-eight other languages. I hope that wasn't your attempt at a joke, Mr. Rocket."

"Not at all." Rupert sat up a little straighter in his chair. "Feel free to test me."

"All right," she said with a grin that showed off a stunningly perfect set of teeth. "*Avez-vous actuellement un emploi?*"

"Yes, I am a dancer, model, and actor." Rupert smiled back.

"Mr. Rocket, it will be more helpful, if you can respond in the same language as the question." She began scribbling notes on a white legal pad.

"*Pardon!*" Rupert apologized. "*Oui, madame, je suis un danseur, mannequin et acteur.*"

"Très bien." She switched from French to Dutch. "*Heb je ooit als vertaler gewerkt?*"

"*Jammer genoeg niet,*" Rupert apologized. He knew she might ask about his experience as a translator, but he thought his omnilinguistic blessing might offset that deficit. "*Zoals je kunt zien aan mijn CV, heb ik voornamelijk in entertainment en kunstadministratie gewerkt.*"

Athiambo pushed her chair back to cross her legs. "I did some research online. I noticed you have a movie due out this summer . . . and you have a fan club. Your name and photo are seemingly everywhere. I even saw your image on a billboard in Times Square. Why would you be interested in working for the U.N. if you have all of that?"

Rupert had anticipated this question as well. He was uncertain whether it would sound too cloying. He took a deep breath and launched into it. "I just turned thirty-eight, Ms. Athiambo. As I've gotten older, I've looked back on my career as an entertainer, and I wonder how much I've helped the world. I had heard about your agency and the work you do helping refugees, and it struck a chord with me. My grandmother Zelda Kellerman was a German refugee almost a century ago, and she used to tell me stories of how harshly she was treated when her family emigrated to Wisconsin. During World War Two, when she was in her twenties, she watched the U.S. government remove several of her friends and neighbors from their homes with no due process and shipped them off to internment camps. They had risked everything to come to America and to escape the Nazis, but the government suspected they were fifth column and locked them

250

away.

"I am keenly aware that refugees are not even halfway done with their ordeal when they escape some calamity. The underappreciated work of resettlement is something I think I might be helpful in doing. I'm in good health, and my celebrity might even come in handy on occasion."

Athiambo's arms were crossed and her chin rested between her thumb and index finger as she listened. "*Maisha ni gweng bana. Inahitaji kujitolea. Unaishi kama kipepeo, kamwe kushika kazi sawa kwa muda mrefu sana. Wewe ni mtu donga. Ikiwa tunakuajiri wewe, Mheshimiwa Rocket, utakuwa na uwezo wa kukaa mpaka kazi imekamilika?*"

Rupert took a deep breath. He had listened to little bits of Swahili in preparation for the interview, but there were all sorts of words he hadn't heard before. He got the sense she was worried about how frequently he had switched jobs, working for different producers and ballet companies. Certain references to children, a butterfly, and a city wall seemed out of place, like they were slang. But Rupert felt the context was clear enough to respond. "*Maisha haijulikani. Labda ningeweza kuanza kama mshauri wa muda?*"

"We will have to see." Athiambo uncrossed her arms and hands and leaned forward with her hands on her desk. "You seem to have picked up a dialect of Swahili you would be unlikely to hear anywhere outside of Nairobi. Have you been there?"

"No, ma'am," Rupert replied. "I'm just really good with languages. Before I came in today, I looked up your name, saw you were from Kenya. I remembered seeing a short Kenyan film at a screening in Los Angeles last year called . . . *Chokora*. I also picked up a couple of old copies of *Taifa Leo* at a news shop in the Village on my way here."

"You read a newspaper in Swahili to prepare for this interview?" Athiambo's eyes got wide waiting for confirmation of a consideration she clearly viewed as overkill.

"Yes, ma'am." Rupert was proud of his performance in the interview, but he tried to keep from looking smug. He aimed for serious and attentive.

"Well then," she began as she finished making a few more notes, "you certainly seem to have extraordinary passion and enthusiasm, both of which are essential in this type of work."

She rose and extended her hand. Rupert grasped it lightly and shook it. "I will put you in our professional talent pool, and then I or one of the other directors at UNHCR will see if you're right for any openings."

"I appreciate that, Ms. Athiambo," Rupert said as he withdrew his hand.

"*Kwaheri! Nimefurahi kukutana na wewe, Mheshimiwa Rocket!*" she called out as Rupert was about to head out her office door.

He turned around and saw her smiling. "*Asante!* It was a pleasure meeting you as well, Ms. Athiambo, and I hope your afternoon goes well."

He met Arthur at a deli near the Flatiron Building. He described the interview for him, and he noticed Arthur seeming a little dubious about Rupert's sudden grasp of Swahili. "You're saying a fifteen-minute film you saw with subtitles last year and scanning two old Kenyan newspapers prepared you to be interviewed in Swahili?"

"It wasn't all in Swahili," Rupert explained. "A lot was in English, and I was able to get enough of the gist of what she was saying to answer back. I wouldn't call myself fluent, by any means."

Arthur just stared at Rupert for a few seconds while he chewed his food. Once he swallowed, his face seemed primed for sarcasm. "And you're going to tell me you picked up French, Dutch, and Chinese in the past few months?"

"I traveled a lot in Europe before I met you." Rupert hoped that that ambiguous statement would serve as sufficient explanation for the other languages.

It had been difficult enough to confess his secret fantasy to Arthur about working for the U.N. during this year of his omnilinguistic blessing. Rupert was sure he wasn't ready yet to clarify all of his odd abilities Arthur had started to notice. He rationalized that after Arthur had lived through enough of them, it would serve as sufficient evidence to make him sound less crazy. There would be no other conclusion Arthur would be able to embrace at that point other than the one Rupert offered: Magic was real, and his luck changed with precision every

252

Christmas morning on the anniversary of his birth.

Over the eleven years since Rupert had met Arthur as a young intern at the Alvin Ailey benefit, Arthur had tried to give him money he didn't have, done whatever Rupert asked, complimented Rupert whenever he saw him, watched Rupert's predictions come true, and rarely won an argument against Rupert. For a year at a time. More recently, Arthur had never been able to hide anything from Rupert, had seen Rupert go from athletic to bodybuilder in a matter of months, had seen Rupert propositioned everywhere he went, had puzzled over Rupert's super-sensitive hearing–all starting and ending on successive Christmas mornings. The evidence was already so overwhelming, Rupert felt, he started to believe he could wait until Arthur confronted him about it.

Not long after Arthur left for work two days later, Rupert was surprised to hear of a follow-up to his interview at the U.N. He saw the number come up as "private" on his mobile phone. The man introduced himself as Parker Kilpatrick, and he said he had seen Rupert's resume in the UNHCR's Talent Pool and wanted to talk to him. Rupert started to ask the man which floor of the U.N. his office was, and Kilpatrick told him to meet him in a rental conference room at the Brooklyn Public Library at Grand Army Plaza.

Rupert donned his usual disguise–dark glasses, baseball cap, and earmuffs– and called a car service to pick him up. On his way out to meet it, he didn't see any photographers lurking; he assumed he was not yet hot enough to warrant any of them waiting for him in the cold for the hours or days he might be holed up in his apartment.

After the driver dropped him off, Rupert hurried up the steps and inside to avoid gusts of cold wind so strong, they almost knocked him off his feet. A woman at the desk inside directed him to the row of conference rooms.

"Thanks," he told her. "Do you know which one might have been rented by a Mr. Kilpatrick? It's my first time meeting him."

The woman looked through a sign-up sheet. "No one by that name has one reserved," she reported.

Rupert stalked back and peered through the glass-front walls of the rooms as he passed them. After he reviewed almost all of them, he walked back to the only one with a single male occupant and opened the door. "Are you Mr. Kilpatrick?"

The man waved him in and didn't speak until the glass door had swung shut behind Rupert. "You must be Rupert Rocket then."

Rupert self-consciously took off the cap, earmuffs, and glasses. "Sorry. I'm starting to have fans and photographers stalking me."

"That's part of the reason I asked you to meet me here," Kilpatrick explained. "My assistant suggested it might be too disruptive to have you show up at our offices."

Rupert sat in a chair with his back to the door. "And where might those be?"

Kilpatrick closed a briefcase that was near him on the tabletop. "I'll get to that in a minute. I got your information from the UNHCR talent pool, as I mentioned over the phone, but I don't work for the U.N.—not directly, at least. I might have some work you could do for our agency that might help you get a better foot in the door to work with UNHCR. If that interests you, I'd like to find out why you decided to suddenly pursue a career in international service. I'm told your modeling and acting careers are going quite well."

Rupert studied the man closely to get some sense of what his angle was. He was shorter and leaner, and his receding hairline formed a dark-brown widow's peak. His eyes were brown and his gaze was reminiscent of a spectator at a chess match. He wore a dark olive-green suit and black tie, and a gray, wool overcoat hung over the chair next to him. "My grandmother was a refugee," Rupert finally said. "I wanted to do something more meaningful than selling clothing and making movies."

"I see." Kilpatrick uncrossed his legs but leaned back again. "And you're single?"

There was something about the way he had asked that made Rupert suspect Kilpatrick already knew the answer. He decided to test the waters a bit. "I'm gay, and my boyfriend lives with me."

"And you have no criminal record?"

Again, the question seemed like it was seeking confirmation of something known. Rupert estimated that he was being tested about how truthful he could be about embarrassing information. "I was criminally charged twice. In one case, the charges were dropped, and in the other, I was acquitted."

Kilpatrick crossed his arms and brought his right fist up to his mouth. He kept that position for nearly half a minute before he lowered his arms and spoke. "I've been told you're quite facile with languages. *Şu an hangi dili konuştuğumu biliyor musun?*"

Rupert had come to learn that he never got a word-for-word understanding of a new foreign language. He only got a sense of the whole question, and it seemed like Kilpatrick just wanted him to identify the language. "Turkish, I believe."

"Let's try one more," Kilpatrick said. "*Aapakee daadee kahaan paida huee thee?*"

Rupert wondered what his grandmother's birthplace had to do with his application to work for the U.N., but he let the answer flow through him with the certainty that the words were right. "*Main apane paitrk daadee ke baare mein nahin jaanata. Meree daadee Zelda Jarmanee mein paida huee theen.*"

Kilpatrick leaned forward and started making notes on a pad. "So, you have demonstrated your familiarity with English, German, French, Dutch, Swahili, Turkish, and Hindi."

"I've also picked up some Mandarin Chinese recently." Rupert smiled. "I have a really good memory for languages."

"Could you learn Russian?"

Rupert smiled again. "*Da. Eto bylo by lyegko.*" He remembered having overheard the words from Russian tourists on the subway.

"Your accent sounds native," Kilpatrick acknowledged.

"I strive for accuracy," Rupert said. He leaned forward on the table on his forearms. "You work for the CIA, don't you?"

Kilpatrick's eyebrows went up. "What makes you say that?"

"Well, I was just guessing," Rupert said, "but that response seems to confirm it. Anyone else would have laughed and/or denied it. You've been studying me very closely, even more so than my old therapist. And when I answered your question, your eyes didn't show any sign of taking the information in. You already knew the truth. Your mouth just changed to acknowledge that I hadn't lied. You didn't seem very surprised that I knew Turkish, Hindi, and Russian. All that suggested you were in the intelligence services; I just figured CIA was the agency most likely to be in constant contact with the U.N."

Kilpatrick didn't acknowledge Rupert's deduction except to move on. "You already have a great cover, Mr. Rocket. Being a celebrity gives you entry into a lot of places it is difficult for our other agents to convincingly penetrate. Also, your high-profile trial about your alleged complicity with the 9/11 hijackers is just enough taint to give you some traction with extremists. We would want you to start working with Jenny Athiambo, the woman you met at UNHCR. She will send you out on refugee relief missions, but every time you get an assignment from her, . . ." Kilpatrick slid a card across the table toward Rupert. ". . . you will call this number and get a code." He took a printed sheet of paper from his briefcase and slid it across the table as well. "You will cross-reference that code against this list of drop-off points. You will need to wait at least two hours to pick up your additional instructions, but not more than six hours. If you miss that drop-off, call the number again to get a new code."

Kilpatrick put his notepad and pen back into his briefcase. "On occasion, we will arrange something to coincide with your modeling and acting work. Further down on that sheet I gave you are keywords divided by months. At the beginning of each month, memorize those keywords, and if you notice anyone approach you and use at least three of that month's keywords, confirm by using three different keywords, and follow them to a secure location to receive instructions. Do you understand what we're asking of you?"

Rupert had a dozen questions. He tried to prioritize them. "I guess you are asking me to spy for the U.S."

Kilpatrick's voice got very low. "Essentially yes. You will be working as a covert operative for the United States. You need to keep this work secret from everyone in your life, including your boyfriend. If news of your work for us gets to the wrong people, it could put you and everyone else in your life at risk."

256

Rupert matched Kilpatrick's low tone. "Can I refuse an assignment? And how do I quit altogether?"

"Jenny will be your handler," Kilpatrick clarified. "If you get an assignment from us you can't or don't want to do, just tell Jenny you refuse the cover job. And if you want to discontinue working with us, just tell Jenny you don't want to work with the U.N. anymore, and we'll contact you like we did today to debrief you."

"What if I get an assignment through an anonymous contact with the keywords?" Rupert asked. "How do I refuse those?"

"You'll need to keep Jenny appraised of your schedule," Kilpatrick explained. "If you tell Jenny you are free at times when we had scheduled you to work for us, we will take that as a refusal." He leaned in even closer and whispered. "I'm trusting we won't have to reassign your operations often though. We do a lot of work to prepare them, and you usually won't have much time before you need to commit to them."

"I understand," Rupert whispered back. "I am not that picky, but I trust you just want me to obtain information, and I won't have to hurt or kill anybody."

"Noted," Kilpatrick said as he leaned back again. He closed his briefcase and grabbed his overcoat. "There may be times, however, when you may have to defend yourself, so we will schedule some time to help train you in that."

"And sometimes I might be sick with the flu or have another job to do," Rupert suggested.

"That's another good thing to mention to Jenny." Kilpatrick grabbed his briefcase as well and stood up. "You will just generally keep her up to date on your availability, so that she knows when she can send you on an aid mission."

"And every time she gives me an assignment, I will get one from you too, if I call that number?"

"That's correct," Kilpatrick confirmed. "I have to get going. Send Jenny your availability for the next two months, and we'll try to schedule some training time." He moved around to Rupert's side of the table and transferred his coat out of his right hand. They shook hands. "Welcome aboard," Kilpatrick whispered. He opened the door and quickly made his way out the front door of the library.

Rupert stood up and gathered the card and code sheet. He stuffed them into a pocket in his jeans. He put his disguise back on and was zipping up his jacket when he slowly followed his new boss out the front door.

When Arthur came home from work that evening, Rupert had two good pieces of news for him: He had signed a lease on a one-bedroom apartment in a high-rise in Battery Park City, and the U.N. had agreed to hire him as an occasional consultant for their refugee resettlement programs. Arthur hugged and kissed him immediately, but later worried that the apartment he described might be too expensive and the additional volunteer work too much of a drain on Rupert's time and energy.

Arthur ordered food to be delivered, as they were doing more frequently lately. While they waited for it to arrive, Rupert emailed his availability to Jenny Athiambo, noting that he was obligated to go on a two-week press junket for his movie at the end of February. He also called Margot to let her know he was available for her as well.

A week later, while Arthur was at work at ABT, Rupert was standing in a mostly empty apartment on the twenty-first floor of a building on River Terrace in Manhattan, directing movers where to put furniture and boxes. Just as the movers were heading for the elevators again, he heard the house phone ring that was reserved for use by the security desk in the lobby to announce visitors. Rupert calmly walked to answer it, wondering who would want him before he had finished moving in. "Hello, this is Rupert Rocket in 2102."

"Mr. Rocket, you have a visitor." Rupert didn't recognize the voice and made a mental note to learn the names of the people that worked the desk downstairs. "Were you expecting a Mr. Hakim Noor?"

Rupert was even more puzzled why Hakim would want to see him in person. He hadn't spoken with him in three weeks or seen him in months. "You can send him up," Rupert replied.

"Very well, sir."

Hakim walked in fifteen minutes later when the door was left open by the movers who were heading out to get another load from the truck. He approached

Rupert with his arms wide, and although he had only hugged Rupert once before during his hypersexuality blessing, he stepped into it and embraced Hakim.

"For living at such a glamorous address, I thought it was strange to see a yellow school bus parked out front," Hakim commented as he stepped back and surveyed the apartment.

"I didn't see it when I was out there," Rupert said. "It must have just pulled up in the past hour."

Hakim sighed and took a couple of steps further into the living room. "Rupert, you've got to study your keyword list better than that."

Rupert's jaw dropped. He thought back to the list of ten keywords for each month Parker Kilpatrick had given him. The words were always arranged to form odd acronyms. This month's was DO BE SINGLY—dead, onion, barber, electric, strange, indigo, nasty, glamorous, longest, yellow. "Wow. I didn't expect you would be one of my couriers."

"I can't tell you anything more until you give me the proper response," Hakim maintained.

Rupert tried to think of something that used the remaining seven words. "I think someone dropped an onion behind the stove, and it's been there the longest time, so it's probably really nasty."

Hakim sat down in an easy chair. "Hmm. Okay. You'll have to practice that a bit more, so it sounds like something a normal person would say."

Rupert walked over and stood facing Hakim. "The movers are going to be back in a couple of minutes, so you better hurry up and tell me."

"Come by my house on Monday morning around ten o'clock. Wear whatever you'd wear at the gym, and plan to stay for three hours. You'll have lunch with me, Azami, and Ichiro afterward." Hakim stood again and hugged Rupert. "I'll see you then."

Rupert followed Hakim out into the hall. "Thanks for coming over . . . I guess."

Hakim stepped into the elevator and said just as the door was closing, "I look forward to working with you again."

Rupert heard the movers wheeling back dollies with more boxes from the freight elevator. He followed them back into his new apartment and wondered if he had, as Arthur feared, overcommitted himself. He considered that five months in prison was driving him to be more active and engaged in the world. He also found himself shivering in a panic, as he realized his flurry of activity also distracted him from the complete exhaustion of the Grogoch's blessing in eleven more years—an event that gave the Pooka's curse full reign and had killed his grandparents and his mother. Suddenly, his life seemed unfairly brief.

CHAPTER 24: RUPERT'S
FIRST MISSIONS

Rupert suggested to Arthur a trip to Beijing to see the 2008 Summer Olympics, so they practiced Chinese together during dinnertimes and read books in Chinese together on the weekends. Since Arthur preferred to work at ABT's offices when they were in New York, it was relatively easy for Rupert to get away to train with Hakim's friend, Mr. Eng, in self-defense. By Rupert's last lesson on Valentine's Day, Mr. Eng declared him sufficiently prepared for his first mission. Rupert asked when that might be, and Hakim didn't know.

Arthur went along on the press junket for Rupert's movie opening on Memorial Day weekend. They visited only cities in Europe, because advance buzz was lagging there compared to the U.S. and Canada. They landed in Paris on February 19, and it was a relief especially to Arthur that they had left behind freezing New York for the warmer air of France in late winter.

Their routine was pretty similar in all the cities the director, the publicist, Rupert, and his co-stars visited. The distributor gave them an easy schedule of only one or two appearances per day, so Rupert and Arthur usually had lunches and evenings together to explore Paris, Berlin, Vienna, Zurich, Rome, and London. Rupert tried to struggle a bit with languages other than German around Arthur, but French and Italian were among the easier languages he had acquired with the help of his omnilinguistic blessing.

They were supposed to finish the tour in London, but the publicist traveling with them informed them the day after they arrived in England that an additional stop in Saint Petersburg had been added. Some of the other actors were nervous about traveling to Russia, but when the distributor kicked in an additional daily pay bump, they stopped protesting. They landed in Helsinki, Finland, late on a Sunday morning and were quickly transferred to an old school bus for the six-hour drive to St. Petersburg. They enjoyed the views of the Gulf between the pleasant meanderings of the highway through winter forests. They stopped for a late lunch in Kotka, and Arthur was already confessing anxiety about leaving the relative safety of London.

"I told you you could have stayed," Rupert said as they climbed back onto the bus. "I could have extended the hotel reservation and rebooked flights."

"I can have misgivings about something," Arthur said, and then more softly, "and still want to explore something new."

Once they had taken seats near the back of the bus, Arthur continued. "I've been trying, ever since I met you to match your fearlessness. You see something you want, and you go after it without hesitation. I'm usually much more . . . careful. I always want to minimize risks, so I tend to want to keep to a routine. Part of why I love being with you is you keep challenging me to try new things, over and over, and I go along with them because I don't want to give in to my fears all the time. Does that make sense?"

"Yes," Rupert acknowledged. "You have to let me know when something makes you uncomfortable then, Arthur. I have no measure of what seems sane to the average person. To me, catching a bus in Finland to go to Saint Petersburg is no big deal. I only recognized perhaps once we were underway, . . . how singularly unique I was in that reaction."

"Without you, I don't know when I would have had such an amazing trip like this." Arthur leaned over and nuzzled Rupert's chest. "I've gotten to visit all of these European capitals, and I've gotten to do them with the man I love." He was quiet for a minute before he spoke again. "And I *have* put my foot down with you."

"About getting the new apartment and the chauffeur?" Rupert asked.

"No, I . . ."

"About showing up in drag to Chantal's Thanksgiving dinner?"

Arthur sat up to get a better look at Rupert's face. "You didn't want to do that?"

"Not at first," Rupert admitted.

"I was just going to bring up my monogamy rule." Arthur settled back down against Rupert's chest. "I knew a nonexclusive sexual relationship was . . . not something I wanted to experience."

Rupert looked out the window at the sun setting on the Gulf of Finland and thought about his relationship with Arthur, and what might happen to it when either one of his two big secrets got revealed. Once again, he had taken on a secret he couldn't share with anyone in his life, and both of them would worry Arthur. He remembered how Jorge used to hate being blindsided by things he had not shared soon enough. Arthur seemed a lot more relaxed about those sorts of oversights, but Rupert had never tested him on something big like either his curse and blessing or his work for the CIA.

Everyone on the bus sat up from their napping and otherwise reclining positions when the bus came to a halt a little over an hour later. Their Finnish interpreter got up and made an announcement in his broken English: "We now enter Russian border crossing control. Find now your passports and visas so you are not making border soldiers wait too long. Better now not to speak unless they ask questions. Not smiling. Not touching anyone. Not staring out window nor at soldiers."

When the bus had inched forward to within 500 feet of the wooden pikes blocking each of the two drives through the border gate area, two Russian soldiers boarded the bus. Rupert could hear only snatches of what they said near the front of the bus. They were mostly disappointed that they did not recognize any of his fellow actors, it seemed. They went down the aisle checking everyone's passports and photos. They asked everyone to take off head coverings and sunglasses.

As one of the soldiers finally got to Arthur and Rupert's seat, Rupert heard the guard mutter a complaint something like, "All these capitalist pigs coming to take advantage of us."

"We are going to be on television in Saint Petersburg tomorrow," Rupert volunteered in Russian. "You can tell your friends and family about that tomorrow and when the film is in theaters in two months."

Arthur gave Rupert a subtle elbow to the ribs. Rupert knew that their interpreter had advised against speaking, but the guard was probably bored and could use a positive experience like meeting movie stars to boost his self-esteem.

The guard raised his eyebrows as he looked at Rupert's passport again. "I don't know any Rupert Rocket."

"You will see me in movies very soon," Rupert assured him. "You will be able to say you met me even before I was a star."

The guard finally cracked a bit of a grin and handed the passport back to Rupert. He asked what the name of the film was, and Rupert gave him the English title and apologized that he did not know what the Russian title would be yet. As the guards were leaving the bus, he heard them brag to each other about which American celebrities they had met.

It took another three hours before they finally pulled up in front of their hotel in downtown Saint Petersburg. It looked like it had been built in the late 1800s. It still had the original carriage entrance in front. An old-fashioned cage elevator took Rupert and Arthur up to their room on the third floor. The hall was narrow, and their room was at the end of it. They had been issued brass keys, and when they opened the door, they saw a canopy bed, brass-and-stained-glass lamps, an ornately carved armoire and matching writing desk, and an entrance to a private bath where Rupert could see a bit of the marble sink and tile floor.

While Arthur went off to find an Internet connection for his laptop, Rupert sat in one of a pair of overstuffed easy chairs and reviewed his schedule for the following day. He heard a knock on the hall door and kept the schedule in his hand as he opened the door. A young woman in a bell hop's uniform stood there and looked up at him and spoke in English. "Mr. Rocket, please excuse the interruption. There is a delicate emergency I must show you before sunrise tomorrow."

Rupert had been practicing his February keyword list religiously before the trip to Europe. He immediately picked up on the use of *delicate*, *emergency*, and *sunrise* from CAN LET DOGS. "God, I haven't been able to find an orange anywhere."

"I will do my best to help you with that," the courier responded. "Follow me, please."

She led him down a back stairwell three floors to the hotel basement, then down a hall and into a laundry room where machines and clattering pipes were making a racket. "This is the only room they haven't bugged," she reported. "We will have to be quick, because I am being watched."

"Go ahead," Rupert said. "I'm ready."

"After your interviews tomorrow, someone wearing a white flower will bump into you. You need to follow him to a vehicle that will drop you off at an address in the suburbs." She handed him an I.D. card and a map. "We believe it is a cyberattack center focused on disrupting Western elections, and we need to confirm who they are targeting and how. Your cover is as a new employee getting training before you start work tomorrow. Study the information on your I.D. and on the back of the map so you will match the records we have inserted for you. Once you have the data, excuse yourself and leave the facility. Your extraction point is four blocks away, marked with an X. Call the number and let it ring just once, and they will be there to pick you up in five minutes. You will need to disguise your features in a way that seems natural. If you are arrested, we may not be able to bail you out, so don't get arrested."

She led Rupert over to a gap in the building's foundation. "Leave your report in there between ten o'clock and midnight tomorrow night. Any questions?"

Rupert scanned both sides of the map briefly. The street names in Cyrillic made his head swim for a moment, but he trusted he would figure it out before it became crucial. "I'm good."

"Good luck then," she said just before dashing out of the laundry room.

The next morning, while getting made up for the first TV interview, Rupert asked the makeup artist if she would mind letting him have a bit of fake hair in his hair color. He explained that it was for a disguise later in the day to surprise a friend, and she laughed at the idea and gave it to him.

During the interview, the host had so much trouble with English, Rupert was about to volunteer to translate between English and Russian for everyone, but he realized the secrecy of his mission required him not to be a showoff where half of Saint Petersburg would see it. After the interview, the two other stars, their publicist, their interpreter, and Rupert were shown to the TV station's cafeteria for a brief lunch. From there, they were whisked off to a film society forum where they were joined by the film's director in a panel discussion.

As the four of them were being led toward a back exit of the theater, one of the stagehands in a dark-green coverall bumped into Rupert going the opposite direction on a staircase. Rupert immediately turned and saw an embroidered rose on the man's back with the words in Cyrillic for "white rose logistics."

Rupert immediately grabbed the shoulder of the interpreter. "I think that guy just stole my wallet!" he whispered. "Take off without me if I'm not there in five minutes. I'll find my own way back to the hotel."

He took off back up the stairs before the confused interpreter could respond. He made his way to the front lobby and caught site of the man in the green coverall getting into the driver's seat of an unmarked gray van in front of the theater. Rupert opened the other door and hopped up into the seat beside the man.

"Close the door and get in back," the man demanded in Russian.

Rupert climbed between the seats and into the cargo area. He found a toolbox with a hand mirror and a flashlight. He set them up to work on his disguise. Careful not to try to do anything when the van was turning a corner, Rupert used the spirit gum he had stolen from the TV station to build himself a moustache and bushier eyebrows. He also took Arthur's spare pair of reading glasses out of his jacket pocket and placed it low enough on his nose, so he could see over it. He turned off the light and put all his supplies in the toolbox before taking his seat in the front again.

The man glanced over at Rupert briefly. "Good."

A few minutes later, without saying anything else in between, the man said, "We are here."

Rupert got out of the van and looked around. There were three buildings with entrances very close to where the van was idling. Rupert looked back inside the van, and the man pointed toward the center building and then drove off. Rupert fished his I.D. out of his pocket. He hoped the shoes he had changed into looked Russian enough.

He was confronted by a security guard as soon as he was through the front door. He held out his palm and said in an odd dialect of Russian, "Identification card, please. Who are you meeting with?"

"Olga Petrovich," Rupert replied as he handed the I.D. over. "I'm new here. Starting tomorrow."

Rupert followed him over to his desk where he consulted a list of employees. He looked over the man's shoulder and saw his alias added in pen at the bottom and relaxed a little.

"You are early," the guard said as he handed the card back to Rupert. "You will go to the second floor and wait for Ms. Petrovich in room 210."

Rupert kept his head down. "Thank you." He headed toward the pair of elevators.

When he got out of the elevator again on the second floor, he scanned the wide hallway. It looked like it had been a hospital at some point in the past. The air smelled vaguely of ammonia. Most of the doorways were open, and the raised black numbers screwed vertically onto the sea-green doorframes nearest him were 221 and 222. He followed the hallway to the left and snatched quick glances inside where the doors were open. They held four to six workers, mostly in their twenties, either typing furiously on keyboards or studying text on colorful screens.

Another guard, this one wearing a sidearm, looked at Rupert suspiciously as they passed each other. Most strangers he had observed didn't make eye contact on the streets and only greeted each other when there was a previous acquaintance. Rupert kept his gaze down until the guard was behind him.

Rupert saw another guard leaning against a wall and consulting a sheaf of papers on a clipboard. Rupert started to suspect that the center was indeed run by Russian military intelligence. The uniforms didn't look like a private company. He passed this guard too with his head down.

Near the end of the long, U-shaped hallway, Rupert saw room 210. The room was twice as large as most of the others. It was set up with three rows of desks facing a bigger desk against the left wall. The late afternoon sun shone brightly through the window opposite the door, so Rupert could only see the outline of a student sitting at one of the desks. As he entered, a bookish woman with braided auburn hair wearing eyeglasses looked up and smiled at Rupert. He sat at a desk behind her.

She turned around in her seat as Rupert removed his overcoat and sat down. "Hello."

"Hello," Rupert called back. "I assume you are not Olga Petrovich." He tried to make it sound like a joke.

The young woman chuckled. "My name is Lana. You didn't have your intake interview with her?"

Fortunately, the CIA analysts had covered this in Rupert's briefing. "I was a late replacement," Rupert explained to Lana. "Someone had to go to the hospital, I heard. My name is Ivan Vladimirsky."

"I'm nervous my French is not good enough for this job," Lana confessed. "Do you know what language group you were assigned to?"

"I don't know yet," Rupert said. This wasn't covered in his briefing.

"You speak several languages then?" she asked as she turned a bit more in Rupert's direction.

Rupert replied in French. "I speak several languages, so it could be any one of them."

"Wonderful," Lana said in French as she clapped her hands together. "Can you help me practice until the orientation starts?"

Just then, six other people entered the room, and Lana turned around in her seat. Rupert watched them take off coats and hats and settle into the empty desks. A minute later, a very severe-looking, short, older woman with streaks of red and brunette hair pulled into a bun whisked between the desks and laid a laptop, clipboard, and valise down on the desk at the front. Over the course of a twenty-minute lecture, Ms. Petrovich described how the government wanted them to study social media discussions in other countries and copy down words and phrases that were political in nature and critical or inflammatory. Once the databases were full, analysts from other departments would furnish them with scripts and target lists in which to deploy them. She told them to gather up their belongings and follow her to the work rooms.

Rupert and Lana were sent to separate work rooms. In his, Rupert was given the task of analyzing discussions centering around British dissatisfaction with the European Union. His database was already started with phrases about "lost sovereignty" aimed at Labour Party backers. When no one was watching, Rupert loaded one of the American databases, which was mostly empty, except for a few poorly worded messages suggesting that presidential candidate Barack Obama was born in Kenya, not in Hawaii.

Suddenly Olga Petrovich was standing over his shoulder. "I thought I assigned you to the British database," she said accusingly.

"I'm sorry, Ms. Petrovich." Rupert searched his mind for a possible excuse. "I was looking for a dictionary to look up a word."

She grabbed his mouse and clicked on a book icon on the toolbar. An English-Russian dictionary opened. Then she pointed at the handbook lying next to Rupert's keyboard. "Read the handbook all the way through before you start clicking randomly in the databases, Mr. Vladimirsky."

"I need to use the bathroom," Rupert lied. He grabbed the handbook and got up from his chair. "I'll continue reading it while I'm there."

She looked partly confused and partly disgusted, but she didn't say anything more. Rupert grabbed his coat as well and headed out the door. He found a bathroom near the elevators and called the number he had predialed on his cell phone. He let it ring once and then disconnected it. He called the elevator and prayed it would come quickly, because he had started to draw the attention of one of the guards patrolling the hallway.

He lurched into the elevator when it arrived and pushed the button for the ground floor. As he passed the security guard at the front of the building, he mumbled an excuse about not feeling well and headed out the front door quickly.

He pulled the map out of his coat pocket as he zipped the coat up. The streets came together at odd angles, so he had to compare the map and the street signs several times before he reached the bus stop extraction point. An older man at the bus stop called out in English as he approached, "The orange line is not running today because of some emergency in the capitol."

Rupert came to a stop in front of the man somewhat out of breath but managed to respond, "God, I can't wait all night and get home at sunrise!"

The man slowly stood up and waved at a black sedan parked across the street and down the block. It pulled into the bus stop, and Rupert opened the rear door and dove in. He saw the man at the bus stop leave as he pulled the door shut and the car sped away.

Rupert pocketed Arthur's glasses and ripped off his fake eyebrows and moustache in the car. When he got to the hotel, he tried to slow his breathing and seem calm. He realized he was still carrying the handbook, so he stuffed it in his coat pocket quickly.

Arthur was sitting at the desk in their room when Rupert returned. He got up as Rupert was taking off his coat and hugged him. "They said you didn't leave with everybody else in the van from the film forum this afternoon. I was worried about you."

"Somebody tried to steal my wallet at the theater," Rupert said. "It was this whole big thing stopping him and making a report to the police."

"You got it back?"

Rupert sighed. "Yes. Did you ever find a printer?"

"No," Arthur said as he crossed back to the desk. "And there is only one place in the whole hotel I can connect online. I want to go back to Western civilization."

"We're leaving tomorrow morning," Rupert reassured him.

Rupert managed to write out his report while Arthur worked on his ABT emails. They ordered dinner in their room, and at ten o'clock, Rupert excused himself and headed down to the hotel's laundry room. An older woman was sweeping the floor in the doorway, so Rupert backtracked to the stairwell. He looked again five minutes later, and the sweeper was gone. He rolled up his report and the handbook and slid them deep into the crack in the foundation in the back of the laundry room.

In early March, Margot booked Rupert in a small role as an American tourist in a Bollywood musical. Since it was supposed to be a short trip, Arthur stayed in New York. In a four-day break in the shooting at a sound stage in New Delhi, Rupert was shuttled off on a bus tour to China. Rupert had two days to investigate the source of contaminated milk killing children there. After going to a couple of dairies and speaking with an inspector, Rupert concluded that the drought had depleted the grain supply, so the cows were underfed, and their milk contained an unacceptable dearth of protein. Some dairies were adding melamine, a plastic additive and fire retardant, to milk and infant formula to raise the milk's nitrogen content, how inspectors measured the amount of protein.

Rupert was surprised when a Tibetan woman stepped out of a crowd on the street in Chengdu and walked beside him. "The market here is a symbolic island," she said in English.

Rupert was getting much better at memorizing his keywords at the beginning of each month. He remembered HOME IS FLAT and told her, "You can trigger harmony with an apple."

"Follow me." She led Rupert further down the main street and then into an alley.

When they were far enough away from the crowds, she gave Rupert instructions to fly to Bhutan to monitor the first democratic election there. When Rupert finally returned a week later than planned, Arthur welcomed him home with a hug and more concern. "Why couldn't you let me know you had changed your plans? I waited for you at the airport."

"I'm really sorry, Arthur." He finally set down his suitcases and hugged Arthur back. "We had to reshoot everything because there was some problem with the booms and the playback in the first shoot. We were . . . on location and there wasn't much cell service. When I could let you know, I was boarding the plane to come home."

"You couldn't ask your assistant to send me an update?"

Rupert broke out of the hug and hung his coat in the hall closet. "I didn't have an assistant this time. I'm really sorry you had to wait for nothing. I'll make it up to you."

When they got back from Arthur's favorite Italian restaurant in Midtown, Rupert emailed his availability to Jenny Athiambo at the U.N. and requested an in-person debrief. She emailed him the next morning, and they met in the late afternoon at her office.

Jenny stood as he entered and offered her hand to Rupert. "*Hamjambo!*"

Rupert shook it and replied, "*Sijambo.*" He sat down. "Can we talk freely in here?"

She sat back down. "If you turn your cell phone off, yes."

Rupert fished his phone out of his pocket and turned it off. "Done. I had two missions while I was in New Delhi shooting that movie. I was sent to China, tromping around farms and meeting with inspectors, and it was just a few corrupt farmers, no government conspiracy. Then I was sent to Bhutan to cover a presidential campaign, and it was clear that the king was still handpicking the government. The royalists were getting all the news coverage."

"I do read all your reports, Rupert," Jenny advised. "Are you coming to a point?"

"I have a cover at home to maintain too," Rupert said. He realized he was starting to get to angry, so he tried to calm down. "I left my boyfriend waiting at the airport for me, and he didn't know where I was until a week later."

"You handled it well," Jenny commented.

"I handled it adequately. This time. I can't stay radio silent if my mission goes beyond parameters. You have to give me some way to get a message to Arthur, and possibly Margot . . ."

"Let me stop you," Jenny interrupted. "I understand your frustration, but it is not unusual for missions to come up at the last minute. You were the only linguist in the area we could get to Bhutan in less than a week. The only solution I can offer you is to stop promising your return date. Tell them you don't know how long it will last, even if you have a return ticket."

In early May, Cyclone Nargis passed through Myanmar, killing thousands. Rupert was ostensibly sent to help with refugee resettlement in its wake, but the CIA had him taking breaks from that work to investigate claims of human rights abuses. He had told Arthur he couldn't accompany him and that he didn't know when he would be done.

As it turned out, a week later, Rupert was diverted to the Sichuan region of China again after a 7.9 earthquake killed thousands and left thousands more homeless. A courier gave him a briefing about an extended mission to Beijing. Rupert quickly scanned through it in the barracks-style warehouse where he had been staying. "This is two missions," he complained. "I won't be back home for over a month. I'll miss the premiere of my film!"

"We will contact boyfriend and agent," the courier said in heavily accented English. "Let them know you have delay."

Rupert switched to Chinese. "No, I have to be in Los Angeles on May 22. That is something I cannot miss." He paged to the second mission in his briefing. "You don't need me to monitor another election."

"I tell them you refuse trip to Nepal," she patiently explained in English, "but you must do Beijing job. No one else can do. China government not give visas to Westerners now because Olympic protests. Military aid meetings happen next week, and you need so much time to build your cover. Very dangerous to make mistakes."

CHAPTER 25: RUPERT TURNS THIRTY-NINE

On the train ride from Chengdu to Beijing, Rupert read through the extensive mission briefing twice. The upcoming operation was a bit of a promotion for Rupert, from linguist to special agent. He was no longer just being tasked with OR (observation and reporting); he was now embarking on an influence campaign. The target he would approach with a fellow agent was a general in the Chinese army named Tong Wu-meng. General Tong was the chief procurement officer, and the CIA was trying to convince him to recommend withdrawing military advisors and supplies from Sudan. The Sudanese government was using China's desperation for oil reserves to force them to supply pro-Arab militias. The Janjaweed were going through the rebellious, mostly African, western region of Darfur raping, burning, and killing everyone they encountered. The CIA analyst who had written the brief did not hesitate to call it genocide.

At that point, Rupert had spent enough time getting around in China, he had no trouble managing the multiple transfers from the train station to his hotel in the Xicheng District near the White Cloud Temple and the Capital Museum. On every train and on every platform, there was no doubt that the Summer Olympics were about to start. Athletes and fans wore Olympic hats and T-shirts, and advertisements for events crowded out almost every other ad space.

When he checked in at the hotel, the desk clerk commended him on his excellent use of Mandarin. In the same hand that passed him a magnetic-strip key card, the woman passed him a note on a folded piece of paper, telling Rupert he had a message waiting. Rupert took the elevator to the tenth floor, opened his room door, and set his suitcase down before opening the note:

Come by 1030 when you're settled. – Guy

The briefing included a blurry reproduction of a photograph of his partner, Guy Al-Misnad, next to a much better photo of Rupert. He grabbed it again from the outer pocket of his suitcase and headed out and down the hall to room 1030.

After he knocked on the door, Rupert heard a man's voice inside call out in English, "It's unlocked!"

Rupert opened the door and stepped into a room that was almost an exact copy of his, except that the colorful quilt and shams on the bed were a different palette. As the door finished closing and latching, the voice called out from behind the bathroom door, "I'll be out in a jiff. Make yourself at home."

When Guy exited the bathroom, he was wearing only a white, terrycloth robe. His curly, shoulder-length hair was wet, and his exposed chest, arms, and lower legs were covered with equally dark hair. His smile raised a square-cut moustache. He looked up at Rupert's greater height as he came to a halt. "Welcome to Beijing," he said in an English accent that reminded him of his old neighbors in Brooklyn.

"It would be edgy to find a xylophone afterward," Rupert said.

Guy chuckled and led Rupert by the arm to the only easy chair in the room. "You got my photo in your brief, and you came to me. IC-work doesn't use passwords as much as you straight OR guys have to." He sat on a corner of the bed. "Hakim Noor sends his regards. He told me you were green. Have you ever been on a mission before?"

Rupert gave him a sarcastic grin. "Yes, this will be my fifth mission, depending on how you count them."

Guy chuckled again. "And you managed to become fluent in Mandarin *and* Arabic?"

"Among a few dozen others, yes," Rupert replied. "I had a question for you."

"Go ahead, . . . Rupert." He said the name as if he thought it was comical.

"So, Guy, why do you have an alias and I don't?"

Guy sighed and looked a bit more serious finally. "You're not kicking around

275

in backwater kingdoms any more. People at this level will recognize you by sight, and at your level of face recognition, it would be hard to disguise you for up-close inspection, so we're capitalizing on your celebrity. Hopefully it will help sell my story as a lawyer for Qatar Petroleum if I have a celebrity as my U.N. translator."

"Should we be talking so loud about covert details?" Rupert asked. "Aren't you worried about bugs?"

"Oh," Guy replied. "On IC missions, unless you're really out in the boondocks, we have techs come in and do a sweep just before we arrive. They'll come back every morning after we leave for the day to sweep again after the maids leave."

"So, the brief said we were supposed to play it like a real simultaneous translation," Rupert said. "So everything I translate has to be exactly what you and General Tong are saying."

Guy got up to put on underwear and socks from his suitcase that was on a stand near the bathroom. "We can't ever be certain the general or somebody listening in isn't checking what we say in Arabic. Leave all the creativity to me. Okay?"

"Okay." Rupert appreciated working with an agent who had more experience, but he knew Guy's cockiness would wear on him over time.

"Go put on something more formal and then come back," Guy suggested. "We're due in two hours at a dinner at the foreign ministry."

When Rupert came back in a dark gray suit and black tie, Guy was in full Arab sheik attire. His headscarf was obviously ironed or starched to maintain such geometrically perfect folds. The rope headband was bright maroon with shining golden highlights. The long white thobe matched the scarf and was covered by a heavier brown robe. "So, Mr. Rocket," he began as he picked up a brown, leather briefcase, "you should henceforth refer to me by my alias."

"Certainly, Honorable Rashid bin Ahmed Al-Thani," Rupert proclaimed in his best Arabic accent. "You don't think the Al-Thani reference to the royal family is a bit too much?"

Guy also replied in Arabic. "If General Tong or his staff even recognize the name, it should impress them. Let's go."

Over the course of the evening, Rupert introduced Guy to a host of military leaders and foreign ministers. The American ambassador even came up at one point just to say hello to Rupert and compliment him for his performances in the trailers for his forthcoming movie. When General Tong finally dismissed his staff to circulate, who had been circling him like flies, Rupert immediately guided Guy in his direction.

As they had planned, Guy only requested a private meeting from General Tong to present a proposal from his supposed employer, Qatar Petroleum. General Tong said that he would consult his schedule when he next connected with his aides. Through Rupert, Guy told him he could be contacted at room 1030 at their hotel, and then they excused themselves. Guy made sure to play his part for a while after their brief exchange with Tong. He made Rupert translate Russian, Hindi, Japanese, and English before agreeing to return to their limousine and eventually their hotel rooms.

Rupert was finally getting used to the time zone and slept the night through. He had room service bring him breakfast and then shot an email to Arthur telling him the earthquake resettlement was going to be over in a little over a week, and he was looking forward to meeting him in L.A. for his premiere on the 22nd. Around eleven-thirty, Rupert's hotel phone rang. It was Guy telling him in Arabic to meet him in the hotel restaurant in an hour.

Rupert brushed his teeth and shaved finally. He put on his gray suit again, and wondered why he hadn't brought a second one. He headed down in the elevator right around twelve-thirty, and found Guy in the restaurant already at a table for four. He wore his same bin Ahmed Al-Thani costume except that the headband was black with red diamond shapes. "Mr. Rocket," he said in Arabic as Rupert sat down across from him, "I have a written report I'd like you to review before we begin."

Guy slid a folded piece of paper toward him. Rupert opened it. It was written in Arabic script:

Sweep this morning yielded bugs. We must remain in character
at all times now. Mission critical communications in writing
only and destroyed immediately after reading.

Rupert nodded at Guy and crumpled the paper and put it in his jacket pocket.

"Destroy immediately," Guy reiterated in Arabic.

"I'll take care of it, your Honor." Rupert found it odd how selective Guy was about which protocols he followed more loosely than others.

"We seem to have gotten their attention," Guy commented.

"Does your translator ever get any time off?" Rupert joked.

"You had the whole morning off," Guy managed to say with great seriousness. "We need to increase the stakes. This afternoon we meet with the Japanese ambassador. I trust that will make General Tong sufficiently nervous to expedite our meeting with him."

After lunch, Rupert arranged for a limousine to take them to the Japanese embassy. The front desk informed him when it arrived, and he went to gather Guy. The embassy was a boxy building that looked like a waffle iron near Chaoyang Park and the U.S. embassy. Like their hotel, it was also next to a busy freeway, but at least Rupert appreciated the trees on the far side of the building.

It didn't take them long to get through security, so within twenty minutes of arriving, they were sitting down with the ambassador and his secretary. He thanked Rupert for agreeing to translate between Arabic and Japanese for him. Guy quickly laid out the same proposal he was going to offer to General Tong: an exclusive joint venture arrangement with China for the next two years. Guy decided to make the ask relatively easy, so he requested lowered Japanese export taxes for Qatari businesses. The ambassador seemed genuinely impressed and promised to get back to them soon. As before, Guy asked them to contact him at the hotel.

When Guy and Rupert returned to the hotel, the desk clerk had three messages for Guy. Rupert carried them to two chairs in the lobby where they sat down and Rupert translated them into Arabic. One was from the Japanese ambassador already requesting a second meeting the following day. One was from the Canadian foreign minister, requesting a meeting. And the third was General Tong.

"We caught more fish than we expected," Guy mused in Arabic, "but at least we hooked the one we wanted."

Rupert went to Guy's room to call the Japanese and Canadian consulates back while Guy changed out of his oppressively hot clothing. Rupert promised to arrange meetings with both of them later in the week. Guy sat down on the bed to listen more carefully to Rupert's side of the conversation with Tong's aide. When he finished the conversation in Chinese, Guy anxiously asked in Arabic, "What did they say? How soon can we see them?"

"The earliest they could give us is in two days," Rupert reported, "and then only at six o'clock at night."

"That's good," Guy said. He rubbed his hands together like he was about to eat something tasty.

"How do you figure?" Rupert asked. He was appreciating all the practice he was getting in Arabic.

"If they make us wait only two days," Guy explained, "they are probably very excited about our offer, but they don't want us to know how desperate they are. And this way, they can see if we are willing to talk with them after Canada and Japan. It will make them feel they have more bargaining power."

Two days later, when they returned to the foreign ministry building where the dinner had been, they were shown into a conference room where General Tong was waiting. He had a notepad and pen, and he was completely alone. Rupert and Guy took seats across the table from him side by side. Guy opened his briefcase and removed a pad and pen as well.

Tong faced Guy and spoke in Arabic. "Can your translator be trusted?"

Guy allowed himself a bit of a smile and nodded slowly in Tong's direction.

Rupert decided to reinforce Guy's response. "It would ruin my reputation if I were indiscrete," Rupert added in Chinese.

"I hear you are offering an exclusive license for joint ventures with your company," Tong said carefully in Chinese.

Once Rupert translated for Guy, and Guy responded in Arabic, Rupert said in Chinese, "I will have to speak with the Japanese ambassador about his lack of discretion."

Guy smiled more broadly and spoke again in Arabic. Rupert translated. "It is a two-year contract I am authorized to offer, but in the case of China, my boss, Director Al-Kaabi, insists on an additional stipulation."

"We are prepared to offer trade incentives," Tong immediately volunteered.

After Rupert translated into Arabic and Guy responded, Rupert finished some notes and then replied, "That is generous of you, General, but it would be difficult to publicize a joint venture with China, when you are supporting ethnic or religious cleansing in western Sudan. To receive the contract, Chinese military advisors in and aid to Sudan would both need to be withdrawn."

"You cannot dictate under what terms we purchase oil from other sources!" Tong blustered.

Rupert dutifully translated the Chinese into Arabic. He could see a stubborn, determined look appearing in Guy's face. Very quietly and efficiently, Guy put his pad and pen back in his briefcase and closed it. As he stood up and started to reach for the briefcase again, General Tong whispered to Rupert, "What is he doing?"

Rupert looked at Guy again. Guy shook his head. He was turning over the reins to Rupert. He tried to come up with the right Chinese words to make it sound polite but condemning. "His Honor, Mr. bin Ahmed Al-Thani, feels insulted that you would not even consider his position for a moment before rejecting it."

Rupert picked his pen and pad up off the table and scooted his chair back also. "What are you going to do?" Tong said with a certain amount of anxiety.

Rupert turned to Guy and translated for him. Guy folded his arms and responded in Arabic. Rupert translated into Chinese for the general. "We had preferred to work with China, but if Sudanese oil is more important to you than Qatari oil, we will seek other partners."

"We would sacrifice all oil reserves from the Sudan," Tong pleaded. "They have made military support a condition of our trade agreement."

After Rupert translated, Guy put his briefcase down on the floor and leaned toward the general with his fingertips on the table. Rupert translated his response into Chinese, "We can double the amount of oil Sudan would send you over the course of two years. What do you get from them? Ninety-two thousand barrels a year?"

"One hundred twenty thousand," Tong corrected. "Are you truly prepared to offer us a quarter-million barrels per year?"

Rupert translated, and Guy sat down beside him again as he replied in Arabic. "Easily," Rupert said in Chinese. "With freight on board at your choice of South China ports. We can draw up the papers tomorrow for your signature."

"I will need time," Tong immediately said as he scribbled notes on his pad. "The approval of my superiors and then the withdrawal you request will take at least a week or more to coordinate."

Rupert translated, and Guy stood and picked up his briefcase as he responded in Arabic. "Mr. bin Ahmed Al-Thani must return to Qatar before then. We will draw up a conditional arrangement tomorrow, but the joint-venture agreement will have to wait until we receive confirmation of your withdrawal from the Sudan."

Once Rupert had finished translating, the general replied, "I will need a security from your government to convince my government that you will not back out of the arrangement once we have already ended our agreement with the Sudan."

Rupert got up as well as he translated the general's request for Guy. Guy opened the door to the conference room as he replied in Arabic. Rupert translated into Chinese. "The Emir will make a public statement to that effect by the end of this week."

Once Rupert and Guy were back in the limo headed to their hotel, Rupert checked that the driver's screen was down and asked Guy in Arabic, "Do you really think you can get the Emir of Qatar to issue a public statement about wanting a joint venture with China?"

"Not at all," Guy quickly replied. "We only have to get the Emir to publicly decry Chinese intervention in Darfur. His ministers have already been saying as much publicly. That should be enough to rattle the correct cages in the Chinese military, and then the dominoes will fall in the Department of Foreign Affairs and Trade. Then we just need to beef up the peacekeeping troops there, and it's a big win."

"I assume you have someone at Qatar Petroleum backing up your cover," Rupert said. "You know, in case they start verifying your story."

"They are willing to keep mum about negotiations for unannounced contracts," Guy reported, "so I'm pretty sure we're in the clear there."

Three days later, Rupert landed at LAX. A limo from the film company picked him up and took him to his hotel. Arthur was waiting for him in his room when he opened the door. Rupert got a big smile and gave him a bear hug. "Hey there, handsome. How did you know I was arriving here today?"

"I checked with Margot." Arthur giggled. "She felt sorry for me when you delayed coming back from India. How was China?"

Rupert had to switch gears. He was writing out notes for his Beijing report right up until the plane landed. "The devastation was horrible. We had to stay on canvas cots in a warehouse with no privacy, spotty electricity, and no running water. I worked twelve-hour days."

Arthur broke out of the hug and flopped down on the king-size bed. "You worked longer days than that on this movie we're going to see tomorrow night."

Rupert flopped onto the bed next to him. "You did hear me mention no privacy, spotty electricity, and no running water, right?"

At the premiere, at Grauman's Chinese Theatre, both Rupert and Arthur were assigned beards. They escorted one of the female leads and her lesbian lover down the red carpet, but they got to sit together in the theater. At the end, the audience clapped, and Arthur kissed Rupert on the cheek. "You liked it?" Rupert asked.

"Do another one!" Arthur demanded. "You were great! It was hard to remember it was you up there."

Rupert ended up having a month back in New York before Jenny called him back in for a new assignment. It was a hot day in early July, and Rupert felt bold enough to wear shorts and a polo shirt. Jenny had gone similarly casual in a top that showed her bare midriff.

"We're sending you to Guinea," she announced. "There's a huge camp there for refugees from Sierra Leone. I'm sending you there to help with the administration for three weeks. They're expanding and they need the time to find more volunteers."

"And will I have time for a side trip somewhere?" Rupert teased.

Jenny smiled. "I'm sure we can arrange for a couple of days off for you to do some sightseeing."

Once again Rupert dissuaded Arthur from accompanying him to the refugee camp. He was surprised how persistent Arthur was becoming, but then he looked at his calendar and saw how much of the past year he had been away. He needed to make a change soon, he decided. It was getting harder to leave Arthur behind.

The refugee camp was much like the one in Sichuan, but the walls and roof were plastic over aluminum poles instead of brick-and-mortar buildings. Canvas cots, bottled water, and meals in cardboard trays with plastic wrap covering them were the standard. Some American and French companies had donated shoes and clothing, and Rupert took great joy in passing them out.

That night, a Jeep pulled up near Rupert's tent. A man leaned into the tent and said in a French accent, "It would be great to be under the moon at midnight."

Rupert had already been practicing a couple of responses to the July passwords. The man had used *great, under,* and *midnight* from U SOMETHING, so he replied in a whisper, "In this shade, even a taco would be invisible."

The man drove him back to the airport in Conakry and ushered him onto a small plane. As the plane was taxiing, he pulled a mission brief out of a pocket in the side of the cabin. "Read this on the way over."

Rupert took the brief from him. He waited until the plane took off to crack the seal.

They had Rupert bring a copy of his new movie subtitled in Arabic to President Abdallahi of Mauritania. The President was so grateful, he agreed to grant Rupert's request to let him stay the night at the Presidential Palace in the capital of Nouakchott. It looked like a cross between the White House and an Arab mosque, and Rupert carefully observed all the security measures when he was given a tour.

Late at night, Rupert left his guest room with a towel and a flashlight and bribed his guard to let him take a swim in the palace's pool. From the rooftop pool, Rupert had a view of the front gate and surrounding guard towers. As he had anticipated from stealing a glance at the daily guard rotation schedule in the security office, the guards started disappearing at midnight. Rupert moved to the edge of the roof and signaled with the flashlight in the direction of the military convoy. He made it back to his room before the soldiers broke in to put an end to Abdallahi's 21-year rule.

On the plane ride back to New York, Rupert typed out a text message to Margot:

> *I've been traveling too much this year and need to spend time with Arthur. Can you get me a movie role that would accommodate both of us until December?*

Once Rupert was back in New York for two days, Margot called him back. "Hey, sexy," she said. "I was putting off this guy from Sony Pictures, so your timing is perfect. You need to be in L.A. for a screen test next Tuesday, but since they requested you, I think it's just a formality. You've got the lead, Rupert!"

"That's great news, Margot!" Rupert shouted. "Email me the time and place, and I'll be there. Do you have a script?"

"I'll send it to you before I leave tonight, sweetie. I'm glad you're back from all that do-gooding and ready to make us some more money."

As Rupert was disconnecting the call, Arthur who was home early because of a dental appointment, came into the bedroom and crawled onto the bed next to him. "Did I hear you got another movie role?"

"I'm gonna' star in this one." He kissed Arthur and tousled his hair. "And you get to come along for once!"

"Where is it going to be?" Arthur kissed him back.

"I don't know yet."

It ended up being shot in Toronto with locations in the forests north of the city, and Arthur's enthusiasm didn't flag at all whether they were at a hotel in downtown Toronto or in a trailer on location. He kept thanking Rupert for bringing him every couple of days over the four months they were there, and Rupert more firmly decided that he had to put time with Arthur ahead of his CIA work. He planned to meet with his handler, Jenny, when he returned to New York to work out the arrangements.

Film shooting wrapped in early December, and so when he met with Jenny on December 12, he was ready to propose a temporary sabbatical from his CIA work. But as soon as he was sitting in front of her, she launched into another assignment. The request that came from UNHCR simply requested he help manage the distribution of new supplies at the same refugee camp in Guinea.

Then she handed him a CIA mission brief to read. This one involved helping a paramilitary team from Sierra Leone cross the border at the U.N.'s refugee camp and into the capital city, Conakry. He was needed to convince the refugee camp management to let them in without too many questions.

She assured Rupert he would be away a week at most. He would be home in time for Christmas. Rupert sighed, rolled up the brief, and put it in his jacket pocket. He stood and started to leave and then turned back. "You've been putting me to work a lot this year," he said slowly, "and I'd like that pace to . . . ease up a bit in 2009."

"I'll see what I can do," she promised.

Arthur was, of course, understanding and made Rupert promise to be home by his birthday. Rupert said he would try.

Three days later, he was on a jet again. Landing in Conakry was becoming very familiar to him. People he knew from the refugee camp met him at the airport and brought him back to their tent city. They fed him some stew and gave him a cot in the supply manager's tent to spend the night. Rupert woke with everyone else the next morning, and he helped uncrate and distribute the new supplies that had arrived when he had. He helped serve food in a brand-new cafeteria line they had built, and because it was December, almost his birthday, it reminded him of going down to the church in Chelsea to feed the homeless. Here were thousands of homeless people he was serving. It started to make him tear up to see their hopeful faces finally catching sight of the food he was dishing out.

He knew the soldiers were due to come through that night, so he bunked down to take a nap right after sundown. He awoke to shouting outside his tent. Someone was yelling, "They have weapons!"

Rupert realized he'd overslept, slipped into his sandals, and scrambled out of the tent. The conversation in French was going too fast for Rupert to parse it. He approached the group of three camp workers and four very large, athletic men with full backpacks and one shorter, more wiry man who was right up in the camp workers' faces cursing at them in French.

"Guy!" he called out. The shorter man turned to look at him. He continued in French. "Stop abusing my staff, please!"

Guy stalked over and gave Rupert a hug. "Good to see you again, Rupert!"

Rupert approached his three colleagues. "I've got this. You can head back to your tents."

"They've got weapons," one of the women whispered to Rupert in English.

"I'll handle it," he whispered back.

After the camp workers dispersed, Rupert led Guy and his four companions to the edge of the compound. "We can't travel to Conakry at night. I'll borrow a Jeep. It will be tight, but if we leave by three o'clock, I should be able to get you guys to the capital by sundown."

"We'll need a place to hide out until it gets late," one of Guy's companions mentioned.

"Fine," Rupert said. "I think I know a place."

Though it was December 22, Rupert estimated he could still bring them back to the border and then turn right around and head back to Conakry for a flight to New York. He could be with Arthur for Christmas Eve. They were stopped by police just outside of the capital, and Rupert said they were his bodyguards and bribed the officers with autographs and photos to let them pass.

Rupert waited with the Jeep at the repair garage in Conakry for hours. Guy and the other four men finally returned at around two-thirty in the morning. One of the men was limping, and he could see lacerations on the arms and legs of two others. Only one of them was still carrying a pack.

Guy ran ahead to talk to Rupert first. "We have to get going!"

Rupert whispered back, "I told you; we can't risk taking those roads at night. It's too dangerous. Especially when it's this cloudy."

Guy pulled Rupert further back into the garage near the back of the Jeep. "It would be more dangerous for us to stay," he whispered. "We have to risk it."

Guy was finally close enough that he saw blood spatters on Guy's forehead and forearms. "What did you do?" Rupert whispered insistently.

Guy started to walk away and called back in Arabic. "You don't want to know."

Driving very slowly and frequently stopping to check the GPS locator, they made it back to the refugee camp by sunrise on December 23. Rupert walked them to the Sierra Leone border and then trudged back to the camp. One of the other camp managers came up to him and asked him if he had slept.

"I'll sleep on the plane," Rupert told her. "Can you drive me to the airport in Conakry?"

Rupert hadn't slept all night. So it seemed like a nightmare when he was driven back to the airport, and it looked like the city had gone through a military coup. Soldiers and military vehicles were everywhere. Everyone was surprised that President Conté had died early that morning. But Rupert pieced together what had happened, and he felt sick that he had been part of it.

Arthur met him at LaGuardia at one o'clock Christmas morning. "I am done working for the U.N.," he declared as he almost collapsed into Arthur's outstretched arms.

"Happy birthday," Arthur timidly called out.

"Anything's got to be better than the past two days," Rupert lamented.

CHAPTER 26: RUPERT TURNS FORTY-ONE

On the bus and train rides home to their apartment in Battery Park City, Rupert could barely keep his eyes open. He had gone almost two days without sleep, so he only managed to grunt in agreement occasionally as Arthur talked on. He roused enough when they were transferring to the train to pick up more of it:

"I decided to just get gifts from both of us for everyone except Jorge. I had no idea what sort of thing you'd want to give him, because I know you two have a lot of history. I just got a Bed Bath and Beyond certificate for your father and a webcam for Mike, so you could do video chats with him."

Once they had settled into seats on the nearly deserted train at 2:45 in the morning, Rupert lay down with his head on Arthur's lap. Arthur took advantage of the brief period of Rupert's alertness to ask questions:

"I don't know if you've gotten any news while you were in Africa, but the ACLU just sued Arkansas over the constitutionality of their gay marriage ban. That's a strategy I hope they can use in other states. Did you get to see any of the Summer Olympics while you were in China? I forgot to ask you."

"No, I had to work," Rupert replied. "I'm sorry. It was impossible to get visas again after I left to meet you at the premiere."

"Do you want to practice your Chinese with me again?" Arthur's tone was far too chipper for three o'clock in the morning.

"No, babe. *Wǒ tài lèile.*"

"Why are you so tired? Is it all jet lag?" Arthur sounded significantly concerned.

"I had to work twenty-four hours straight just before my flight." Rupert moaned to emphasize the sacrifice he had made. "Why are we riding the train anyway? Why didn't you hire a driver?"

"I'm sorry," Arthur said. "I had kind of gotten used to using public transit again while you were away, and I forgot."

It was after three-thirty on Christmas morning before they arrived home and Rupert found himself facing his old bed. He managed to get most of his clothes off before he collapsed. He vaguely remembered Arthur repositioning him at some point, but otherwise he slept soundly.

When he next roused, the bedroom blinds were open, and Arthur was not beside him. He got up to use the bathroom, and Arthur wasn't there either. He checked every other room in the apartment, and Arthur wasn't in any of them. And the Christmas tree lights were unplugged, which Arthur only did when he was the last to leave the apartment. Rupert wondered if some emergency had occurred, and in Arthur's hurry to leave, he had forgotten that Rupert was there and unplugged the tree.

Then it dawned on him. One of his two most-hated blessings had visited him that morning: the invisibility blessing. When he had first received it at age ten, he had wondered why the Grogoch or the universe or whatever was responsible for picking blessings thought that invisibility was a blessing. It meant being ignored and overlooked, and that was hard for Rupert to imagine as being a gift.

Rupert imagined that Arthur had gotten up before Rupert, used the bathroom, and then completely missed seeing him still in bed when he came back. He had probably left the apartment to go look for Rupert, after concluding that Rupert had left, just as had happened so many times when he was a boy struggling with the approximation of invisibility he had suffered through for a year.

He fished his cell phone out of the pocket of the jacket he had worn last night. There was a missed call from Arthur's cell phone on it, from two hours before. He immediately called Arthur back. "Hey, Arthur. Where did you run off to?"

"Rupert? Rupert, are you okay? I couldn't find you after I woke up this morning. I was surprised you didn't tell me where you were going. Where are you?"

It was obvious to Rupert that he needed to take the blame for crossed signals. "I'm sorry. I had a really bad stomach pain from something I ate and went out to get something for it. I'm home now. Where are you?"

Arthur sighed. "I just left that church in Chelsea you used to volunteer at on Christmas Day."

"I stopped doing that when we started dating," Rupert argued.

"I thought maybe you got nostalgic for it. I don't know. I'm headed home now." Arthur paused for a moment. "Please, sweetie, don't ever take off like that without letting me know. It really freaked me out."

"I'm sorry," Rupert said with as much humility as he could muster. "I will try to do better next time."

"If it was an emergency, I understand," Arthur conceded. "At least you let me know as soon as you could."

As Rupert waited for Arthur to return home, he tried to catch up with the pre-planning he had been doing on his new blessings before he started traveling so much. The way he had dealt with the invisibility blessing as a boy was to announce himself frequently, and plan on arriving a little late so he could find the other party instead of waiting for them to find him, which they never would.

But Rupert had a tool now that could make it easier to be noticed: his cell phone. If they could avoid looking where Rupert was, they could not ignore him calling them.

The issue with Arthur was a bit more complex. He couldn't call Arthur every time he went into another room. He might need to keep close to Arthur when they were together. The invisibility effect seemed to engage whenever he was out of someone's fairly continuous sight. He couldn't even rely on being at home or at his desk when he promised he would be. Arthur could walk right by him and not see him.

Tag teaming with one or more friends or acquaintances was something that had helped him as a boy. When his mother came back from the kitchen wondering where Rupert had gone, his grandmother or Mike, who had remained with him, could point out that he had not left their vicinity. His closest relatives had been in on the invisibility blessing, however, so they eventually adapted. After being away from Rupert, they had learned to expect he was where he should have been, and they occasionally had to pretend they were playing hide-and-seek and call for Rupert to reveal his hiding place.

But that depended on the other person recognizing that some supernatural force was giving them a year-long blind spot. Rupert considered that he might need to tell Arthur about his curse and blessing to keep him from thinking he was going crazy.

When Rupert heard Arthur return, he rushed toward the door to check in with him immediately. He hugged Arthur. "I'm sorry I . . . took off without letting you know," Rupert repeated.

"It's okay," Arthur said as he disengaged from the hug to take his coat off. "Are you feeling okay now?"

"Yeah, I'm fine," Rupert said as he bounded in the direction of the Christmas tree he had plugged in while he was waiting. "Let's open presents."

That strategy seemed to work best for Arthur: Rupert would check in with him before he could panic that Rupert had disappeared. It was a lot easier than Rupert had anticipated, and he relaxed into a pattern once the holidays were over and Arthur made his daily trek to ABT's offices. He made plans with friends, went to the gym and ballet class, and checked in with Margot periodically. He hired a chauffeur named Randy who drove a black Ford Explorer with tinted windows.

After getting through the first full week of January 2009 with no substantial hiccups, Rupert finally wrote to Jenny to tell her that he wanted to quit working for the UNHCR—and thereby quit the CIA as well. Within ten minutes of pressing send on the email, Rupert's cell phone rang.

"Rupert, I haven't gotten a chance to read your report on the refugee camp in Guinea," Jenny began before Rupert could speak. "Did something go wrong?"

Rupert sighed. He wasn't sure how to communicate his distaste for being blindsided with something so revolting as covertly aiding a bloody coup. "It was very much like my last trip to Guinea, except this time it was considerably messier."

"Ah." She seemed to understand his subtext. "You know, Rupert, we don't always know how a situation will develop once we get in there. It might have been planned to go very cleanly and efficiently, but the circumstances required a bit more . . . effort."

Rupert sighed. He wondered if she was trying to cover up what had been the plan all along. "Given the people I was working with, I think a messy situation was inevitable."

"Very well." She paused for a moment before continuing. "I am leaving tomorrow for some meetings in Washington, and then I am staying for Mr. Obama's inauguration."

Rupert suddenly remembered his manners. "Oh, I forgot you said you knew him. You must be happy that he won."

"And you are not?" she teased.

"No, I am, too. Were you invited to any events?"

"Two balls," Jenny reported. "I have a lot of packing to do. I will pass your message to the appropriate parties so no one else solicits you for assignments."

Rupert knew she meant Parker Kilpatrick, his CIA boss. "Tell him I'm free to meet anytime next week."

"Will do. *Nilifurahia kufanya kazi na wewe!*"

Rupert had spoken Swahili with Jenny often enough to remember a lot of common words and phrases. "It was good working with you also, Jenny!"

On the following Tuesday, a few minutes after Arthur had left for work, Rupert got a call from Kilpatrick. "Parker," he said with unaccustomed familiarity and a tinge of sarcasm, "so good to hear from you again!"

"I'll be in Washington Square Park at noon," he said without acknowledging Rupert's tone. "We can catch up then."

It was a chilly mid-January day, so Rupert bundled up in many layers, wearing a scarf and stocking cap in addition to his mandatory dark glasses. He called for Randy to pick him up in front of the building as he called the elevator. By the time Rupert had descended from the twenty-first floor and crossed the lobby and the courtyard, the black SUV was waiting for him.

He got in the back seat, because it had a TV, and he liked to watch the morning news shows. He asked Randy to drop him off at the north side of the park nearest the big arch. Rupert figured that it was the most obvious place to meet, and he waited for Parker to arrive.

Rupert checked his phone frequently, and when it was almost ten after twelve, he got a text from Parker:

R u running late? Where r u?

Rupert laughed. The seasoned CIA operative had fallen victim to his invisibility blessing too. He texted back:

Check beneath the arch.

He saw the shorter, well-dressed man approach with earmuffs bracketing his exposed widow's peak. Rupert started to take a step in his direction to get his attention, but then he decided to tease him a bit. It would be interesting to see if Parker lost his trademark nonchalance. Parker walked past him once without looking up at him. He passed by Rupert a second time, still not seeing him. He finally stopped and texted Rupert:

Did u mean under or near arch?

Rupert couldn't help but giggle. He texted back:

Right beneath the center of it.

This time when Parker started to pass him by, Rupert tapped him on the shoulder and said, "Boo!"

Parker jumped as if he were being attacked. He looked startled almost to the point of fear at first, but then he settled back into his usual calm and stood more casually. "There you are. I don't know how I missed you."

"I know why you did," Rupert continued teasing. "For the next year, I'm going to be world champion in hide-and-seek." He broke into laughter.

Parker guided Rupert by the arm away from the other people taking partial refuge from the wind in the arch. "That's a skill we could use in the agency. Are you sure you want to quit?"

"I told you I didn't want to hurt or kill anyone when I agreed to work with you." Rupert lowered his voice. "That includes driving the getaway Jeep for a group of paramilitary assassins."

"I should have discussed that with you in advance, I suppose." Parker pointed at a bench far from anyone else, and they both sat. "I didn't think it counted if you were just the transport guy. *Mujhe maaf kar den.*"

"I'm sorry. My grasp of Hindi has faded. Languages were last year, invisibility is this year."

Parker quickly turned to look more directly at Rupert. "What did you just say?"

"I was just trying . . . to explain." Rupert stumbled to get the words out. "I have only been practicing Chinese, Swahili, Russian, and French enough to stay fluent in them. And German, of course."

"There was a guy like you . . ." Parker started to point his finger at the trees in front of them, as if they held the memory he was searching for. "When I was training at CIA University, one of the older instructors, when we got him drunk, would tell stories of the early days of the CIA back in the 1940s. One of the lead spies recruited to help run the agency back then was a guy he only referred to by his code name: The Spook. He was the one that started that nickname for all CIA spies. He had been born around the turn of the century, and he died fairly young—a year after the agency formed."

Rupert looked at Parker. He seemed to be really recalling something, not fabricating a ruse.

"The instructor told us that the Spook would have these uncanny abilities for a year at a time, and then they would switch. One year he could see ghosts of people who had died. One year he healed really fast. One year he could understand and speak every language. . . . just like you did last year. And now . . . I know I walked through that archway over there at least three times and never saw you until you tapped me on the shoulder. So, you have some sort of invisibility thing going on now?"

Rupert studied Parker more closely. He didn't look like he was humoring him. "Are you sure you want to hear about this?"

"Hey, if it helped me do my job, I'd believe in the Tooth Fairy again. What'cha got, Rocket?"

Rupert explained how his family had been cursed by one Irish fairy, and another had blessed him on the day he was born. He described the luck echo that began when he was twenty-five, and how he could now anticipate what each year's new ability would be. He explained how the invisibility blessing worked, and Parker insisted on testing it again. And again.

Before they parted and Rupert called Randy to pick him up at the same location, Parker promised to transfer Rupert to another division. He would move out of CI-work with the "Freedom Flag" operation and become a courier.

As Rupert rode in the SUV back home, the transfer made sense to him. The biggest problem the couriers he'd worked with had had was evading surveillance. For the rest of the year, it would be a piece of cake for him to shake someone tailing him. And he would be far enough from any direct action to keep his conscience clear.

Just at the point in February when it seemed everything in his life was finally going well, he was at a Valentine's dinner with Arthur. And Arthur got very quiet right after the waiter had taken their orders. Rupert finally spoke first. "Is something bothering you, Arthur?"

"Yes." Arthur paused for almost a minute before continuing. "For the past few weeks, I feel like you've been ducking out on me a lot. I feel like I'm searching for you all the time. I was hoping you could explain what's going on."

Rupert folded his arms and let out a frustrated sigh. This didn't seem like a good time to tell Arthur about the curse and blessing. But there he was, asking for an explanation for a pattern that couldn't be ignored. "Well, you've commented before how I seem to have strange things happen with me on Christmas morning every year."

"Yeah, that hyperacusis especially." Arthur seemed to relax in anticipation of the answer he had been seeking. "It was bizarre how your ears got so sensitive and then back to normal exactly a year later."

"Good example," Rupert commented. "You remember when we first met, how you were trying so hard to give me money?"

"Yes. I was trying to borrow money to give you. You really seemed to need it. That is related to this?"

"And the year after that, you did whatever I asked without question."

He noticed Arthur trying to connect the disparate things he mentioned. "I cared about you. Of course I wanted to make you happy."

"But you don't remember saying no to me that year, right?"

Arthur thought for a moment. "I don't remember."

"How about the year I could predict the future . . . 9/11 and that other stuff?"

"That *was* freaky."

Rupert waited for the busboy to finish filling their water glasses. "There was that year when I was muscle building really fast."

"That's related to this too?"

"It is," Rupert confirmed. "They all started on one birthday and ended on the next. You commented how frequently I was getting propositioned the year after that. Everywhere we went. Men and women, gay or straight."

"That started and ended on your birthday, too?"

"Yes. Christmas morning sometime between eight-thirty and nine-thirty. Last year I could understand and speak any language I heard. This year, people have trouble keeping track of where I am. You remember how many times lately you've gone off looking for me, and I was in the room you'd just left?"

"I keep thinking you're gaslighting me or something," Arthur confessed, "but I don't think I can wait until April First. What does it all mean?"

Arthur listened politely and quietly while Rupert narrated the story of his grandmother Zelda meeting the Grogoch, the spiteful Patricia the Pooka had mentioned, and the luck echo that was repeating the odd twists in his fate from his first twenty-five years.

"I met the woman you call the Pooka?" Arthur asked.

"About five and a half years ago at that Italian restaurant in Midtown you like."

"The one with the waterfall." Arthur paused, looked up at Rupert, paused again. "I have to say, your story makes a certain amount of sense, as far as explaining some of the weird stuff you can do, but you're asking me to believe that you've been enchanted. By a fairy. And that worries me. Did you talk to your therapist about all this?"

"Y-yes," Rupert stammered. He was concerned that he had blown past Arthur's easy-going tolerance.

"You're an amazing guy," Arthur said as he took Rupert's hands in his across the table. "And you're sexy and kind and generous, and I love you." Arthur sighed and released Rupert's hands. "And I'm worried you may be a little insane. So, after dinner tonight, I'm going to go back to our place, pack some things . . ."

"No, you don't have to go!" Rupert pleaded. "I can get a hotel room somewhere. You can stay at the apartment."

Just then, the waiter brought their food. Before he set down Arthur's plate, Arthur asked him to wrap it to go. When Rupert asked for the same, Arthur suggested he finish his at the restaurant so that Arthur would be moved out already when Rupert returned home. Before Rupert could think of some other reason for Arthur to change his mind, Arthur had already left. The bouquet and the heart-shaped box of chocolates were still in his backpack. And the steaming plate of food he had ordered just turned his stomach.

When he returned home, Rupert noticed Arthur's suitcase was no longer next to his in the hall closet. Arthur's backpack was no longer on the floor beside the desk. The drawers in the bedroom where Arthur's clothes had been were empty. Rupert sat down on a corner of the bed, put his head in his hands, and started sobbing. His mind kept switching from Patricia to the Pooka to the

Grogoch as targets for the anger that was slowly building in his stomach. Another boyfriend driven away by his twisted blessings. No more Arthur to spoil with expensive dinners and shows. No more Arthur to wake up beside him. To fold laundry with him. To play video games with. To take on trips, to practice Chinese with, and to have sex with. No more Arthur. It seemed impossible after so many years of devotion, but his absence was inescapable. He didn't brush his teeth. He didn't even get under the covers. He jostled and lay awake for hours before he finally passed out.

In the morning, he wondered if he should call Arthur. He hoped Arthur had changed his mind after a night of sleep, assuming he'd slept better than Rupert had. He stared at his cell phone for forty-five minutes, occasionally scrolling back through Arthur's texts nostalgically. He decided to wait for Arthur to contact him first. He was the one who broke it off.

Rupert ran into Guy Al-Misnad again in March. He delivered to him a brief for another Freedom Flag operation in Madagascar.

Rupert figured after three weeks he needed to at least let Arthur know that he was still open to reconciling. He texted Arthur to see how he was doing. Arthur texted back:

Don't contact me. I'll contact you when I'm ready.

By early April, Vermont, New Hampshire, Iowa, and Sweden had all made same-sex marriage legal. Rupert wanted to talk about it with Arthur. He called Danny instead. After that he called Margot, begging her to find him a nice long movie to shoot. She came through, and he spent most of the next four months on a sound stage in Los Angeles. He wanted to tell Arthur that he could stay in the apartment while he was gone, but he couldn't. He asked Chantal to get the message to him.

He heard from Denise and Michaela. Despite the passage of the infamous Proposition 8, they were still legally married, and they were moving back to New York to join a lawsuit to get same-sex marriage passed there. He wondered if they had told Arthur. They wouldn't reveal if they had.

He arrived in Taiwan in mid-August to help refugees in the wake of Typhoon Morakot. He frequently took breaks to help with the surveillance of the corrupt president of Taiwan, Chen Shui-bian, and his cover was never blown. President Chen was arrested on 9/11 in 2009, so Rupert was sent home to New York. There was still no evidence that Arthur had been there in his absence.

A couple of weeks later, Jenny passed along the news that two of the volunteer managers he knew from the refugee camp in Guinea were massacred along with 155 others by the Guinean military for protesting the coup Rupert had helped succeed. Jenny made herself available if Rupert wanted to talk through the grief. He called her once after that, and they talked for twenty minutes.

Chantal invited Rupert to a Halloween party to help celebrate the Matthew Shepard Act, the first U.S. law to offer any protection to transgender people. Rupert went in costume. He was pretty sure Arthur was not there.

Danny and Max took Rupert out to see *Avatar* at the cinema in Times Square for his fortieth birthday. Rupert wished he could go back to the church and feed the homeless. But with the release of his third film and his fourth due out next summer, he had to remain in disguise when in public.

The passing of his invisibility blessing was a relief. The new omniscience blessing was easier to deal with. It just made him seem a bit too pedantic. He appreciated when someone asked him something for which the answer was ambiguous or uncertain, and he could finally say he didn't know.

Parker Kilpatrick had discreetly let it slip that there was another Spook working for the CIA, and Rupert spent most of 2010 answering emails and phone calls from data specialists trying to locate fugitives and foreign spies and terrorists. He flew down to Washington, DC, at one point and met briefly with President Obama, who encouraged Rupert to focus on tracking down Osama bin Laden. Between then and the end of the year, Rupert had given the military leads on bin Laden's locations, but he moved too quickly and too often and always avoided capture.

Danny and Max took Rupert out for his forty-first birthday as well. They went to dim sum in Chinatown, and once Rupert had posed for a sufficient number of selfies, the other patrons left them alone. At one point, when Danny got up to use the bathroom, Max revealed that several of their friends in common were trying to convince Arthur to give Rupert another chance. He also heard that Arthur was living in Astoria and had gotten a promotion to General Manager, when Rick Kassel had retired.

After almost two years without any other information or contact with Arthur, Rupert felt Arthur might never be back in his life. He had rarely had sex and hadn't dated anyone at all. He wondered if he needed to move on. He looked at Max just as Danny was returning to their table. They kissed briefly before Danny sat down, and Rupert's eyes started tearing up.

Danny glanced at Rupert crying and then glared at Max. "What did you do this time?"

CHAPTER 27: RUPERT TURNS FORTY-TWO

John Gomez had grown up in Texas, the Anglo-Saxon adopted son of Mexican parents. Rupert had met John at Julliard. They ended up in several dance classes together, and they bonded as part of the smaller proportion of male ballet dancers there. Rupert had always found John very attractive, so back in his teens, it was no burden at all to hang out with him and listen to John's stories about the women he dated. As their friendship advanced through their twenties, Rupert didn't seek out his handsome, straight friend as often anymore. They more often just greeted each other and shared small talk when they met on the street, at a dance class or performance, or when mutual friends had invited both of them out.

So it was a surprise to hear from John again for only the second time since Rupert got out of jail. He wanted to meet one-on-one. Rupert apologized that meeting in public was getting more and more difficult for him to do without constant interruptions from adoring fans with questionable personal boundaries. John invited Rupert to meet him at his apartment in the East Village just south of 14th Street. Rupert was in the midst of a blessing whose effects were easy to control, so that reduced his stress, and he proposed meeting on a Thursday afternoon in early February 2010.

Randy dropped him off in front of the building across from the Hyatt on Fourth Avenue at two o'clock, as agreed. John immediately buzzed him in, and Rupert jogged up the four floors and knocked on John's door. John opened the door wearing jeans and a tank top, and his feet were bare. Rupert glanced down at what he himself had chosen to wear, and his Oxford shirt, cashmere sweater, pleated slacks, and Prada shoes—which he had come to think of as casual when he was getting dressed that morning–were clearly still too formal. "I have to go to a meeting downtown after this."

"It's no problem," John said as he closed the door and extended his hand to take Rupert's wool jacket. "I don't usually wear too much here, so I just threw on some jeans."

John had used furniture to subdivide his main room into a living room with a couch, coffee table, and easy chair; a small dining area with a round wooden table and four metal folding chairs; and a computer desk in the corner beside shelves for a scanner and a printer. Rupert sat on the couch facing the coffee table. It held an empty bud vase John's adoptive grandmother had given him when he graduated from Julliard. There was a woman's engagement ring his fiancée had left behind when she had stormed out two days before. And there was a photograph in a frame of John and Brenda smiling at an anniversary party nine months earlier. It seemed obvious why John had called him out of the blue. Rupert had learned when he first got the psychometry blessing at eight that he needed to pretend he didn't have foreknowledge of certain things. He tried to lead their discussion in that direction. "Who is the beautiful woman in the photo?"

John sat in the chair and sighed. He tried to look at the photo that was really more tilted in Rupert's direction. "That's Brenda. She and I broke up this week."

"Sorry to hear that, John. How are you doing?"

"It was my fault," he volunteered. "I fucked it up." John seemed on the verge of tears.

Rupert tried to imagine what would sound conciliatory. He had certainly been in the same situation with Arthur. "If she really cares about you, it's possible she would forgive you . . . eventually."

"Not this time." John dwelt in his gloominess, breathing a bit faster for almost a minute. "I cheated on her, and she didn't believe me that it will never happen again."

"Even that," Rupert maintained. "I was in a similar situation with the guy I was dating, and it just took a year of platonic dates to win his trust back."

"No, this is different," John argued. Tears were starting to form in both of his eyes. "I cheated on her with a guy, and she said she didn't think that temptation would ever go away. She broke off our engagement." He pointed at the ring on the table. "She left her ring here. It's over."

Rupert saw the tears starting to roll down John's cheeks, and he tried to remember how he'd seen straight men comfort each other before. Pats on the shoulder or back were not practical in this situation. Rupert scooted over on the couch and gestured for John to join him on the couch.

John rocked in his chair for a moment, seemingly undecided about whether to switch seats. He dove for the couch, put his head on Rupert's shoulder, and started bawling. Rupert brought John's head to his chest where it was a bit more comfortable and hugged him with one arm. In the midst of his tears, John managed to choke out, "And this isn't even why I wanted to see you!"

Rupert allowed him to weep a little longer before asking, "What else did you want to tell me?"

John quickly got his tears and breathing under control enough to sit up and then cross the room to a shelf for a tissue. He dabbed his eyes and stood there for a little while. "I hooked up with a guy who said he knew you. He said he hadn't worked much since *The Titanic* closed on Broadway, and I mentioned you worked in that show too. I didn't think it was a big deal, but he said the two of you had sex for a while after you left the show. With your acting career taking off and his stalled, he started to get in his head that he would blackmail you."

"That had to be Charlie," Rupert surmised.

"Yeah, I think he said that was his name," John confirmed. He went back to the couch and sat down next to Rupert. "He figured he could out you if you didn't help him out financially."

"Don't worry about it, John," Rupert advised.

"Why not?"

"I don't worry about guys like that," Rupert explained. "They make their claims and insinuations, and rumors start, but without more people willing to corroborate his story, it gets buried pretty quickly. I wondered why he was trying to get me to come over again a couple of years ago. I'll probably come out in the media on my own after this next movie comes out. It will be my fourth heterosexual role, so I'm pretty sure it won't affect my ability to get more."

The demand finally came two days later to Rupert's personal email. He forwarded it to Margot saying he wasn't concerned about it. She called him back the following day and suggested he try to get out and do some media interviews and appearances to drown out the rumor mill. Rupert had only ever used publicists provided by the producers of his various films and shows, so it was with a little trepidation and befuddlement that he hired his first personal publicist. Her name was Nadia, and she came highly recommended by one of his co-stars on the last film.

Nadia sent him a list of talking points to study within two days. She sent him an itinerary to appear on talk shows in New York, Wisconsin, and California over the following five weeks. In the thriller he had just finished shooting last August, he played a spy, and the producers gave him a new trailer to roll out as he toured. Most of the interviewers were fixated on the fact that he did most of his own stunts in the movie. They asked him to speculate about his chances at an Oscar. They speculated what he might be hiding about his personal life, but they never gave much credence to the online blogs Charlie had managed to interest in his boring story.

And when the discussion got to his fans, Rupert always tried to tell the story of a crazy, old, Irish woman who cornered him and a friend at an Italian restaurant a few years earlier. He mentioned how he worried that his dinner companion was taking her too seriously. Rupert had developed a theory that the Pooka had cornered Arthur in order to poison his mind against Rupert, and that she might still be influencing him either with words or through whatever control she held over the expression of her curse. He tried to trust that the pressure from their friends would suffice until Arthur realized that the person he had fallen in love with was still there.

In the midst of Rupert's local media tour, when Rupert was in the back of Randy's SUV headed home from a very early call at Good Morning America, he got a call from Parker. It was immediately clear who it was, because he had been starting and peppering their conversations with a nickname he was trying to get Rupert to accept. "Hey, Spook!" Parker shouted into the phone when the call connected. "Where are you right now?"

"Heading down . . . Twelfth Avenue on my way home. Why do you care? Are you back from D.C.?"

"I am at the corner of Eighteenth and Ninth. Come pick me up."

Rupert had gotten used to Parker's curt phone manner. He calmly knocked on the privacy partition. Randy opened the transparent window in the partition and said, "What can I do for you, sir?"

"We're picking someone up on Eighteenth at Ninth Avenue in Chelsea," Rupert relayed. "I'll watch for him and let you know which side of Ninth to stop on."

"I will approach slowly. Just let me know when our party is in sight."

When they got to the intersection, Randy had to stop for a red light. Rupert heard someone tap on the right-side rear window. It was rare anyone did that, because the tinted windows made facial recognition from outside the car nearly impossible. He assumed it was Parker and opened the door.

The smaller man hopped onto the seat sideways and knocked the slush from the gutter off his boots before turning forward and closing the door.

"Welcome," Rupert said in his general direction.

"Are we continuing on Eighteenth?" Randy asked as he slowly pulled through the now open intersection.

"Just drive for a few minutes," Parker suggested.

"Like he said," Rupert confirmed.

Once Randy had closed the window in the partition again. Parker began speaking very softly. "I gave you a few weeks off, like you requested, but now we need to put you to work. You're in the psychometry blessing now?"

Rupert caught a glimpse of the yellow tie with diagonal blue and white stripes showing from his partially open jacket. "The tie you're wearing was given to you by your son but picked out by your wife at Macy's in the Westfield Mall in Potomac, Maryland."

"Oh. Okay. So, if I just showed you a photo of the tie . . ."

"I would only have information about the photo," Rupert clarified. "I have to be able to see and ideally touch the object to get a clear sense of its origins."

"So, if I let you touch my tie—which you should not—you might be able to tell me what?"

Rupert folded his arms to put Parker at ease. "What types of fibers were in it. Maybe where it was manufactured."

"So, you're essentially a one-man forensics lab," Parker summarized.

"That's one use of it," Rupert agreed. "It usually only works with objects, but I also get a more vague but often helpful vibe from living things, including people."

Parker faced forward and seemed to be musing to himself. "Maybe security clearances? Nah. Forensics is better." He turned to face Rupert again. "I think we'll add you to our forensic experts list. We'll try to be selective in the cases and evidence we ask you to weigh in on. Since your revelations are only lead-producing and don't serve as evidence, hmm."

"I usually only think of it as a party trick," Rupert said to break the tension.

"I'll let you know." Parker knocked on the partition window. When Randy opened it, he called out, "Just drop me at the next bus stop."

Jenny was still trying to convince Rupert to help her out with relief efforts in Haiti. Now he could say that between his January vacation and his new assignment from courier to forensic consultant, he would leave the task to others.

About the time Rupert finished his media tour in California in February, the Winter Olympics were about to start in Canada, and he wanted so badly to take Arthur there, because he hadn't been able to take him to the Summer Olympics two years before. But there was still no word from Arthur. He couldn't imagine what was going through his mind. To stay away, without even casual, friendly contact, Arthur had to be thinking of him as dangerous. Arthur had always said that he enjoyed all the new things Rupert introduced him to, but fairies, curses, and blessings had been a step too far.

Jenny continued to check in with Rupert. A record-breaking earthquake in

Chile left tens of thousands homeless. *No, sorry.* His new movie came out, and while on another media tour, hundreds of thousands in Pakistan were displaced by torrential flooding. *Sorry, busy.* Hundreds of thousands fled a volcanic eruption in Java. *I'm doing too much work for Parker to leave.*

The CIA flew Rupert around the country to analyze bomb fragments, drug shipments, contraband, murder weapons, and documents–reams and reams of documents. It was kind of boring work for Rupert, but it kept him distracted enough to keep him from focusing on Arthur. The one highlight was that he identified some evidence that led to the capture and killing of Osama bin Laden. It felt a little like revenge for Dorian's death.

In late June, almost at the exact point when Rupert had decided that two-and-a-half years of mourning was sufficient and that it was time to move on and start dating again, Rupert was walking along Broadway near Madison Square Park looking for a Starbucks while waiting for Randy to pick him up. He saw Arthur walking toward him in a suit, carrying a briefcase and reading something on his cell phone. Rupert stopped. He wasn't sure what to do. Arthur had requested he not initiate contact. But if they met by chance, wasn't that something else?

As Arthur was about to pass Rupert, he put his phone back in his jacket pocket and looked up. He did a double take when he saw Rupert. Rupert took off his dark glasses and tried to smile. "Hi, Arthur," he said tentatively.

"Were you following me?" Arthur seemed somewhere between curious and accusatory.

"No," Rupert said carefully. "I had a meeting a couple of blocks away and I was looking for coffee." He paused for a moment. "And *you* came up to *me.*"

"I was on my way to a meeting," Arthur commented. He seemed conflicted about staying to chat politely or running away.

Rupert couldn't wait any longer to test his theory. "I have to ask you something. After that first time in the restaurant in Midtown eight years ago, did you ever see the Pooka again?"

Arthur pulled out his phone again and looked at it. "I'm sorry, but I really have to get going."

"Just, please, answer that one question, and I'll let you go." Rupert moved to be a bit closer and more directly facing Arthur. "Have you seen the Pooka more than once?"

Arthur put his phone away and sighed. He studied Rupert's face for a few seconds. "I have. Twice."

"Okay, thanks," Rupert said as he stepped aside and put his dark glasses back on. He fully expected Arthur to walk away at that point. "I thought that's why you didn't want to hear from me for over two years."

"She told me you were keeping other secrets from me," Arthur volunteered. "It's true."

"And I believed her when she said you were . . . I guess it doesn't matter. I've been talking to Danny. He reminded me that he's known you for twenty-five years, and he still loves you, and thinks you're a great friend. And he reminded me that I used to feel the same."

Arthur looked at his phone again. "If you have to go, I understand," Rupert said.

"I do," Arthur conceded. "But I'll contact you soon to arrange to talk."

Rupert took another step away and timidly said, "Okay."

"I will!" Arthur repeated as he took off down the block.

The following day, Rupert received an email from Denise. She and Michaela invited Rupert to a celebration of their victory in Albany: Same-sex marriage had finally passed in New York, the sixth state to do so. Rupert had an audition for a commercial that night, but he called Margot to postpone it. Denise had hinted that a certain "Asian geek" friend of theirs was going to be attending and said it was okay to invite him too.

On Friday night, Rupert asked Randy to drop him a few blocks away from Denise and Michaela's co-op in Washington Heights. His publicist, Nadia, had been harping on Rupert to meet his fans in person more. He had a shoulder bag of his headshots and a Sharpie, and he left his dark glasses, hat, and hoodie in the SUV. At first, people just stared, not quite sure if it was really Rupert Rocket. Then people started pointing. A few stopped him to compliment him on a particular role in a movie. Some took photos from a distance. Some politely asked Rupert if he would pose for photos with them. And he handed out autographed photos to anyone else who wanted one. By the time he got to the correct address, there was a small crowd of people following him, and cars were double parking to take a look. He buzzed to be let in, and he turned and waved before he went inside.

Michaela met Rupert at the apartment door which was ajar. "Rupert!" she exclaimed as she threw her arms around him and kissed him on the cheek. "I'm glad you could make it."

"It's my pleasure." Rupert pulled a bottle of wine with a ribbon around it from his shoulder bag. "I wasn't sure if you wanted people to bring anything."

"That's fine," Michaela said as she grabbed the bottle from him and pulled him further into the room.

"Congratulations on the legislative victory," he said as Denise joined them.

"Thanks for coming," Denise said. "You were the reason Michaela and I met, so we wanted you to be here."

"I remember," Rupert joked. "You were so cute to give me that 'get out of jail free' card from Monopoly. I still have it. I haven't needed to use it."

"Come say hello to everyone," Michaela urged.

As they led him into the living room, Rupert saw Danny and Max, a bunch of women he didn't recognize, Chantal, John, Theo, Jorge, Luke and James, and Arthur. John was closest and stood up and hugged Rupert. "I watched your last movie," John told him. "I am so glad you're still doing all right."

John released him, and Rupert said, "Thanks. It's good to see you. You look happy."

"Most of the time," he acknowledged.

Chantal stepped around John to kiss Rupert on the cheek. She wore a tall Afro wig, long dangling earrings, and a black dress with straps. "So nice to see you again, sweetie. Are you staying out of trouble?"

"Yes, ma'am," Rupert said.

Theo got up and hugged Rupert next. "Hey, Rupert," he said. "Thanks again for that referral. I booked the job!"

"Congrats, Theo," Rupert said as he stepped out of the hug and patted him on the shoulder. "I'm glad it worked out."

Arthur moved into the room a bit more from the kitchen doorway, but he didn't approach Rupert. Rupert moved around Theo and stood in front of Arthur. "I'm glad you came," he told him.

Arthur looked like he was suppressing a grin, and he pulled Rupert into the kitchen by the arm without saying anything. When they were in the kitchen with only Denise arranging raw vegetables on a serving tray, he whispered, "I meant to call you to talk one-on-one, but I got busy, and then this . . ."

Rupert put his hand over Arthur's mouth. "It's okay. I'm just happy you felt comfortable showing up when you knew I'd be here. We can talk another time."

Denise tried to squeeze by them with her tray of vegetables. As she passed by Arthur, she whispered to him, "You okay?"

Arthur nodded, and she left. "I have missed you," he admitted. "I watched some of your interviews, and I noticed you referred to me as your friend."

"You were then, and you are now," Rupert said. He wanted to hug Arthur, but he kept his distance.

"I've got my own place in Astoria now," Arthur reported.

"That's nice." Rupert didn't want to reveal that Max had broken Arthur's confidence about his news.

"And I'm GM at ABT now," Arthur continued. "I have a very stable, predictable life now."

"I guess that's good," Rupert said. "That's what you wanted."

"Except it's not." Arthur moved a bit closer and put his hand on Rupert's arm. "When I was with you, I was jetting off around the world, meeting new people, trying new restaurants, seeing amazing performances, and having fantastic sex and talks and walks and adventures . . . with you."

Rupert put one arm around Arthur's shoulders and gently pulled him in closer.

"I haven't done any of that in the past two years," Arthur concluded.

Rupert waited a moment and then pulled Arthur into a full hug. Michaela appeared in the kitchen doorway, noticed them, and immediately went back into the living room. "Just so you know, I wasn't lying. My current blessing is psychometry. With it, I can tell you that you bought your shirt at a second-hand store on the Upper West Side last summer, and your shorts were a gift from your parents the Christmas before last."

Arthur leaned back just enough to look up into Rupert's face. "That's . . . right. That's amazing."

"I have to get on a plane to DC tomorrow afternoon, but I'll text you when I return, if that's okay."

"Yeah." Arthur sounded like he was getting choked up. "So will you be able to tell me your other secret when you get back?"

Rupert smiled and pulled Arthur in tighter again. "I just have to check with someone else first. It's not just my secret to tell."

When Rupert arrived at CIA headquarters that Saturday afternoon, the guards at the front desk made Rupert wait there instead of sending him in to the forensics division as usual. After a few minutes, Parker appeared behind the turnstiles and waved at the guards to let Rupert through. "I have another al-Qaeda recording," Parker said as he led Rupert to a conference room.

A woman there was playing a videotape with a still photograph of Osama bin Laden. The voice playing on the monitor's speakers was definitely speaking Arabic. The man on the tape was promising retribution for the death of their leader.

"Can you translate it?" Parker asked him.

"I am getting the gist of it," Rupert acknowledged. "I got a lot of practice in Arabic working with Guy."

"Excuse us for a second," Parker said as he walked up to the VCR and ejected the tape. He carried it over to Rupert. "We need to verify where it was recorded."

Rupert took the cassette in his hand. His mind immediately lit up with the history of the tape, moving backward from CIA headquarters, a field office in Kabul, an al-Qaeda informant, a production studio somewhere in Saudi Arabia, and an audio tape there. "It was recorded at an Al Jazeera studio in Saudi Arabia.

I don't know where the audio tape on the soundtrack came from."

"Any more details?" Parker asked. "Where in Saudi Arabia?"

"That's it," Rupert replied.

"Okay," Parker acknowledged. "Thanks for coming down on a Saturday."

"I had a couple of questions for you yet, if you've got a couple more minutes to spare."

Parker pulled out a chair at the conference table and sat down as the woman left the room. "Have a seat, Spook." He gestured toward the chair near him.

Rupert sat down. "I'm getting paychecks now from the State Department. Is that supposed to be happening?"

"You haven't done any work for UNHCR this year, so we couldn't justify paying you through their expense reimbursement system any more."

Rupert wondered how he was going to explain it if anyone found out he was a paid consultant for the State Department. "There's one other thing. You said I shouldn't tell anyone about my work for the CIA. You said it would put them at risk. What if I told someone and made them swear not to tell anyone else? Is there any way you would permit that?"

Parker's eyebrows went up, and he leaned forward with his forearms on the table. "Who were you thinking of telling?"

"Arthur."

Parker lowered his tone. It seemed almost reverent. "I thought you two weren't together anymore."

"We may be reconciling now," Rupert reported. "And I think he's already suspecting. Is it really dangerous to tell him?"

"If he's already suspecting, then it may be better to tell him, so he doesn't pass along a suspicious piece of evidence or intel," Parker said carefully. "We just advise our agents and consultants not to divulge their employment with the agency, because the more people who know, the easier it is for someone to slip up and blow your cover. That doesn't just mean an end to your career here, Spook. It puts any operations you've ever been involved with in jeopardy, including other agents currently working them."

Rupert nodded. "I understand. If it looks like there will be a problem, I'll resign immediately."

"It's a heck of a secret to keep, Spook," Parker acknowledged. "I still haven't told my family. My wife and I just celebrated our tenth anniversary." He paused for a moment. "She would worry herself sick if she knew I was an international spy."

Rupert sighed. "Arthur knew I was going to potentially dangerous locations just from my cover work with the U.N. I'm not sure this secret will bother him as much as learning I was a freak with special abilities."

"You're doing good work," Parker said as he leaned back in his chair. "You're serving your country, keeping it safer, and you're a decent guy. I hope it goes okay for you. Let me know if it doesn't."

When Rupert next met with Arthur for lunch in the reserved back room at a café in the Village Rupert frequently patronized, Arthur said he was ready for Rupert's other secret. As Rupert described his recruitment by the CIA at the same time he started cover work for the U.N. refugee agency, he could see a change happening in Arthur's face. He had been steeling himself for something traumatic, but he started to tear up and smile at the same time.

"Are you okay?" Rupert asked him.

Arthur pulled a handkerchief out of his pocket and dabbed his eyes with it. "You've been doing that for the past three years?"

Rupert nodded. "If it bothers you too much, I can quit. I don't want you to worry. I always try to be careful, and I've asked them to keep me as far as possible from . . ."

Arthur got up from his chair and hugged Rupert. "I wouldn't ask you to do that," he choked out. Rupert could feel Arthur's tears against his own cheek. "I'm just so proud of you, Rupert." He slowly released him and went back to his chair. "You surprise me–all the time–how you go where you're needed, even when it's hard. You're incredibly brave and selfless . . ."

"I don't know about that," Rupert interrupted. He grinned and wondered if he should be hugging Arthur instead of just sitting across the table in the empty back room watching him cry. "I have plenty of weak moments. I get selfish."

Arthur laughed through the tears. "And you're humble. I've been following discussion online in your fan forums, and that word keeps coming up in everyone's descriptions of you. You seem humble and nice. They say you're even more soulful than Keanu Reeves. And they compliment how you seem to so completely inhabit your roles, however different they are. A few even compare you to Meryl Streep!"

Rupert was blushing, so he tried to change the subject. "I can see how being a movie star isolates you from the world, makes you start thinking you're above others, makes you think you deserve special treatment. One of the best things for me has been following Nadia's advice and making time to meet my fans."

"Who's Nadia?" Arthur asked as he finished wiping his eyes.

"My publicist," Rupert replied. "I have a chauffeur now too. His name is Randy."

Arthur smiled. "I met Randy already. He's been working for you for three years."

"Oh. Yeah." Rupert forgot there had been six weeks of Arthur in the SUV with him before they separated.

"I think I've already told you all of my news, so why don't you catch me up on you?"

Just as before when Rupert came back from having sex with Trevor in Wisconsin, Arthur slowly agreed to more platonic dates throughout the rest of the year. They arranged to meet on Christmas morning for brunch at a diner in Chinatown. Rupert was pleasantly surprised that the staff and few other diners there were leaving him in peace. He risked taking off his dark glasses, and no one except for Arthur seemed to be paying attention to him.

"I'm glad you could meet me again so soon," Rupert remarked. "I just saw you two days ago."

Arthur grinned. "I couldn't miss celebrating your birthday. I hope you didn't have other plans."

"Honestly, Fred and Britney invited me to San Francisco, but I was kind of

314

hoping I could spend the day with you."

"So, what new blessing did you get this morning?" Arthur seemed curious but worried about Rupert's answer.

"Empathy," Rupert replied. "I get a read on the emotional state of everyone I'm talking to for the next year."

"Oh." Arthur considered the information for a moment. "So, what are you getting from me right now?"

Rupert smiled. "I learned something very early on when I got this blessing the first time thirty-five years ago."

"What was that?" Arthur leaned forward, seemingly expecting an involved story.

"Revealing someone else's secrets rarely ends well."

"That's it?" Arthur asked. "You're not going to tell me?"

"Nope." Rupert smiled again. He knew that Arthur felt comfortable with him and excited about the future. And Arthur was falling in love with him again.

CHAPTER 28: RUPERT TURNS FORTY-FOUR

Rupert had another movie to shoot starting at the end of January, and he wanted Arthur to come along with him. Arthur had a job that required his on-site presence now, and that was hard to get around. He poured over his investments and savings, and he calculated that he was worth over ten million dollars, and even with all the jetting around and the expensive rent, he still had more than enough money to support both of them. But Arthur didn't want to retire; he wanted to work. Rupert already had so many riders on his movie contracts, Margot was concerned that he was starting to get too picky and turning off some producers and directors. "It's not like making sure there are green M&Ms in your dressing room, doll," she said at one point.

He called her any way. "Margot, I need an amendment to my contract for the next movie."

Her otherwise low, raspy voice raised by a few tones. "Hon', how many times have I had to tell you, enough with the special conditions?"

"I need to make Arthur an executive producer, or at least my assistant on this film, Margot. It's important to my relationship and my future happiness."

"Rupert, sweetie, you know I love ya' to death, but I've already gone way outside my comfort zone for you. You're my only actor client. I did that for you. I'm an agent for models. I know advertising and fashion. When you start talking about renegotiating such a fundamental part of your movie contract, I throw up my hands. You need to be dealing directly with an entertainment attorney. I'll get our lawyer to send you some referrals."

Rupert was shocked that Margot was essentially firing him as a client. He

316

couldn't believe it. "You don't want to represent me anymore?"

"Rupert, listen to me," Margot began. "I could still get you modeling jobs, no problem. But that's small potatoes for you. You're signing contracts for millions of dollars. I appreciate the commissions, but you need somebody who knows your business better. After this contract, you need to have someone else representing you. It's for your own good, sweetie."

Margot's referrals came two days later, and Rupert talked to all of them on the phone and then met with a woman he described to Arthur as a short Vietnamese bulldog: Victoria Tran. She had a pixie cut and wore wire-frame glasses, a floral blouse, and dark slacks at the interview in her office in Hell's Kitchen. She was even more aggressive than Margot. She scanned through Rupert's contract for his next movie role, and after a minute, she declared, "Yeah, we will definitely need to renegotiate this. Actors not as hot as you are are making more than this, and Margot and I will need to split the agent's commission now."

If Victoria could deliver on her promises, Rupert still had one additional hurdle to jump. Even if he could convince Arthur to quit his job at ABT, he was very cautious, and Rupert didn't want to wait so many months like the last time to get back together. He needed to move courting Arthur into high gear, if he wanted all this to happen in two weeks.

He took Arthur to his favorite Italian restaurant in Midtown. In the SUV in the ride uptown, he told Arthur all about his meeting with Victoria. As the hostess led the two of them past the waterfall to their usual table in the far corner, she said, "So good to see you again, Mr. Rocket."

"This is my boyfriend, Arthur," he told her. "This is his favorite Italian restaurant in the whole city."

"Nice to see you again as well, Arthur." She waited for them to sit down and handed them menus. "Your server will be Berto, and he'll be here shortly to take your orders."

Arthur set down his menu and shot Rupert an incredulous stare. "Okay. You are freaking me out, Rupert. You not only called me your boyfriend, . . . you did it in public, and gave her my name?"

"Well," Rupert began slowly, "you have been my boyfriend, and I'm hoping we get there again soon."

"Don't you have to be more discreet about your sexuality? Your producers had us entering restaurants in L.A. separately and escorting women at your first premiere."

"I've been thinking about coming out publicly for a while now," Rupert recounted. "Nadia thinks it might help sell the next movie because I'm playing a bisexual. I'll be kissing a man in it, if they don't cut that from the script."

"That's a really big step," Arthur acknowledged.

At that point, Berto came to take their orders and gather their menus. After he left, Rupert spoke a little softer. "It's an important step, I think. There are still so many Americans who think they don't know any gay people. That makes it especially vital for us entertainers to do it. The only issue is that this is not just my secret anymore. If I come out, you're inevitably going to come out, too."

Arthur sighed. "I hate hiding how I feel about you when we're in public."

"And how do you feel about me?" Rupert asked. He smiled to suggest it was a tease.

"Oh, well, yeah, come on," Arthur sputtered. "You already know how I feel."

"I want to hear you say it."

"I really like you, Rupert."

Rupert folded his arms and leaned back against the seat cushion. "Like?"

Arthur dislodged one of Rupert's hands and brought it into his lap to hold. "I first met you about fourteen years ago, when I was still a grad student interning at Alvin Ailey. I've had a pretty close relationship with you most of that time, first as your assistant, and then as your boyfriend. When I look back at all those years with you, and the time before and the two times we separated, it is like night and day for me. You were this shining knight who swept me up and carried me off into a life of fun and adventure."

"Really?" Rupert teased. "Shining knight?"

"Stop making fun of my clichés!" Arthur scolded. "You were this dazzling light in my life. Amazingly passionate about everything, so generous and caring

318

and compassionate, and . . . I miss holding you. And kissing you. And waking in the middle of the night and having sex with you."

"So, move back in with me!" Rupert was getting a sense that Arthur just wanted his fears persistently challenged.

"I have four months left on my lease . . ."

"I'll pay any penalty for breaking it early," Rupert offered. "At the very least, you can be living at my place here in Manhattan and use Randy to take you to ABT. I leave in a little over two weeks to start shooting in L.A."

Arthur squeezed Rupert's hand tighter. "That's very generous of you . . ."

Rupert could feel Arthur's emotions shifting. He was getting so close to saying yes. "I'd rather have you with me in L.A., though."

"I can't leave my new job at ABT," Arthur argued. "I'm supervising over twenty people."

"Victoria said she can get you a job working on the film," Rupert said. He grasped Arthur's hand in both of his. "I still love you, Arthur." He leaned over and kissed him on the ear.

Rupert felt the dam break in the two seconds before Arthur scooted over to hug and kiss him. "I don't know why I keep fighting it," he whispered into Rupert's shoulder.

"I'm a bit of a rollercoaster," Rupert admitted. "Not everybody's brave enough to attempt this ride." He hoped Arthur wouldn't notice or at least wouldn't care that he was quoting a line from one of his movies.

"Let me think about it," Arthur said as he finally leaned back away from Rupert. "This is a lot for me to process."

"Take your time," Rupert said as he straightened the silverware in his place setting. "Just not too much time."

Rupert brought in a maid to clean his apartment before he left for L.A. Arthur was working as Randy drove him to JFK, but he texted Rupert:

Bon voyage, mon amour. Hǎoyùn!

"I just got a text from Arthur in French and Chinese," Rupert commented through the open partition window.

"He's a very talented man, as are you, sir," Randy said.

"All I've done with you is tell you where to drive me," Rupert argued.

"Not so, sir," Randy countered. "I've seen ballets Arthur helped produce that moved me deeply. And I've watched your movies, sir. You are a formidable actor. Your performances amaze me. I hope you don't mind that I tell my friends I'm your driver. They think you're an amazing person. They know about your work for the U.N., and they are impressed that with all your money, you still volunteer to help refugees."

Despite the compliments, they seemed a bit empty to Rupert—especially because he hadn't done much work for Jenny in the past year or two. He resolved to get in touch with Jenny on one of his days off.

Arthur did agree to move back into Rupert's apartment in Battery Park City, and whenever Rupert had two days in a row off, he flew back to New York to be with Arthur. He told Arthur that Nadia and Victoria and the producers were in discussions about the optimal timing for Rupert to come out as gay in the media. He wanted Arthur to be part of the considerations as well, so Victoria copied him on her emails about it.

They settled on June 24, 2012. It was the Saturday before Gay Pride in New York City. Rupert's director promised he would have that weekend off. Rupert put Nadia in touch with Michaela and Denise to make sure Rupert was on the list of speakers for their event on the steps of City Hall at a rally. It commemorated eleven months of same-sex marriages in New York, and they sought support and publicity for the ACLU's suit against the Defense of Marriage Act or DOMA. Arguments were being heard in Windsor v. United States, brought by a lesbian widow whose inheritance from her wife's estate the IRS said was subject to estate taxes no other married couples were required to pay. Michaela emailed Rupert the next day thanking him for his courage and support. She had worked out a strategy with Nadia to tease the media by telling them the event would include the coming out of a prominent celebrity, so Rupert's participation was to remain a secret until the day of the rally.

Randy picked Rupert up at JFK the night before the rally. Riding back to Manhattan, Randy seemed eager to talk. "I hope you don't mind my saying so," he said as they were crossing the Brooklyn Bridge, "but I wanted to draw your attention to the fact that Master Shu did not accompany me to meet you this time."

"He texted me," Rupert said. "He said he was busy and would meet me at the apartment."

"I picked him up at Party City and then at a bakery earlier today," Randy revealed.

"Ah." Rupert checked his emails on the new phone he'd picked up in L.A. "Thanks for the warning, Randy. Please stop by that bodega on Barclay; I suspect I need to pick up some roses."

Both of the security guards in the lobby were smiling conspiratorially when Rupert walked past toward the elevator. When it let him out on the twenty-first floor, Rupert could already hear multiple voices coming from his apartment. He brought the bouquet of roses up to a more accessible position and set his suitcase down to try the door handle. It was locked.

He fished his key out of a pocket in his shorts, and as soon as it entered the lock, voices on the other side of the door hushed. When he opened the door, a group of about twenty friends and acquaintances scattered between his living room and dining room cheered. Some started chanting his name: *Ru-pert, Ru-pert, Ru-pert.* Arthur ran up to him trailing a couple of the streamers hanging from the ceiling and kissed him on the lips. "Welcome home, sexy," he half-shouted above the chanting. He looked down at the bouquet. "Are those for me?"

Rupert kissed him again as Danny approached them. "Of course. So, what's the occasion?"

"Arthur invited us to celebrate gay pride, your coming out announcement tomorrow, and you and Arthur getting back together!" Danny shouted.

Rupert turned back to Arthur. "We got back together?"

As Max and Chantal joined them as well, Arthur replied, "Yes. I just gave my two-week notice to Rachel today. I'm going to go back to L.A. with you on

321

Sunday."

Rupert was confused. "I only have two more weeks of filming."

"I don't have to show up there anymore," Arthur explained. "I'm taking my last two weeks of vacation starting Monday."

Max and Chantal hugged Rupert and congratulated him as well. Rupert stopped asking what they were so happy about and just enjoyed the company of his friends. Michaela and Denise had some last-minute details to share about the rally. Hakim and Azami had brought their thirteen-year-old son Ichiro, who competed strongly for the guests' attention. As he made his way through the throng into the dining room, he noticed his childhood friend Trevor there.

Rupert rushed up to him and hugged him. "Trevor! Buddy! What are you doing here?"

"I'm here to support you," Trevor reported. "I'm going to your rally tomorrow."

"Who invited you?" Rupert worried that whoever knew how to invite Trevor might not know what a sore spot he was for Arthur.

"Your boyfriend wrote to me and suggested it," Trevor revealed as he pulled out of the hug and nodded toward Arthur in the next room.

Rupert looked at Arthur amazed and then back at Trevor. "Where are you staying?"

"I'm staying on the couch at your friend Theo's place," Trevor replied. "Someone named Max arranged it for me."

Rupert spent time talking to and thanking Danny, Max, and Theo for helping Arthur with the invites and party planning. He also chatted with Jorge, Luke, John, and Chantal. Once the last four of them left after midnight, Arthur turned to Rupert and said, "I'm trying to challenge myself more."

"You're doing great. Thanks for the party."

"Thanks again for the roses," Arthur said as he smiled at them in their vase on the dining room table. "I want you to know that if you want me up on stage with you tomorrow, I'm willing to be there."

"You don't have to do that," Rupert said.

"It's fine," Arthur reassured him. "I've let my family and other friends know, so it won't be a surprise to anyone I care about."

The following morning, when Rupert revised and rehearsed the speech he had begun writing on the plane, he kept going back and forth about how to refer to Arthur, or if he should refer to him by name at all. Part of the point, as Nadia had explained to him, was to settle the rumor mill so the focus would go back to his acting work, and a mystery boyfriend was ripe for gossip if Arthur didn't come out too.

And since the event was all about gay marriage, he wondered how to include that without speculating about the direction of his relationship with Arthur. He had told Rupert before that being with him was enough—that a marriage license was just a meaningless piece of paper. Rupert even considered proposing marriage to Arthur just to thwart the Pooka's curse, but there was no way to predict how she would react to that destruction of her plans. She might increase the pressure on the curse so that he might die even before his fiftieth birthday—when even the echo of his blessing was due to evaporate.

The next day, Arthur and Rupert waited in the SUV a few blocks from City Hall waiting for the cue from Denise to drive up and take the stage suddenly. When the text came, Rupert told Randy to go, and both Arthur and Rupert looked at each other. Rupert could tell Arthur was more nervous than he was. When they got as close as they could to the stage, Rupert and Arthur made their way to the back of the stage just as Michaela was starting to introduce the mystery guest. A few reporters on the edge of the crowd noticed Arthur and Rupert dashing past and snapped photos. Denise took Rupert's arm as Michaela finished her introduction: ". . . and he's here today on a short break from shooting a movie role as a bisexual detective hunting down human traffickers. Please welcome, the amazing Rupert Rocket."

Denise pushed Rupert toward Michaela and the mic and kept Arthur backstage. He scanned the crowd as he stepped up to the mic. There were people of all types, ages, and races. A few had signs that supported same-sex marriage, and most of them were cheering his arrival. He figured it was at least two hundred.

Not bad for a Saturday afternoon before the biggest gay holiday of the year.

"My fellow New Yorkers and friends from other places, thank you for letting me speak today. I just wanted to share a story. It's maybe not as tragic as Edie Windsor's, but I think it's poignant. My grandmother Zelda fled Nazi Germany in the 1920s. She seemed to have a strong sense of right and wrong. When I came out to her as a gay man . . ."

At that point, the crowd erupted in awe and cheering. When it died down a bit, Rupert continued. ". . . when I came out to my family, my grandmother told me that my 'choice' was wrong. I wasn't doing the right thing. But I didn't know if I could do anything else. I later learned that her main objection to having a gay grandson was that he would never marry.

"Now for lesbian and gay people in New York, that sort of equal treatment has been legal for the past eleven months. It means we can declare our love publicly, visit our loved ones in the hospital, live without fear of discrimination, adopt children, and not lose our home because the IRS doesn't honor our marriage licenses, as happened to Edie."

More cheers interrupted Rupert. "In the movie I'm shooting in Los Angeles, part of the plot involves an ex-lover trying his hardest to break up my character's marriage to a woman. It takes place in the past when a gay or bi man's only option for public acceptance and raising children was to bury part of himself and marry a woman. Of course, the same was true for lesbians and bi women at the time.

"It's important to remember that there will always be resistance to progress in the direction of our equality. But we should never, ever give up fighting just because the battle is hard. Six states allow gay marriage. Denmark just became the twelfth country to allow same-sex marriage within its borders, and that includes our lovely neighbors to the north in Canada."

Rupert waited for a small contingent of Canadians to finish cheering and waving their maple-leaf flags. "Another three states have gay marriage initiatives on their ballots this fall, and the ACLU tells me that no matter what happens in the Second Circuit, Windsor versus United States is headed to the Supreme Court, and cases in Michigan, Ohio, Kentucky, and Tennessee could be headed there as well, paving the way for the United States to be the lucky thirteenth country to welcome gay marriage equality."

Rupert got his loudest cheers. He wondered if the crowd thought he was done. He decided to wrap it up quickly. "My partner Arthur is here today." Suddenly Arthur was by his side with his arm around Rupert's waist. The crowd's cheer rose again briefly. "We decided to put a face that people know to the gay people too many Americans find it easy to demonize. We hope it will encourage more of you to come out. Every one of us who comes out means another dozen people for whom gay prejudice and bashing is no longer an option." He waved at the crowd, kissed Arthur on the lips, and added, "Happy Gay Pride, everyone!"

That night, Rupert and Arthur went up to Washington Heights to watch coverage of the rally on the evening news. Arthur blushed when the television showed him being kissed by Rupert. Rupert nudged him playfully. "Get used to it. You're dating a movie star."

"It was just a little kiss on a stage downtown in front of a couple hundred people," Arthur said, somewhat in a daze as he continued to look at the TV screen. "Suddenly people all over the world are seeing it. It is blowing my mind."

Denise patted Arthur on the back. "They'll stop playing it in a matter of days," she suggested. "The world's media will inevitably move on."

Indeed, the Presidential Election immediately grabbed the focus back, but the tug of war continued even on the day when Obama won his second term. Voters in Maine, Maryland, and Washington State approved propositions allowing same-sex marriage. In some of those places, interviewees and commentators called out Rupert and other celebrities who had come out as instrumental in their success.

From the beginning of December, Rupert was counting down the days until his birthday. He couldn't wait to be rid of the empathy blessing. It was certainly far from his most annoying one, but it made acting especially difficult. He had to keep reminding himself of the words and feelings of the other characters in his scenes, and not focus on the powerfully projected feelings of the actors themselves. He remembered having to do multiple takes in a scene with his movie wife. He was supposed to be declaring his love for her, and he kept being distracted by the actress' subsurface feelings of hunger and annoyance.

On December 14, however, Rupert stopped focusing on himself. A gunman had opened fire at an elementary school in Connecticut, killing six adults and twenty six- and seven-year-olds. It brought up all of his nightmares about his spy work. He tried to talk about it with Arthur, but Arthur couldn't comfort him. He eventually called Jenny.

She lived in Connecticut and knew one of the mothers who had lost a child at Sandy Hook. She had lost two nieces in the pipeline explosion in Nairobi the previous year. Her advice to Rupert was just to keep living and dreaming of a better world.

On his forty-third birthday, Victoria called him with another movie offer. It was a smaller independent film but a juicy role. Rupert told her to send him the script. He found it hard to be enthusiastic.

At breakfast, Arthur got excited about planning a vacation with Rupert. He said he realized that morning that he needed to take more responsibility for planning their social life. The epiphanies blessing had begun.

Arthur seemed to get a new inspiration for some project or another every day he saw Rupert. Meeting with Victoria inspired her as well, but Rupert started to prepare her for the career direction he wanted to go at the end of the year. He also warned Arthur it was coming up. He didn't seem concerned. Rupert tried to relax about it. His mother and grandmother had certainly adapted to it.

Rupert was invited to meet with Edie Windsor at a small gathering in the Village celebrating her Supreme Court victory on June 26. At that point, England, France, and Brazil had also legalized same-sex marriages. By the end of 2013, five more states adopted marriage equality–New Mexico became the seventeenth on December 19. Rupert had shot a small budget film in Europe, and then he and Arthur had toured the continent for a few weeks after filming ended, so he mostly only had to deal with Arthur's plethora of epiphanies: painting the bedroom walls, getting corrective surgery on his eyes and braces on his teeth, wearing more blue or more white, developing plans for several businesses, and joining Occupy Wall Street.

It wasn't until Christmas Eve that Arthur asked him about his upcoming blessing. "I'll let it be a surprise when we wake up. I'll give you a little hint. I'm scheduled to perform at a club downtown on New Year's Eve."

In the morning they woke at around eight o'clock. Every gift either of them opened was another impetus for Arthur's brainstorming. "I'm glad this is about to end," Arthur admitted. "I've been feeling pretty frenetic all year." He was sitting on the floor in front of their Christmas tree.

"Sorry." Rupert kissed Arthur on the top of the head. "I'm thinking the next blessing is also going to be a bit rough on you."

"What is it?" Arthur stood up to look at Rupert more directly.

"My mother said it was pretty exhausting at first when I got it at age five, but she got used to it." Rupert watched the clock in the hallway approach nine-thirty.

"Can you at least tell me where you're performing on Tuesday night?"

"Wait for it," Rupert advised.

"Wait for what?" Suddenly Arthur broke out into laughter.

"Bingo," Rupert remarked.

"Bingo?" Arthur said between chuckles. "That's so funny."

"I'm performing at a comedy club on New Year's Eve. Welcome to the laughter blessing."

Arthur thought that was incredibly funny and couldn't stop laughing for a full minute.

CHAPTER 29: RUPERT TURNS FORTY-FIVE

Rupert barely remembered the laughter blessing when he was five. He remembered running and hiding in the bushes in his grandmother's backyard, or in the back of her closet, just to get away from the constant giggles, guffaws, chuckles, chortles, snickers and titters, hoots and tee-hees. He remembered his mom and grandma trying desperately to suppress the urge to laugh when he was around, and they managed for only a few seconds at a time before they would have to turn away and release at least a snigger. One or the other of them would, at least once a day, say she needed to "take a break from Rupert"–usually because her sides were aching from hours of laughing.

Young Rupert returned to nursery school after New Year's Day. Initially his caregivers thought it would grant them respite from all the laughing. But that didn't work out either. When Zelda would pick him up afterward, he was always in tears, because the other children had responded to his new blessing by making fun of little Rupert.

It was only in the adult world where Rupert felt like he could manage– transforming the laughter into adoration when he performed at his family's restaurant. When he got onstage and sang and danced and told stories, he could imagine that his performance was garnering the laughter–pushing to the back of his mind that standing on the little raised platform and doing nothing at all might achieve the same result.

It was standing room only at the club in the Financial District near Wall Street, because Rupert was now an A-list celebrity. Everyone was curious if he could do comedy, since all of his previous movies were dramas. From the cameras and microphones, Rupert counted nine members of the press corps, two of whom he knew from his media tours. He smiled broadly as the host introduced him. He did a bit where he tried to decide if he was going to sit on a stool or not. The audience laughed. He continued the gag with uncertainty about using the mic stand. The audience laughed louder. "My name is Rupert Rocket. Some of you may have heard of me before."

A combination of laughter and cheers greeted him. He was glad to know he had fans there besides Arthur. "When I was a young child in Sheboygan, Wisconsin . . ." (even the mention of his hometown brought titters) ". . . my mother used to take me to our family restaurant, and I would climb up on a little raised platform they used for special events and do a five-year-old's version of a song-and-dance number. I performed 'I'm a Little Teapot' and 'Itsy Bitsy Spider' and waved my hands and shuffled my feet, and the diners couldn't get enough of it. I got requests for encore after encore."

Until he paused, most of the audience waited to laugh and applaud. Rupert sighed and tried to look like he was embarrassed by the attention. "It really wasn't a big deal."

The audience laughter reached a crescendo with the last comment and the mugging. Rupert waited for it to die down a bit more before he continued. "They loved whatever I did, I guess because they didn't have a five-year-old of their own to watch acting silly. My mom encouraged me to expand my repertoire and take more chances, so I started rehearsing at the full-length mirror in my grandma's bedroom after school."

Rupert paused to acknowledge the additional chuckles. "I agreed to take dance classes so that my performances would be a bit more polished. The only classes being offered for kids that young in Sheboygan was ballet, and my mom signed me up. When I was there, I felt a freedom I didn't feel anywhere else. It took some bullies in first grade to make it clear that being the only boy in a class otherwise filled with little girls was not a good thing."

Rupert made another embarrassed face, and the laughter rose again. He looked away and then looked surprised that they were still laughing. "Seriously, I was teased almost every day of first grade, and my grandma and mom kept telling me to ignore it, that the ridicule would eventually stop. I didn't believe it, but by second grade, no one went out of their way to tease me. By third grade, one other brave boy joined me in ballet classes. It felt like things were turning around. I was doing well in school. I was managing the bullies well."

The audience had died down to chuckles, so Rupert skipped forward in his routine. "And then, when I turned ten, I became . . . invisible."

The audience exploded with laughter again. Throughout his twenty-minute set, he told stories, and when it had been too quiet too long, he would make a face or say something ridiculous to get them going again. At the end of his set, he got a standing ovation, but he just grabbed Arthur by the hand and led him out the exit. Randy had exactly timed his arrival to be parking in the loading zone as Rupert and Arthur got to the curb.

In the ride back to Battery Park City, Arthur managed to stay serious for almost a full minute. It was encouraging to Rupert, because that was a record in his experience with the laughter blessing.

"You did great, Rupert!" Arthur said. "I loved hearing those stories about your childhood, and I really truly think you could have gotten a similar response without your new blessing." He paused for a moment, "And I've started to realize that when you're not saying anything or doing anything too dramatic, I can suppress the laughter. I was worried I wasn't going to be able to sleep next to you, but once you fell asleep, you just looked handsome and adorable again, and it was easier."

"So, all I have to do is not speak and not do anything?" Rupert said. "Let me get back to you on that."

Of course, Arthur laughed again then. But Rupert watched him over the following days, and indeed, silently walking past Arthur did not seem to get a rise out of him. Eating across from him sometimes only brought a smile to Arthur's face. Rupert reverted to his old strategy during the dominance blessing and pretended he was mute. Writing or typing out notes to hand to Arthur seemed to keep his giggling in check.

The change in Victoria's gruff personality was almost disturbing because she seemed so uncomfortable laughing at Rupert, whether over the phone or in person. She managed to explain what he needed to know about contract negotiations without snickering, but as soon as Rupert would ask a question, she would start again. She seemed to wrestle each chuckle to the point of surrender. It looked and sounded like the exercise was tiring her, so he tried to keep interactions with her brief.

Since Rupert rarely saw Randy's face when he was riding in the SUV with him, he had no idea what contortions he performed to stifle his laughter. Audibly, it sounded like he was simply clearing his throat after Rupert spoke. He did comment more than once that chats with Rupert were becoming more amusing.

Rupert went for a screen test in Queens for a comedy film. The script had intrigued him, partly because there were once again stunts he felt it would be easy to perform without relying on a stunt double. It also had him shirtless in some scenes, so he spent every day for the two weeks preceding the screen test lifting weights at the gym.

The film was set in and shot in New York, which also appealed to Rupert. He could go home every night. Arthur was allowed to watch him work when he wanted and spent the rest of his time nibbling on food at craft services or hanging out in Rupert's trailer. The director and the director of photography had enough experience working on comedies to stifle their laughter when Rupert worked. The sound designer kept complaining that he could pick up someone laughing on most of the takes, which the director claimed they could mask in post. They went through three boom operators before they found one who could work without shaking the pole. And each new actor had to work really hard to maintain a straight face in scenes with Rupert.

Rupert's stunt coordinator was a hopeless case. He laughed throughout their training, and the director banished him to the makeup trailer as he set up each new shot. Most of the stunts were easy falls and jumps, and they were a piece of cake for Rupert, who had done fight scenes in previous movies.

The accident occurred on a shoot early on a Saturday morning in mid-July, near the end of shooting at a sound stage in Queens. He and Arthur had gone out dancing the night before, and Arthur felt too lazy to accompany Rupert so early. Rupert had managed to sneak in a workout in the building gym where they lived before heading to Queens.

Rupert had been practicing the trip-and-fall combination for a couple of days, and while he was going through hair and makeup, he tried to visualize it in his mind. Before getting into costume, Rupert went onto the set to get a better look at where he would be performing the stunt. He had to wait for the lighting techs to raise the lighting truss out of the way. It was a complex dream sequence, so they had dozens of spotlights on the truss. Four techs pulled on the ropes that raised it high above Rupert's head, but only one of them had started to tie it off when Rupert entered the middle of the stage to get a look at the springboard and pad placement.

Rupert was told much later what had happened. It involved one of the lighting techs yelling at Rupert to get off the stage. A woman nearby screamed. And then Rupert felt the heat and weight of nearly a half-ton of spotlights and steel trusswork smash him to the stage floor, burn his shoulders and neck, and turned his body to jelly in the moment before he blacked out.

The sound of the ambulance siren brought Rupert briefly back to consciousness, but the intense pain in his jaw, chest, arms, and legs made him pass out again.

The renewed pain of being transferred from a gurney to the operating table also brought Rupert back to consciousness for a moment, and then he passed out again.

Rupert drifted in and out of partial consciousness for what seemed like days. He felt like his bones were being broken again. He felt like he was being choked. He imagined the Pooka standing near him laughing. Near the end of the phantasm of nightmares, he felt like a long python was slithering out of his mouth.

He blinked his eyes. He couldn't move his arms, legs, or jaw. His chest hurt every time he breathed. He saw Arthur's smiling face with raw, red skin around his eyes appear above him. "Are you awake again, Rupert?" he asked.

Rupert didn't remember waking the first time, at least not since that morning after they stayed up too late dancing. He tried to communicate this to Arthur, but it came out like, "Errrr. Uh. Errr."

Arthur laughed for a second and then stopped. "I'm sorry. I shouldn't have asked you a question. Your jaw is still wired shut and your tongue is probably still swollen." He went away for a couple of seconds and then came back and rubbed Carmex on Rupert's lips with a finger. "Um, let me try to remember what you need to know." He went away again for a couple of seconds and then reappeared unfolding a piece of paper. "I made a list. You've been unconscious for about two weeks. You were in an accident at the movie set. A bunch of spotlights fell on you. You have fractures in one arm, one shoulder blade, your jaw, both legs, and five of your ribs. You got second-degree burns on the back of your neck and shoulders. You have a catheter on your penis. Your arms and legs are strapped down and have braces on them, so you can't move them."

At that point, Arthur traded his list for a handkerchief and wiped the tears streaming from his eyes. "One of your broken ribs punctured a lung, so you may feel like you're not getting enough oxygen some times. It's healed now, but the lung never fully reinflated. The doctor said it is probably still painful for you to breathe, so you're getting pain medication and fluids through a port on your left arm."

Arthur swallowed hard and blew his nose. "Your director said he could finish the last two scenes using a double, since there wasn't much dialogue. You'll still get your full pay, plus the insurance money eventually. Your father and Britney are staying at our apartment and are on their way here. Mike has visited a couple of times to help me with the bills, your investments, and dealing with Victoria and Loretta."

Rupert wondered why Fred had decided to come and why Loretta, his criminal defense lawyer, was involved again. It didn't seem like such a big deal to him until Arthur started crying again as he told him, "You've lost a lot of weight, and you . . . have a big scar on the right side of your face."

Arthur disappeared again from Rupert's visual field. He was propped up at an angle, but he couldn't turn his head to the side. He could hear Arthur weeping. And he wished he could say something to comfort him. His own eyes started to tear up and he tried to blink the tears away. Arthur reappeared with the handkerchief and gently dabbed around Rupert's eyes. "I was terrified that you were going to die, but the doctor said you seemed strong, and eventually the burns will fade and the bones will knit back together, and you'll be able to . . ." Arthur paused to wipe his own tears again. ". . . eat solid food again."

That mention of food made Rupert realize how incredibly hungry he was, but the dull pain every time he inhaled made the prospect of swallowing anything scary. He tried to imagine what it had been like while he was unconscious. Arthur said he had worried that Rupert would die. That was probably what brought Fred and Britney to New York for the first time since his graduation from Julliard. Arthur probably hadn't slept much. With Fred and Britney at the apartment, Arthur was probably sleeping on their couch and coming to visit Rupert's inanimate body as much as he could, waiting for Rupert to wake up. He was probably an emotional wreck. All of the listening and thinking and keeping his eyes open was making him tired, so he decided to close his eyes for a bit. Arthur said something about an irregularity in Rupert's heartbeat that wasn't that serious at the moment.

The next time Rupert awakened, it was in the middle of an argument with a dream character, a bag lady in Central Park, about the effects of his blessings. He argued that his immobility during his recovery at what he assumed was a hospital was not going to evoke any laughter, especially given the seriousness of the injuries Arthur had described to him. She said he was supposed to have this accident during his rapid-healing blessing—that he'd made a mistake in having it this early during his laughter blessing. He countered that he could already be in another one of the blessings described in his mother's journal, like the clairvoyance one. The bag lady just laughed, so he knew he was still in the laughter blessing. He was still only forty-four. He hadn't missed a birthday.

"Rupert, wake up," he heard Arthur say. "Fred is here."

Rupert opened his eyes and looked down his body and past the metal braces on his legs where his father was standing in a gray sweatshirt and wearing eyeglasses and a pained expression at the foot of his bed. "Err," Rupert said to acknowledge that he was awake.

Fred waved awkwardly toward Rupert, almost like he was shooing a fly. Maybe he was. "It's good to see you awake finally, son," he called out a little louder than he needed to. "Britney and I came out from California last month when we heard about your accident."

Rupert's thoughts were: *Duh. I can see you're here. Is being awake inherently better than being asleep? I'm really hungry. Have I really been laid up here for a month?* Rupert only managed to say, "Uhhh. Errr."

"We're here in case you need anything," his father continued. "We were worried about you. Arthur said he didn't know if you were going to survive the surgery."

It's good Arthur finally got to meet my father and stepmother. I don't know what you can do for me now. Say something comforting to Arthur for me. He moved his eyeballs in search of Arthur and said. "Errr-uhhh."

"He doesn't look that bad," Fred commented to someone beyond Rupert's right-side field of vision, presumably Arthur, but maybe Britney was there too. "He has a bit more color to his skin."

Arthur's voice preceded Arthur's face by a couple of seconds. "The physical therapist has been starting to stretch his arms, legs, and back a little bit, and he's able to consume soft foods now. He's off the liquid diet. He won't be able to chew anything though until the wire comes out."

Rupert didn't remember any physical therapist, or any food for that matter. He wondered if he had forgotten, or if they had happened while he was sleeping. Arthur put more Carmex on his lips, and it felt good.

"When will that happen?" Fred asked.

Arthur smiled and looked down at Rupert. "They're going to do a new set of CT scans next week. The wire could maybe come out after that, but he'll still be limited to soft foods for a while, because his jaw will be sore."

"How about the arm and leg braces?" Fred asked as he gestured up Rupert's body.

"They'll scan them too," Arthur replied as he pulled his head away to the right again. "He may be okay with just the casts after that. In the last scan, all but one of the cracks in the ribs were healing nicely. They may have to do surgery again to insert a metal plate on that one."

Ten days later, when the metal braces came off and the jaw wire came out, Rupert was in a new world of pain, but at least he could describe what he needed. The room was dim, so Rupert assumed it was nighttime, and Arthur's face and hand appeared periodically from his right side and delivered a spoonful of vanilla pudding into his mouth. He let it sit on his tongue for a few seconds before swallowing it, because his tongue was still a bit raw from frequently brushing against the ends of the jaw wire. When the spoon stopped appearing, Rupert moaned, "More!"

"All gone," Arthur apologized. "You already ate everything that was on your tray."

"Still hungry," Rupert grunted.

Arthur laughed. "I know, sweetie. You're used to eating more, but you've had close to zero exercise for the past two months, so we have to take it slowly, or it's all going to become fat."

Rupert looked down at his body. "Look at me! I'm as skinny as I was when I was thirteen!"

Arthur laughed again. "You don't look that bad . . . considering what you've been through. You're still sexy to me."

"I guess my laughter blessing is still working," Rupert observed.

Arthur just looked down at Rupert with curiosity on his face. He let a titter escape and then said, "I haven't laughed in weeks."

"That's gonna' change now." Rupert carefully maneuvered his mouth into a smile, which didn't hurt as much as he thought it would.

Arthur laughed again, and it made Rupert happy. He was slowly reentering the world.

The big change happened in mid-December when Rupert's casts came off, and he was allowed to go home. Rupert was excited at the prospect of sleeping in his own bed and getting some decent food finally. Randy picked them up and actually got out to help Rupert out of his wheelchair and into the SUV. Rupert was surprised and disappointed that the wheelchair was going into the back cargo area. He was glad that Arthur held his hand once he was sitting next to him. Rupert's spirits sank again, however, when he saw the rented hospital bed set up in their living room.

Every day thereafter until Christmas Eve, Arthur scheduled a different one of Rupert's friends to visit one at a time. The first night, it was Danny, then Max, Chantal, Theo, Michaela, John, Denise, Jorge, Luke. And on the evening of the 23rd, Rupert looked over from his hospital bed set up in the living room and saw Arthur escort a huge spray of flowers and palm fronds through the front door of the apartment. When Arthur took the flowers into the dining room, Jenny Athiambo was standing there in the same yellow dress and matching jacket she had worn years before at his first interview with her.

"*Hamjambo, Mheshimiwa Rocket.*" She smiled and her teeth seemed brighter to Rupert than the Christmas tree lights she stood beside.

"*Sijambo, Bosi!*" Rupert gleefully shouted back. "Come closer so I can see you!"

Initially, she laughed. But as she approached, her smile faded into a look of sadness. "You look so different. How are you feeling?"

Rupert only had one day left on the laughter blessing, and he was determined to do some good with it. "I feel like I was crushed by hundreds of pounds of metal, went through half a day of surgery and four months of recovery, and lost forty pounds. I get winded easily, I have trouble walking on my own, and they only let me start chewing solid food a week or two ago. I'm peachy. How are you?"

Jenny tittered. "That's the Rupert I remember: Indomitable!"

Arthur returned from the dining room. "Can I get you anything, Ms. Athiambo?"

"Just a chair, so I can sit closer to Rupert," she said. "And please, just call me Jenny, Arthur."

"I'll bring one in from the dining room, Jenny," Arthur said as he took off again.

"I have to tell you, Rupert, it's been a rough couple of years." Arthur set a chair down behind her, and she sat. "I'm hoping 2015 brings us fewer natural disasters and wars, because I could use a break. I'm sorry I couldn't visit you sooner."

"They told me they would only allow Arthur and Fred to visit until I was out of critical care."

Jenny looked at Arthur, who was standing near the foot of Rupert's bed. "How did you manage that if you're not family?"

"Mike arranged it," Arthur replied.

"He probably bribed the hospital," Rupert suggested, and both Arthur and Jenny laughed. "I can only sleep on my back propped up like this. I'm hoping I can get back into my old bed in a few weeks." He smiled at Arthur. "I miss being cuddled."

Jenny chuckled, but Arthur guffawed once. "I do cuddle with you!" he retorted. "I was just up there with you this afternoon!"

"It's not the same," Rupert said with mock petulance.

"I'll try to come by again next month," Jenny said as she got up from the chair, "and I can help you brush up on your Swahili."

"I don't know when I'm ever going to use it again except with you." It made Rupert a little too depressed, but Jenny and Arthur both chuckled as if he'd said something precious.

"I'd love to have you come back and work for UNHCR," she said as she rebuttoned her coat.

"And the CIA?" Rupert asked hopefully. Jenny cast a concerned glance at Arthur. "I told him about that work already."

"Well, you'll have to speak with Parker about that. You mean he hasn't even called you yet?"

Rupert looked at Arthur to answer, but Arthur also looked puzzled. "I don't think so," Rupert replied.

"That is going to change," Jenny vowed as she headed toward the door.

Arthur rushed toward her to open the door for her, and she turned back, chuckled for a moment, and said, "Have a merry Christmas and a happy birthday, Rupert Rocket. And don't push yourself too fast. We'll still be here when you're back to your old self."

When Arthur came back from closing the door, he came up and put his hands on the side rails of Rupert's hospital bed. "You look so sad. I thought you'd enjoy seeing Jenny."

"That was great," Rupert admitted. "Thank you for arranging all those visitors." He could feel himself tearing up, and Arthur immediately had his handkerchief out, dabbing his eyes. "I'm just feeling sorry for myself. I've got scars on my face and neck and shoulders . . ."

Arthur giggled. "Surgery can get rid of that."

". . . I can't act in films any more . . ."

Arthur tittered for a moment. "I'm talking to Victoria about that."

". . . and I feel like I don't deserve such a wonderful, kind, generous, beautiful young man taking care of me."

"I love you, Rupert Rocket." He giggled for a moment and then changed the subject. "So what is your next blessing?"

"It's one of the C's," Rupert replied. He didn't remember what had originally come before his laughter blessing when he was four. And it had been so long since he had looked through his mother's journal or his blessing schedule on the computer. "Either charisma or clairvoyance."

"I guess we'll find out in about thirty-six hours," Arthur calculated.

The day before Rupert's forty-fifth birthday started out with lots of phone calls. Parker did call and wish him a speedy recovery; he had not closed Rupert's agency file yet. Mike called to deliver early birthday wishes; he was planning on spending Christmas day in Chicago at his girlfriend Laura's. The director of Rupert's last film called to check how he was doing; he said he had just finished editing the film and they were able to fix the soundtrack. Fred called to check on how Rupert was doing; he advised Rupert to be really nice to Arthur because he'd been through a lot. And Michaela and Denise called to tell them they were on their way to pick up the Christmas dinner.

Rupert was in the bathroom in his wheelchair when he disconnected the last call. "Arthur?" he called out.

Within seconds, Arthur was there, somewhat out of breath. "Are you okay? What do you need?"

Rupert laughed, and after a moment, Arthur joined him. "That was Denise and Michaela. They said they're on their way over. What's going on?"

"Did they say anything about Max and Danny?" Arthur asked.

Rupert couldn't decide if he was angry about being kept in the dark or excited at the possibility of having more than one visitor at a time. "No! Why would they?"

Arthur explained that Victoria had purchased a holiday dinner for six for Rupert, and Arthur had invited the two other couples they were closest with to eat. Rupert thought the turkey, the stuffing, the mashed potatoes, the cornbread, the green beans, and the pumpkin pie were amazing. But it was the company, laughing around his dining table, even if he was in a wheelchair, that made him even happier. He had known all of them for decades. They had become his family of choice, and yet he tried to imagine what his grandma Zelda and his mom would say if they saw this little gathering:

We're proud and happy you've found a place in the world, dear Rupert, he imagined them saying. *A place where you are surrounded by people who love you.* And Zelda would start singing that song she loved: *Oh wie wunderbar! Nichts ist so wies war! Durch ein winziges Wort: Heirat.*

And Rupert found himself whispering the translation out loud in a momentary lull in the conversation around the table: "Oh, how wonderful! Nothing's as it was! With one tiny word: marriage."

They all chuckled briefly at the non sequitur. "That's that song you used to sing all the time when we were roommates," Danny said.

"I used to sing that?" Rupert asked.

Everyone chuckled. Arthur leaned over and kissed Rupert on the cheek. He whispered, "I think you're still going to be funny even after tomorrow morning."

"We'll see," he whispered back.

When Rupert awoke early the next morning, the Christmas tree lights were still on. For some reason, just staring across the predawn gloom in the living room at the tree and the wrapped gifts beneath it on the floor made him start crying again. "*Oh wie wunderbar! Nichts ist so wies war!* . . ." he softly sang.

Arthur had been sleeping with the bedroom door open, so he was quickly up and in the doorway looking over at Rupert. "Are you okay, Rupert?" He approached a little closer. "You're crying. What's wrong?"

"I need a cuddle again," Rupert choked through the tears.

Arthur climbed up into the bed and threw one arm and one leg over Rupert. "What's making you sad?"

"I'm going to miss all this." Rupert turned his head and wept audibly into his pillow.

"Where are you going?" Arthur asked. He sounded a little scared.

Rupert sighed and tried to staunch his tears. "At the end of each twenty-five years of blessings, someone in my family always dies at the hands of the Pooka's curse. I only have five more years."

"You can't know that for sure," Arthur whispered.

"It happened to my grandfather, my grandmother, and my mom." Rupert immediately regretted bringing Arthur's holiday mood down. "I'm sorry," he whispered.

"It's okay," Arthur insisted. "We'll get through this somehow. Later this morning, you're going to wake up and have a brand new blessing that starts with C and start a brand new year."

They both laughed. "Happy birthday, baby," Arthur whispered.

A couple of minutes later, Rupert fell asleep. Arthur was still holding him. He felt a tiny sliver of hope still clinging to his heart.

CHAPTER 30: RUPERT TURNS FORTY-SEVEN

Rupert had Randy load the wheelchair in the back of the SUV just in case. Over the month of December, during his physical therapy, he had practiced walking with a walker. He still fell down when he tried to use a cane. He could, with effort, stand up and sit down without someone helping him anymore. He didn't shave the beard he had been growing for the previous four weeks, because it covered around half of the pinkish elliptical scar that ran from the top of his right cheekbone to the corner of his mouth. The hairs on the scar itself were sparse, but the surrounding hair could be combed over it.

When they pulled up in front of the Time-Warner Center at Columbus Circle, Rupert put on his dark glasses and picked his folding walker up off the backseat floor. Since he had a beard, his hair was longer and beginning to gray at the temples, and he was almost fifty pounds lighter than the morning of the accident in July, he didn't need more of a disguise.

Randy opened the door for him and made sure he didn't fall getting out of the car. Rupert waved at him and started to head toward the posts protecting the entrance. Randy jogged up and in front of him and put a hand on the front of his walker to stop him. "Perhaps I could get a concierge to help you inside and upstairs?"

Rupert fished his cell phone out of the little bag hanging from the front of his walker and held it up for Randy. "I can always call you if I run into problems. I need to try this on my own."

The foot traffic in front of the building and heading in and out of the entrance was minimal. It was a Friday, but since New Year's Day had been the day before, most New Yorkers seemed to be extending their holiday straight through the weekend. A young woman held one of the swinging doors open for Rupert, and he nodded, still unaccustomed to accepting help and not being recognized. He had usually used the escalators here, but Rupert decided to roll off in search of an elevator.

When he got on the elevator, he pushed the button for the third floor and tried to straighten up. The walker always had him leaning forward slightly, and it made his back sore and tight to use it for too long. Just before the door opened, Rupert had a mental image of finding Parker still wearing his gray wool coat, sitting at one of the lower tables in the café.

Evidently Parker had made eye contact with him first—or at least heard the clattering of his walker wheels on the tile floor—because he was standing, still in his gray coat, and looking in Rupert's direction. Parker took off his coat and draped it over the back of the chair where he had been sitting as he waited for Rupert to slowly make his way closer. Rupert looked at the higher chairs along the bar looking out into the atrium and then at the lower chair Parker was pulling out for him, and he decided that back support was more important than view or ease in access. Rupert sat in the chair slowly. Parker watched anxiously, as if he were prepared to catch Rupert if he tumbled out of it.

"I'm surprised we're meeting so early in January this year," Rupert commented. "Are you eager to have me working for you again?"

Parker finally sat down. "First of all, I'm glad you survived, and that you're doing so well in your recovery."

"I think my film and modeling careers are effectively over," Rupert said. "And with my current disability, I don't blend in very well either. I'm not sure what good I would be to you."

Parker grinned. "It depends, Spook. What'cha got for me this year?"

"Clairvoyance." Rupert had figured it out late on Christmas Day, when Arthur had gone out. Rupert wondered where he was going, and a moment later, he felt certain he knew. "It seems to work best if I'm at the place or it's a place I've been to or a person I've met. I can often get details from photos. Seeing behind walls and other barriers seems the easiest."

"Hmm." Parker looked like he was running scenarios in his head. "I can picture you helping with manhunts, bomb squads, abductions, . . ."

"I could also maybe help with surveillance again," Rupert volunteered.

Parker held his palm out. "Let's not get ahead of ourselves, Spook. You don't look particularly mobile right now. I'll have to see what I can start you on from your home, or at least a desk somewhere. How about if we send you photos and documents by email first, and you tell us what you can about them?"

Before Rupert could answer, a waitress took their orders. Rupert wasn't hungry for once, so he just ordered tea. Parker got a quiche and a salad. "That sounds fine. My balance is getting better, so I should be able to graduate to a cane soon."

Parker was pretty quiet until after his food came. He stopped after two bites of the quiche and put his fork down. "The big boss wanted me to thank you for helping track down bin Laden. It had been dogging him for years, and he was really glad to add that notch to his belt."

"It was an honor to meet him," Rupert said. He took a sip of his tea before continuing. "Thank you for arranging that."

"It was at his request, Spook. The director reported you were consulting for us, and the President reads all of those reports." Parker finished his quiche and wiped his mouth with his napkin. "Luxembourg just passed same-sex marriage yesterday. You and Arthur could go there to tie the knot now."

Rupert assumed his CIA supervisor was teasing him, but he responded any way. "With my health the way it is, we're trying not to add any more stress to my life."

"I can understand that, Spook, but you never struck me as the cautious type." Parker started picking at his salad. "Up until your accident, the only thing you ever balked at was wetwork. You've actually been one of our longest-lasting deep-cover operatives. Most burn out after a year or two."

"You don't think getting this banged up gives me the right to being a bit more cautious?" Rupert joked.

"The scar, the beard, and the walker—they give you character." Parker laughed. "You were kind of boring and white bread before. You look more like a spy now."

On the ride home, Rupert turned Parker's comment over in his mind. He had thought boring and conventional was a better cover, but perhaps he was right. A person using a walker or a cane was less likely to seem like a dangerous spy.

Rupert had texted Arthur when he was on his way, so after Randy dropped him off, Arthur was supplanting the doorman at opening the lobby door for him. Rupert was getting a little winded, and Arthur noticed. "I wish you would have let me go with you. You look exhausted."

Rupert kissed him on the cheek. "It was a good test of my endurance, and Parker would never have let you sit in on my briefing."

"I could have just been nearby," Arthur argued as he walked with Rupert toward the elevator. "I'm terrified that you're going to fall over. And hurt yourself worse."

Arthur was referring to his tumble on New Year's Eve when he tried to traverse the entire living room using just a cane. "I have to keep pushing myself," Rupert said. "I was an athlete my entire life, and I don't want to give in to my injuries and give up. I want to have sex with you again. You deserve that."

Arthur waited for the elevator door to close. "There's no need to rush that."

"Can we at least get rid of the hospital bed?" Rupert begged. "I could probably be in bed with you as long as I sleep on my back a little longer."

"The doctors said you need to lie at an incline a little longer."

They got out of the elevator and headed down the hall. Arthur ran ahead and unlocked the apartment door. "So, I'm still banished to the living room?" Rupert teased.

"You're so melodramatic sometimes."

"Occupational hazard," Rupert joked.

"I can still climb into your bed," Arthur reminded him.

A week later, Rupert was walking more reliably using his cane in the apartment and just using the walker when he went out. He got a phone call when

345

he was wheeling himself back into the building lobby after a medical checkup. He stopped and pulled out his phone. "This is Rupert," he said.

He heard the voice of his handler from the U.N. "Hello, Rupert. I heard you met with Parker last week."

"Hi, Jenny. He's been sending me stuff by email to work on. Give me just a second to get in out of the cold." Rupert found a seat in the lobby and spoke into the phone again. "How are you doing?"

"I'm fine," she replied. "Are you up for some international travel?"

"I'm walking with a cane more often," Rupert reported. "As long as I don't have to run or walk long distances . . . or climb lots of stairs, I might be okay."

"We have an urgent need for linguists fluent in English, French, and Arabic," Jenny explained. "Troops from Chad have crossed into Nigeria and massacred thousands. Many of those who survived have fled to Cameroon. We need people who can process the refugees and be vigilant for Chadian insurgents among them. You are one of the few I could turn to for that combination of languages and experience working in Africa. Can you help?"

Useless. It was the word that kept coming up in Rupert's mind so consistently over the previous five months he had been recovering. First it had been his whole body that felt useless. Now it was just his diminished lung capacity and his unsteady balance that was making him feel useless. So, when Jenny begged Rupert to go to Cameroon, it was hard to let go of the possibility that he could be useful again. He knew Arthur, cautious Arthur, would be against it, but maybe if he could bring Arthur along, he would worry less. "Let me talk to Arthur about it and get back to you."

He disconnected the call with Jenny and called Arthur. "Hey, Arthur. I'm in the lobby on my way upstairs."

"How was the appointment?" Arthur asked.

Rupert stood up and readied his walker for the trip over to the elevators. "My ribs and arm are completely healed, and I should be able to slowly reintroduce weight-bearing exercises."

"That's great," Arthur said. "I got a call from Hakim. He said he tried to reach you."

"I had the ringer turned off during the exam," Rupert explained.

"He's coming over."

Rupert was still resting on the couch when Hakim arrived an hour later. "Hello, Arthur," he said as he entered. When he got to the living room, he was silent for a moment, taking in Rupert's altered appearance since the accident. "It's good to see you, Rupert. How are you feeling?"

Rupert forced a smile. "I have had a pretty big day so far, so I'm taking it easy. Would you like to sit down?" Rupert gestured toward the nearer easy chair.

Hakim took off his coat and handed it to Arthur. "Would you mind giving us a bit of privacy, Arthur?"

Arthur grinned. Rupert had told him that Hakim was working as an undercover CIA courier. "I'll be in the bedroom, with my earbuds in," he replied.

Once Arthur closed the door, Hakim continued. "I'm not sure I would have recognized you if I'd run into you on the street."

"I don't have to worry about paparazzi anymore," Rupert commented. "Although I don't know if that will change when my movie premieres in August. They'll probably want me to do publicity."

"The CIA wants you to accept the relief mission to Cameroon," Hakim announced.

"Why is that?"

"You may have heard about the attack at the headquarters at the editorial offices of Charlie Hebdo in Paris last Wednesday," Hakim replied. "It was carried out by a Yemeni terrorist cell working with al-Qaeda. We need you to go to Yemen and help us find their base in Sana'a. We would fly you in and out from Cameroon."

"You think I can do it in my current condition?" Rupert asked.

"Analysts have done all the risk management, including your most recent scans this morning, so I'd give that a conditional yes. They wouldn't have green-lighted inviting you to the operation otherwise."

Rupert checked to make sure Hakim wasn't joking. His eyes looked very earnest. "I'm impressed and a little bit shocked if your analysts already got access to scans even I haven't seen yet."

"Well," Hakim said as he sat down on the couch next to Rupert, "as a rule, I power down my cell phone when I'm not using it, and I put any of my private digital files on removable media. If you want the agency in less of your business, you have to make it harder for them." He patted Rupert on the knee. "So, I can't stay long. What should I tell them?"

"Arthur?" Rupert shouted toward the bedroom door.

A moment later, Arthur opened the door and started taking out his earphones. "Do you need something?"

Rupert lowered his volume only a little. "How would you feel about a trip to Central Africa?"

Arthur was wary, but Rupert was right. Arthur was only willing to let him go if he tagged along. Rupert decided to leave his wheelchair and walker behind and rely on Arthur and his cane to get around. The bus trip to the far north of Cameroon began in N'Djamena, Chad, and was the most difficult for Rupert for two reasons: The bumping of the bus made his bonier butt sore, and he suspected Chadian spies were following him and Arthur as soon as they left the airport.

The car that had been following them out of Chad kept heading west toward Gambaru when the bus turned north toward Makari. The bus was frequently passed by convoys of trucks with red crosses on them. The refugee camp was set up at the end of a cow path ten miles north of Hile Halifia, already a tiny desert town at the end of the paved highway in northern Cameroon. It was a tent city on a dairy farm's pasture, and it looked like the trucks that had passed them might only have been the second or third shipment there. Hundreds of frightened Nigerians arrived just after they had, bringing the population of the little camp to almost a thousand.

Arthur and Rupert helped as much as they could answering questions and directing refugees to services. On their second day, Rupert thought he heard Arabic being spoken, but he decided he would follow up on it after his return from Yemen. He explained to Arthur that he had to attend to his "other job," kissed him, and left for Sana'a alone in the cab of a returning aid truck early the next day.

The work in Yemen was actually a lot more comfortable. Rupert got to stay in a hotel. He was taken through the streets using his clairvoyant blessing to peer into buildings as they drove past. On his second day there, he found the al-Qaeda hideout and was back at the refugee camp in Cameroon after only three days away.

The other CIA agent at the camp helped Rupert slip back in unnoticed, so Arthur's lie about Rupert being sick for three days seemed plausible to everyone else who had noticed his absence. Rupert found the two Chadian spies in the camp the next day, and they were ordered to leave. Rupert was proud that he had been able to make it through the entire mission, even with its long commutes and long hours. He felt like he was getting stronger.

Arthur was exhilarated by the trip. It was the sort of adventure he seemed to love. But when a return to Yemen in March and a trip to Syria in June came up, Arthur convinced Rupert not to go. By June, eleven months after his accident, Rupert was no longer using the walker and only using the cane to go out.

Rupert was getting more focused on the upcoming presidential campaign. He liked the candidacies of both Bernie Sanders and Hilary Clinton, both of whom had announced in April. When an ex-beauty pageant producer, ex-reality-TV star, and sleazy real estate developer from New York entered the race, Rupert couldn't stop laughing at the absurdity of it.

With the Supreme Court's ruling on June 26, 2015, Rupert was able to forget about the election for a while. They had ruled that the denial of marriage licenses to any citizen violated the Fourteenth Amendment to the Constitution, essentially making the count of states allowing same-sex marriage suddenly jump from thirty-seven to all fifty, including the ones most hostile to gay rights: Arkansas and Texas.

Rupert and Arthur had conceded to Michaela and Denise's pestering and stood on a small stage in the Village with Edie Windsor celebrating the victory. Rupert declined to speak, but some of the reporters recognized Arthur on his arm and took some photographs. The following day, Nadia called Rupert in a panic. "We have to get you to a photo shoot pronto," she told him. "There are photos from the rally yesterday that are surfacing in the tabloids that make you look sickly and not very attractive."

"I haven't seen them," Rupert admitted.

"Book it soon," Nadia advised. "I'm gonna' need new shots to send out by Tuesday night at the latest."

Arthur searched for the photos online. They weren't hard to find. They both agreed with Nadia's appraisal. Rupert looked pained and upset, and the scar on the right side of his face was red and prominent.

Rupert finally shaved his beard and started lifting light dumbbells to prepare. Arthur hired a makeup artist and hair stylist to meet them at Horst's studio in the meatpacking district. They worked their magic and found lighting and clothed poses that favored the unscarred left side of his face. Arthur remarked when they reviewed the proofs that Rupert looked like an enchanted nymph.

The movie producer loved the shots too, and it motivated Rupert to get even more exercise. By the time of the premiere at the Ziegfeld Theatre in Midtown Manhattan just before Labor Day, Rupert had transformed himself into a leaner and more-athletic-than-muscular version of his former self. His stamina had increased to where he could keep going on the publicity tour for two full days before he needed a half-day of rest. And he slept in the same bed with Arthur every night again.

He and Arthur spent time publicizing discrimination against gay and bi men in blood donation after the tour. Argentina, the Netherlands, and France had all lifted their lifetime bans. The U.S. FDA responsible for the safety of America's blood supply dithered and sputtered about how perception of the blood supply was as important as its scientific safety and finally gave into the growing trend just before Rupert's forty-sixth birthday. They adopted the new standard, which was essentially like the old lifetime ban because it required gay men to not have any sex for a year before donating blood, and very few men Rupert knew would stay celibate that long just to donate blood. They didn't ask the same waiting period for heterosexuals, so it was still discriminatory.

Between Christmas and New Year's, almost all of Rupert and Arthur's friends dropped by to say hello. It was one of the effects of his new charisma blessing. Rupert considered surgery to have his facial scar removed, because he liked to imagine that the year of charisma would be a good opportunity for his Hollywood comeback.

However, Rupert kept putting off the surgery. Through most of 2016, Rupert lent his charisma and not-completely-faded star power first to the Sanders campaign, and then to the Clinton campaign. Just word of his appearance at a rally guaranteed a huge crowd that couldn't resist his charisma blessing. They hung on his every word, and he tried to direct as much of the attention as he could toward the former Secretary of State.

In late October, just days before the presidential election, Rupert was waiting in front of the Clinton campaign headquarters in Brooklyn for Randy to pick him up and take him home to Battery Park City. He looked both directions on the street, unsure which direction Randy would come from. People passing on the street smiled and said hello, but none of them asked for selfies, which Rupert appreciated. Now that he was getting in shape again and putting on some muscle, he was more fixated on the facial scar. He didn't want it to appear in any of his photos.

So, Rupert was facing the other direction when he heard an older woman with a strong brogue walk up to him. "So, we meet again, Rupert Rocket!"

He turned quickly and saw her. She hadn't changed at all in the twenty years since he'd seen her last at the church in Chelsea. Her hair was the same gray-highlighted red. She wore the same patchwork coat, and her ears were as large and pointed as he remembered. "This is beyond a surprise, Grogoch. To what do I owe the honor?"

The Grogoch's laugh was somewhere between a giggle and a cackle. "I've been trying my darnedest to avoid you these past months, Rupert. But that charisma charm is a strong one."

"So, I've noticed," Rupert agreed. "While I've got you here, I'd like to ask you about something related to your blessing."

351

"If I can help, I certainly will, m'dear."

Just then, Randy's black SUV pulled up. Rupert waved at it to indicate he was busy. "When Grandma Zelda's blessing ended, my Grandfather Thomas died. When my blessing ended, Grandma and Mom died. Do you have any idea what will happen to me when my luck echo runs out in about three years?"

"Oh, I know that's distressing to contemplate," she said as she patted Rupert on the shoulder. "I had one young man many years ago much like you, blessed at birth, and he did pass away at fifty, but you're only my second case like this—with the blessing on the day you were born and the curse twisting it a bit as it progressed."

Rupert heard Randy turn off his engine. The Grogoch continued taking a step away from the car. "I really can't predict if the same will happen to you, dear Rupert. I've been following you since the day we first met. You've had an amazing life. You were a great dancer, a world-renowned actor, a humanitarian, and a spy. And you've been in love with the same person now—despite any ups and downs—since just after I last saw you. Most people in this world don't get to experience one tiny sliver of what you already have had now at forty-six. And who's to know what the next three or more years will bring?"

"Will you come see me again?" Rupert asked.

The Grogoch smiled and scratched one of her pointed ears. "I gave you my best pep talk, boyo. That will have to hold you. I promised your stepfather I'd help him in his last few years."

As she turned and started to walk away, Rupert called after her. "You mean Mike is going to die soon too?"

Randy rolled down his window. "Are you ready to go yet?"

Rupert looked back and forth between the departing patchwork coat and the SUV. He thought the exact form of Randy's question was ironic. He just nodded and climbed into the back seat.

Rupert was a blur of activity until election day—traveling all over the country trying to get Democrats out to vote. He saw so many people wanting to believe but feeling hopeless. On the night of November 8, 2016, Rupert was over at

Danny and Max's with Michaela, Denise, Arthur, Theo, and Chantal watching the returns come in. For the first two hours, everyone felt hopeful, but by eleven o'clock, the outcome was too depressing to face. A man who had bragged about molesting women, who said he could shoot someone in the middle of Fifth Avenue and it wouldn't hurt him, who said that Mexicans in the U.S. were all rapists and drug dealers, who denigrated a fallen war hero because he was Muslim, and who publicly begged the Russian government to assist him in beating his opponent—that man lost the popular vote, but won the election based on the outdated American electoral system, which made votes from sparsely populated areas count many times more than those from denser areas.

Arthur and Danny kept talking about moving to Canada. Rupert and Max both maintained that the American public would only need to see a short stint of the man in office to recognize their mistake and impeach him.

Rupert tried to cheer himself by meeting with Victoria again. She conceded that facial surgery and makeup could definitely revive his career. He'd only been out of the public eye for a matter of months since his last movie had premiered.

On Christmas Eve, Arthur got into bed with Rupert and asked him what to expect the next morning when the charisma blessing ended. Rupert refused to give up that particular secret. "I told you, I wanted it to be a surprise."

"Will it be a nice surprise?"

"I think so."

When they woke around nine o'clock, Arthur scanned Rupert and then took off out of the bedroom. He slowly walked back into the bedroom a minute later. "I don't see anything different. I give up. What's your new blessing?"

Rupert touched the right side of his face with his hand. The scar was still there. "My mom said I had rapid healing just before the charisma blessing. I don't know what's going on."

CHAPTER 31: RUPERT TURNS FORTY-EIGHT

In the first two months of 2017, Rupert was fixated on two shocking realizations. First, the country seemed to elect a 70-year-old man who was openly racist and sexist, didn't understand the Constitution, was functionally illiterate, and evidence was mounting that he was under the thumb of the Russians. He appointed Cabinet secretaries who were openly hostile to their departments' goals. His E.P.A. administrator wanted to roll back environmental protections. His education secretary wanted to defund public schools and make college harder to pay for. His secretary of state wanted to abolish Russian sanctions when they were invading Ukraine and were demonstrably guilty of meddling in our election. His secretaries of housing and urban development and of energy had no understanding of the workings of their agencies. And his policy proposals were ridiculous fantasies: building a patently useless wall along the Mexican border, fighting Muslim extremists by banning all Muslims from entering or reentering the U.S., tax cuts for the rich supported by the tired lie of "trickle-down" economics, and replacing a health plan that covered preexisting conditions with one that did not.

And the second one that he couldn't believe was that his rapid-healing blessing didn't cover preexisting conditions either. He still got winded when he ran more than a couple hundred feet. And the scar on his face persisted. His doctors claimed that his damaged lung had mostly healed and reinflated, and they were at a loss to explain his fatigue. He tried to stretch on his own, but ballet classes were beyond his capability now. The scar on his right cheek was so large, his doctors recommended surgery; less-invasive techniques were unlikely to make a difference, they said.

When the day came for the surgery in March, Rupert was feeling odd about it. He wanted to put himself out there for additional movie roles and possibly live theatre again so he could stay in New York, but the discoloration and swollen look of the scar made that close to impossible. And in his darker moments, he would think to himself: *What's the use? I'm likely to die in three years, so maybe I should just retire and enjoy the time with Arthur and my friends.*

The surgery was performed with local anesthesia, and Rupert tried not to look at what they were doing to the right side of his face. He wondered if he wouldn't have been better off with general anesthesia, despite the plastic surgeon's recommendation. He wanted to fall asleep and just wake with it done, but the minutes dragged on seemingly forever.

The orderly transported him in a wheelchair to his recovery room where Arthur was waiting. "They said they just have to observe you for a couple of hours, and then I can take you home," Arthur reported.

Rupert gently patted the bandage covering the right side of his face. "I'm excited and scared to see what it looks like."

"Don't take off the bandage yet!"

"I'm not," Rupert said. "Thanks for being here."

They were quiet for a couple of minutes. Rupert was trying to imagine what it would be like to need only a little foundation to cover the remaining scar. Arthur spoke first. "You got another call from Parker while you were in there," Arthur reported. "I hope you're not going to take another mission from him."

"Don't use that word," Rupert cautioned in a whisper. "Call it a job."

"Sorry." Arthur looked toward the door as if checking whether someone else had heard him. "If your . . . most recent birthday gift doesn't cover your previous injuries, you should still take it easy."

"That shouldn't matter. According to my mom's notes, everything that happens to me for the rest of this year should heal completely in a day or so."

Arthur sighed. He looked like he was on the verge of crying. "It can't heal you if you die, Rupert. Parker's . . . jobs put you in dangerous situations."

"By that logic," Rupert argued, "I shouldn't act in films anymore either. That's where I got hurt the most."

Arthur wiped his eyes with his handkerchief. "That was a freak accident. Parker's jobs put you around people who are actively trying to kill you."

"They don't have to," Rupert said more softly. "I can ask for easier assignments."

"I'll drop the subject," Arthur promised. "Please just consider retiring from that work."

That was how most of their arguments ended lately. Arthur was able to make his point and then drop it. Rupert turned it over in his mind sometimes for days afterward, but not around Arthur.

When Rupert and Parker finally did connect, Rupert apologized for putting him off for three months. He said he didn't feel like his rapid-healing blessing was of special use to the CIA. Parker made a sound like he was thinking for several seconds. When he finally spoke again, he promised to get back to Rupert after further strategizing with his team.

Rupert first dared to remove the bandage to shower after a week. The new scar still looked red and puffy, but it was much, much narrower. After showering, he put a new bandage over it, and didn't look at it for another week.

Two weeks after the surgery, Arthur got his first look at it when he removed the bandage for the last time. It was difficult for Rupert to read his expression. He seemed somewhere between curious and disappointed. "It looks better," Arthur said.

"Makeup is still not going to hide it," Rupert said dismally.

"Ordinary makeup maybe," Arthur countered. "Movie makeup can probably cover that with some sort of prosthetic skin, right? Like you had in your first movie?"

"Maybe," Rupert acknowledged.

Rupert met with Nadia and Victoria at Victoria's office a week later to discuss options. They were both kind but skeptical. They said they would need new headshots that showed how he could look on film. Nadia said she would make an appointment for Rupert with a special effects makeup artist.

The artist had a workshop in the Red Hook neighborhood of Brooklyn. It looked like it had been an auto body shop previously. The woman took a cast of the remaining scar, poured latex into that, and fitted it over the scar with a little adhesive. She smiled. "Take a look," she suggested as she held up a hand mirror.

Rupert examined her work. The edges of the prosthesis were so thin, he worried that it could be torn easily, but it left a smooth contour to the right side of his face. "I'll probably need a few of these," Rupert commented.

"Oh, they're single-use," she said as she pulled the latex off his face with a tweezers. "I'll make you a more durable mold and set you up with some supplies so you can make as many as you need. If the scar heals more, just come back for a new mold. I just need your mailing address for the supplies and the invoices. Be careful not to open your mouth too wide when you're eating or yawning; the prosthesis may become detached, and you might have to glue it down again."

Once the supplies arrived, Arthur begged Rupert to let him be in charge of them. Rupert arranged for the makeup artist for his photo shoot to work on him at home and teach Arthur how to do the concealment. Once in the studio, Horst examined Rupert's face closely. "We will still have to be careful with the lighting and the angle," he said as he released Rupert's chin.

"Are you sure?" Rupert asked. "It looks pretty natural to me."

"It doesn't have the elasticity of normal skin," Horst said. "Maybe we should wait until it heals more?"

Rupert whispered to try to keep Arthur from overhearing. "I'm going crazy doing nothing every day. Let's please do these photos and see how they come out."

When Nadia saw the photo proofs, she was not enthusiastic. Victoria declared, "These will be fine. Ask the photographer to send both of us high-res digital files, and we will coordinate in sending them out."

Since Rupert wasn't hearing from Jenny or Parker, Rupert didn't wait for Victoria to send him scripts. Once a week, he would comb through submissions himself in her office, even before she had looked at them. Because his last film had been a comedy, and it had done very well at the box office, most of the scripts tended to be comedies. He found himself more drawn to unique scripts, often dramas with small, independent production companies.

Victoria had enough income from Rupert's royalties and residuals and from her other clients, so she didn't fight Rupert very hard when he turned down more commercial scripts. She sent an email to a small production company in Seattle, informing them that Mr. Rocket was interested in accepting the lead role in their feature-length sci-fi film about a man diagnosed with split-personality disorder who is actually a shape-shifting alien with amnesia.

The role didn't require him to be on set all the time, so Rupert and Arthur rented a cottage across the bridge in Bellevue. They took day trips to Vancouver, Glacier Peak, Bainbridge Island, and Mount Ranier, and spent two weeks renting a yacht to tour up the Pacific coast and explore the islands of British Columbia. Rupert fell when they were hiking near Glacier Peak, but his bruises and cuts all healed within a day. The older scar on his face had actually started to heal more, but the latex prostheses he wore only on the set still fit without slipping much.

Near the end of filming at the end of August, Rupert was asked to stay late for a night shoot in downtown Seattle. Arthur was too sleepy to stay and went back to their cottage in Bellvue near the start of shooting at nine o'clock. When shooting wrapped at four o'clock the next morning, Rupert didn't even bother to take off his makeup there. He changed quickly out of his costume and found a driver to take him back to Bellvue to rest before the following night's shoot.

Rupert was half-asleep when the crash occurred. It had been explained to him later in the hospital that he had suffered multiple lacerations from flying glass, a broken collarbone, and massive contusions on his upper body and head when his driver was going too fast down an exit ramp and collided with a car stopped in traffic that hadn't turned on its emergency blinkers yet. The driver in the front seat had been bashed into the windshield and gored with pieces of the steering wheel and dashboard and didn't survive.

Rupert's right arm was in a sling, and he had bandages over his many cuts when Arthur arrived around seven o'clock in the morning to take Rupert back to their cottage. Arthur took Rupert by the left arm and led him slowly to the vehicle waiting for them in the hospital loading zone. "Go slow!" Arthur admonished the driver as he helped Rupert into the back seat and then climbed in to sit beside him.

"They said my collarbone broke close to my shoulder, so I have to get x-rays in two days to see if it's healing properly," Rupert reported. "That's going to be a bit awkward."

They had come up with a shorthand for talking about Rupert's blessings. "Your 'birthday gift' is going to heal something this serious by then?" Arthur whispered.

"The most serious thing my grandma said I had when I was two was a dislocated shoulder. That was back in its socket in less than two hours, and it didn't hurt any more after two days."

"Your luck seems to be degenerating pretty fast," Arthur observed.

"Just the one fall hiking and then this," Rupert countered.

"No," Arthur argued, "you also fell several times when you were recovering from being crushed. And that was just over a year ago!"

"I'll heal from this too," Rupert reassured him. "The next one will help me avoid danger, so I should have minimal consequences from the Pooka's curse for these two years at least."

Rupert decided to skip his follow-up appointment two days later. The shoulder was still a little sore, but he didn't need the sling anymore, and the medic on the set verified that Rupert was good to continue shooting. All of his cuts and bruises had healed.

After a long break for Labor Day, the film continued with a week more of reshoots, and Rupert's were done in the first two days. Arthur applied Rupert's prosthesis and makeup, they packed up, and they were driven from their cottage in Bellvue to the airport. Randy completely surprised them by showing up at the baggage claim at JFK. "Do you have everything?" he called out as he approached the luggage carousel.

"Randy." Rupert set his suitcases down again and approached his chauffeur, the very proper and reserved young man he had hired nine years before. "You didn't have to park and meet us here. We were fine just calling you when we were getting ready to depart."

"I was just about to text you," Arthur confirmed.

"I feel like I've been remiss with you for far too long," Randy apologized. "My colleagues have admonished me for barely giving you the service of a common taxi driver. Sadly, it has taken your absence these past several months and the memory of your convalescence, sir, to make me get out of the driver's seat and help you to the car. I hope you will let me carry some of your luggage at least."

Arthur was about to beg off having one of his bags carried, but Rupert put his hand on Arthur's arm and whispered, "Let him do it." Rupert could see the pain in Randy's eyes that reflected years of frustration and regret. If Randy wanted to be of greater service, he was the last to fight it. It was an impulse he himself had felt pulling him back toward his U.N. and CIA work in the last couple of months of filming in Seattle.

By October, Rupert had already settled into a routine of putting on his prosthesis and makeup, heading to the gym in the morning, taking a brisk walk along the Hudson on his way home, and using the afternoon to catch up on emails. Nadia had been handling all of Rupert's fan mail, and he picked up a bag of it from her office to go through.

Some of the letters and emails were very sweet and complimentary. Some had questions about his personal life. Some were just letting him know they were praying for his recovery and return to their movie theaters. A very few were critical of his performances for reasons that seemed based in personal taste alone. He chose four to answer personally and gave the rest back to Nadia to process.

One of the fans he had written to directly was a ten-year-old boy from the Bronx who signed his name Tony Jalisco. Tony was living in a foster home as a ward of the state after his mother died and his father beat him to the point where Tony had a permanent limp. Tony had seen all of Rupert's films, even the minor role he had in the Bollywood musical, back when Tony was only a baby. Tony had searched YouTube and watched every one of Rupert's interviews and live performances as well. He felt certain Rupert would be a good father, even if he was gay. He wrote that that wouldn't bother him.

The implication that Tony was asking Rupert to adopt him was pretty clear. When he wrote back to Tony, he asked if he would be interested in going to the New York Botanical Garden. Tony wrote back incredulous that a celebrity like Rupert had written back to him and even wanted to meet him.

Rupert delighted in following the young boy. Despite his obvious limp, Tony galloped along with the other children in a special tour for them of the gardens. Tony seemed especially fascinated with the underwater plants and with the birds they pointed out to him when it was his turn to look through the binoculars. As he rode back to Tony's home from the Botanical Garden, Tony asked him as if it were the most natural thing, "What would you like to do *next* weekend?"

Rupert chuckled. "We don't have to wait for weekends. I'm not working right now."

"I have to go to school," he reminded Rupert.

"Oh, yeah." Rupert smiled. "Have you ever been to the Bronx Zoo?"

Tony looked at him cautiously. "Not really," he finally said.

Rupert grinned. "Either you have or you haven't."

Tony's first word took several seconds to finish. "Well . . . I went a couple of years ago as a field trip from my school, but I didn't get to see very much."

"So would you like me to pick you up and take you there next Saturday?"

"Um," Tony began, "my foster parents are taking me trick-or-treating on Saturday. I could go Sunday."

"Ah. I almost forgot Halloween was coming up. How about if we save the zoo for another time and we go to a haunted house on Sunday instead?"

"That would be totally rad!" Tony slapped both his knees and smiled up at Rupert.

That night, as Rupert and Arthur were getting ready for bed, Rupert came up behind Arthur in the bathroom as he was brushing his teeth. After he spit into the sink, Arthur looked at Rupert in the mirror behind him and said, "It looks like the scar is fading more. Maybe the healing blessing is helping a little bit."

"I'm not sure," Rupert said. "So, ACS told me that Tony is . . . he's available for adoption."

Arthur finished rinsing his mouth and turned around to face Rupert directly. "Is that something you're seriously considering?"

"I'll only be . . . " Rupert thought better of projecting his life past the next two years. "You'll only be . . . fifty when he's eighteen. He wouldn't be that much trouble, would he?"

"We'd have to get a new apartment," Arthur said as he walked past Rupert into their only bedroom.

Rupert followed him out. "We can afford it. Between savings and investments, we have over twenty million."

"So, you'd want to jointly adopt him?" Arthur sat on the corner of the bed.

Rupert sat down next to him and massaged his shoulders with one hand. "I think it would have to be one or the other of us only unless we . . ."

"Unless what?" Arthur asked.

"Unless we were married," Rupert finally said. "But that isn't necessary. I can talk to Loretta about . . ."

Arthur interrupted him quietly. "I would consider that."

"Consider adopting, or consider marrying?" Rupert stopped massaging to study Arthur's reaction better.

"Either? Both?" They were both confused when they looked at each other. "What do you want, Rupert?"

"I think Tony would be a great thing for both of us . . . maybe. I've been considering going back to working for Jenny and Parker because I wanted to feel useful. This seems like a lot less risky way to feel useful."

"You've only met him once," Arthur pointed out.

Rupert tousled Arthur's hair and stood up to face him. "We corresponded a bit before that. You saw his photos and video on the website. You don't think he'd be great to take care of and teach?"

"I am concerned you're dashing into another adventure without thinking it through," Arthur cautioned. "Kids get into trouble. They get sick. They say things to hurt you. They even try to run away. None of that worries you?"

"You should meet him." Rupert pulled Arthur up into a hug. "He's smart and funny, and he's got a great attitude."

"Have you scheduled your next buddy outing yet?" Arthur asked.

"You can come along! I said I would take him to a haunted house on Sunday."

Arthur made a distasteful face. "I don't like scary movies. Why do you think I'd want to go to a haunted house?"

Rupert picked up Tony in the Bronx, and Randy drove them down to a haunted house in Midtown Manhattan. On the way there, Rupert gave Tony a cell phone, and Tony was ecstatic and made Rupert show him how to activate it and set it up before they got out of the SUV at the haunted house.

Tony and Rupert exchanged texts almost every day when Tony got home from school the following week. Arthur went along with Rupert to pick Tony up the following Saturday to visit the Bronx Zoo. Tony and Arthur bonded immediately as they made their way around the paths between the enclosures. They traded trivia about the animals or where they lived, Arthur proudly announcing when he had seen some of them in the wild.

After a home visit by Tony's caseworker in mid-November, Rupert was approved for an overnight visit, conditional on them renting a cot for Tony to sleep on. Rupert assured her that if the adoption went through, he would get a new apartment with a separate bedroom for Tony.

On Thanksgiving, Tony got to meet Arthur and Rupert's closest friends. Chantal had agreed to let Rupert and Arthur host this time, and a generous gift to Tony's foster family convinced them to let him go on an important family holiday. Hakim and Azami brought their now seventeen-year-old son Ichiro, and the two boys and Arthur bonded over Arthur's collection of video games. Michaela and Denise had also adopted a daughter, but she was much younger and staying with a babysitter. They took Rupert aside as they were leaving and gave Rupert tips about navigating ACS and the adoption process. They were both worried they were too old to conceive their own children, and they thought he and Arthur would make good parents.

Hakim and Azami finally tore Ichiro away from the games to take him home, and Arthur turned off the power and told Tony to go get his backpack and use their bathroom to brush his teeth and get into the pajamas he'd brought. Rupert wore sweats and a T-shirt for once to bed and got up when Tony was ready for bed and followed him into the living room to tuck him in. He noticed Tony immediately reaching for his phone, so Rupert crouched down and grabbed it away. "No phone in bed," he reminded Tony. "Bedtime is for sleeping, not texting or surfing the Web."

"Just let me return the texts from my friends that came in while I was playing Arthur's game?" Tony begged as he reached for the phone.

"You can do it in the morning." Rupert remained firm. "Did you have a good time tonight?"

Tony grinned. "The food was great. Chantal was funny. I had fun playing Baldur's Gate with Ichiro and Arthur. I helped win the Slythe fight with my Burning Hands spell."

"Sounds good," Rupert commented. "So I guess they might have told you that we're applying to adopt you. We haven't signed the papers, and it could be up to a year before it's final, but is that something you think you might want to do?"

Tony didn't speak. He just sat up and leaned over to hug Rupert tightly.

"I'll take that as a yes," Rupert said as he hugged Tony back.

By Christmas, Rupert got permission to become a foster parent to Tony while he was awaiting the approval for the adoption. Tony came to live with him and Arthur on Christmas Eve. Rupert had signed a new lease on a bigger two-bedroom apartment on the twenty-fourth floor, and they moved in the first week of January.

Once most of the new furniture had been moved in, Arthur and Rupert brought Tony up to see the new apartment, and as Tony dashed into the second bedroom to luxuriate in his first-ever private bedroom, Arthur hugged Rupert. "Here we go, sexy," he whispered to Rupert. "Hopefully your new danger-avoidance blessing will cover Tony too."

"Probably only when I'm with him," Rupert suggested. "But that's more than most kids get."

"Well, so far I've been lucky not to get any of the fallout from your curse," Arthur pointed out. "I wasn't on set when the spotlights fell on you. I wasn't in the car when it rear-ended that other one in Bellvue."

"Maybe that was by design," Rupert said as he led Arthur over to Tony's bedroom door to watch him open boxes. "The curse is reserved for members of my family."

"So, when will the curse consider Tony and I part of your family?" Arthur whispered as they stood in the doorway.

"If we don't get married, it may leave Tony alone until I officially adopt him," Rupert concluded. "Maybe you should be the one to adopt Tony instead?"

Arthur hugged Rupert tighter. "If you think that would help, I'll do it."

CHAPTER 32: ARTHUR

Arthur Shu was born on April 4, 1976, in King of Prussia, Pennsylvania, the first of three children and the only son to an electrician and a housewife in this suburb of Philadelphia. His family had already gotten used to diminishing returns by the time Arthur came along. His mother's mother had been a college professor. His father's father had been an electrical engineer for a defense contractor. They were content that Arthur was a good student and loved to read and never pushed him toward a career in law or medicine as their friends seemed to with their children.

At fifteen, Arthur got inspired by his high school art classes. The idea of taking stories to the next level and bringing them to life as colorful, graphic representations seemed like a natural next step to him. He dreamed of getting good enough to create the art for video games, and with the help of scholarships, he was admitted into the Bachelor of Fine Arts program at Moore College of Art & Design.

In college, Arthur's professors appreciated his dedication, but they repeatedly suggested that his artwork lacked inspiration. Some said it lacked daring, that his choices were regularly too safe. Arthur heard the feedback for two years, and then he promptly switched his major to art curation. In that, Arthur excelled, and his academic advisor suggested he continue on at the Columbia University graduate program in New York.

During the final semester before submitting his master's thesis project, Arthur took an internship with the Alvin Ailey American Dance Theater. He was helping them plan their 40th Anniversary Gala. After he got his MFA, he stayed on to help them with their special events. He was on duty to greet guests at a fundraiser for their South African residency when his supervisor quickly pulled him aside, pointed out a tall, young, Germanic-looking man in a suit and tie, and told Arthur to introduce himself and to stay with him until he left.

Arthur wasn't sure of the purpose of the assignment until he started talking to the man. He seemed surprised that Arthur didn't know who he was. He introduced himself as Rupert Rocket, the development director for a rival dance company in Brooklyn. It became clear that he was to make it harder for Rupert to poach Alvin Ailey's donors. He handed Arthur a business card and suggested they remain in touch. Arthur thought he caught a twinkle in Rupert's eye that suggested something beyond professional interest, but he dismissed it and pocketed the card.

Arthur had been dating a young man he met in grad school, and it was his insistence that Arthur should learn to network more that got Arthur to call Rupert. Rupert invited him to tour his company's offices and studio in Brooklyn. Twice thereafter, he got an email or a call from Rupert begging him to come be his assistant. He realized his internship was not going to turn into full-time work, and he accepted the offer to work in development at Rupert's ballet company.

Arthur found himself frequently worried about his new boss's finances and asked him every day if he needed a loan or at least some money for lunch. Rupert always reassured him that his salary was sufficient, but Arthur kept checking anyway.

After working for Rupert five days a week for seven weeks, Arthur was overjoyed with the novelty of being paid not to work in the week between Christmas and New Years. On Christmas morning, he had intended to get on a bus to Philadelphia to visit his parents and sisters, but a strange, seemingly extrasensory feeling made Arthur think he needed to stay available for Rupert, in case he needed him for something.

Rupert had told him that he would be volunteering to feed the homeless at a church in Chelsea during the day, so Arthur debated whether to arrive before or after that, took the train down from Harlem to Lincoln Center, walked up to the building, and pressed the buzzer. Arthur had addressed so many packages to Rupert's home address, he had it memorized.

He climbed up the stairs and knocked on the door. Rupert seemed surprised to see him, but Arthur felt he was where he needed to be. This was his boss, and he needed to do whatever was asked of him. They ended up having sex and spending the night together.

Over the next twenty years, even when they were not seeing or communicating with each other for up to two years at a time, Arthur was completely fascinated with Rupert Rocket. He was so engaging. He made Arthur feel like he was the most important thing whenever they were together. He kept introducing Arthur to new things, and he couldn't believe he had been missing out on so much of what life had to offer.

Arthur finally convinced Rupert to retire once Tony started to live with them as a foster child. Tony had said he was okay transferring from his school in the Bronx to the private one in Manhattan Rupert had picked. Every day Rupert would accompany Tony in the SUV, drop him off at his new school, and be there when he got out.

By mid-January, Rupert already regretted giving Tony the cell phone. He complained to Arthur that it was turning him into an obsessive introvert. When Arthur suggested that the boy was old enough to get to and from school on his own, and that that might give Tony more opportunities to hang out with his new school friends, Rupert seemed unconvinced.

Rupert's solution was to take Tony to the Canadian wilderness for the three-day President's Day Weekend to stay at a remote cabin with neither television nor phone, far from any cell tower, and go snowshoeing during the day for exercise. Arthur got concerned that snowshoeing might be too difficult with Tony's disability, but Tony begged Arthur to let him go, and Arthur eventually accepted it. On the Monday they were to return, Arthur got a text from Randy, their chauffeur:

> *Meet me in front of your building in 10 mins. Rupert/Tony in emergency room.*

Arthur's mind lit up with horrible visions of both Rupert and Tony barely clinging to life after Rupert's curse brought yet another instance of bad luck into their lives. He was already waiting at the curb when Randy pulled up.

When Randy dropped him off at the emergency room entrance, Arthur texted Rupert:

I'm on my way. There in 2.

Arthur walked into the emergency room waiting area, and he saw Rupert sitting in a chair near the triage station, calmly typing on his cell phone. He started calling out to him just as his phone pinged that he'd received a text. "What happened? Where's Tony?"

The details came out in an odd order, but Arthur eventually pieced together what had happened on their weekend in Northern Ontario. Late Sunday afternoon, as sundown was approaching, Rupert and Tony were hurrying to get back to the cabin, and Tony slipped and fell down a hill, then down a small cliff. It took Rupert several minutes to climb down and reach him, and the snow around the boy's body was already turning red with his blood. As their ride home wasn't due for another eighteen hours, Rupert carried Tony the two miles to the home of a nurse who served as the nearest emergency medical service. She had admonished Rupert for not trying to staunch the bleeding with a tourniquet or bandages, and Rupert felt guilty that he had never learned first aid. Tony's wounds weren't too serious, but he'd lost so much blood he was starting to go into shock.

The nurse had no blood reserves, and there was no time to verify Rupert's blood type as O negative, so she put pressure bandages on the wounds, and then worked on getting Rupert set up for the transfusion. She called for an air ambulance, and it arrived as Tony's heartbeat and blood pressure were stabilizing. They checked whether Rupert's blood was potentially incompatible with Tony's in Toronto. In New York, they were checking whether the loss of blood had damaged Tony's heart or brain.

"But you're okay?" Arthur whispered insistently.

"Some bruises from climbing down to find Tony, but otherwise okay," Rupert reported.

"How is Tony?"

"He's been sleeping through most of it," Rupert said as he put his hand on Arthur's knee. "I think he's going to be fine."

Tony confirmed later that he'd had fun on the trip despite his fall. Arthur started to see why Rupert and Tony had bonded so well. They were both unrelentingly cheerful and adventurous most of the time. Arthur decided privately that Rupert's new danger-avoidance blessing had protected him, but not Tony, and he wondered if Tony was going to get Rupert's deflected bad luck through the end of the year.

Rupert had more panic attacks at night in bed mostly. He seemed terrified that he only had months left to live. In most cases, Arthur was able to calm him down. Occasionally Rupert dashed for the computer and watched cute, funny, baby-animal videos on YouTube for a few minutes and then wandered back to bed.

On Arthur's forty-second birthday, Rupert and Tony planned a big day for him. They made him breakfast in bed, and then once he'd showered and dressed, they took him out on the town. They had burgers at Johnny Rockets near Penn Station, walked along the High Line down to the meatpacking district, got family portraits done at Horst's studio, went to Joe Allen for dinner, saw the revival of *Carousel* at the Imperial Theater, and ended the evening at Junior's for cheesecake.

It was Rupert's turn to tuck Tony in and listen to him read aloud from his current book, *Great Expectations* by Charles Dickens. Tony was still near the beginning, and Arthur had heard him read the introduction to Miss Havisham the night before. Tony seemed engrossed in the plot already.

Arthur was still loading the dishwasher when Rupert came into the kitchen a few minutes after he left for Tony's room. "I feel funny," Rupert said.

Arthur stopped what he was doing and took a step closer to examine Rupert's face. "Funny how?"

370

"I think I need to go to a hospital."

Arthur thought about six different options at once and narrowed it to two. "Should I call Randy or 911?"

"Nine-one . . ." was all Rupert got out before his eyelids fluttered and he collapsed to his knees and then fell toward Arthur.

Arthur caught him and guided him to the floor away from the open dishwasher. Arthur checked Rupert's pulse first, and it was weak but steady. He called 911 first and then John, because he could get there the quickest to watch Tony. He went into Tony's room where Tony was sitting up in bed with the book open. "Is Rupert coming back?" he asked meekly.

"Why don't you turn out the light and try to get to sleep?" Arthur suggested. "Rupert and I are going to have to go out in a little bit, but Uncle John will come by very soon in case you need anything while we're gone."

Fortunately, Tony was willing to comply. Arthur glanced over to where Tony's phone was charging on his nightstand. Usually, they took it into their own bedroom when they left after the story, but Arthur decided it might not matter as much tonight.

There was no problem with the paramedics. They entered as quietly as they could with their gurney, and they turned down their walkie-talkies and spoke softly to keep from waking Tony as they moved Rupert's unconscious body to the living room where there was more space to check his vitals and transfer him to the gurney. And they didn't question Arthur riding along in the ambulance.

As Rupert's gurney wheeled past into one of the emergency exam rooms, Arthur was stopped by a nurse to get all of Rupert's information. She asked Arthur to describe any of Rupert's symptoms before he fainted.

"We had had a busier day than usual," Arthur told her. "Rupert had an accident a couple of years ago, and it punctured one of his lungs. He gets fatigued easily now, but he wasn't complaining of that today. Maybe because it is my birthday. I don't know. He was just in our son's bedroom listening to him read, and then he came into the kitchen and said he felt funny and collapsed."

"His heart is healthy, as far as you know?" the nurse asked.

Arthur went through everything he'd heard about Rupert's medical condition in the past two years. "His doctor's noticed an irregular heartbeat two years ago during his coma after the accident."

The nurse promised to pull up Rupert's medical history and to let Arthur know if she heard any news on his condition. Arthur took a seat in the waiting room. The adrenaline rush was fading, and he was feeling his eyes starting to overflow with tears. He considered taking out his contacts, but he still needed to be able to read his phone.

Then his phone made a tone. He had a text from John:

> *Made it here. Tony woke up. I told him I didn't know where you guys went. Let me know how Rupert is.*

Arthur thanked him in a return text and tried to decide whom to call next.

Rupert was discharged thirty-six hours later. He had had a stroke. His doctor said that it wasn't life threatening, but it could lead to brain damage. All Arthur noticed at first was that Rupert couldn't remember where they went after leaving the theater that night. Arthur tried to think back to uncover some hint of anything wrong earlier, perhaps when they were at Juniors, one of the events he couldn't recall.

Once he brought Rupert home, there were other instances of things that had happened earlier in a day that Rupert forgot or confused with other days. He frequently left the bedroom or got out of Randy's SUV and couldn't remember where he was going. Simple arithmetic made him reach for the calculator app on his phone.

Rupert's condition didn't change much in the seven months that followed. In November, ACS announced that Tony's adoption by Arthur was approved, and the three of them met Danny and Max at Alice's Tea Cup on the Upper West Side to celebrate the following morning for breakfast before Tony left for school. Max and Danny had made buttons for Rupert and Arthur to wear—one said "Daddy" and the other said "Dad."

"I have just been calling them Rupert and Arthur," Tony explained to Danny. "Should I call them Dad and Daddy now?"

"It's your choice, little warrior," Danny replied. "What did you call your birth father?"

"He wanted me to call him Papa." Tony looked over at his two fathers. "I think it's better to call them Arthur and Rupert. That way it's easier to brag that one of my dads is a movie star."

"Rupert was an international fashion model and ballet dancer when he was younger," Max volunteered.

Tony turned and put his hand on Rupert's chest. "Did you have to wear tights?"

Rupert grinned. "All the time."

A few weeks later, on Christmas Eve, once Tony had read to Arthur, Arthur climbed into bed with Rupert and initiated their usual discussion about the changing of Rupert's blessing. "So, what can we expect to happen when you turn forty-nine tomorrow morning?"

Rupert tried to make it sound like a joke, but Arthur knew all to well it was the truth. "You can expect me to be a bundle of anxiety because it will be the beginning of my last year . . . before the last bit of my luck echo goes away."

"I meant," Arthur clarified, "what is your next blessing?"

"I don't know."

"I thought you had them all plotted out," Arthur argued. "Your mom didn't include that in her journal?"

"She was a new mother," Rupert explained. "She was twenty-five and taking care of me with only Grandma's help at first. I remember my grandmother telling me I hardly ever cried in my first twelve months."

In the weeks that followed, Arthur analyzed almost every interaction with Rupert. It seemed that he often anticipated Rupert's desires and needs a little better, but Arthur dismissed it as being the result of two decades of familiarity.

The big hint came at the end of March, when it was only a week away from Arthur's birthday. Arthur got a feeling so strong it felt like Rupert had told him he was getting him a Kindle for his birthday. When his birthday arrived, every gift he opened was a surprise until he got to Rupert's: a Kindle Fire. That night when Rupert came to bed after tucking in Tony, he shared his theory: "I think your blessing has something to do with secrets, Rupert. I knew about a week ago that you were going to get me the e-reader. I think you can't keep a secret. Is that possible?"

Rupert looked over at Arthur while he thought about it. "I wish you would have reminded me about the doctor's appointment I missed yesterday."

Arthur didn't see Rupert's point. "I didn't know about it."

"That's my point," Rupert clarified. "It was information I was keeping from you that I wasn't broadcasting to you. There has to be some other explanation."

The key ended up being Tony's twelfth birthday on May 10th. Tony was sitting between his two dads on the couch and opened Arthur's gift to him. He was truly surprised that it was a new video game. When Rupert handed his gift to him, Tony smiled and said, "You've been thinking about this for the past couple of days. I already know what it is."

"What do you think it is?" Rupert challenged him.

"A baseball glove." Tony ripped off the wrapping paper, and indeed there was a baseball glove in the box.

Arthur couldn't wait to test his theory with Rupert. "It has to be about secrets you are *intentionally* trying to hide from us."

"I don't know." Rupert seemed to want him to drop the topic.

"What are you guys talking about?" Tony asked.

"I knew what Rupert was getting me for my birthday too. A week beforehand. I even told Max he was giving me a Kindle."

"Yeah, like when we were in the Village last week." Tony tapped Rupert on the chest twice. "I said we can get ice cream, if you want, and you said you were just thinking about the Big Gay Ice Cream Shop."

Arthur looked past Tony to Rupert. "Other people can read your mind!" he declared.

"That's a weird superpower," Tony commented.

"I've had weirder ones," Rupert teased.

Arthur was shocked that Rupert was essentially admitting his blessings to Tony. But Rupert started to tickle Tony, and he decided that was the better note to strike. Make it a silly coincidence.

There were times in the following months when Arthur felt Rupert was back to his old self—not getting confused as easily and his memory more reliable. He was still leaner than he had been before the accident, but he was getting his muscle tone back. So, it was a surprise when Arthur got a text from Randy on a Friday morning in October:

Rupert at hospital again. Can pick you up in 25 mins.

On the ride to the hospital, Arthur asked lots of questions of Randy to prepare himself. Rupert had been coming back from a doctor appointment in the back of the SUV and had told Randy he wanted to lie down. Randy had pulled the car over and checked Rupert's pulse as he lay across the back seat and then rushed him to the emergency room. He had texted Arthur immediately thereafter and had no other information. Tony was in school, so Arthur texted Michaela to see if Tony could go to their place after school in the likely case that they would be at the hospital for hours. That Rupert had arrived there unconscious made Arthur worry about another stroke.

By the time Randy brought Arthur back, Rupert had already been moved to a room in the intensive care ward. Arthur had been there before, so he found his way there and asked the nurse at the reception desk which room held Rupert Rocket.

"Only members of his family are allowed to visit his room," he announced. "The doctor is still examining him, so we don't have anything to report."

Arthur considered that the new nurse didn't know who he was and was just following protocol. In his rush, he had forgotten to bring Rupert's medical power-of-attorney form. "I have to run home and get his paperwork," Arthur explained, "but I'll be back."

When Randy took him back home, he more calmly packed some food and drink, copies of Rupert's medical history, the power-of-attorney form, and he dug through the desk to find the journals Rupert's mother had kept starting in the late sixties when Rupert was born. By the time he got back to the hospital, he was able to get the basics from Rupert's examining doctor: Rupert had had another stroke and was in a coma again.

They let him visit briefly in Rupert's room. Rupert looked pale, but otherwise he just looked like he was sleeping. He could see his eyeballs moving beneath closed lids, and Arthur got a strong impression that Rupert was trying to win a game show in which the prize was a gargantuan birthday cake. *Great,* Arthur thought. *Now I just get to know what he's dreaming.*

But instead of waking up two weeks later as he had last time, by the middle of December it had lasted just over two months. There were moments when Rupert seemed to stir, and Arthur sensed Rupert's need for fluids, or being touched, or repositioning his leg for better circulation. Mike flew out from Wisconsin to help Arthur talk to the doctors at the hospital about their prognosis and options for caring for Rupert at home. They had the rented bed and all the supplies transferred to their living room again, and on some level, Arthur got the sense that Rupert appreciated the familiar surroundings.

Tony was emotional at first, and for a while, he refused to visit Rupert in the hospital, because it made him sadder to see him so sick. When they brought Rupert home and had round-the-clock nurses there, Tony seemed to calm down and be more accepting. Arthur asked him about that as the two of them ate dinner one night.

"I got this feeling that he loves me and cares about me," Tony remarked. "And I feel like sometimes, when he moves or says something, he is trying to tell me that he's trying to come back—to wake up."

"I never get that," Arthur admitted. He was reporting information from Rupert's last blessing like it was a conversation he'd had. "He just wants me to moisten his lips or move his arm or something."

"I know he cares about you too," Tony said. "I think he's thinking that right now."

Arthur didn't know if Tony was really getting that. Perhaps Tony was just trying to comfort him. When they were both in Rupert's presence, they tended to get the same impression from him.

When the doctor came to visit just before Christmas, she advised Arthur that a coma lasting more than two months rarely led to waking up again. His organs were starting to shut down, and he might have only days before he died. She gave instructions to the nurse on duty to administer a morphine drip, because the pain might be making it harder for him to stay awake for more than a few seconds, as he seemed to do about once a day or so.

Tony broke down and cried again when Arthur told him that it was likely Rupert would die soon. Tony suggested a big party on Christmas Eve, to celebrate Rupert's fiftieth birthday. He seemed convinced that was what Rupert would want.

Mike helped Arthur plan the details. Rupert's stepfather handled hiring the bartender and the server and ordering the drinks and hors d'oeuvres. Arthur reached out to everyone who had ever meant something to Rupert to invite them. Even Fred and Britney arrived from San Francisco and Trevor and Samantha from Wisconsin. Jenny Athiambo brought her daughter along as did Michaela and Denise. Hakim and Azami even convinced Ichiro to come home from college early and attend. Tony felt so swept up by the occasion, he started putting *Grandpa* in front of Mike's and Fred's names.

During the height of the party as the server was starting to put pieces of birthday cake on plates and passing them out, Azami, whom Arthur had always thought of as quiet and reserved, grabbed him by the lapels of the dark-blue dinner jacket he was wearing and insisted, "We must perform a marriage tonight!"

Hakim seemed somewhat concerned about this rare outburst and was at her side in a moment. "Darling, are you okay?"

She let go of Arthur's lapels and tugged on Hakim's arm instead. "Rupert and Arthur need to get married tonight! I know that is what Rupert would want!"

"It's a nice idea," Arthur admitted, "but I don't see the point."

377

"It might help you with probate," Hakim suggested.

"We don't have anyone to officiate," Arthur argued.

"Azami is certified to perform weddings," Hakim said. "You have plenty of witnesses, but it is just symbolic until you get a marriage license, and Rupert would have to show up at the city clerk's office and be responsive for you to obtain that."

"That doesn't seem worth the trouble then," Arthur decided.

"It is important to Rupert!" Azami insisted. "It is like he told it to me."

Arthur remembered that Rupert's blessing didn't just apply to him and Tony. Anyone in Rupert's vicinity could sense his thoughts and feelings. "All right," he conceded. "I'll make the announcement. Let me know if you need anything, Azami."

All the guests stood facing the corner of the living room where Rupert lay, frail and gasping, in his bed. Fred stood closest to Rupert, Tony put his arm around Arthur, and Azami stood between them. "When two people find out that they cannot live apart from each other for very long, they fall in love. And after being in love for so long, as Arthur and Rupert are, it is natural to want to proclaim a family, along with their son Tony, so that everyone they know can support them in a process we call marriage. When I was meeting Rupert for the first time, he was funny. He was interested in everybody he met. He loved being around people. It was no surprise to me that Rupert found a smart, sweet, generous man like Arthur Shu a couple of years later. They treat each other nice, and you know when you see them together that they care so much about each other. You see it when they look at each other.

"So, we ask both Arthur . . . and Rupert to indulge us now on Christmas Eve in 2019, and let us hear them commit to each other. We start with Arthur. Arthur, do you promise to continue loving and caring for Rupert, forsaking all others, for the rest of your life?"

"Yes," Arthur said, and then a bit louder, "I do."

Azami turned to the bed where Rupert lay, suddenly a bit restless, turning his head to the side slightly and twitching his hands. "Rupert, do you promise to continue loving and caring for Arthur, forsaking all others, for the rest of your life?"

The room got very quiet, as if they were expecting a miracle. When Azami put her hand on Rupert's chest, it seemed like Rupert said something, but Arthur couldn't quite understand it.

"We will take that as yes," Azami reported as she turned back toward the other guests. "With that agreement, we ask Rupert and Arthur's friends and family if you do agree to help support them in their life together, for however long that will be? If you do, please respond, 'We do.'"

A chorus of voices, mostly in unison, replied, "We do!"

"By the power vested in me by the State of New York, where we are now, I am pronouncing Rupert Rocket and Arthur Shu husband and husband. Arthur, you can do the kissing part now."

Arthur rushed over to the bedside and kissed Rupert on the lips. A cheer rose among the gathered guests. Arthur couldn't stop crying as one guest after another came up to him and shook his hand or hugged him. Many stopped to talk to Rupert as well.

After everyone had eaten a piece of the dual-purpose birthday-wedding cake, they started to make their way to the bedroom for their coats and other belongings. Arthur and Tony stood near the door as most of them left. John volunteered to help Tony get ready for bed.

John had closed Tony's bedroom door to go in and listen to him read from *Great Expectations*. The last of the guests were getting ready to leave, and Arthur accompanied them all the way to the elevator. They let a woman off the elevator and then boarded. Arthur waved at them and watched the elevator door close.

The woman stood a few feet away down the hall looking back at Arthur. She was an older woman with graying red hair and really large ears that seemed to come to a point near their tops. She wore a patchwork coat and smiled broadly at Arthur. "I hope I'm not intruding," the woman said with a strong Irish accent. "I knew Rupert Rocket, and I was hoping I might steal a moment with him, if it isn't putting you out."

Arthur had noticed that there was a woman at the party named Sherry, another named Shannon, and a man named Charlie whom he'd never met. He assumed one of the other guests had invited them, as they may have for this late-comer. "Everyone else has left, but if you want to come in and see him for a minute, I guess it's okay. How did you know Rupert?"

As they walked into the apartment, she gently placed her hand on Arthur's back. "His grandmother introduced me to Rupert on the day he was born."

Suddenly it all clicked for Arthur. Rupert's verbal description and his mother's journals he had read in the hospital made it clear who she was. He turned to face her. "You're the Grogoch!" he whispered.

"And you have to be Arthur," she commented. "I was so glad to hear that Rupert finally found someone to love. He was a bit of a restless wanderer in his youth, and I wondered if he was ever going to settle down."

They stopped beside Rupert's bed. "His last blessing ends tomorrow," Arthur said. "He turns fifty in the morning. He was afraid he would die, and it's starting to look like that might really happen. His doctor said he doesn't have long now."

She held Rupert's hand for a moment and then let it go and looked around the room. "It appears you were having some sort of party," she commented.

"It started out as a birthday celebration for Rupert, and we ended up getting married."

She looked excited and animated. "Could you repeat that please?"

"One of our friends is a minister, and she married Rupert and me tonight."

The Grogoch rushed to the living room window with both fists raised and shouted out to the Hudson River below. "Do you hear that, sister? Rupert just got married!"

"I heard!" another female Irish voice called from the apartment doorway.

Arthur turned and saw the same woman he'd seen three times before. The Pooka was unmistakable with her short reddish-gray hair, asymmetric eyes and off-center nose. She wore the same wool coat and long, dark-green dress she always wore. "You shouldn't be here!" Arthur called back defensively.

She stepped into the apartment. "Well, that's too late then, isn't it, Arthur? I'm here."

"I didn't think you'd show up and admit defeat," the Grogoch taunted.

Arthur turned back to the Grogoch. "What do you mean?"

"Rupert's family curse was supposed to keep anyone after Zelda from marrying," the Grogoch replied. "It didn't work, so I think that means the curse has ended."

Arthur heard Rupert stirring and when he turned to look at him, he noticed Rupert's eyes open. "He's awake!"

"Yes, yes," the Pooka grumbled, "the curse doesn't just vanish in a poof. It sort of pops or explodes, and that usually erases at least the most recent of its effects." She turned to face the Grogoch. "This is the ninth time you've done this, sister. It's really getting on my nerves!"

The Grogoch chuckled. "Oh, you had your fun! Now just leave them alone. You can easily find someone else who wants revenge and is willing to pay your price."

The Pooka still seemed pissed off. "What about *your* price? Have you ever charged him for your blessing?"

The Grogoch laughed even louder. "Despite your curse, Rupert made millions of dollars. His name is known all over the world. He helped thousands of homeless people. That is enough for me."

The Pooka stormed out without another word. The Grogoch turned to Arthur with a hesitant look. "There is one thing I generally do ask," she announced. "I didn't want to mention it until my sister left."

Arthur's attention was drawn to Rupert's hand moving up to scratch his ear. He turned back to the Grogoch. "Whatever it is, I'll pay it."

"Would you happen to have a cup of cream for me?"

Arthur didn't drink coffee, and since Rupert hadn't needed coffee for months, he hadn't gotten more. "I don't think so," he said at first. "Wait. Let me check."

He dashed to the kitchen and opened the refrigerator door. A small carton of cream was indeed tucked into one of the lower shelves. He got a teacup from the cupboard, filled it with cream, and handed it to the Grogoch. She bowed her head in thanks and then started sipping it, smiling after every swallow. Arthur felt it might be too disruptive to interrupt her, but he was too anxious not to ask. "But we weren't really married," he argued, "so how did that break the curse?"

She stopped sipping the cream and smiled. "People have been getting married for centuries. A piece of paper from some bureaucrat doesn't matter as far as I'm concerned. It was enough."

"Arthur?" Rupert croaked.

Arthur turned and saw Rupert trying to sit up, so he put his hands on Rupert's shoulder and back to help him up. "I'm here," Arthur whispered.

Once he was sitting up with his tubes trailing, he cleared his throat and asked, "I had another stroke?"

The Grogoch was already out the door when Arthur finally turned to check on her. The empty teacup was sitting on the dining room table. He turned back to Rupert. "Yes. You've been in a coma for a couple of months."

John appeared from Tony's room. "It's almost midnight," he observed quietly as he approached Arthur. "Tony finally fell asleep."

"Did you buy cream and put it in the refrigerator?" Arthur whispered.

"Yeah," John said. Then he noticed Rupert sitting up. "Rupert, you're awake!"

"I'll take your word for it," Rupert quipped.

"Should I tell Tony?" John asked.

"No, let him sleep," Arthur suggested. "It will be an additional gift for Christmas morning."

The night nurse who was supposed to come on duty at midnight knocked on the door gently.

"It's midnight," Arthur said. He leaned over and kissed Rupert on the cheek. "Happy fiftieth birthday, sweetie!"

"I didn't think I'd make it." Rupert smiled.

"By the way, we're married," Arthur mentioned.

"I had a dream about that," Rupert said. "So does that mean I'm officially

Tony's father too now?"

"You may have a stronger connection to him than I do," Arthur concluded. "He has your blood in him, remember?"

Rupert just grunted his assent. John went into the kitchen to get another piece of cake and snagged the teacup to rinse out on his way. The night nurse approached the bed with her eyes wide. "This is a miracle!" she declared.

"Oh," Arthur told Rupert, "I paid the Grogoch for your blessing."

Rupert looked skeptical. "What did she want?"

"It doesn't matter," Arthur said. "I'm just glad to have you back."

"I'm looking forward to tomorrow and a gift I've been waiting for my whole life," Rupert said as he lay back against his pillow. "It's going to be my first time without a curse or a blessing. I'll get to feel what it's like to be normal."

"When you look at it from the big picture," Arthur said, "your life isn't that different from mine. I've had my ups and downs, my victories and disappointments too. Normal is overrated."

The nurse listened to Rupert's heart and lungs and checked his eye tracking. She said she would ask Rupert's doctor to come by in the next couple of days to take him off the catheter, the IVs, and the gastrostomy tube. Then she gave Arthur instructions about how to reintroduce fluids and soft food and left. After John left as well, Arthur took off his shoes and jacket, climbed into the hospital bed with Rupert carefully avoiding all his tubes, and fell asleep at his side.

Printed in the USA
CPSIA information can be obtained
at www.ICGtesting.com
JSHW020500180324
59338JS00004B/125